THE COMGY

Cover Design by www.damonza.com

ISBN: 9781790885541
(print edition)

Trotting Fox Press

Contents

PRINCE OF THE MAGIC

BOOK ONE OF THE SON OF SORCERY SERIES

Robert Ryan

ISBN-13 978-0-9942054-7-6
(print edition)

Trotting Fox Press

1. Murder and Mayhem

Nightborn. The sound of the name was bitter in Gil's ears. It was what the other boys called him, and he did not like it. Worse, he knew that he was about to hear it again. But he would not let that stop him from doing what he had to do.

For a little while he had watched as Elrika, daughter of the palace baker, struggled to fend off the sword strokes of the group that had set upon her. It did not matter that they were only wooden practice swords – they still hurt. Welts had risen on her skin, and a cut on her forehead dribbled blood toward her eyes. Bravely, she brushed it away with the back of her wrist and tried to defend against multiple attackers.

This was meant to be a sparring session. It was supposed to be one against one. But it was more violent than it should have been, and when the leader of the boys, older than everyone else, had nodded for his friends to join in it had suddenly become very personal. They all hated Elrika, for she was a commoner and they were of the aristocracy. It did not matter that her father owned baker shops scattered throughout the city and was richer than most of their own parents. She was not of the blood as they were, and they despised her for it.

Dust rose about their feet as the girl gamely dodged and turned, trying to fend them off. And she was good too. Very good. That infuriated them even more. She was nearly their match, but she tired beneath the hot afternoon sun and the constant blows that came from all sides no matter how fast she twisted and spun.

Gil glanced at the Swordmaster. The man watched from where he sat on a padded chair, slowly smoking his pipe. He had done nothing to intervene. The Swordmaster was of the aristocracy himself, and had inherited the position from his father twenty years earlier. No, he had done nothing, and it did not look like he was going to. He was a baron, and his sympathies lay with the boys rather than the daughter of a baker.

Elrika stumbled and the attackers struck her hard several times. She fell, rolled, and came to her feet again in one motion. The boys were surprised, and then laughed. But soon they moved in on her again.

Gil had seen enough. "Stop!"

The boys turned to him, and the eldest, their leader, sneered.

"Stay out of this, *elùgrune*. Or you'll be next."

There it was. Elùgrune. The old word for nightborn, but the voicing of the insult did not intimidate Gil. Instead, it filled his veins with fire. Still, he controlled his temper.

"The task we were set," he said calmly, "was to spar one on one. This isn't fair."

One of the other boys, emboldened by the ringleader's insult, took it further.

"Go back into the dark, elùgrune. Go back to whatever black pit spawned you."

They all laughed at that. Gil, the fire in his veins starting to throb, did not answer. He breathed slowly to try to calm himself, but they mistook his silence for fear, and that emboldened them even more.

Elrika seemed forgotten, and they turned on him. The eldest boy pushed him. It was not a hard push, but it sent Gil back a few paces. Still, he did nothing. He did not want to fight them.

The taller boy pushed him again, much harder this time. Then the other boys lifted their wooden practice blades and yelled insults. They were working themselves up to what must surely come next.

Gil glanced once again at the Swordmaster, but the man just sat there puffing smoke, staring at them all coldly with heavy-lidded eyes.

A thought flashed through Gil's mind when he looked back to the boys. He remembered the advice of Brand, his *real* teacher. *Go for the leader first when confronted by a group. He's the one who gives spine and willpower to the others.* It had been just like that here. Gil could almost hear Brand's voice continue. *Often, the many can be defeated by the destruction of the one.* That, Gil realized, was what Elrika had done wrong. She had tried to fight them all at the same time.

The ringleader went to push Gil once again, but just as he made contact Gil rocked his weight back a little and turned to the side. The older boy was suddenly pushing at nothing, and he was off-balance.

Gil struck. He did not use the blade of the wooden sword, but rather the rounded pommel. With a crack, he thrust it hard against the back of the other boy's head.

The ringleader dropped, his legs seeming to lose the ability to hold any weight, and he collapsed like a felled tree. Gil felt panic rise within him. A blow to the back of the head could be lethal, and he had struck harder than intended.

He did not look back though. With a leap he was among the other boys, but they scattered from him like leaves blown on the wind. Only Elrika stayed where she was, an intense look on her face that he could not interpret.

He heard a movement behind him and turned. The ringleader was struggling to his feet. His face was red with anger or shame, and blood dripped from his nose. He had fallen face-first onto the ground.

With a shaky movement the boy used the back of his hand to wipe the blood away. "Elùgrune!" he said, and his voice was a hiss of hatred. "Nightborn! Born of the blood of a witch! You'll pay for—"

He got no further. Gil struck again, this time a swift blow with the heel of his left palm. It caught the other under the chin and sent him sprawling backward onto the ground once more.

Quickly, Gil darted forward and kicked the sword out of his opponent's limp hand. Then he whipped around to face the other boys, but they had not moved.

His heart thudded in his chest, and his anger threatened to break loose. He almost went for the other boys even though they now made no move against him, and they saw that look on his face and feared it. They backed further away.

With a long breath he steadied himself and stayed where he was. His anger was no longer directed at them. He was seething at the insults that had been cast at him. *Elùgrune. Blood of the witch.* He had heard them all his life, but no one had ever explained to him exactly what they meant. That would change, and soon, he decided.

At last, the Swordmaster came over. For all that he sat through most of the training sessions on his cushioned chair, he was not that old. He walked over briskly, and anger distorted his face.

"Fool!" he said, stopping directly before Gil. "This was a sparring session, not a fight!"

"But they were—"

"Enough! You should be ashamed of yourself. In all my years, I've never met such an arrogant boy. Do you think you can get away with this? Do you think Brand will protect you? I don't care that he's regent. In this practice yard, I rule."

Elrika stepped forward. "Sir, he was only trying to help me." She paused, seeing the look on the Swordmaster's face.

"Be silent. I'll deal with you later."

He turned back to Gil. "Apologize. Apologize now."

Gil glanced behind him. The boy he had hit was standing once again, but he did not look well. No, not well at all. But he had deserved everything he had received, and Gil made his decision.

He faced the Swordmaster. "No."

The man looked as if he were about to fly into a rage. "What do you mean, no? No one says no. Not here. Not you. Least of all you!"

"By no, I mean no. I won't apologize. They were picking on Elrika. They could have hurt her, and you did nothing to stop them. So I did."

"It's not your place to stop anything boy!"

Gil held his ground. His heart pounded more than it had in the fight, but he was not going to back down. Right was right, after all.

The Swordmaster glared at him coldly. "I won't have my authority or my actions questioned. You're expelled. There's no place for you in this practice yard. You may go now."

Gil looked at him. He thought about arguing, but that would be pointless. Then he caught the hint of a smirk on the Swordmaster's face. Finally, he understood. The man had set him up for this. The whole thing had been a trap, and like a fool he had fallen into it. The aristocracy hated him even more than they hated commoners, but for a different reason.

There was no help for it now. He had done what he had done, and he was not sorry. He turned to walk away, but the Swordmaster was not quite done.

"Be sure to tell Brand exactly why you were expelled. If he doesn't understand, he can come here and I'll explain it to him personally."

Gil did not answer. He kept walking, but he *did* wonder how he was going to explain this to Brand. That was not something to look forward to.

He thought about Brand as he walked to the palace. Brand was regent, taking the place of the king who had once ruled the great city of Cardoroth. There were many stories about him. So many, and all hard to believe, yet they were still true. Gil was old enough to remember some events himself, or at least to have heard about them from people who had been there. And he had learned more as he had grown older.

Brand of the Duthenor, they called him. He had come from a wild tribe that lived in the wilderness far to the west. Quickly he had risen in the ranks of Cardoroth's army, and he had won the king's favor for feats of bravery that made other men tremble.

But it was not for bravery alone that the king had kept promoting a stranger. It was for his loyalty as well. Brand's word was his bond, and not once had he failed the king, either in a matter of trust or of courage. Gil knew that for a fact, because the king had told him so himself. The king, after all, was his grandfather. He had always spoken in the highest terms of Brand.

Gil walked ever more slowly. The more he thought about it, the more he worried about telling Brand of his expulsion. It was Brand himself who had sent him to study under the Swordmaster, and the last thing Gil ever wanted to do was disappoint him. Brand was in many ways like a father to him.

11

His own father was dead. His mother was away on a long journey, and Brand was his guardian. In a way, Brand filled in for his parents just as he filled in for his grandfather.

His grandfather was old. Old, and weary after long years of hard service. Only the wit and military strategy of that man had kept his realm's many enemies at bay. Cardoroth only existed today because of the old king, and Gil was proud of him.

But even great men wearied. The old king had served most of his life, and he had suffered greatly under the strain of incessant attacks to the city from without, and constant treachery from within. With only a few years left to live, he had made his most trusted and competent servant regent. Regent for his only heir, Gil himself. But no one asked Gil what he thought about all of that. There were lots of things they never asked him.

He slowed even further, dreading his return to the palace in shame. At least his grandfather would not know of this. He had left the city, trusting Brand implicitly. Where he had gone, no one knew for sure. But he was with his wife, Gil's grandmother, and Gil did not begrudge the short happiness they would have together, free of troubles, even if he missed them terribly. After what they had endured in Cardoroth, they deserved that.

Gil let out a long sigh. He should have seen through the Swordmaster's scheme. If there was one thing the aristocracy hated more than a foreigner being made regent, it was a prince too young to ascend the throne. For though Gil was of the aristocracy, here now was their chance to try to maneuver one of their own families into the kingship. They would have to be bold to do that, but the attitude of the Swordmaster showed they were capable of it. Still, Brand would never let that happen.

Gil walked through the palace gardens. The well-tended grounds were lush with new growth and flowers, and the hot afternoon sun burned above. It was a beautiful day, but more and more he dreaded telling Brand what had happened. Brand was many things to him – regent, hero, warrior. But most of all he was a tutor. Brand taught him as a father might a son, and the way of the blade, of combat and military strategy, was the least of it. Brand taught him how to be a king, and how to defend himself and the realm that one day he would rule. That knowledge was needed too, for both he and Cardoroth had many enemies.

All of these were good reasons that the old king had made Brand regent. But he still missed his grandfather. And now his mother also, who had left to visit with his grandparents. She knew where they had gone, even if she would not tell.

Out of habit, he looked about him as he walked through the gardens. Sure enough, he caught glimpses of the bodyguards who trailed him wherever he went. It was proof that he had enemies, and it made him uncomfortable.

At last, he entered the palace and walked freely through its halls. He knew where he was going, could have found his way blindfolded if he had to. He had grown up here, and he had long since discovered and explored its every nook and cranny.

He knew exactly where he was going now – the throne room, even if he did not really wish to. But, at this time of day Brand would still be there, though the official audience period was finished.

He came to the great doors, which stood open. There he paused a moment, and though he did not see them he sensed the bodyguards, much nearer now, behind him. They paused also.

13

He did not wait long. It would not do to let anyone see his hesitation. So, with a brisk step he entered the throne room.

His steps echoed loudly. The marble floor was white and polished, and his boots made a slapping sound against it that he could not hush. Worse, the vaulted ceiling that rose to a dizzying height seemed to swallow the sound and then cast it back a thousandfold.

He saw Brand straightaway. There was a woman with him, old and gray-haired, but her eyes were very sharp. The two of them appeared to be finishing a conversation. The stranger gave Brand a bow, gathered some papers, and left. She did not look at Gil on her way out, but he sensed no animosity.

Gil approached the regent, but despite himself his pace slowed. Brand looked as he always did. He was dressed in well-fitting, but rather plain clothes. They were of the same sort that ten thousand other men might now be wearing on the streets of Cardoroth. And Brand's physical appearance was the same – ordinary.

The regent was not tall nor short. He was, perhaps, a largish man because his muscles were well-developed and could be discerned even beneath his clothes. But if so, it was no more than any laborer in the city. About his every move was a sense of lithe alertness, as though he could transform from stillness to sudden action quicker than the eye could follow, but that too was not unique. It was the look of a warrior, and there were many such in a city long beset by enemies.

But then Brand turned his blue eyes upon him, and as always Gil sensed the raw charisma that set him apart. Here was a man of power. Here was a man who commanded by inspiration, trust and loyalty. Here was a man who looked into the hearts of others and saw their strengths and weaknesses – saw, forgave, and encouraged. Here was a man warriors would follow to death. *Had* followed to death, and that the people of the city loved even if the aristocracy did not. Here was the man who had been the city's greatest hero in the recent war. Cardoroth would have fallen if not for him, and even though Gil had not been old enough to fight, he had heard firsthand from his grandfather exactly what Brand had done.

Gil made up his mind. Brand was not the sort of man you lied to, or even tried to present yourself to in a favorable light. You just told him the truth. He respected that, the good or the bad, and the consequences of Gil's actions would be … whatever they would be. He took a deep breath and accepted that.

Brand raised an eyebrow. "You're back from training early. What happened?"

There it was. Straightaway the man knew something had happened. Not much ever slipped past him.

Gil looked him in the eye. "I'm sorry. The Swordmaster expelled me."

There was a pause. A flicker of emotion played across Brand's face, but Gil did not think it was surprise. Had he already known?

"It seems you've had an interesting day. Tell me all about it."

So, that's what Gil did. He told Brand everything. He held nothing back, including his fear that he had struck the other boy too hard on the back of the head, and his relief that the boy had stood up afterward.

Brand asked some simple questions, then finally shrugged.

"I see no fault in what you did."

Gil was amazed. He had been expecting some kind of punishment.

Brand looked at him curiously, evidently sensing his surprise.

"It's a case of properly attributing causes and effects," he explained. "You did the right thing. Some would argue that you should have tried harder to reason with the other boys. Truth is, though, some people can't be reasoned with. This was one of those situations. The other boys were always going to do what they were doing. The only question was, what were you going to do about it? In the end, you may have saved Elrika from serious injury."

Brand leaned back in his chair. "The effect of being expelled was beyond your control. Just because a man tries to do the right thing, it doesn't follow that the end result is good. So, it's not the end result a person should be judged by – it's the intent they started with."

Gil was startled. He had never thought of things in that light before. Brand was always opening his eyes to other ways of seeing things.

"Well, I'm glad you think so," Gil said. "I still feel bad that I was expelled though. Word of that will get around the city, and not everyone will see things as you do."

Brand considered that. "What matters more is that you know the truth. You can't worry too much about other people. As for being expelled, well, the Swordmaster overstepped his power there. Go to training tomorrow as normal. I'll send Lornach with you so that there'll be no trouble."

Gil was surprised all over again. He had not expected that, and he had no desire to see the Swordmaster at all, but if Lornach was going to be there then he had nothing to fear. In fact, he could hardly wait to see the look on the Swordmaster's face. Lornach had a way of dealing with these sorts of situations. It would prove memorable. Then he remembered something, and suddenly felt less buoyant.

"The other boys called me elùgrune again," he told Brand. "Am I? Is what they say true?"

Brand straightened in his chair. Once again there was a flicker of emotion, but it was gone before Gil could read it.

"Let no one tell you who you are," Brand answered. "You are the sum of your own thoughts and your own actions. The first becomes the second, and the labels of other people are meaningless. At least, unless you give them power yourself. Remember that."

Gil held out his hands. "Then what do these marks really mean? No one ever answers that properly."

Brand did not even look at the marks, the two small dots of white skin, like eyes. They had been there all Gil's life, were a part of him. But they made him different from everybody else, and he did not know why. Brand had seen them before. So had the boys at the practice yard. It was from that moment that they had begun taunting him. Again, he did not really know why.

With a shrug, Brand leaned back.

"If you're old enough to ask the question," he said, "I think you're old enough to know the answer. The Camar people, that great race who swept out of the west and came east to form cities and realms, including Cardoroth, tend to think of the sign of Halathgar – a constellation of two stars like eyes, just like the marks on your palms, as a sign of sorcery. In Cardoroth, that mark is known as the Seal of Carnhaina."

That much Gil already knew. He knew what the marks were called, and he knew that Queen Carnhaina was his distant ancestor. He could not quite remember how long ago her reign was though, perhaps as much as seven hundred years.

Brand went on. "What you have probably also heard is that Carnhaina delved into sorcery. So, in Cardoroth, the constellation of Halathgar is associated with dark magic. She took the constellation as her own sign, and also as her royal seal."

Gil held his palms before him and studied them. The marks on each hand were pale, more or less white spots devoid of any pigment. They were not quite round, and indeed looked like eyes, especially when he held both hands together. But all of this he had already been told before, if not quite so directly.

"Then what people have said all my life is true. Ultimately, I'm born from a witch." He could not make himself say anything about the words nightborn or elùgrune.

Brand scratched his chin. "Well, many in Cardoroth would say so."

"And what do you say?"

"I say this. Maybe the sign of Halathgar, or the Seal of Carnhaina – call the mark what you will, represents dark magic. But among my own people, among the lands of the Duthenor, there's a different view."

This was something Gil had not heard before. Brand rarely spoke of his homeland, so Gil listened closely.

"I remember my father taking me for a walk one evening. I was younger than you are now. Far younger, but I remember it clearly. It was a cold night, and still. It was also very late. Frost lay in the hollows, and the stars were piercing bright. We came out from beneath the night-shadow of a great oak, and he pointed suddenly to the glittering sky. 'See, my son! Bright Halathgar shines upon us!'"

Brand paused, seemingly lost in memory. Gil knew that his father must have died not long after that night, for it had happened when Brand was quite young. It brought back memories of his own father's death, and he suddenly felt very close to this unusual man.

Then Brand, almost imperceptibly, straightened in his chair.

"My father told me then that the constellation was a sign of good luck. From then onward, I look for it every time I go out into the dark. But you, Gilcarist, need never search it out. You will carry it with you all the days of your life."

Gil felt suddenly very strange. He also wondered why Brand had used his full name. Come to think of it, Brand *did* do that quite often. It made him feel as though he were being treated as an adult, and he liked that.

Unexpectedly, Brand went on. He obviously had more to say on the subject, and Gil was fascinated.

"But, truth be told, there's an older meaning than either the Camar or Duthenor really know."

Brand paused, considering his words. Gil remained perfectly still. The great hall was silent and brooding, as though it too listened.

"The constellation of Halathgar has an ancient significance. The immortal Halathrin call it the Lost Huntress. To them, it's a sign of surpassing good luck. The legends they tell about it are among the most hopeful, among the brightest and most beautiful stories you will ever hear. Some men falsely call it a sign of ill fortune, but in this world the ignorant say many things that aren't true. And the firmer they are in their view, the less likely it is that they're right. Remember that."

Brand spoke now with real passion, which was a thing he rarely did. Gil listened, and he recalled that Brand was one of the few men to have spoken with the immortal Halathrin in the last thousand years.

"Forget what you hear in the practice yard," Brand continued. "The Lost Huntress is one of the great heroes

19

of the whole land of Alithoras. The constellation is named after her, and she is revered by the Halathrin. Indeed, she has another name. They call her also Arangar, which means noblebright. And you bear her sign on your very hands. It's no curse, but rather a blessing."

Gil felt suddenly special. He felt better. For some reason he felt that he could face down a thousand boys insulting him. He could look them in the eye with unflinching pride. Brand was good at doing that, good at giving people hope and dispelling the dark. But this once it was still not quite enough.

"But *why* do I bear the marks?"

Brand shook his head. "That, I don't know. It's a mystery, though legend says you're not the only prince of Cardoroth to have done so."

"No, that I've heard. But the other princes were born and died long ago. And it's not said that any of the royal line since Carnhaina herself have possessed magic." He paused. What he was about to say next was a secret that few knew, but Brand was one of them. In fact, he was his instructor in this as he was in so many other things. "Yet I do. Why am I different?"

Brand sighed. "I really don't know. But in no other time during the history of Cardoroth, since Carnhaina herself, has the kingdom been so threatened. I know nothing for certain, but I don't think you have the gift by accident. If you have it, you will have need of it. Fate works like that. At least in my experience."

Gil thought on that answer. He never spoke of the magic to anyone but Brand. None of the few who knew about it understood what it meant to possess it, but Brand did. He possessed it too. He taught him its uses just as he taught him many other things. The answer he had just been given felt right: if he possessed the power, he would have need of it.

Gil remembered something. "Is it true that you have met her ghost? The spirit of Carnhaina, I mean?"

There was a long pause. "Yes."

Brand removed a silver band from his finger, a signet ring, with a flat emerald set on top. Carved on the face of the stone was an image of a tower. Two diamonds, like the twin stars of the Lost Huntress, like the marks on Gil's palms, glinted above it.

Unexpectedly, Gil wanted to know something. "What was she like?"

"What was she like?" Brand folded his arms and closed his eyes. When he spoke, it was almost to himself.

"She was imperious. She was complex. She was powerful. Above all, she had a commanding presence. Her spirit only rose from death but briefly. It was a moment of great urgency, for the fate of the city hung in the balance. But when she spoke, I listened! Whatever else people say about her, she was a *queen*."

Gil thought about that. His grandfather had been something like that too. He wondered if one day people would ever listen to him, really listen. He had trouble imagining it.

Brand went on. "This was a lesson I learned from her. We are born into the world with nothing, and we leave with nothing. Nothing, except the name we make for ourselves. Thus are we remembered – so make your time count."

Brand sat back in his chair, and Gil considered what he had said. For some reason, it struck a chord with him. There was truth in that statement, hard-won truth. He stored the idea away to ponder sometime in the future.

He sensed that Brand had revealed all that he could, or would, about his heritage. It was not enough. He wanted to know *why* he had those marks. Was it just some random coincidence, or did it *mean* something? Did he possess magic for some specific purpose? But he would learn nothing more on those subjects now, so he brought the conversation back to where it had started.

"Why must I learn from the Swordmaster? Especially now? He'll hate me if you force him to do it. I practice with you every day at dawn, and you're better by far. Can't I just do that?"

Brand looked at him, as though assessing him.

"Gil. The Swordmaster *already* hates you. He hates you for who you are. But I don't send you there to learn swordcraft."

That was a surprise. The first part of the comment was brutally honest, but he appreciated that Brand always told him the truth. The second, he did not understand at all.

"But if I'm not going to the Swordmaster to learn what he teaches, then why am I going at all?"

"Because the other boys you train with are of the aristocracy, as are you. One day they'll be captains, generals, judges and the like. You'll spend your time as king dealing with those sorts of people. I send you there to get to know them, to understand them."

Gil thought about that. He saw immediately how much sense it made. It had nothing to do with swordcraft at all. He was about to ask why he also helped the stablemen to heap manure and look after the horses as one of his chores. But he did not. He saw for himself that he had been set that task to understand horses. That was critical for a king who might one day command an army, including cavalry regiments, in defense of the realm. Even more importantly, he would also gain an understanding of what it meant to be a common man or woman, what was important to them and what their

22

worldview was. It was people like them who were the backbone of the realm.

Gil had a new insight into his training, and a deeper awareness of Brand's methods. He had much to think about.

Their discussion ended soon after. Messengers came to Brand, and the business of being regent cut short their time. Gil went away, his mind sifting through all that he had learned.

He passed once more through the tile-floored corridors of the palace. It was time to get something to eat, and though it was early the kitchens would be open, their preparations for dinner well underway.

He was not looking forward to tomorrow. The Swordmaster had expelled him, but Brand was going to disregard that. Sending Lornach to ensure there were no problems was sure to produce trouble of its own. Lornach was a commoner, but he had an attitude of supreme confidence that would set the Swordmaster's teeth on edge. There was going to be conflict there…

A voice came from behind him, startlingly close. "Why so deep in thought, young man? The troubles of the world aren't your own yet."

Gil looked around and smiled. It was Arell. She was said to be Brand's lover, but he had never seen any sign of it. But whatever the case, he liked her for she was beautiful and kind.

He opened his heart to her, and told her what had happened and what Brand had said.

"Listen to him," she advised when he was done. "Trust in Brand, and all he says. Men would follow him into the pit of hell."

Gil was a little taken aback. She was so certain in the way that she spoke.

"Why would anyone do that?" he asked.

Her response was swift. "Because he would do the same for them. Loyalty breeds loyalty," she said. Then she smiled and winked at him. "Remember that."

Her choice of words was no accident. She echoed one of Brand's sayings, the words he used to give special emphasis to something that would be of use throughout Gil's life.

He parted with Arell then, his mind a little clearer. Tomorrow would bring whatever it brought, but he would just face it and see what happened. And with Lornach going with him to see the Swordmaster, anything was possible.

Lornach was the Durlindrath, or at least one of them. There were two now. They jointly headed the royal bodyguards, the Durlin. One group guarded Brand, the other him. But Gil's group was bigger. Brand had been Durlindrath to the old king, and he did not need much in the way of guarding. No man in Cardoroth was his equal as a warrior. But if any came close, it was Lornach, and somehow Gil knew that when he met the Swordmaster tomorrow things would not go well.

He tried to put it all from his mind. It had been a long day, and he was hungry. He ate a quick meal, then went to his room. He was exhausted, and he pulled off his boots and got into bed in his clothes. No one would know.

Sleep came quickly. But just as quickly came the strange dream that had troubled him lately. He tossed and turned, rising up toward wakefulness, but then falling again into a deeper sleep. The dream gripped him this time and did not let go.

His body drifted through a dark place. The only light came from a sickly moon, yellow and blotched, partly concealed behind scudding clouds.

He slowed, and a forest grew about him. Trees stood tall and silent, as though watching. Their dark limbs reached forth beneath the fitful light, and shadows played across their leaves, making them seem like fingers that curled and clawed, always seeking.

Suddenly, he knew this place. It was in Cardoroth, but a part of countryside that few ever traveled. It was the pine woods that surrounded Lake Alithorin, only hours from the city. Its reputation was grim.

Gil felt malice in the air. It was like a chill wind that blew right through him, yet nothing moved in the dark place except the shifting dance of yellowed light and forest shadows.

And then the trees seemed to arch, to form an aisle, and he saw beyond them into a dead-grassed glade, and wished that he had not.

His feet did not move. But he glided once again, ghost-like, and entered a world within a world. The grass below him was withered. The leaves of the surrounding trees hung limp, like dead fingers. The moon glared down now, free from its shroud of drifting clouds, peering like the watchful eye of a cruel cat, hunting, stalking, playing with a mouse caught in the open.

Gil shivered. In the center of the glade was a woman. Tall, thin, cloaked in shadow. Evil fell from her like leaves from a dead tree. Cold and hard was her swift glance, devoid of life, and her pale hand, pallid beneath the sickly moon, rose slowly but surely and pointed at him.

The woman spoke. Her voice welled as though from the earth itself, or an ancient tomb newly opened. But she did not address Gil. Rather, she chanted, and her hollow voice slowly filled the dark.

Murder and mayhem. Mayhem and murder. Seep from the ground. Rain from the sky. Float in the air all around. Malice and wrath, betrayal and treachery, bring the world woe and bring the world deviltry. Let the earth weep blood. Bring all to ruin. Crush hope and devour light.

Gil moaned. The woman paid him no heed. Her finger still pointing at him like a marker of doom, she turned her head and looked down. Beside her, Gil now saw, kneeled an acolyte. The man stood and took a step forward at some hidden command. In his hand he bore a curved knife. It glinted with dull moonlight.

Though the acolyte served the woman, there was terror in his eyes. That fear grew and spread. It gripped Gil. His breath caught in his chest, and he could not breathe. He tried to scream, but found no voice for his horror. And like a shadow that leaped and danced, it spread from the glade and filled the forest.

The forest trembled, and then the dark fear was out, out into the wide lands beyond, and Gil wondered if this was no mere dream but the casting of a spell.

The marks on his palms burned as though with fire, and suddenly a second lady stood in the glade. Tall she was, and a great spear she held in her jeweled fingers. One glimpse he caught of her, and then he woke.

Sweat drenched his pillow, and he lurched upright on his bed and gulped in the sweet night air. There he sat and trembled, waiting for his terror to subside.

2. The Tower of Halathgar

Dawn came after a long night, but Gil was already up. The dream hung over him like a cloud, stronger and darker than he had ever felt it before, but he tried to shrug it off.

Most mornings started in a particular way for him, and he liked the routine of it. The half hour before the sun came up was a time of peace. It was time that he spent with Brand, and it was the part of the day that he loved most and where his real training was conducted.

First, came the weapons practice. That was mostly with a sword, but Brand was introducing him to new things lately: daggers, staffs, spears and bare hand fighting.

This morning, it was a long sword that they used. Brand's was his own blade, the one he carried with him always, but Gil used a wooden training weapon, at least for sparring. For practicing techniques in the air, he used a real blade, sharp and dangerous.

The dawn air was still cool, and the sweat that soaked his tunic felt cold and clammy every time he rested. Where they practiced now, in an outside courtyard attached to the Durlin chapterhouse, a breeze blew through the lattice work and vines that blocked away the outside world. It made things even cooler, but the fresh air was vitalizing, and Gil inhaled deeply.

He slowed his breathing as Brand had taught him, using his abdomen rather than his chest. He felt relaxed as he sparred his teacher, moving sure-footed and purposefully. Without warning, he dropped low and swept his wooden blade at Brand's legs. It was a move the Swordmaster had showed the boys, but it did not work on Brand. Quicker than Gil would have thought possible, the other man stepped forward and brought his blade down to stop suddenly above Gil's head. It would have been a killing stroke in a real battle, and Brand had executed it while Gil was still trying to perform his own technique, even though he had moved first.

Brand stepped back. "Don't use flashy moves, Gil. You left yourself unguarded there to perform it. No matter how good a move looks, always ask yourself how a skilled opponent would combat it. Add nothing to your repertoire until you fully understand its strengths and weaknesses."

Gil nodded. "I should have known better. I thought that surprise might have outweighed leaving myself open."

"Surprise is a factor in fighting, but not if it comes at too high a price. Anyway, that move isn't really intended for surprise. It does serve a function though."

"How should it be used, then?"

"It's for a man on foot fighting a mounted warrior. The target is the horse, rather than the rider. Dropping low gives you access to the horse's legs, and because of the rider's height, it takes you beneath his slashing blade. But it still must be timed just right, or you can get trampled or stabbed."

Gil suddenly saw how it would work that way, but he did not like it.

"It's a cruel thing to attack the horse instead of the rider."

Brand looked away. "So it is, but war is a cruel master. A man must sometimes do things that he would rather not, if he is to survive. What's the alternative?"

Gil had no answer for that. As was his way, Brand was teaching more than just swordcraft, no matter that they were in the middle of a sparring session. Always, he prepared him mentally for the things he practiced physically.

They continued to spar for a while longer. The sun rose slowly, and then Brand took him through a new technique. It was the same forward step and overhead blow that Brand had used earlier.

They went slowly at first, Gil standing a little behind and to the side so that he could copy the movements.

"Picture it in your mind first," Brand advised. "Whenever you practice the technique, see how the feet move, see how the sword is lifted – still held protectively in front of the body. Visualize it coming up, but not too high, and then imagine the footwork and arm movements coming together with a sudden hammering motion." Brand cut down in the final sequence of the technique, dropping his bodyweight to add force to the blow.

Gil tried it several times. It was not as easy as it looked.

"Keep on practicing, Gil. Imagine it first, and then execute it slowly. As with everything else I teach you, you'll gradually unify thought and action. Eventually, the two become one. The aim is to reach a point where the body acts by itself. It adjusts, and it does what's necessary without your conscious thought. When you can do that, then you're truly fast."

Gil wondered if he would ever reach that stage. It seemed beyond him, but so too had many things that he once doubted he would be able to do that were now second nature to him.

The sun was now fully risen, and the vines on the latticework cast dappled shadows across the paved floor of the courtyard.

"Time for another exercise," Brand announced. "Put away the sword."

Gil hung the wooden blade in one of the racks on the wall, and then he came back.

"Sit down, and face the sun," Brand instructed.

Gil sat cross-legged. Excitement built within him, for as much as he loved the way of the blade, he knew what was coming next and he loved it even more. It was for this, he felt, that he was born.

"Close your eyes," Brand continued.

Gil did so, and he attained a measure of peace and tranquility, though he knew as he progressed he would have to do the same thing with his eyes open. One day, he might have to do it under the stress of battle.

"Reach forth with your mind," Brand instructed. "Feel the light and warmth of the sun."

Hesitantly, Gil did so. He was still new at this, but the procedure was becoming familiar.

"Become one with it," Brand said. "Bring it into yourself … and then focus on the palm of your hand. Let it out, transform it into fire."

Gil struggled at this point. He had no mastery of the magic yet, for all that he knew it was his passion in life. Sometimes it worked for him, and sometimes it did not.

But this time he felt it flutter to life. Flame leaped from his palm, and then it fluttered and dimmed only to flare again. It was unsteady, but it was there.

He opened one eye a slit and saw that Brand held a small ball of flame in his hand. It burned with a bright light, and neither flared nor dimmed. It was a constant thing, and Gil envied him that control.

"Lòhrengai is alive," Brand whispered. It was the true name of the magic; it was a name from the old tongue, from the immortal Halathrin themselves.

Brand passed the ball of flame from one hand to the other with casual ease.

"Lòhrengai is alive," he said. "The magic is all around us. We reach out and take it. We transform it, but it is alive. It's unpredictable. Perhaps it even has a will of its own. And even as we shape it, it works to shape us. Remember that."

Gil was having trouble concentrating. As sometimes happened when he used lòhrengai, his palms itched. Suddenly, he remembered the dream from the night before and he lost the ball of flame completely. It dimmed and then died out, and his hand felt cold and empty.

Brand twisted his hand and his own ball of flame dissipated into the air as though becoming mere sunlight again.

"I had a dream last night," Gil said. "Do you think that a dream can be a dream and yet be true at the same time?"

Brand did not answer at once. He cocked his head as though in thought, and then he shrugged.

"Not normally," he replied. "But you are not quite normal. The magic you possess and your heritage make it so."

Gil tried a slightly different approach. "Have you ever had a dream that turned out to be real?"

Brand looked at him solemnly. "No, I have not. But that doesn't mean anything."

"Why not?"

"Because I'm not you."

31

It was a simple answer. But as was Brand's way, he had said something as a simple fact that also had a deeper meaning, and Gil could follow his train of thought. Just because people were similar on the surface did not mean they were not profoundly different from each other.

"Well," he said. "I had a dream last night, and at the time it seemed as real as the two of us talking now."

"Tell me of it," Brand said. There was a note in his voice that Gil could not quite place. It might have been unease. Or perhaps not, for there was no sign of it in the other's eyes.

So Gil told him of the dream, and that last night was not the first time. It was a dream that he had been having for weeks. But it had somehow become more vivid, more real.

"And it was the first time that I saw the other woman," he added.

Brand looked thoughtful, which was far better than the attitude of dismissal Gil had feared. He should have known that Brand would take him seriously.

"Tell me more about the second woman."

Gil tried to remember the details. "She was large. She was dressed very well, and extremely regal. But she held a spear in her hand, which was rather strange, though she seemed like she knew how to use it. But she didn't. Instead, she watched and said nothing."

He paused, remembering more details. Which also was strange for a dream. Normally, they became vague rapidly, but this one seemed easy to recall.

"When I looked into her eyes," he continued, "the marks on my palms burned."

Brand seemed suddenly alert. If he had looked interested before, now his eyes glittered with an intelligent fierceness that he did not attempt to hide.

"What does it all mean?" Gil ventured.

"Nothing," Brand answered. "Or everything. Who can say with certainty? But the lady with spear, I think, was Carnhaina. She is quite distinctive, and her presence, or at least the presence of her ghost, makes me wonder what else of the dream may be true, and that whatever it portends will turn out to be of great significance."

Gil was not sure if he really believed any of that. Why should a long-dead queen appear in one of his dreams, even if they were related?

"What should we do?" he asked.

Brand turned to him after several moments of thought. "You've never been to the tomb of Carnhaina before, have you?"

"No," Gil said.

"Then we'll go there. And we'll do it tonight. It's part of your heritage anyway, and you should pay your respects."

Gil wondered what exactly Brand had in mind. No one visited tombs at night.

"Do you think she'll appear, as once she did for you?"

"No," Brand answered. "She has only ever appeared at times of great need. But we'll go there anyway."

Gil knew that Brand was worried, but it was not his way to show it. Nor was there any reason to suppose Cardoroth was in any great danger. He had only had a dream, after all. But not even his grandfather had ever taken him to Carnhaina's tomb before. He really did not know what to expect. Perhaps, in Brand's own words, everything or nothing.

33

Their practice for the day was over, and Gil went to the stables for rest of morning. It was not that far away, and he quickly found Brand's black stallion. The horse was old now, but he had sired many of the finest horses in Cardoroth. Gil and Brand were the only ones who ever rode him, but there was no time for that today.

"Hello, boy," Gil said, after letting himself in the stall and stroking the great horse's flanks.

The stallion snorted his own greeting, but as he moved Gil noticed something was not quite right. He took the horse by the halter, and got him to move around a little.

There it was. The shoe on his left rear leg seemed loose. Gil studied it a little more, and then fed him a ration of chaff and grain.

He left the stallion then, carefully closing the stall door behind him, and went in search of the farrier.

He found him in his work shed near the grain bins and equipment rooms. He was a tall man, normally quiet and grim, with black hair and a bristling black beard streaked with silver. Just at that moment he was shoeing a horse, quickly hammering in a nail while holding the horse's leg up at the same time.

Gil waited until the man was finished. "Good morning, master Fereck," he said.

The farrier nodded, but did not speak.

"Brand's black has a shoe coming loose, I think," Gil said into the silence.

The other man slipped his hammer through a loop in his trousers, and then he wiped his hands down his leather apron.

"I'll have a look and see this morning," he answered.

"Thank you, sir," Gil said. He followed Brand's example and showed respect to men such as this. The farrier, and the men like him that Gil knew, were men of skill and they deserved it. Not to mention, as Brand pointed out, the craftsmen who shoed horses, forged swords, constructed bows and the like did things upon which a warrior's life depended. It was wise to acknowledge that, and to stay in their good graces.

Gil turned to leave, but the farrier, for all that he seldom spoke much, was not done.

"One last thing," the man said.

Gil turned around, somewhat surprised.

"I know what you did," Fereck said.

"I beg your pardon?" Gil replied, confused.

"In the Swordmaster's practice yard, young man," the farrier explained. "I know what you did for the baker's daughter, and it was well done."

Gil blushed. "It was nothing, sir."

"It was more than nothing, and I for one will not forget."

The farrier turned away then, going about his business. He had said all that he was going to, but Gil felt a thrill run through him. The farrier was a quiet man, a reserved man, and praise from the likes of him was always understated and rare. That made it special to hear.

Gil went away, feeling on top of the world. As he walked, a realization came to him. The aristocracy tended to stick together, but so too did workers and tradesmen. Word had traveled fast of yesterday's events, and he did not doubt that many now knew the story, and he had gained some friends he had not had before. It was a good feeling.

Brand, of course, must have foreseen that he would learn lessons like that, and that he would gain a better understanding of such people, of human nature itself. It was why he had been asked to deal with them in the first place, but he found that he liked them too. They were in many ways more real, more down to earth, more honest and just plain likeable compared to the run-of-the-mill aristocracy.

Gil spent some time in the palace library after that. He had been given a schedule of history books to read, mostly the memoirs of kings. They could, at times, be fascinating reading. So it was now, and before he knew it the afternoon had arrived and it was time to set aside a treatise on a centuries-old battle and head toward the Swordmaster's practice yard a little way into the city.

There was no sign of Lornach. But the Durlindrath was a busy man, and perhaps he was not free to come. If so, Gil was going to have trouble explaining his presence when he got to training. He had been expelled, and he had no business being there. Still, he did not think Lornach would let him down. He would be there, and his presence, though very much wanted, was also very likely to cause trouble. Gil could not guess how things were going to go between him and the Swordmaster.

When Gil arrived, the other boys were already there. They were practicing in pairs, and he felt their looks on him and heard the whisper of "nightborn" from some.

He passed down their line, and the looks and whispers ceased. But when he came to the baker's daughter, she stopped what she was doing and spoke to him.

"Hello, Gil."

He nodded and smiled, even if it was nervously. "Hello, Elrika."

He had no further chance to talk to her. The Swordmaster had seen him, and he had removed himself quickly from his seat and was in the process of striding over.

"How dare you—" he began, but that was as far as he got. Lornach was suddenly there. Where exactly he had come from, Gil did not know, but he was relieved.

He turned to look, and noticed that Brand's friend was not wearing the white surcoat of the Durlin, which signified his office. Instead, his clothes were plain.

"That's enough," Lornach said.

"And who the blazes are you?"

Lornach did not answer that. Instead, he delivered a message.

"I bear word from the regent," he said. "You're dismissed from your post. Another Swordmaster will take your place. Today."

The Swordmaster looked incredulous. Then he stood tall, towering above the much shorter man.

"The *regent* does not have that right. I was appointed by the king himself."

"No," Lornach said matter-of-factly. "Your *father* was appointed by the king. You weren't. The title of Swordmaster is honorary, and you have never been honored with it. You have no business here, and you are dismissed."

There were noises of shock from the line of students. The two men ignored that, and stared at each other.

"I'm the best swordsman in Cardoroth," the Swordmaster said. "No one can take my place. Who would even dare?"

Lornach seemed amused. "You're not the best swordsman in Cardoroth. You're a pompous ass. You have no skill with the blade. At all. And that makes you unfit for the job, besides never being appointed to it."

"How dare you!"

"I dare, because Brand has made me the Swordmaster. Now, once more, you are dismissed."

"You can't dismiss me!"

Lornach shook his head slowly. "I just did."

The baron drew his weapon. "This is an insult," he said through clenched teeth. "I will not permit it. Draw your blade, peasant. I will show you a real Swordmaster."

Lornach looked intently at the other man. His expression was no longer amused. It was cold, cold as ice, and Gil felt fear grip him. The Swordmaster had gone too far in drawing his weapon.

"I would not injure you," Lornach said clearly. "But if you don't sheathe your blade, I'll not guarantee your safety."

The face of the Swordmaster was red, and when he spoke he almost spat the words.

"Enough talk, peasant. Tell me your name, and nothing else. I would know that before I kill you."

Lornach sighed. "I'm generally known as Shorty, at least by my friends."

"An apt name. Now draw, or I'll spill your blood where you stand."

"We don't have to duel," Lornach said. "Accept the regent's decision, and move on with your life."

"This isn't a duel. Only the nobility duel against each other. You will never be that, no matter how you serve the regent, who is only a peasant himself. Now draw!"

Lornach's expression hardened, and the blade of his sword slid from its sheath with a quick rasp. Nevertheless, he did not look like a man ready to fight. If anything, he looked supremely bored.

Gil felt someone shuffle close behind him, and heard a whisper in his ear.

"Your friend is a dead man."

It was Turlak, the ringleader of the boys. Gil had heard that he was the son of a duke, but they had seldom spoken. He did not take his eyes off the scene before him, but whispered back.

"You don't know who he is, do you?"

"I know a dead man when I see one."

Gil grinned tightly. "He said his name was Shorty. But most in the city know him better as Lornach. You *have* heard of the king's champion and one of the great heroes of the war, haven't you?"

The older boy did not answer that. He had not known, for he and his father did not come to court and had not seen Brand's entourage.

Gil paid the boys gathered behind him no more heed. The Swordmaster had stepped into the open and assumed a long fighting stance. It was not one he had ever taught his students. Not Gil, anyway.

Lornach still seemed casual, and his sword wove tight but lazy circles in the air before him.

Suddenly the Swordmaster lunged. It was fast, faster than Gil had ever seen him move, but Lornach must have seen it coming. He stepped nimbly away to the side and did not even use his blade to deflect the other's.

Lornach grinned. "Really? No one taught you to keep the shoulder of your sword arm still so you don't signal your intention to strike? That's a basic error."

The Swordmaster went white. There was death in his eyes, but Lornach merely laughed.

Three more times the Swordmaster struck. Each effort failed, but for each of these attacks Lornach flicked out his sword, deliberately striking the other's body with only the flat of his blade and then dancing out of range.

The Swordmaster had become enraged. His face was twisted and his hands trembled. He tried his best to kill Lornach, but the king's champion was more than his match. When he was ready, Shorty casually disarmed his opponent with a short flick of his blade, a move that Gil had never seen, and the Swordmaster's weapon flew through the air.

The Swordmaster leaped to regain it, but Lornach was quicker, the point of his sword flashing to stop an inch from the other's neck. They both froze where they were, one crouching and reaching toward a blade, the other poised. They both knew that one wrong move would end in death, and it would not be Lornach's.

"I would leave now, if I were you," Lornach said. "Retrieve your sword some other time."

With great care, the Swordmaster straightened and stepped back. He shook violently, and cold fear was etched on his face.

"You are dismissed," Lornach said softly.

The Swordmaster left, but he drew himself together enough to manage a parting shot at Gil.

"I hold you responsible for this!" he hissed. "But your time will come. Think on this, meanwhile. Brand is regent. But he will usurp the throne. You will never be king. *Remember that!*"

Gil did not answer. He looked over at Lornach instead, but if the Durlindrath had paid any attention to what was said, he gave no sign.

Lornach, not even a little out of breath, addressed the students.

"Class is dismissed for the day. You may return tomorrow at the same time. But think on the two lessons you have just learned. Never underestimate an opponent. Never. No matter what they look like. And talk is cheap. If you wish to become accomplished, in any field, take these lessons to heart. The sweat of practice is worth more than empty words. Class dismissed."

The boys trailed away, beginning to talk among themselves as they left. Some cast dark looks at Gil, but Elrika smiled at him.

When they were gone, Lornach spoke. "Forget what the baron said. Brand will see you king. He'll not usurp your throne."

Obviously, he *had* heard the Swordmaster's words. But no more was said after that, even though Gil sensed that Lornach wanted to add more.

It was not the first time Gil had heard the Swordmaster's claim. He shrugged it off though. He did not believe it, but still, human nature being what it was, he was forced to accept the possibility. In a way, it did not matter. He had no wish to be king, no wish for all the responsibilities. He had seen what that had done to his grandfather. He did not want that. Not at all. What he wanted was to keep learning lòhrengai. That was his true passion. With that knowledge, with the gift that was in him, he could make the world a better place.

But no one ever accepted that. He would be king, they said. He half wished that Brand *would* usurp the throne, but that would be a breach of trust, and just the thought of that possibility, of an action like that from a man such as Brand that he admired so much, struck Gil like a blow.

It was a quiet walk back to the palace with Lornach, for they both seemed to be occupied with private thoughts.

They said their goodbyes once they were within the ancestral home of the kings of Cardoroth. And now, Gil realized, Brand's home. Much had happened, and Gil needed to think. Not to mention that at some time during the night he would be going to Carnhaina's tomb. That would undoubtedly be a sobering experience.

Much seemed to be happening these days, and Gil wished he could talk things over with his mother. But she was not there, and he did not really know when she was coming back. She had said she would be with his grandparents, and that was not hard to believe. She was as close to them as she was to her own parents, but Gil had a feeling there was more going on. It was almost as if he had been left in the care of Brand for some other reason. He felt slightly abandoned, but then he dismissed that thought. It was not true, and whatever his mother had done she had done for good reason. And her trust in Brand was just as deep as that of his grandfather's.

The rest of the afternoon passed, and the evening drew on to night. Gil slept, but he woke instantly when he heard a soft knock on his door. He got out of bed, already dressed and in his boots, and opened the door. It was Brand, come to take him to Carnhaina's tomb, but strangely there was no one else with him.

Brand must have sensed exactly what he was thinking. "We go alone, for this," he said.

They spoke little after that. Like dark wraiths they slipped out of the palace. There were no bodyguards. There were no palace staff. There was no one save him and Brand.

Out through the gardens they went, and into the city beyond. It was late, near the midnight hour, and the streets were quiet. They saw few abroad, and those they did see were revelers well-steeped in drink, or the furtive cutthroats who lurked in the dark to prey upon them.

Neither was a problem for Brand. He ignored the first, and the second he seemed to spy out with an uncanny prescience that amazed Gil. He would slow, place a hand on the hilt of his sword and stare into the hidden shadows until whoever hid there knew their ambush would fail and scuttled away.

Brand's eyes were bright, almost eager for battle, and the hunters who hid must have sensed that in his every move and glance. There were easier targets, and they did not long survive on the streets themselves unless their instincts told them when to fight and when to run.

They went through a park. There was no light except for the stars above, and cold fear settled over Gil. This was no place to be at night. Yet Brand walked with sure purpose, his gaze searching the shadows and his strides relaxed and easy.

Before Gil knew it they had come to a cobbled street again, and there before them was the Tower of Halathgar. It reached up into the night, bordered by the park and the trees that grew there. There was light here, some cast by fitful street lamps and some that spilled out of the structure's lower windows.

Gil looked up. Only the base of the tower was lit. Higher, it disappeared into shadows, and somewhere

43

within was the fabled sanctum of Queen Carnhaina. Here, legend held, she came to study the stars away from the palace lights and to work magic while the city slept. Looking at the dark tower now, wreathed in night-shadows, a silhouette of tightknit stone blocks that thrust from the earth like an arm reaching up from the grave, he believed it.

They came to the door at the base of the tower. Two guards stood there, wearing the livery of soldiers of Cardoroth. They did not seem surprised to see someone, least of all the regent and the heir to the throne, and Gil surmised that they knew of this visit.

Brand greeted them, and they saluted him. Quickly, the door was opened and Brand led Gil through. One of the soldiers passed the regent a burning torch, and then the door was closed again.

Gil stood behind Brand while they waited for their eyes to adjust. His heart raced, but Brand seemed as calm as ever. There were signs of a trapdoor on the floor, and beyond that the beginning of a spiral staircase that wound toward the top.

Brand paused, as though in momentary doubt, but Gil caught a glimpse of his face in the ruddy light and saw that his eyes were far away. He was remembering something.

With the slightest of shrugs, Brand started up the stairs.

Gil was confused. Surely that was the wrong way, and they should be opening the trapdoor to go down into the basement.

"I thought we were going to her tomb?" he asked, and even his whispered voice seemed unnatural and loud in the quiet.

"We are," Brand answered. "But it's not in the basement as men think. Instead, it's atop the pinnacle of the tower. You'll see."

Brand did not pause. He walked up the stairs, sure of his way as always, and Gil envied him his confidence.

The stairwell circled the inside of the tower wall and they passed a series of doors that led to inner rooms. They reached the ninth level, and there they found another two guards. No one spoke, but they exchanged nods, and Gil felt the eyes of the soldiers on him, weighing him up.

They came soon to a door that opened onto the top of the tower. It was closed, but apparently not locked, and Brand opened it with a soft touch of his hand. The ancient hinges made no noise.

Brand stepped through first, and he rested his torch against the wall. When Gil stepped through, the regent closed the door behind them.

Gil looked around. He saw an open platform and above the great vault of the sky, star-laden and vast.

Brand led him forward, stepping on soft feet, and Gil followed closely. A chill wind blew into their faces. The city stretched out below. It lay beneath a blanket of shadows, but lights twinkled here and there within it, and the torchlit main streets wound through the dark like rivers of fire.

In the center of the platform a stone monument rose knee-high from the floor. Brand, without hesitation, moved toward it. The structure's sides were slabs of red marble, engraved with strange script and sculpted with scenes of battle. Carved carrion crows, their wings cut sharp-edged and lifelike into the stone, circled above battling armies while wolves prowled the horizon. The single slab that served as a top was tightly fitted to the four sides, but there were groves in the stone as though

45

once it had been removed without care. And black stains, perhaps scorch marks, covered it.

Gil felt a sudden chill beyond even the breeze that blew across the high pinnacle of the tower.

"We should not have come here. Not at night."

Brand turned his gaze upon him, and his eyes were bright.

"I'm too busy during the day."

Gil did not quite believe that. He thought Brand was holding back. However open he seemed to be, he *did* have secrets. Then the words of the Swordmaster rose sinuously in his mind. This, the Swordmaster had said, was the man who would usurp his throne. And he was alone with him in the tower of a long-dead queen. Alone, and no one knew where they were except a handful of guards, and those guards were loyal to Brand.

Gil dismissed such thoughts. They were unworthy. Brand was a great man, a hero, and trusted by all. Instead, he concentrated on the slab that formed the top of the structure. An image of Carnhaina was on it. He was sure it was the same woman from his dreams. She was unmistakable.

He thought back over the long history of the city. It was old. Near a thousand years had passed since its founding, and Carnhaina was there close to its beginning. It was she who had defended it from the hordes that had come from the north. She had beaten them, as she had also beaten the hordes that came from the south. Each had been led by mighty sorcerers of antiquity, but she had defeated them all. But why was she so forgotten? Little was known of her, except that she was also named the witch-queen. Was she a hero or a villain?

A sudden noise broke his thoughts. There was movement too. He looked out over the pinnacle of the tower and into the park. There, he saw the tops of the trees. They seemed very close, and they swayed in the breeze. But something moved among their branches.

Gil strained, searching the darkness. There were crows there. Something had disturbed their roosting and they flapped and hopped from branch to branch. He heard also their rasping call, a croak that sounded oddly human, as though there were words in it. But there were not.

The breeze picked up, and then went still unexpectedly. The crows seemed to go mad, flapping and cawing and some even took to wing in the shadowy air.

Above, the stars twinkled bright. Halathgar was there above the tower, the two stars shining bright against the black sky, looking down like eyes.

The marks on Gil's palms itched. And then they seemed to burn like fire. He held them up, but they looked as they always did.

Brand was not still. He stepped back, back toward the door. In one hand the cold steel of his sword glimmered. In the other, he held once more the torch.

The regent came forward, slowly. The crows cawed and flapped as the light flared and sputtered. The branches of the trees creaked, and the great trunks groaned as the breeze stirred to life again. It came and went according to some rhythm beyond Gil's guess or understanding.

And then, suddenly, everything went still again. The trees did not move. The wind did not blow. In the branches, the now-silent crows merely watched the tower with beady eyes.

Gil's palms burned all the more.

3. Four Horsemen Shall Come

Gil stood perfectly still. Something was happening, but he did not know what. He glanced at Brand, but the regent did not move either, and there was an expression on his face that Gil had never seen before. It might have been awe. It might have been fear. He could not tell which, but that he had never seen it before was unsettling.

The dust on the flagstones of the tower floor rose and seethed. More than that, the top of the monument rattled, and dust sprayed out from its edges. Light glimmered, over and above the fitful flicker of Brand's torch, but it seemed to have no source unless it was the stirring dust itself.

And that dust began to take shape. An ethereal form rose from it in a swirl of color, and Gil staggered back. Brand did not move.

Gil had thought the slab was a monument. Now, he understood that it was a sarcophagus. The image of a woman, tall and majestic, solidified from the dust. She gazed down at the man and the boy, her eyes terrible and stern. They were blue, cold as Lake Alithorin in winter, but her skin was pale, and her unbound hair shone like spilled blood. Luxurious curls ran down her back and shimmered in the shadowy air. She was a massive figure, heavy-boned and thick-limbed. A gold torc gleamed brilliantly about her neck, and her body was clad in a tunic of many colors. In her right hand she grasped an iron-headed spear as though ready to strike.

Her stare bored into them. "Who comes hither? Who disturbs my rest?"

They did not answer. The eyes of the long-dead queen burned upon Brand, and there was recognition in them.

"You," she said, pointing at him with her spear. "You I know. Brand you are called, though other names you might yet earn. If you live."

Her chill gaze fell on Gil. His blood turned to ice, but his hands felt like they were on fire.

She studied him long before she spoke. "You also I know, blood of my blood, heir to my realm. You I know, though you do not yet know yourself."

She paused. The breeze blew across the top of the tower, and her hair ruffled and moved. But Gil could see through her, see that she was at once real, and not real. It made his heart thud in his chest, but the blood in his body seemed frozen in place.

"Do you know who I am?" she said to Gil, her spear poised, but her glance sharper still. "Speak!"

Gil found his voice. "You are Carnhaina. Once you ruled this realm. Once, you were Queen of Cardoroth."

His voice failed him after that. But she did not seem to notice.

"Yes, that was me." She spoke almost as though she were talking of someone else. "And you are Gilcarist. Heir to my throne." She paused again. "You are younger even than I thought."

She glanced thoughtfully at Brand. "There is danger abroad," she said.

Brand held her gaze. "When is there not?"

She laughed at that. The crows in the trees flapped madly.

"Well spoken!" she replied. "You will be ready, but being ready is not enough. Not this time." She seemed as though she would say more on the subject, but then she broke the regent's gaze momentarily before looking back and saying something obviously different from what she had intended. "Is the boy ready?"

Brand shrugged. "Ready for what? But I have brought him here, so you can ask him yourself."

"Then I shall!"

She looked at Gil, and he felt the weight of her mind upon him. He wondered how Brand dared speak to her as he did.

"Well, boy. Are you ready? Are you ready to learn who you are?" Her gaze scrutinized him, measured him, found out all his innermost secrets. "Are you ready to learn what you most desire? To know why your palms are marked? To know your destiny?"

Gil nodded. His voice was a whisper. "Yes."

"And if you do not like what you discover?" she pressed him.

He did not know what to say, and the fear that he felt irked him, so he followed Brand's nonchalant example and shrugged.

"Why don't you tell me, and then we'll both know."

She stared at him a moment. Starlight glinted on the tip of her spear, and it seemed as though the whole night held its breath. But then, with a backward toss of her head, she roared with laughter.

After a moment she fixed him with her glinting gaze. "I guess you're as ready as you can be. Brand has taught you well, and your blood shows."

The once-queen of Cardoroth stood silent a moment. The night was still. The crows were subdued, and the starlit heavens twinkled and shone amid the great dark.

"It will be dangerous," she said, her voice now turning soft and solemn. "Learning who you are, and

51

more importantly who you can be, will not be safe. Do you accept that danger?"

Gil looked into her eyes. "I do," he answered boldly.

"You would know the meaning of the marks on your palms?" she challenged.

"I would."

"You may not like what you discover."

"So be it," he answered.

The spirit that was Carnhaina drew herself up. "Then look and learn!"

She swept up the arm that carried her spear, and the air shimmered. When it stilled, Gil looked no longer upon reality but a vision. His eyes fixed upon it, drawn as if by a will beyond his own.

He saw the tallest mountains of the land, the far northern borders of Alithoras. They were cold, and the great stretches of pine forests that clad them were draped with snow. Ice covered the ridges. Yet there was peace there, a sense of tranquility. And cold though it was, the sky was blue and the sun shone down benevolently.

Gil sensed Brand stir beside him. Then the vision flickered. Swift images came of a lake that might have been Lake Alithorin. Then there were cities and realms and wild lands of hill and forest. There were battles. Battles with men and creatures that were not men. There was sorcery and magic, and a great sweep of time and distance. There were castles and farms and endless leagues of long grass, and then the vision cleared and stilled once more.

Now, the land was dry and desolate. The hot sun hammered down. The sand and dirt shimmered. Gil felt a sense of malice, a threat of ill-will in the very air. This was Grothanon, the land of the ancient enemy, the land that threatened all of Alithoras, and there was a presence there. Gil concentrated on that, focused his mind upon the source of that hatred. But even as he did so Carnhaina quickly swept her hand down and the vision ceased.

The witch-queen gazed at him, and there was something unreadable in her eyes. Gil had the feeling that she had intended to show more, but had stopped sooner than she planned.

"Alithoras!" she said, her voice ringing. "Our land. A great land, but there is evil within it. And only by the deeds of heroes is that evil kept at bay."

She leaned upon her spear, and turned her gaze upon Brand.

"You," she continued. "You have fought in that battle, and have a sense of what threatens the land. But you sit on a chair as a play-king, not upon the throne of Cardoroth. But if you wished it, you could take the throne itself. None would stand in your way. You have proven yourself worthy, and the land *needs* you. Think, man, of the power you could wield. Why have you not taken it?"

Gil could not believe what he was hearing. This was his own great-grandmother, many times removed. Was she suggesting Brand usurp the throne of her own descendant?

Brand did not move. Still as a carven stone he stood, but he answered her.

"In truth," he replied, "I have considered it. I know exactly how to become king of Cardoroth, and I could do it in less than a week, if I so chose. But I have no interest in that."

Carnhaina gazed at him, then spoke. "You would be a great king. Perhaps even the greatest who ever ruled in Alithoras. Think on that, Brand of the Duthenor."

Her spear swept up again. Suddenly an image of Brand stood there, gazing back at himself. This Brand

53

was older, but not yet old. A mighty crown rested on his head, and liegemen knelt before him. Behind, misted and swirling, were other cities and other lands. This Brand ruled them all, and his glance was piercing as a sword. Wisdom was in it, and great joy and sorrow. It was Brand, and not Brand.

The regent laughed. "You seek to test me, Carnhaina, but you know what I want, and it isn't that. My goal is far less lofty, and even so I guess now that I will never achieve it. Not directly anyway. My destiny, if there is such a thing, is different. And I accept that."

"Destiny," whispered the queen. "Destiny is what you make it, and I know you perceive that. Still, I will not say that your answer is wrong."

Gil had a feeling that they were taking about things of which they both understood, but he knew none of it. Though it did occur to him that Brand would be a great king, better than he would, and that if the regent usurped the throne it would relieve him of the responsibility himself. He had, in truth, no desire to rule. He wanted to learn more of the magic. Lòhrengai was his love, and with that he could make the world a better pace.

But he had no time to think now. The gaze of the queen fell upon him, and it was as though she read his every thought. She was a spirit creature, dead long centuries, but who knew what powers she had in life, and retained still in death? He trembled under her scrutiny, but did not back away though his every instinct was to turn and run.

"And you?" she said. "What of your destiny? Would you know it?"

"Yes," Gil answered, and it seemed that the air in his throat had turned to ice.

"Then," the queen replied, "behold!"

Up swept the spear again, and it pointed straight at him. He could not blink. He could not look away. And suddenly he wished that he had indeed fled, but his feet were rooted to the spot just as his eyes could not turn away.

He saw himself. He was in the forest surrounding Lake Alithorin again. The trees were dark and shadowy about him. At his feet lay Brand. Dead. Blood covered the regent. Blood from some mighty battle, some struggle that not even the great Brand could survive. His eyes, lifeless, stared up at the sky. The vision swept away, and the marks on Gil's palms burned and ached.

He looked up at the witch-queen, confused but defiant. "That tells me nothing. Tell me why I have these marks!" He lifted up his hands and white light glimmered about them. "Why? And why show me such visions? Brand can't be both dead and king in the future. Tell me the truth!"

Carnhaina gazed at him steadily. Her face was a mask, hiding any trace of what she felt. Just like Brand, Gil thought.

The witch-queen answered, and her voice was softer than it had been.

"The truth is that destiny must be discovered. Or made. Made from the day-to-day events that shape your life. Made from the choices that you make. Both visions are true. Both are false. And I can explain it no clearer than that. But you will understand when you are there, when you are faced with choices. For now, know that the marks serve a purpose. Through them, you shall find yourself."

Gil knew when someone was hiding the truth from him. Not lying, but not revealing all that they knew.

"Those are just words," he said. "They mean nothing."

Carnhaina fixed him with her glittering eyes. "Words, is it? You will learn that no force of arms, no power of magic, no strength of will is as great as words. One day, you will know that. But in the meantime, I give you this. Pay heed, for the eyes of the dead see what is to come, or what has already passed. Pay heed, for this shall shape your life. And Brand's."

Carnhaina straightened. Midnight shadows darkened her hair, but the light of stars was in her eyes and she looked fierce, regal, deadly. Deadly and more dangerous than any person Gil had ever met.

"Four horsemen shall come," she said. "And that you shall know them, these are their names. First, Death. Next War. Then shall follow Time. Last, and greatest of them all, Betrayal."

The dead queen lifted up her spear as though it were a scepter of authority.

"Beware! For things are not always as they seem. Before the sun sets tomorrow you shall see Death. It shall mark a beginning, for from thence forward a hidden assassin will try to kill you. He may or may not succeed. But success or failure is still victory for him."

Gil did not understand the queen's words. How could a horseman be called Death? How could a failure be success? It made no sense, but he felt nonetheless a chill run through him, and he saw that Brand looked at the queen intently.

"Discover the identity of the assassin. You will have friends to help you. When you know, the truth shall protect you."

Carnhaina turned to Brand. "You have seen your death," she said. "In the dark forest around Lake Alithorin it shall come to pass. The boy will witness it."

"So be it," Brand answered. There was no trace of emotion in his voice. "No man lives forever."

Carnhaina leaned once more upon her spear, but the intensity of her eyes did not diminish.

"In truth," she said, "you are a fitting heir to me. You are a warrior and a lòhren – a user of magic. You could take the throne and live. It is yours, if you want it."

Brand shrugged. "I know temptation when I hear it. I also know that Cardoroth's army is my friend," he paused. "The aristocrats are irrelevant."

The queen laughed. A cold laugh, without mirth. "They always were. So, take the throne!" she urged. "Take it!"

Brand shook his head. "No. I don't want it. And even if I did, I still wouldn't take it."

Carnhaina studied him, and there was some emotion on her face that Gil could not decipher.

"Then," the queen said at length. "Know this. If you do not, the vision I showed shall come to pass. You will perish within the forests of Lake Alithorin."

Brand, as ever, showed no reaction. But he stood very still.

"As I say, all men die."

Gil thought the regent's voice was cold as the void, but notwithstanding that Brand showed nothing of what he felt, Gil still sensed the hot emotion that lay somewhere beyond sight.

Carnhaina laughed, and Gil suddenly wondered if she was sane.

"So be it," she answered, and she bowed her head.

Gil realized that she had begun to fade. She had seemed so present, but now there was no mistaking that she was a shade, an echo of someone who once had lived.

She lifted her head briefly toward Gil. "Remember the Mark of Halathgar," she said. "When you need help the most, call upon it …"

It was yet another puzzle to Gil. She was the queen of enigmas, and he sensed that although much was said that he did not understand, many things were the opposite of what they seemed. He felt that strikingly as her gaze rested on him. There was the promise of answers in that glance, and a hint that despite what she had urged Brand to do, she was really looking out for Gil, and for Cardoroth, in a way that made no sense now but would later.

Suddenly, the breeze gusted. Brand's torch guttered. When it flared to life once more, the spirit of Carnhaina was gone.

4. I am Death

Brand led Gil down the tower stairs in silence. If the guards had heard anything, they gave no sign. Nor did they speak. They looked ahead as though no one was there, and Gil did not blame them.

Out on the dark streets, Brand remained quiet. He was a man deep in thought, his face shadowed and his head bowed. He did not look like he wished to talk, but Gil risked a question.

"The stories of Carnhaina, the few that I've ever heard, are all strange. She proved that tonight. But what I want to know is … well, is she good or bad?"

Brand gave thought to that question before he answered. His pace did not slow, but his head came up a little and he cast a sideways glance at Gil.

"She was one who delved into sorcery," Brand said. "In truth, there is little difference between magic and sorcery, between what we call lòhrengai and what they call elùgai. Yet, I'm told that though she delved into elùgai, she did not go deeply down that path. The difference is not in the power itself, but in the use to which that power is put."

Brand slowed a little now. He looked over at Gil, assessing how much he understood of this.

"In short, the line between a lòhren and an elùgroth, an adept in dark sorcery, is finer than most think. But know this. It's far more important than labels. Often, we forget what people say, but we never forget how they make us feel. Remember that. And think on how

Carnhaina made you *feel*. That will answer your question."

Gil considered that. Carnhaina certainly scared him, but she had treated him like an adult, too. Only Brand really did that. So, how did she make him feel? On reflection, he realized that in talking to her that he felt a part of something, a part of something great, a part of a long history of defiance against the evil in the world. And thinking of her last glance toward him, he sensed love there, and concern. No matter that she did not say it directly, *it was still there.* That was what he felt. He had learned another of Brand's lessons, and it was one of the best.

They spoke no further after that. Each had much to think about, and no one troubled them on the streets. It was late when they came back to the palace, and the guards admitted them into the building without comment.

Gil went to bed and fell swiftly asleep, but it was a troubled slumber and frequently his mind, drifting between waking and oblivion, pondered all of Carnhaina's words. But though he turned them over and over in his mind, he made little sense of them.

Eventually, he fell into a deeper sleep and straightaway he dreamed once again of the woman in the woods. It was the same as always, and yet somehow different too. This time, it went further.

The woman placed her bony hands on the acolyte. Whether to calm him or hold him against his will, Gil did not know. But the acolyte, though filled with terror, did not move. Still as a statue he stood, his face pale and his bulging eyes white in the moonlight, while the woman lifted her sickle shaped knife.

That part of Gil's mind that was aware even in the midst of a dream recoiled. It sought out the aid of Carnhaina who had in some way saved him from seeing this last time, but she was not there. Yet, on thinking of her, he found strength of his own and drew back to wakefulness.

He woke with a start, the dream shadowing him as though real and reluctant to let him escape, even when his eyes were open. Eventually, though, that feeling faded.

He fell asleep again after that, and was not troubled any further. Yet it seemed that he had only just fallen asleep when he woke once more. Time must have passed though, for light streamed in from the windows.

His first thought was that he was late for his early morning training with Brand, but he did not think that would be an issue. Not after last night. Brand would have slept in too. His second thought was that something was wrong.

He got up and dressed quickly. There was much noise out in the city streets while he did so. He heard it dimly even in the palace, and there were many passing feet out in the corridors, many more than usual even for this later hour of the morning. Worse, he heard muffled conversations as people hurried past his door, but one word was repeated and he heard it quite clearly. *Devil.*

When he was ready he opened the door and went out into the corridor. No one was here just now, not even the Durlin who usually guarded it at night.

He walked along a little further, and after a few turns and twists there were suddenly people everywhere. They looked frightened, and when they saw him they

61

scattered. They knew what was happening, but had no wish to tell him for some reason.

Gil made up his mind. He would go to the throne room and talk to Brand. He would get the truth that way, and he knew Brand would be there. That was where the city leaders gathered in times of trouble, and Gil had a sense that trouble had come.

As he moved through the passageways they became increasingly busy. People were everywhere, standing and talking, and soldiers and messengers filled the gaps.

Gil was not sure what to do, for the way through seemed blocked, and he became increasingly alarmed at hearing the word *devil* repeated in low whispers. Something terrible was happening, and he could not get through to see Brand.

He was about to try to push his way ahead when suddenly he came face to face with Elrika, the last person he had expected to see. He saw her seldom even though her father was the palace baker, but hers was a friendly face so he greeted her and asked if she knew what was happening.

"I think so," she said, but she got no further. A group of soldiers pressed through and separated them, heading toward the throne room.

Elrika reached out for him and took him by the arm. "Follow me. We'll get separated if we're not careful."

She led him back the way he had come, but the press of people was growing and it was now almost as hard to go back as forward.

"Have you had breakfast yet?" she asked.

Gil shook his head. "No."

"Then we'll head to the kitchen."

Gil wanted to ask her to explain what was happening, but the kitchen was not far away and they could talk properly there without the noise and racket that filled the corridors.

They passed along a few more passageways, and then Elrika turned down a corridor that was much quieter. At its end was a stairwell. This they followed for several flights until they came out again in a passageway Gil was more familiar with. Before them was a set of oak doors, old and worn, and though he was not sure if he had ever been through them before he knew they were at the back of the kitchen, the entry the servants used.

Elrika went through. The doors swung closed behind them, and straightaway the noise died down. There were people here, working away at chopping vegetables and dicing meat. They gave Elrika a quick glance and then paid her no more heed. They had seen her many times before and if Gil was with her, then he was nothing to worry about either. They did not seem to recognize him, and he liked that.

They passed through several other rooms, one of which contained a long bank of hearths with great brick chimneys, but there were few fires lit this morning. At lunch and dinner there would be more.

Gil had been here before, but he had been much younger. He barely remembered any of it, but Elrika knew where she was going and she quickly turned into a side room. This was the bakery, and hundreds of loaves of still-warm bread cooled on wooden racks along with many varieties of pastries.

Elrika reached out and grabbed one of the pastries and then sat down at a small table in the corner.

"Hungry?" she asked.

"Starving," Gil answered.

She carefully tore the pastry in half, and gave him one of the portions. It was filled with a combination of savory meats and dried fruits.

She took a bite of hers. "My favorite," she said.

Gil tried his piece. He had never had it before, and he found it delicious.

She took another bite and then leaned forward over the table toward him.

"This is what I know," she said. "My father heard it direct from the first messenger this morning who came in from the West Gate." She paused to take another bite of the pastry.

"The Arach Neben," she said, using the old name for the gate, "is closest to the dark forests that surround Lake Alithorin. The messenger said that a devil had come from there, a devil such as Cardoroth has never seen before."

There were many legends about those woods, and Gil had heard plenty of them. Dark things were said to dwell there, and he believed it, though he had never seen any himself. The forest was out of bounds to him.

"What did the messenger mean by the word devil, though? Some sort of creature?"

Elrika shook her head at once. "No. Not a creature. A man, or something like a man. And he rides upon a horse."

Gil went perfectly still, and his stomach churned with sudden fear. He remembered back to last night. It had seemed like a dream in the light of day, but he knew it was not. What had Carnhaina said? He could hear her voice in his mind. *Four horsemen shall come.* That was what she had told him. And the first would be called Death.

He made himself speak. "And what does this rider want?"

She was looking at him strangely, but she answered him quickly enough.

"He has not spoken nor moved since he arrived. Other messengers have come to the palace since the first. He waits, motionless on his horse, before the Arach Neben."

Gil sat there, his mind racing. What else had Carnhaina said? But Elrika interrupted his musings.

"You already know this, don't you?"

"No. Not really. Not at all," Gil said, still thinking of last night.

She gave him a long look from the other side of the table, but did not speak. Gil knew he had a friend here, but friends did not keep secrets. If he did not tell her what he knew, she would draw away from him, and suddenly that was the very last thing he wanted.

"Last night Brand took me to the Tower of Halathgar."

There was a reaction in the girl's eyes, and surprise was a part of it.

"The tower in the park? Isn't that where…" she trailed off.

"Yes. Whatever rumors you've heard are probably true, and far more besides."

He confided in her then. He was going to tell her just the basics, but instead he told her everything. He left nothing out, and she listened quietly. If she was surprised at Carnhaina's spirit appearing, as she must have been, she did not show it.

"Thank you for telling me that," she said when he was done. "It's a long story, and honestly, I'm not sure if

I could have believed it except for the fact that the rider has come."

Gil knew what she meant. He was not sure that he would have believed it in her position at all.

Elrika took the last bite of her pastry and chewed it thoughtfully.

"So, what do you think the rider wants? Why does he just wait?"

Gil had not considered that, but instantly he knew.

"He's not going to try to come into the city. He's waiting for someone to go out to him. He's waiting for Brand."

Elrika looked at him. "I heard some soldiers talking. They said Brand was going to confront this thing, whatever it is. But I ignored them. I didn't think the regent would get involved personally. I thought he'd send someone."

Gil shook his head. "No. This whole thing reeks of sorcery, and Brand is the only one in the city who can deal with that."

They exchanged looks. They both wanted to go to the city wall and see the horseman, and they both wanted to see what Brand would do about it.

They did not even speak. It was in their eyes, and they stood and raced away out of the kitchen. Brand had probably already gone, so they would have to hurry to get to the city wall in time.

As they raced ahead Gil wondered about his bodyguards. In the confusion this morning he was unguarded, and that was unusual. He was not supposed to go out onto the streets without at least one Durlin, but it would take too long to find anybody now and get to the wall in time, even if they would take him there.

66

They raced out into the palace gardens and Elrika made for the streets.

"Wait!" he called. "It's too slow that way. We'll need a horse."

She stopped and looked back at him. "I don't know how to ride."

"Never mind," he said. "Follow me."

He led her to the stables and picked a quiet mare. Quickly he saddled her and got her ready, and then he helped Elrika up.

"She's quiet this one, but fast."

When Elrika was in the saddle he mounted and took the reins.

"Hold on tight!"

Her arms wrapped around him from behind and he nudged the horse forward into a trot. When they were out of the palace grounds and into the streets he kicked the horse into a much faster pace.

The streets were full of people. They always were, but riders were common and the city-folk kept a way clear on the side of the road. They did look though, for the mare rattled through at a fast pace and the clatter of her hooves over the cobbles was loud.

Gil felt a thrill run through him. He was free of the bodyguards, free of the palace and its constant undertone of politics. He was out in the city, a member of the population just like anybody else, and he had not felt that for a long time.

He knew that he led a privileged life. In many ways, he liked that. But it came with a burden of expectation. He would be king one day, and he did not really want to be. There was no freedom in that. It was a prison. He had learned as much from his grandfather, and it would shackle him to Cardoroth and his duty to rule the city and the realm. Such expectations left no room for what he really loved.

Even as he rode he felt the magic deep within him. It was always there, ready to stir at his will. He did not have much control of it yet, but that would come with practice and age. But in his case, as he grew older and took on more responsibilities, his opportunities to practice would lessen. What then of his dreams? To rule Cardoroth was something, but he could do more. If he mastered the magic, if he became a lòhren, he could be a force of good for the whole of Alithoras, not just one of its realms.

They raced through the streets and Gil was conscious of Elrika's arms wrapped tightly about him. She had not ridden a horse before, and she was scared. He could feel it in the way she gripped him. But at the same time he sensed that she was exhilarated too, and he was glad that he had confided in her.

They sped ahead. Tall buildings loomed over them. Dark alleys opened to either side, the sorts of places that were dangerous at night but were now filled with people and life. Above, red-tiled roofs glittered in the morning sun and high-arched windows flitted by. Gil did not hold back, desperate to get to the gate in time to see what would happen. He urged the mare forward, and she sprang ahead.

They saw the wall well before they came to it. It was the city's main protection. Throughout the history of Cardoroth no enemy had breached it, though, in the recent war, that had nearly happened. The people called it the Cardurleth.

Gil saw something ahead, and abruptly slowed the mare.

"What is it?" Elrika asked.

"Soldiers," Gil answered. "Lots of them."

He felt her lean sideways to look out past his body. "I see them. What are they doing?"

Gil was not sure. "They don't seem to be blocking the way. And many are mounted. I wonder…"

"What?"

Gil had gained a little more on them now. They only travelled at a trot.

"We're not too late," he said. "Brand rides at their head. I just caught a glimpse of him."

Gil deliberately stayed some distance behind. If he was seen now, he could be ordered back to the palace. Elrika did not say anything about his slowing down, and he guessed that she understood exactly what he was doing.

Nevertheless, they were nearly at the Cardurleth anyway, and within a few minutes Gil veered away down a side street. Then, he urged the mare forward again and they raced toward a spot he knew just a little away from the Arach Neben. It would take him far enough from the gate so that Brand would be unlikely to see him, and there was a wooden set of stairs leading up to the battlement where they would have a view of the encounter between Brand and the waiting horseman.

They came quickly to the wall. Once there they jumped down from the mare and Gil tied its reins to a hitching rail. Without hesitation after that, they raced up the stairs. The top of the battlement was filled with people, and Gil worried that he would not get a good view, but the two of them managed to press through

69

until they came to a spot near the tower that protected the gate. There were some soldiers there who recognized him, and they made room so that he could see. Perhaps they would not have if they knew he was there without permission, but he was not going to tell them that.

They peered out over the battlement. The horseman was there, below them, motionless. They could not see much, and Gil was at first unsure why the people were calling this man a devil.

The horse he sat upon was black, but his robes were all of white. A white cowl covered his head, and he sat perfectly, even unnaturally, still. Then the black horse snorted, and Gil saw its nostrils flare. Inside, they were red raw, and a flicker of crimson flame curled within them. It was an eerie sight. But then he wondered if he had imagined it.

Even as the horse moved, the rider moved a little to keep his balance, and something stranger still occurred.

There were flies. A cloud of them rose, thickening the air, and then they landed upon the rider again and were still.

The rider stirred again, of his own accord this time. For a moment he looked around uncertainly, and then his gaze shifted to the Cardurleth, shifted straight to Gil, and fixed upon him.

Gil gazed back, enthralled. He could not understand it, but he sensed beyond any doubt that the rider knew exactly who he was.

And then, as if to confirm it, the rider lifted his arm and pointed right at him. A bent blade was in the figure's hand, sickle-shaped and wicked. The black metal of the strange weapon gleamed dully.

Gil felt a sudden stab of fear. It was overwhelming, but then the horse shifted its stance, the attention of the rider faltered, and Brand was there.

The regent came through the gate. His sword was sheathed at his side and in one hand he bore a white staff, the staff of a lòhren. He walked casually, seemingly unafraid, as though he strolled through the gardens surrounding the palace.

Gil felt movement beside him. Lornach was there. How the Durlin had found him, Gil did not know, but neither spoke. All that Lornach did was glance at him, and Gil felt suddenly embarrassed. He knew that he had done the wrong thing sneaking away from the palace, but there was no opportunity to say anything just now.

Below, a macabre scene unfolded that could not attract less than the full attention of every person who stood upon the battlement.

The rider urged his horse forward a few steps closer, approaching Brand and becoming more visible to those who watched. He came to a stop then, and pulled back his hood. The flies swarmed again, and a sudden stench filled the air.

Gil saw that the rider was no living man. Where a head should have been, there was a skull. Tufted hair sprouted from it. Skin clung to it in a few places and hung loose in others. Maggots fell from what had once been a face to ground. The eyes were writhing, bubbling pits of horror, and they fixed on Brand with unwavering hatred.

Some on the Cardurleth vomited. Many turned away. Gil closed his eyed and whispered, or perhaps merely thought to himself, he did not know, *Can Brand endure this?*

71

Lornach answered, or maybe guessed his thought. "Watch." His voice was hoarse, but there was a strange confidence in it.

Gil opened his eyes.

The rider was still again, but now he spoke. "I am Death," he said coldly, and his voice carried up to the battlement and beyond by some art of sorcery.

Brand gave a nonchalant shrug. "You certainly look dead enough."

There was silence for a moment, and then a grim laugh came in answer. It sounded like the rattle of bones rising from a deep pit.

"Death is where all living things go. Only I was there first. And I will be there last. And I will be there when no life is left at all, unchanged. Death is the only thing that survives death."

Brand straightened. "Well, you talk a lot – for a dead man. But let's get to the point, shall we? What is it that you want?"

The horseman smiled. His mount shifted its footing and neighed. Red fire flickered at its nostrils, curling up to lick at the air before its eyes. Gil was sure of it this time.

Brand remained relaxed and still, and Gil felt in awe of him. The presence of the rider was overwhelming even up on the battlement, yet Brand was right next to him and seemed unconcerned. What had that man endured in life to forge his will into a thing of such iron?

"I am Death," the rider responded slowly. "I want you. Many times have you cheated me, but you cannot cheat me forever. But this I will give you. It is a respite. If you take up the crown of Cardoroth, I will let you live … at least a little while longer."

72

A chill went through Gil. Carnhaina had also said that Brand would die unless he usurped the throne. What was going on here?

"I've been threatened before," Brand replied, and there was a new edge to his voice. "But my enemies are all dead."

The horseman laughed, and he seemed genuinely amused.

"Dead? Are they? *All* of them? I tell you this much, if no more. One at least lives."

"And who is that?" Brand asked.

"Ah! You will discover that. Eventually. But she knows you well. Yes, long has she studied *you*, and learned all your secrets."

"What does she want?"

"Revenge. And she shall have it."

Brand seemed puzzled, but his gaze did not leave his enemy.

"Revenge for what?"

The horse shook its head and pranced for a moment where it stood. The rider moved in the saddle to keep his balance and the flies swarmed and settled again.

"That is enough. I am done, for now at least. My message is delivered. Rule Cardoroth and live. Become king, and live. Anything else, and die."

Brand would have spoken more, but the rider and the horse both began to writhe. The stench that had come from them before increased. Maggots dropped to the earth like rain, and the bodies fell apart, seeping into the earth.

The rider was gone, but his words lingered, and doubt was in everyone's heart. What would Brand do?

The regent, for his part, studied the ground a moment as though in mild surprise and then casually turned and walked back through the Arach Neben. He disappeared from view.

Gil heard the crowd begin to whisper, and he felt eyes upon him. He was recognized by more than the soldiers now that people's attention was no longer focused below, and his name was on the lips of many. He felt suddenly very uncomfortable.

Lornach ushered him and Elrika away toward the back of the battlement.

"Time to return to the palace," the Durlindrath said.

Gil was worried. He exchanged a look with Elrika, and he saw fear in her eyes. It was not of the rider though, but rather of the words that had been uttered.

Without doubt, Gil trusted Brand. He trusted him with his life. The man was a legend. No one in the city could do what he just did, save perhaps Lornach or Taingern, the other Durlindrath. Yet still, between the words of Carnhaina and now this, Gil began to wonder. Brand would not be human if these warnings did not go to his heart. What man could ignore the same warning that came from friend and foe alike?

5. Other Servants than You

It was dark, and yet a glimmer of light came from the stone basin. The liquid within it moved, stirred to sluggish life by the images that played across its surface.

Ginsar watched. Her gaze was steady, but her pale hands trembled with excitement.

"It begins," she whispered.

Her acolytes, crowded behind her to try to see what she saw in the basin, did not answer. But their black-cloaked forms shuffled nervously.

Ginsar sensed their fear. She understood it, for the horseman that she saw in the basin, the horseman that confronted Brand, the horseman known as Death, had been one of their number. She had sacrificed him, and they had watched, and into the shell of his body she had summoned a force from without this world. And this she would do three more times.

The acolytes were right to be frightened. A smile played over her red lips, and she licked them in anticipation.

But her eyes never left the images she saw before her. She was drawn to Brand. Fascinated and repelled at the same time. Her hatred stirred, but she calmed herself and listened. By her arts she could do that, do what none of the acolytes could do, though they were sorcerers. And she liked what she heard.

Had she the power she would watch Brand all day, study his every move and word, and fuel her hatred of him. But she could not. She saw and heard only because her servant was there.

Somewhere in the dark of the chamber water dripped. It was always wet here. She hated it, but it was home. The cave had been home to her brother before, and to her master also. But they were gone…

Ginsar did not let her thoughts stray in that direction. She focused again on what was happening, and her heart leapt as she saw puzzlement on the regent's face. How she hated Brand! How she *loved* to hate him. It was exquisite to see him thus, pretending to be unafraid but all the while sensing that doom was catching up to him.

The horseman had delivered his message and seeped back into the earth. But he would come again, would rise for the confrontation that was inevitable. Inevitable as death itself.

The images ceased. The glow of light in the liquid faded away. It was still now, a dull red. And as the power was withdrawn from it, the blood in the basin began to congeal.

Light flared behind her, harsh and orange. One of the acolytes held a torch. With its flickering end he lit another set in the wall. On he would go, for many torches were needed to light this underground chamber. But her other servants gathered about her.

"It is done," she said. "The wheels are set in motion."

"Why not just kill them, man and boy both?" one of the acolytes asked.

Ginsar gazed at him and he shrank back. The acolyte beside the speaker looked at his brother. For a moment, a wicked smile played across his face, but then was suppressed. Oh, how she loved it. She could read their every thought, see their every strategy. They hated one another, mistrusted one another and gloried in each other's errors. They vied for her attention, always seeking to be her favorite, and she loved that too.

Ginsar took a slow step forward. With her left hand she suddenly struck the acolyte who had spoken across the face.

The man reeled back, stunned by the raw force of the slap. He sagged to his knees and held his face in both hands, cowering.

With slow steps Ginsar approached. She stopped just before him, and drew herself up. There she towered above her servant, and he prostrated himself at her feet, whimpering.

Ginsar breathed in of the air, breathed in and trembled. How simple, how easy to snuff out this man's life. The temptation possessed her, made her heart flutter wildly. She lusted for it and her eyes blazed.

Slowly, she drew herself back. Not now. Not yet. His life meant nothing, but she would spend it wisely. A time would come later, would come for them all. They were only instruments to further her purpose, and when her purpose was achieved … she would celebrate.

She smiled. With a soft hand she reached down, caressed the man's cheek and drew him up to his feet.

When he stood, she lifted his chin and gazed into his eyes.

"Remember this. The power of life and death is mine. Brand and the boy will both die. But not just yet. First, they must suffer. They must suffer now, for after death they are beyond my reach."

The acolyte did not speak, but he trembled at the touch of her hand. She loved this power over him, over them all. They thought her mad, but they could not leave her. Thus they served, hating her and loving her by turns. Fawning for her favor, hating each other, desperate to learn from her store of secrets and power.

Ginsar let her hand drop from the man and turned away. She glanced at the basin. It was void of light now, a mass of thick blood, congealing. It would show her no more this day, but her plan was underway, and nothing could stop it.

Brand would die. He would pay for killing her brother. But that was not all. Her hatred for him was fierce. She would do anything to destroy him. She would destroy the world itself to get at him, but her hatred went deeper still.

She turned back to the acolytes and surveyed them. They were dark things, cloaked in black and filled with hatred like herself. They were sorcerers all, elùgroths, adepts of the dark powers that moved and substanced the world. But they had not her power, nor her knowledge, nor her foresight.

"Listen," she said to them. "I teach you the art that you desire to learn. I teach you elùgai. You know that in an age long since passed my own master was Shurilgar. From him I learned much, but the sight that I have, the foresight that blesses me, is my own. I was born with it, and I can see what was, and what is, and a measure what may yet be."

She paused to look at them, to gauge how much she should reveal.

"My sight stretches back to that age. My memory also, and I remember the founding of the kingdom men call Cardoroth. I remember it, and I remember also the rise of Carnhaina. It was she who taught my master defeat,

78

and that was a bitter lesson to him, and to us who served him."

The elùgroths remained still, listening to her every word. The cavern was alight now with smoke-reeking torches, but the forms of the sorcerers remained shadows.

"That queen is long since dead, but her line endures. And while it lives, so too does our enemy. For though the queen is dead, yet still can she work through him to stymie my plans. I will not suffer that. I will not suffer her line to walk upon the earth. And I will not suffer Brand who killed my brother."

Her voice rose, and anger flashed in her eyes. "Think not that these things are unrelated. A battle is underway, the same battle that commenced a thousand years ago. Verily, Shurilgar was my master, and still is. We both serve the Dark, and Brand is of the Light. He is the key. Kill him, and the Light dies in Cardoroth. Kill him, and the death of the boy will follow. Kill him, and the long battle is at last won!"

There was silence when she finished speaking. The only sound was the constant drip of water. Into that quiet one of the acolytes, braver than the others, spoke.

"What now, Mistress?"

Ginsar smiled at him, rewarding his courage, showing him favor above the others.

"I have agents in the city," she said. Yet, seeing surprise on their faces, laughed. "I have other servants than you! But do not fret, my beloved. They are as nothing. They have no power, not of sorcery anyway. Yet still, they have uses."

She smiled again, to herself this time. She had set things in motion, perceived by the power of her second sight how they must proceed. It would not be long before revenge was hers, and the taste of that was sweet in her mouth. And when she closed her eyes, she pictured every detail.

"Now," she continued, "we must wait. Fate and human nature will unfold as they must."

She saw the puzzled looks on their faces, knew they did not understand. But they would.

As would Brand and the boy.

6. Dagger of the Duthenor

Gil was alone. After Lornach had seen him and Elrika back to the palace, they had all gone their separate ways. He was heading to his bedroom to study; a treatise on infantry tactics awaited him, and he treasured the feeling that walking the palace passages by himself and the prospect of several hours of uninterrupted study gave him.

Time alone was rare these days, and he enjoyed not having his every move watched by the Durlin who guarded him. It was true that they were subtle, that many of the city people and palace staff would not even have noticed how they trailed him, or spread out before him. But *he* did.

There had been much commotion after the horseman, and everyone's routines had been disrupted. There was sure to be a guard waiting outside his door when he got there, or one would arrive as soon as Lornach sent him. They were always outside his door, and he did not much like that either.

He walked through the empty passages, so different from how full of people they had been when news of the rider broke, and he heard a noise behind him. He turned and looked, but there was nothing there.

Moving on he came to a flight of stairs and ascended them. There was no further sound, but as he came into another passageway and strode down it, he heard a noise again.

Once more he turned, and this time he saw a man. Gil appraised him quickly, wondering who he was. He was not a soldier nor a palace servant. But he seemed nondescript and ordinary, so Gil gave a mental shrug and walked on. His room was close now.

It was a mistake, and he knew it instantly. No sooner had he turned to the front again than there was a flurry of movement from behind. The man had raced toward him.

Gil turned. He saw the flash of a blade, dull and frightful. He had no time to do anything except twist to the side. There was a thump, and the man seemed to bump into him. It was all too fast to be sure of anything.

Straightaway the man fled. Gil stood there in shock, unable to think clearly. Should he chase after his attacker, or call for help?

It was only when he felt the throbbing begin in his left shoulder that he realized he had been stabbed. He looked down and saw that blood stained his shirt and dripped to the floor. There, its blade glinting red, lay the dagger.

"Durlin!" he yelled, as he had been trained to do. His voice was loud, and there was a waver in it that scared him. "Durlin!" he called again, trying without success to keep his tone even.

He did not have to wait long. His room was only around the corner, and in a moment the bodyguard waiting there came rushing.

The man assessed the situation swiftly. His eyes were alert but calm, and Gil took reassurance from that. The Durlin took a cloth from one of his pockets and pressed it against the wound. Gil took hold of it and held it down himself.

"That way," he said, nodding with his head toward the stairs. "He went that way. Catch him!"

The Durlin looked at the stairs, and then back at him. "No," he said emphatically. "I'll not leave you unprotected."

Gil bit back his initial response. He had been unprotected just before. Then, as he thought about that, doubt washed over him in a wave.

Was it possible? Had it been arranged that no guards were present just so that an attempt could be made on his life? Was it possible that Brand could do such a thing?

Gil could not believe it. Yet here was the guard refusing to chase down the attacker. It was suspicious that the man would make no attempt to pursue an assassin, although it made sense that he did not want to leave him alone either. Gil calmed himself. He trusted the Durlin with his life, and Brand and Lornach and Taingern most of all. They would never betray him. None of them. Yet still, the doubt would not quite go away.

The Durlin lifted the cloth a little and studied the wound.

"You're lucky," he said. "Very lucky. It's only superficial."

The man studied the empty passage a moment, then pushed Gil's hand firmly against the cloth.

"Keep it pressed down hard," he instructed.

With a few quick strides he went to the stairs and yelled for help. It was not long before a palace servant came. They talked quickly, and Gil saw the eyes of the servant dart to him nervously several times as the Durlin gave him orders. Then the man was off, running down the stairs to get help.

The Durlin returned. He was cool, calm and professional as the guards always seemed to be. Brand chose his men wisely, and they were all loyal to him until death. There seemed to be no emotion there, and Gil could sense nothing of what was going on in the man's head. That, and the Durlin's loyalty to Brand, did nothing to ease his doubts.

The man helped Gil to sit, and there they waited together. Gil tried to turn his mind to other thoughts. He would not think ill of Brand. The man was his hero.

He soon began to realize just how lucky he was. The attacker had been almost free to strike without fear of discovery or retaliation. Gil knew he had turned and disrupted the man, but his reaction had been too slow to offer any real resistance. Luck alone, it seemed, had directed the blade into his shoulder rather than his heart.

A moment later, Brand was racing up the stairs. How he had gotten there so quickly, Gil could not guess. It seemed impossible that the regent should arrive before other help. It seemed as though he had already been nearby for some reason … as though he had been expecting something to happen.

A chill ran through Gil, but as Brand approached and knelt down beside him, they looked into each other's eyes. All doubt left him then. There was concern there, and a depth of feeling beyond a regent for his charge. Brand's gaze was clear and steady, void of any deceit. Here was a man for whom his word was a bond. There was no betrayal in him, if Gil was any judge of character at all.

Yet a moment later surprise flashed over Brand's face. It was a look that Gil had rarely, if ever, seen before on the other's face.

He followed Brand's gaze and saw that it fell upon the bloody dagger on floor. Gil wondered why it should surprise him so, but before he could ask Brand had picked it up and slid it behind his belt.

"Why did you do that?" Gil asked. "Why did the dagger surprise you?"

Brand looked away and hesitated. Then he turned to Gil again.

"It's not an ordinary dagger. At least, not in this part of the world. I haven't seen its like in many years."

"I didn't see anything unusual about it," Gil said.

Brand looked quickly at the wound in Gil's shoulder. He had seen many such and knew, as did Gil, that even though it bled profusely it was not dangerous.

The Durlin kept the bandage pressed firmly against it, and Brand evidently decided that there was no reason not to talk while they waited for more help to arrive.

The regent withdrew the dagger from his belt. "See here," he said, tracing his fingers over the small pommel. This is shaped as a wolf's head. In Cardoroth, pommels are usually round. And look at this." He trailed his finger down the bone hilt. There were fine markings there, some sort of decoration or perhaps even writing. "This is scrimshaw. Many people carve in bone, but this pattern, this design … these markings are distinctive. It is a Duthenor dagger, somehow come from the far west, and I wonder how it got here for I'm the only one of my tribe to ever travel this far. At least, so I've always thought."

Brand looked away again, and Gil saw that the regent was puzzled. But the Durlin stirred uncomfortably. He must be thinking, just as Gil was himself, that he would have known if someone of his own race had entered the city. Surely, they would have contacted him, brought him news of his homeland, for it was well known in Cardoroth what his origins were.

Yet if there was no stranger in the city, no wandering Duthenor tribesman as Brand had one day been, then how had the dagger come to be here? Unless it had been Brand's …

7. Worse than Death

Brand returned to the throne room after Gil's wound had been cleaned and dressed. The boy rested now in his room, but for himself, there would be no respite. Now was a time to think.

The throne room was quiet. But soon his advisors would come. Some were already there, those that he trusted most in all the world. They were few, but their opinions were vital. He was never afraid to act on his own, to do what was necessary, but likewise he was not scared to receive advice, to weight it up and judge it, to change his view or his course of action when a better way was shown.

He did not sit on the throne. Rather, he sat on a far less ornate chair beside it. The throne was for kings, and he was not a king.

Shorty was there, the man that most people knew better as Lornach. Taingern also. These were his oldest friends in Cardoroth, the men he had chosen to share the role of Durlindrath, his own previous title. But it was more than a title. It was an honor, a duty and a burden. It had broken men in the past. It had nearly broken him, but he had found a way through all difficulties to arrive at where he was today. And they were not there because they were his friends. They were there because they were great men, and he trusted them.

Arell arrived now, coming through the great doors of the throne room, as beautiful as always, her sharp eyes looking at him, reading his mood, discerning his thoughts as no other ever could. There was a trace of blood on her shirt, for she was the best healer in Cardoroth. The heir to the throne was not treated by just anyone.

A fourth person entered immediately after her. It was another woman. She was older than the rest, an old woman in fact. The others knew her, but not well.

The old king had told Brand that her name was Esanda. She preferred to be called Sandy though. Brand doubted anyone knew her true name, for secrecy was her stock in trade. She was the head of the king's secret intelligence service. Or, as the old king had told him once, the eyes and ears of the world. When she spoke, Brand listened. If he wanted to know something, she set her spies to find it out. He had come to rely on her, and he had also learned to trust her judgement. She knew better than anybody who was doing what, and why, and how best to influence them. And a king, or a regent, had need of such services.

They gathered before him. The Durlin at the door to the throne room knew no one else was coming, and closed it silently. They were alone, and Brand finally stirred.

He drew forth the dagger that had been used on Gil. It was clean now, the boy's blood removed, and Gil held it before him.

"You all know now that an attempt was made to assassinate the prince. This is the blade that was used. Look at it, and tell me what you see."

Their eyes fixed on it. The two men studied it professionally. They were warriors. Sandy looked, but gave no sign of what she thought. Arell gazed at it with distaste. She had seen the damage it had done, and remembered the many other wounds such weapons caused that she had healed, or tried to heal without success. Those men had died, and she thought of that now. He could sense her mood as well as she sensed his.

Shorty broke the silence, being direct as usual. "What of it? It's a dagger. That's all I see."

"Yes," Brand replied. "A dagger. Even an ordinary dagger, at least where it comes from."

Sandy sat back in her chair. "Well, it doesn't come from Cardoroth. You've just said as much yourself. But I don't think it comes from any other Camar city either. Not Camarelon or Esgallien or any of the others. So, where does that leave?"

Arell sat very still. She did not look at Brand when she spoke.

"I can guess," she said. "It's from the homeland of the Duthenor."

Brand knew that she did not want to say that. She understood well enough what it meant. She also knew that he would not have asked the question unless he wanted the information to surface.

"Exactly," he said. "It comes from the Duthenor. But I'm the only Duthenor tribesman in Cardoroth."

They all looked at him in silence. He saw trust in their eyes, and he knew that none of them thought he was responsible for what had happened.

He slid the blade of the dagger behind his belt. "So, what now?"

Sandy was the first to speak. "Likely enough, if there was another Duthenor tribesman in the city we would have heard of it by now. Nevertheless, I shall send word to all my … associates. If a tribesman has come into the city, I'll find out about it, eventually."

"It's a big city," Brand said. "Where would you even begin to look?"

"Well," she replied matter-of-factly, "the brothels are usually a good place to start. Foreigners always seem to end up there sooner or later. Usually sooner. Especially those who don't come from another city."

Brand smiled. "A good theory, but I didn't find my way to any such place when I first came here." He deliberately did not look at Arell.

"Maybe not, but as I recall you were pretty busy with other things at the time. Besides, you've never been an ordinary man."

"Nice of you to say so. Anyway, that'll take time. So, what do we do in the immediate future? Word of the dagger will get out. That, combined with what the rider at the gate said, will make people suspicious of me. There is a crime, and I have a motive."

Taingern scratched his chin. "The people may not be so quick to judge you as you think. They trust you, as do we all."

Brand thought about that. "Perhaps. Perhaps not."

"The aristocracy don't," Sandy said. "And they hate you to boot. They'll use this against you, try to destabilize your position. Indeed, for that matter, they must be the prime suspects in the whole business. How hard, after all, would it be to seek out such a dagger? A deliberate scheme to vilify you would hardly be beyond them."

Brand nodded. "That's true, but your ... associates keep a close eye on most of them. If they were planning some such thing, you would probably have heard a whisper of it by now."

Sandy gave him a guarded glance. "Maybe so. But there could be a conspiracy that I haven't yet discovered. I'll get my people to keep an even closer eye on things. Or a closer ear, anyway. It's marvelous the sorts of things a cleaning maid or stable hand can overhear, by accident."

Brand winked at her, but did not answer. Likely enough even his own servants were in her employ, one way or another. This was his way of letting her know that he knew.

He turned to Shorty and Taingern. "What of Gil? How will you ensure his safety? What happened today may well be tried again."

Taingern looked at Shorty, but it was the taller man who answered.

"We have no choice but to assume that another attempt on the prince's life will be made. We'll increase the guard on him."

"And," Shorty added, "we'll make sure that he's never left alone again. Ever."

Brand allowed himself a small smile. "Good luck with that. Gil is now of an age where he resents supervision, or guarding. He'll take it as a personal challenge to escape your watch."

Shorty shrugged. "I'll take it as a personal challenge to see that he's not successful."

There was not much more to say on the subject. Shorty and Taingern were the best at what they did. But Brand had one more thing to add.

"At the moment, you split the thirty Durlin between me and the prince. That must change. He's in the greatest danger at the moment, so all thirty Durlin will guard him."

"No!" Shorty said.

"Impossible!" Taingern added.

The taller man leaned forward in his chair. "You're the closest thing that Cardoroth has to a king. Should something happen to you, the realm would fall into turmoil. The aristocracy would be fighting in the streets to get one of their families on the throne, and our outside enemies could seize such an opportunity to strike. No, you must remain guarded."

Brand looked at them. He felt their loyalty as a palpable thing, and it moved him deeply. All the more because they had reason to doubt him just now, but did not do so. But though they were correct in what they said, there was a higher truth still.

"You're right," he said. "But you're wrong also. The boy needs you more than I do. I can defend myself, against blade or magic. Gil is still learning both."

The two Durlin began to argue, but Brand put an end to that straight away.

"I've made my decision, and it's final. The Durlin, all thirty of them, will guard Gil."

The two men looked less than happy, but they did not reply. Sandy, however, did.

"Don't be a fool," she said bluntly. "No one, no matter their skills, is immune to assassination. And it's possible that an attempt on the boy's life was made to provoke such a rash decision from you. You're predictable, at least in some ways, and a good assassin might have planned all this out."

Brand always admired that Sandy spoke her mind. She cared not a whit whether she spoke to kings, regents or peasants. She treated them all the same. Few could get away with such a thing, but she did.

"What you say is true, but I don't think you believe that's what's happening. Nor do I. I have a feeling that my greatest threat comes from the rider we saw at the gate. And the Durlin cannot protect me from that."

It was Arell who spoke next, and there was concern on her face no matter that she tried to hide it.

"The Durlin may or may not be able to protect you, but they should still know all there is to know. Tell them."

Brand hesitated, but he decided that she was right. So he quickly told them of his visit with the prince to the Tower of Halathgar and the warnings of the long-dead queen. When he was done, they looked at him in silence. There were few in Cardoroth who would believe such a tale, but those gathered here did. Shorty and Taingern because they had witnessed such things themselves, Arell and Sandy because they trusted. And because they had seen sorcery and lòhrengai in the not so long ago war that prepared them to accept the impossible as possible.

"Everything is vague," Sandy said into the ensuing silence. "Yet this much is clear. Cardoroth has enemies, and trouble gathers. It's said that the Forgotten Queen appears at times of great peril. She has given warning of these horsemen, and we have seen the first. An assassin stalks our city, and there is evil in the air. We know so little, but a battle of some sort is looming. We must prepare, and I sense that the assassin would be a good place to start. Learn his identity, and the rest will become clearer."

"That's true," Brand said softly.

Arell gazed at him, and there was sympathy in her eyes. "I know that you seldom speak of this, but it may help if everyone better understood why you left the

93

Duthenor. Especially as it was a Duthenor dagger that struck Gil."

Brand shrugged. "You all know the story, at least in a general way. Most of you know that I have enemies in my homeland. But I have friends there too. In short, my father was chieftain of the tribe. When I was but a boy, younger even than Gil, a usurper murdered my family. He would have murdered me too, but I escaped. He rules in my father's stead, supported by foreign warriors. Otherwise the Duthenor would have rejected him. I vowed that one day I would return and avenge my parents. The very fact that I still live must worry him. I'm the heir to my father's chieftainship, and if I ever returned I could fan the fires of rebellion."

Arell folded her hands in her lap. "That's reason enough that the Duthenor, or the one who now leads them, might seek to discredit Brand himself, or help others with that goal. Perhaps even try to kill him, if he could. But there's even stronger reason than that. Tell them, Brand."

Brand felt sadness well up in him. He remembered as though it were only yesterday the night his parents were killed. They were good people, deserving more from life than they had gotten. A deep longing to see them, to talk to them just once more, rose within him like a wave. He knew that Arell understood how he felt, and she was right to encourage him to speak of it.

"I was a fugitive," he said quietly, "but the people would have had me one day as their leader if they were given any choice. But neither I nor they had one. Having escaped the massacre, I was hidden by brave farmers as I grew, often moved from family to family and farm to farm because assassins sought me without stint.

"I realized as I matured that one day my luck would run out. One day, I would be found and killed, and those who sheltered me as well. Not yet full grown, but not a child anymore, I decided to leave the lands of the Duthenor to protect those who protected me. But I would not go without sending a message to the usurper.

"One night, I crept into the hall-yard that was my home in better days. Why would the guard dogs bark at someone who had played with them?

"I knew the ways of the old hall and picked a safe path among the sleeping men with slow steps until I came to the usurper's chamber.

"There, with great care and trembling hands, I opened an old chest and reclaimed the sword of my father, and his forefathers before him. With the ancient blade in my hands, I was tempted to kill the man who murdered my parents. But fear overcame me. I would not escape if I did that. Nor did I want to kill a sleeping man, even one such as he. Instead, I reached down and boldly slipped my father's ring, an heirloom of chieftainship, from his finger.

"But the usurper woke and gave a startled cry. Before it left his lips, I was already running. Men groped for their weapons all about. 'Awake! The hall is afire!' I cried, and in the confusion I somehow managed to slip away.

"The ruse did not last long, though. Soon I was pursued. On a ridge above the village, a sliver of the moon riding low in the midnight sky, I gave vent to my feelings. 'I am Brand! I will return one day, and death will come with me. I am the true chieftain, and when next I see the usurper my sword will slake its thirst for justice!'

"It was an empty threat, for I had no means to fulfil it, nor would I until I reached manhood, and not likely even then. I fled into the wilderness, but the story of my daring grew and spread among the people like a wildfire.

"Summer waned to autumn, and autumn turned to winter, and with my enemies ever pressing closer, I was forced to cross the frozen Careth Nien river. I nearly died then, several times.

"After that, I sought to lose my pursuers by traveling the many lonely miles toward Cardoroth. I thought that I had succeeded, but it may not have been so. Perhaps they followed me, made sure of my destination and returned to the usurper. But one such as he does not forget, nor less forgive, and I remember well the naked fear on his face when I fled the hall. No, one such as he does not forget. He hates me not just because of who I am, but also because of what I did."

Brand let out a long sigh and fell silent. They had all heard bits and pieces of this before, but not the whole thing. Only Arell had ever heard that.

No one spoke. They looked at him anew, reassessing him. He saw pity in some eyes, admiration in others.

Shorty eventually cleared his throat. "Perhaps it happened like that, your pursuers following you to Cardoroth. Or maybe not. Your fame has spread now, and stories of you must even have reached your homeland. That might explain why this usurper has only now taken action."

"Perhaps," Taingern said thoughtfully. "But the assassin went for the boy and not Brand. There's something more to this, something more complex than what I think this usurper would devise."

They all looked at him then. "The whole thing," Arell said, "is designed to make Brand look bad. Especially the words of the horseman."

Brand shrugged. "It could be. It's true that my Duthenor enemies would rather just kill me than anything else."

"Something else is going on, all right," Sandy said. "Perhaps someone is maneuvering to take the throne. If they kill the prince and discredit Brand at the same time, the way would be open."

"That could be," Brand said. "But I feel there is more to it than that. Much more. And none of these things explains the horseman. There was sorcery going on there, far darker and stronger than my enemies among the Duthenor or within Cardoroth possess."

"We'll never know," Shorty said. "Not unless we catch this assassin. First, we must better protect the boy. Then you, Brand."

Brand shook his head. "No Shorty. It's decided. The Durlin, every one of them, will guard Gil."

"You're too important," Shorty argued again. "If you die, the realm will fall into turmoil. The old king entrusted the regency to you for a reason. Cardoroth has many enemies. Only you can lead us."

"Well, that's not quite true. Gil is well liked by the people, and more importantly, by the army – at least the ordinary soldiers. Not only that, even though he's still young, he shows much promise. He has intellect and great courage. He also possesses magic. He'll make an extraordinary king, and his time is coming soon."

"All that is true," Shorty answered. "But as you just acknowledged, he shows *promise*. Promise is not enough. We need a leader, and we need one now. Cardoroth cannot afford to lose you."

"Enough," Brand said quietly. "I appreciate all that you say, but the Durlin will protect Gil. I'll look after myself."

Shorty sat back in his chair, and he said no more. He did not like it. None of them liked it, but that was the way it had to be.

Sandy looked at him, her expression inquisitive. "Just how good is the boy at magic?"

It was a simple question, but Brand liked it. He knew its purpose, and approved. Sandy, as ever, was thinking ahead. She wanted to know how effective Gil would prove as a king, for Cardoroth's enemies, when they attacked, employed not just armies but sorcery.

"As with all that Gil does, he learns swiftly. It doesn't matter if it's swordplay, or military strategy, or economic theory. He grasps the concepts quickly. His skill with magic, with lòhrengai as it's properly known, is no different. He has great talent for it. In truth, he would be a lòhren if he was not born to rule Cardoroth."

Sandy considered that. "I've heard tell, that indeed, he would *prefer* to be a lòhren."

It was another good point, and Brand saw its purpose also. She continued to look to the future, weighing, evaluating, judging whether or not Gil would be a good king, whether or not he was best for the role.

"Gil makes little secret of that. He saw how kingship aged his grandfather and how responsibility weighed him down. He does not want the same thing to happen to him. He would prefer to use his talent with lòhrengai, to study it all his life and take it out into the world, to share his gift with Alithoras."

"And is that a quality to be sought in a king? A person who would rather be something else? I don't ask out of disrespect for the boy. I ask in the interests of Cardoroth."

Brand smiled. "That is the *best* sort of person to make king. The one who seeks such responsibility, who manipulates to achieve it, does not have the temperament to rule. Beware such a one as that."

The meeting ended soon after, and Brand was left alone in the throne room. He was alone often these days, and he thought much on the future of Cardoroth, and his own future, as he always did at those times. He had said that responsibility weighed people down. How true that was! Yet it had its benefits. You could not have the good without the bad.

His thoughts turned to Carnhaina. How well she would have understood all this. But the moment he thought of her he remembered her warning, or was it prophecy? Unless he took the throne, he would die. And the horseman had pronounced the same doom. One his friend and one his foe, but the warning from each just the same. It could not be ignored. It could not be acted upon.

Brand let out a long sigh and stood. There were no answers to be found, not today. But they were out there. And whatever they were, he knew that nothing was as it seemed. On that he would bet his life. But he had a feeling that his life was no longer his to bet. His destiny was become a pawn in a game that he did not understand.

He gritted his teeth and walked from the room. He would do what he must, and to *hell* with destiny.

8. Anything is Possible

Gil slept fitfully. His shoulder hurt, but the medicine that Arell had given him reduced that greatly. Far worse than the pain, though, was the dream.

It was not like before. Now, everything was vague. Yet he found himself in the forest again, and it was dark and gloomy. Shadows moved and shifted, and the black boughs of the trees swayed even though the air was still.

To the side was a lake. It was Lake Alithorin, though he had never seen it before. He turned his back to the water, and faced the forest. Things moved within it, dark things. They filled the woods, and they crept toward him.

Here and there he glimpsed a face, or the pale gleam of malevolent eyes. Now and then a twig broke, or dead leaves rustled beneath a furtive step.

Yet, this seeming army of enemies, though their ill will for him was palpable, waited. It was not long before Gil understood why.

Something bigger moved through the shadows. It made noise, not bothering to try to conceal its presence. Within a few moments the shape of the thing loomed. It was a horse. No, it was a horse and rider.

Gil took a step back. Death was come. The horseman paused, and the red nostrils of his mount glowed like living embers within the gloom. The rider slowly drew his sword, a bent blade, its wicked curve like a farmer's scythe.

The dark eyes of the rider fixed on him. They were hollow, hidden by shadow. They were pits of darkness, and yet still Gil sensed the movement of them. He knew there were no eyes there, but roiling maggots.

The rider grinned at him. Or maybe that was just the look of its skull-like face. And then Death charged. His mighty horse sprang forward, and the bent sword lifted high, high for a killing blow.

Gil had nowhere to go. He stood, still as a stone, bound by fear, or bound by the dream. The rider hurtled toward him.

Behind, Gil sensed the lake stir, and a light rose from it. Pale, silvery, mist-like. The rider faltered, and the nighttime sky shone brilliantly, suddenly awash with a countless multitude of stars. Halathgar twinkled brightest of them all.

Gil could not move. He sensed power behind him, and he felt that it was Carnhaina. Ahead, the horse reared and tore the air with its hooves. Grim and skeletal, Death sat astride his mount and his curved blade caught the light of the stars and turned it into wicked glimmerings.

For a moment, all was still. Then the forest, the rider and the silvery light all faded. Last to go was the mantle of the starlit sky, and then all was dark and Gil knew that he slept once more in his bed within the palace of Cardoroth. He stirred in his sleep, but did not waken.

The next morning, he trained with Brand. They could not spar because of Gil's injury, but he watched as Brand performed several routines, starting with warrior's exercises for the body that kept it supple, and finishing with a drill involving two knives.

Gil followed it all as best he could, studying and learning. At length, they sat upon a bench as the sun rose and talked about many things.

After a while, Gil turned the conversation to the horseman.

"How is it that you faced the rider so calmly? How do you prepare yourself for such a thing so that you don't become rooted to the spot with fear?"

The regent gave him an appraising look, his blue eyes gazing with sharp intelligence, and Gil wondered if there were any secrets this man could not discern just by looking. But whatever he had perceived of the reason behind the question, he said nothing and merely answered.

"This is how I approached it. I'll tell you all, because you may learn something valuable from it. Firstly, some advised me to ride out to meet him. The thinking was that no leader should talk to someone from a lower position. They did not think it seemly that a regent should stand to address a mounted messenger."

Brand gazed directly into his eyes. "I dismissed that. There's some logic to the sentiment, but it's more a matter of pride and show. Those things have no place in a potential fight. And that was what I was thinking of when I went through the gate on foot. If it came to a fight the horse would hinder my opponent, for such a conflict would not just be a physical battle but a contest of lòhrengai against elùgai. In that situation, I would be more agile on my feet than if I were mounted, nor would I need to worry about the safety of my horse, which would have no protection against such attacks."

That made sense to Gil. It was practical, free of self-importance. It was the outcome that counted, not the outward appearance.

"But how did you stay so relaxed?"

Brand smiled, if ever so slightly. "It was an act. Simple as that."

Gil was shocked, and the regent saw it. His smile widened.

"Of course it was an act. My guts were churning and my palms slick with sweat. How else could it be in such a situation?"

"But you looked so brave!"

"Brave? If there is no fear, then there is no bravery. Brave is doing something, doing something that you *fear*, not doing something when you know that you can succeed. Remember that."

"Then how did you manage to act like you weren't afraid?"

"Ah, that's a different thing altogether. Practice is the only answer to that. It wasn't the first time I've faced death or danger. My advice is not to seek it, *never* to seek it. But when it comes, look it square in the eye. A man makes many fears, draws them out of the very air and gives them form. But what will be, will be. You cannot worry about what *might* happen. That only gives your fears life. Instead, concentrate on the task at hand. Think of that only. Consequences will come after. That is their proper place. If you think of both the task at hand as well as the future, well, then you're fighting two battles instead of one. And likely enough you'll win neither."

Gil knew there was more to that advice than he understood. But, as Brand always asked, he'd remember those words. As time went by he would understand them better.

"What else did you do?"

Brand shrugged. "Not much else, really. Mentally, it was just a matter of not showing surprise, no matter what was said. Never let an opponent surprise you, or at least never give him confidence by letting him see that he has done so."

Gil asked the obvious question. "And what about physically? You've mentioned why you went out on foot, but what else did you do?"

"Only the basics really. Most of this you know already. Firstly, I ensured that my right hand was free. So, when I crossed my arms to make it appear that I was unconcerned, my right hand rested on the outside of my left arm, rather than trapped *beneath* it. It's only a slight difference, but it allows for swifter movement, no matter how slight."

"Did you use the sun?"

"Not really. By necessity, I came through the gate and it faces west. The sun would have been in the rider's eyes, but it was morning and the tall wall of the city put us both in shadow from the rising sun."

"What about the terrain? Could you positon yourself on higher ground and the rider on lower?"

"That, I tried. But the road there is flat. There was a pothole, but the horse stepped aside from it."

Gil could think of nothing else to ask, but he knew there would be more.

"What else did you do?"

"I observed if the rider was right or left-handed. And I think he was right-handed – at least the positioning of his scabbard on the left hip indicated that, along with the fact that he held the sword in his right. The latter doesn't mean much though. A trickster might attempt to deceive you that way and swap the weapon to his other hand during a fight. But he's much less likely to alter the position of his scabbard to reinforce that trick. So, I stood ready to move to the left of the horse where the rider would have less mobility and power in his strikes."

Brand paused, considering his actions and evaluating them.

"Probably the most important thing in such a situation is this. Don't let your opponent see doubt. You must be confident, supremely confident. It's not a matter of bragging, or a case of *false* confidence though. Those things are useless. It's a matter of trusting in yourself, of believing in yourself. And that only comes through training and practice. You have to do the hard work first. You must sheath your mind with an iron-like determination. Decide what you need to know in your life, and then acquire those skills. It's as easy, and as hard, as that. When you've done so, then anything is possible."

Gil had much to ponder. Soon, though, their training session ended. He went then to the kitchens in search of breakfast. No sooner had he sat down than Elrika approached, and he pulled out a chair for her. Suddenly, he wanted the company of someone his own age. Talking to Brand was great, but sometimes it made him feel a hundred years old. And even if he ever did live to be that age, he wondered if he would understand all that the regent told him.

Between helpings of buttered bread, ham and well-aged cheese, they spoke.

"Were you scared of the rider?" Elrika asked.

Gil thought about that. He had been, especially when the horseman looked straight at him.

"A little," he said. "But I knew Brand was his match. There wasn't even a fight. I think the rider was scared of *him*."

Elrika seemed to consider that. "Maybe," she said. "Or maybe their time to fight hasn't come yet. I get the feeling that it will, though."

Gil ate more bread. He had also had that feeling, and it worried him for some reason.

"How's your shoulder?" Elrika asked.

Gil knew that the bandages were visible above his collar, but he wondered how she had so readily known that he was wounded.

"There are no secrets in the palace," she said. "I heard last night that you had been attacked. Do they know who it was yet?"

"No. Not yet." He said nothing about the Duthenor dagger, but he did not doubt that rumor of it had also spread.

"It may have been the aristocracy," she ventured.

Gil finished eating and leaned back in his chair. "It could be. They hate me enough. And I hate them, for the most part."

"Really? Why's that?"

He thought about the reasons he had, and he wondered if he should tell her. But it felt good to confide in someone.

"Mostly," he said, "because they call me elùgrune. Or nightborn."

"Does it really worry you that much?"

He wanted to say no, but did not. Instead, he looked at the marks on his hands.

"In truth, it does. I *hate* it."

Elrika seemed to consider that. "I can see why, but if it weren't that, then it'd be something else. They try to intimidate you because of *who* you are. Not *what* you are. But anyway, you should know that not everybody thinks the marks on your palms are evil. Without Carnhaina, we would long ago have been destroyed. My dad says the same sign is in many places in the city. He saw it once in the palace itself, in an old store room. It had been closed for many years but opened one time when an excess of grain had to be stored. He said it was a strange room, but the mark of the Forgotten Queen was everywhere inside it."

Gil thought that he knew every room in the palace, but he had never seen that one. He wondered how that was possible.

"Will you show me where it is? I'd love to see it."

The girl looked at him seriously for a moment. "Of course," she agreed. "But it'll have to be later. My father has chores for me to do now."

He smiled at her. "I know the feeling. The chores never seem to end."

She left soon after that, and Gil filled in time wandering about the palace in search of his attacker. He found nobody who looked like him, and grew tired of the attempt. Almost, he felt sorry for the Durlin who trailed him wherever he went, closer today than they had ever been before. He did not like it, even though he understood it.

In the afternoon, he made his way to the training yard where Shorty had taken the place of the Swordmaster. He would not be able to join in, but he could still watch and learn.

He noticed that some of the usual boys were not there, but most were. Unfortunately, Turlak, the older boy who had recently caused him so many problems was one of the ones who had returned. Gil wondered why.

He had been the old Swordmaster's favorite, and surely must now hate Shorty.

Shorty himself showed up moments later. He demonstrated a sword form that none of the other boys had ever seen before, and then he led them through it step by step.

The form was swift, unbelievably so when Shorty demonstrated it, and it seemed designed to teach the type of footwork that enabled fast and powerful strikes. There were leaps, squats and pivots, and Shorty explained as he took them through it that it was all about learning to use the body first and that a sword was only an extension of it.

"You'll learn the form," he told them, "and then break it down technique by technique. After that, you'll put the moves into practice on each other with the wooden swords. Finally, you'll introduce the techniques into your sparring sessions."

Gil listened carefully and watched Shorty very closely. There were many techniques here that he had not seen before, but he recognized some that Brand taught, even if there were slight differences. This perplexed him, but after a while he realized that the differences were only to be expected. Brand was tall and Shorty was short. *Make every technique your own*, Brand had often told him. Now he understood that advice better. Every individual was different, and no matter how sound a technique was in itself it must be adapted to suit differences in height, strength, speed, temperament and the like.

Gil was pondering this when he saw a finely dressed man approach. He knew him for the father of one of the boys in the class, and also as an earl.

The man beckoned his son over and then called out to Shorty.

"A word with you."

Shorty strolled over. There was that look to him that he always bore, relaxed and yet somehow ready for anything. Gil had seen it many times, and he also noticed the ever-so-slightly narrowed gaze that signaled intense concentration.

The earl pointed at his son, and light glinted off several diamond rings.

"I have come to withdraw my boy from this school."

Shorty looked at the man steadily. "As you wish."

The earl seemed slightly taken aback by Shorty's acceptance of the situation, but he continued in his smooth voice.

"I will do you, sir, the courtesy of telling you why."

"Somehow, I rather thought you would," Shorty answered.

The earl frowned at him, but Shorty had not really said anything offensive, though the tone of his words made it clear that he was not concerned with anything the earl had to say.

The boy's father crossed his arms, and the diamonds flashed again against his black silk shirt.

"You do not seem, sir, very interested in learning why."

Shorty gave a slight shrug. "I already know why."

The man seemed less and less certain of himself, but he drew himself up and continued.

"I do not believe so. This is what I would have you understand. The regent, though perhaps I should say *King* Brand, has promoted many uncouths such as you. But know this!" Here, his annoyance at Shorty began to show. "Brand will not endure. One day we will be free of foreign rule, nor do we accept that the whelp of a previous king, marked by the stain of an ancient ancestor's dabbling in the dark arts, and to whom Brand teaches his foreign ways, will rule Cardoroth either. Other families of ancient and noble lineage will one day see their time under the sun…"

The man stuttered to a stop. Shorty had changed while he spoke. No longer did he seem carefree. Now, there was a look of cold death in his eyes.

"Insult me if you like," Shorty said. "I've heard the same words from many mouths before this. Insult Brand, if you will … he cares less about what you think than I do. Your opinion is as nothing to him, for though you walk on two legs you're not a man. While Brand and I risked our lives in the last war to save this city, you drank fine wine and buried your wealth in hidden vaults beneath your mansion. Don't deny it! Brand knows exactly who you are, and many things about you that you would prefer to keep secret. But if you insult the heir to the throne, infer that you conspire with others to supplant him … then that is treason."

Shorty, slowly and deliberately, placed a hand on the hilt of his sword. A hush settled over the practice yard, and no one even seemed to breathe.

"So, was that treason my Lord, or did I mishear you? Speak swiftly! Or, in case you've forgotten, I'm not just Durlindrath but also the old king's champion. As such, I may just now deliver the king's justice. And that will be a duel that ends with my sword in your guts."

If it were possible, the silence deepened. The earl blanched. Though he wore a sword, he, along with everybody else, knew that he was no match for the Durlindrath.

With great care the earl clasped his hands together behind his back. He wanted to ensure there was no mistake. He had no intention of fighting. Then he smiled slyly.

"It is not treason to repeat hearsay rumored on the streets of the city. Good day to you, sir."

With a dismissive nod he turned his back on Shorty, drew his son around with him and began to walk away.

"Coward," Shorty said. His voice was quiet but clear.

The earl paused in mid stride, and then pretended not to hear the deadly insult. He walked away.

The class continued after that, but it was subdued. Gil could not help but wonder if what the earl had hinted at was true. Did the aristocracy really believe that Brand would usurp the throne? And for their part, were they really trying to maneuver so that one of their own would start a new line of kings? If either of these things happened, what of him? A prince, not yet come to manhood, had no place in either situation.

9. A Door to the Past

That night, Gil slept. And for the first time in a long while his dreams were not troubled. He woke early, and unusually hungry. Even though it was one of his days off, and he had no training with Brand, nor chores nor any study to do, he got out of bed while it was still half-dark and headed to the kitchens.

Of course, there were two Durlin at his door when he opened it. They had been there all night, and he felt sorry for them. Guarding a room was a boring duty. But they seemed resigned to it, and after a perfunctory greeting they followed, quietly, but very closely.

He went to the bakery area, and sure enough Elrika was there as he hoped. She spotted him and smiled, knowing straight away what was on his mind.

She brought him over a meat pie and a pastry, and they sat together and talked while he ate. She would have noticed the two Durlin, but she said nothing about them.

"So," she said in a whisper when he was finished with breakfast. "Is today the day?"

She had made no comment about the Durlin, but obviously she did not want them to hear what was being discussed, and Gil was grateful. What they were about to do, the room she would lead him to with the mark of Halathgar, was somehow intensely personal. He respected the Durlin, all of them, but this was for him alone, and for his friend.

"Are you free today?"

She smiled. "I am, until lunch at any rate. Let's go before my dad sees me and decides I'm being too idle."

Gil had not been sure if she would be available, and suddenly things were happening very quickly. A sense of anticipation rose within him, and with it came some nerves. This would be something new, perhaps even something that Brand did not know about. Although lately he had begun to wonder if Brand was not somehow aware of every single thing that happened in Cardoroth.

They left the kitchens, the silent Durlin close behind them. Down they went, working their way through corridors and descending flights of stairs.

Elrika leaned in close and whispered to him. "Do you want to leave your guards behind?"

Gil enjoyed the feel of her so close to him, but it made him nervous too.

"Yes, but I don't see how. We can't just try to run away from them."

She flashed him a smile. "Just be ready, and follow me when the time comes."

Her quick words only made him more uneasy, but he dared not ask any questions. The Durlin were only a dozen or so paces behind them. Not so close as to get in his way, but close enough to reach him within a few heartbeats if he needed help. And when other people were around, they drew closer.

They descended another set of stairs, and then entered a long corridor. Gil could sense Elrika suppressing excitement beside him. She seemed to be nearly jumping out of her skin, and he knew that whatever she had in mind was going to happen soon. Nevertheless, she did not quicken her pace, and

113

continued to walk with the same measured stride that she had used since they began.

They turned left at a bend in the corridor, and there before them was a landing and several stairways rising and falling from it. This was a juncture point that Gil knew, a place where servants came to have quick access to most parts of the palace. He had been here before quite a few times, so what Elrika did next surprised him.

Suddenly, she was all motion. With swift hands she reached out and opened a panel in the wooden wall that Gil had never even seen before. It was small, but she jumped though it and pulled him in after. Quickly she closed it, and there was a faint click and then silence. In the dim light he saw her put her fingers to her lips.

It was only a moment before the Durlin came around the corner and reached the same spot. Gil could sense their astonishment even though he could not see them, and then there was the sound of running feet and yells.

The Durlin raced to the stairs, checking them for any sign of their charge, but Elrika took his hand and led him carefully to the left. Immediately, they were on a new flight of stairs, their own pathway to freedom that was hidden from the outside world. In moments, the clamor of shouting receded, and soon after their eyes adjusted to the dimness.

"Where are we?" he asked.

Elrika shrugged. "Sometimes servants don't want to be seen. There are several staircases like this throughout the palace. They offer an occasional escape from the condescending gazes of the aristocracy when we just want to go about our business. And sometimes it provides a means of communication between two parties who would prefer – who would like to keep their visits to one another's rooms … that is, people who really just don't want anybody to see them, er, communicating."

Elrika's quiet voice trailed off and Gil blushed. He was glad of the dark, and neither of them spoke for a while as she led him downward.

His thoughts wandered back to the two Durlin. He would apologize to them later, and he would explain to Shorty and Taingern that it was not the fault of the guards. He did not want to see them get in trouble.

There seemed to be more light now, or perhaps their eyes continued to adjust. At any rate, he glanced over at Elrika. He found that she was looking at him. There was a curious expression on her face. It was almost like she knew what he was thinking, because her expression seemed to indicate that she understood well enough why the Durlin had been following, and she knew also why he wanted to be free of them. She *understood*, and that somehow strengthened the bond between them.

Down they went to the very bottom of the palace. There were no doors, no corridors, no nothing. There were only the stairs. They were narrower than the usual stairs in the palace, and in need of repair in several places, but still safe enough.

After a while, it grew darker again. There was very little noise, and Gil began to have a sense of how a place such as this was a refuge for the servants. They should not need one, but they did. Once again Gil appreciated Brand's foresight. His training, his exposure to the aristocracy and to commoners alike, was opening his eyes to things that he would not otherwise have seen.

It grew darker still, and he began to have misgivings. What if he ran into the assassin again in a place like this?

Should he really have left the guards behind? There was no help for him down here if something happened.

Elrika reached out and took his hand. "Nearly there," she said, once again seeming to sense his feelings.

They shuffled along a little while longer through the dark, and then it began to lighten once more. Soon they came to a recess. The stairs ended, and a blank wall began. But Gil was not surprised this time when Elrika reached up and placed her hand on the timber. There would be another hidden panel there, but she did not open it straight away. Instead, she placed her face against it for several long moments and listened.

"I can't hear anybody outside," she said.

Slowly, she tripped the mechanism that held it in place. There was a click, and she peered carefully through the slit in the wall that had appeared before opening it up all the way.

They stepped through into a normal palace corridor, and Elrika closed the panel behind them.

Gil knew where they were. He had been here too. He had thought he had been everywhere in the palace, though that belief was now shattered. Still, he remembered this corridor well.

"The wine cellars are beyond," he said.

Elrika nodded, and then leaned in close to speak softly.

"They are, but there's usually a caretaker down here. We'll want to avoid him. Otherwise he'll want to know what we're doing and where we're going."

She led him forward, her shoes soft and soundless on the floor, and he followed like her shadow.

To each side there were doorways. Elrika carefully scrutinized each entry before passing the openings.

116

Brand saw rooms filled with cheeses, and others with hams that hung from the ceiling. Yet others were filled with cured sausages, hanging and drying in the cool air. There was a strong scent of smoke, one of Gil's favorite smells, and he was suddenly hungry again. But Elrika led him on.

They came now to the wine cellars, and these branched off down several narrow tunnels. There were racks against the wall and endless bottles and flagons. Gil was not even sure if they were man-made corridors or just caves beneath the palace. Either way, it was growing dark again, but they both paused in mid stride as a shadow moved at the far end of one of those long wine tunnels. There was a shuffling sound too, and then a husky voice coughed.

"The caretaker," Elrika breathed into Gil's ear.

They dropped slowly into a half crouch and moved carefully past the opening. There was another cough and a few muttered words as the caretaker spoke to himself.

They had not been seen, and they moved quickly and quietly ahead. They came swiftly to the end of the corridor. There, an ancient door barred their way. It was, perhaps, of oak, but it was an aged thing now, still solid no doubt, but covered by mold and stains.

Elrika glanced behind her once, and then took hold of the ancient brass door handle. It was dull and dirty. Slowly she turned it, and then pulled the door open. The hinges creaked in protest, but not loudly.

They slipped through and Elrika closed it behind them. Then they waited a moment in the dark, listening. The caretaker may have called out, having heard some noise. Or maybe he just spoke to himself. Whatever the reason, they heard his voice briefly and then it grew deadly silent. Gil could hear nothing after that, nor could he see much.

Elrika moved in the dark beside him. There were several scratching sounds, and suddenly there was a flash of light. She had lit the wick of a candle, and she held it up before her face.

Gil smiled at her. She had been prepared for this, but a moment later he looked around, keen to see the nature of the room she had led him into.

Shadows danced and slithered. The air was heavy with the smell of ancient smoke and dust. Wooden crates, perhaps centuries old, slowly fell apart in the endless dark and there was a sense of antiquity. No matter how much the city had changed above, this place had not altered in many, many years, nor ever would. No one came here, and if they did so once in every few decades, they left again, happy to leave it just as it was.

The two of them moved forward through the wreckage of dilapidated crates and the rotting remains of hessian bags. No doubt these were the remnants of some grain sacks from the time that Elrika had spoken of. There was nothing in them now but dust and old shadows.

They came to the middle of the room and Elrika held the candle above her head. Eerily, the ceiling sprang into view. Cobwebs hung from it. Plaster and paint cracked and shriveled over it. But there, in the very center, a brilliant blue constellation glittered. Halathgar. The Seal of Carnhaina. If time had touched the rest of the room, it had left that paint alone. Like eyes, the twin stars stared down from above, and Gil had the unnerving feeling that they watched him.

Elrika shivered beside him, and he reached out to hold her hand. The one that lifted high the candle trembled, and Halathgar twinkled in the shivering light.

Now, Gil looked about him, drinking in the room, breathing in its age and the dust and the cobwebs as forgotten as the years that passed by in endless succession of dark days and darker nights. Now, he saw more images.

The queen was there, Carnhaina herself. There was no mistaking her, nor the spear in her hand, even if the ages had chipped and peeled away at the paint. There were other images as well, of things that Gil did not recognize, or so damaged by time that they could no longer be made out with certainty. And bright Halathgar was there in several more places, though smaller and less impressive than the representation on the ceiling.

A good while they spent there, just observing these signs from a past age, awed by them and their antiquity. They did not speak, but often their eyes met and Gil saw as much wonder in Elrika's as no doubt was in his. This was something special. No matter that it had been locked away and forgotten by most in Cardoroth. Maybe even many in the city would not care. But Gil did. This was something that connected him to his great ancestor. Here, no doubt, she must have stood herself in a time that was long ago. And the artist who had made these images had also once been alive. He had crafted her semblance, but to do so with the accuracy that he had he must have seen her and heard her speak. He had conversed with her. Time had buried that event in a mass of years, but the evidence of the moment still endured.

Gil exchanged another glance with Elrika. They had explored it all, had peered at every image. They knew they would come back another time, but the outside world pressed. The Durlin would be looking for him, and it was time to go and to face the consequences of his disappearance.

He took a final look at the room, but something tugged, ever so faintly, at his senses. He was puzzled, for he had never felt such a thing before. Elrika raised an eyebrow at him, sensing his hesitation and that something was happening, but did not voice a question.

Gil calmed himself. He breathed slow and deep as Brand had taught him. He allowed his mind to open, to expand, to become one with his surroundings. And the tugging sensation increased. More, he knew its source.

He glanced at the far wall of the chamber. It was covered in dust and grime and the disintegrating threads of an ancient spider web. There was an image on it of Halathgar, worn and faded. He had looked at it several times so far, but now he knew that it was the thing that triggered his instincts. There was something else about it too that was unusual: even though it was a constellation, it was placed on a wall. All the others were on the ceiling, which seemed a more natural location for them.

He went over a for a closer inspection, and Elrika came with him.

"What is it?" she asked finally.

Gil shook his head. He did not know. "Something…" he said absently.

The image was chest high. He reached out with his right hand and brushed away the spider web and some of the dust. He felt a tingling in his palm.

He paused a moment. An idea occurred to him, and he wondered if it was a wild and stray thought born of imagination, or if his instincts were seeping through to his conscious mind. He decided to put it to the test.

Slowly, hesitantly, he brought up his left hand and pressed it against the second star. Instantly, he felt a thrill of power in both palms. There was lòhrengai in this wall, ancient and slumbering, but brought now to wakefulness.

Stone ground against stone, a rumble as though the earth itself moved in its sleep. A crack appeared, straight and vertical. It was not natural, but made by the art of man. And then the wall moved.

Gil flinched and withdrew his hands. The wall split in two, sliding to the left and the right, leaving a doorway. Dust puffed out of the two corners of the room where sections of wall slid a foot or so into some hidden recess.

It was dark as night beyond the door. Silently, Elrika held up the candle. By its light they saw a narrow tunnel, and beyond was a set of wooden stairs. They seemed ancient, and Gil wondered how long since anyone had seen them or trod the path they made.

"They're no servant's stairs," Elrika said softly. "Where do they go?"

Gil straightened. His apology to the Durlin would have to wait.

"Let's find out." He looked at her, and she gazed back at him. He saw fear there, but also a curiosity as great as his own.

10. Hail, Master!

The elùgroths gathered around her as moths drawn to a flame. Ginsar reveled in their adoration. It pleased her as much as their fear. And, right at this moment, she sensed both swirl in the dark air with a force that intoxicated her.

She, the greatest among them – she, sole disciple left living of the great Shurilgar, was about to perform a summoning that defied the laws of the earth. Well might lesser creatures tremble as they milled about her, for tonight was a night like no other. It would be like no night they had ever seen.

The elùgroths fell back as they reached the shores of the lake. They knew this was where the summoning would happen. They stood silent, their bickering, their petty rivalries and their intricate schemes forgotten; at least for the moment.

She stepped forward a few paces by herself. It was the dark hour before the beginning of dawn. The night was dying, but the sun had not yet birthed the slow graying of the sky. It was that moment when the world stood poised in transition, when there were worlds within worlds and the power that governed all things ebbed. Dark was the pine forest behind her, its shadows stalked by death, by the hunted and by their hunters. Ahead, the water of the lake was impossibly still. A silvery light was on it, gleaming and glistening like dew laid down by the moon. But there was no moon.

Ginsar studied the water. It was beautiful, or so she had been told. To her, beauty was power and obedience. Nevertheless, whatever the lake was now, it was about to change.

She straightened and stood to her full height. As she did so, those behind her cringed. They were scared, and well might they be. But she paid them no heed. Out, out her mind spread, out over the water. She plumbed its depths, became one with it, flowed with its currents and felt everything between the muddy bottom that cupped it to the mirror-like surface that topped it.

Beneath the dark fringe of the forest four riders appeared. She did not see them, but rather sensed their presence. She had brought them into existence and knew at all times where they were and what they were about. They were hers to command, and yet they made her uneasy.

She turned her mind to the deed at hand. Her mouth moved, and in a whisper that slowly grew she chanted. Her words filled the air, and then gained substance and descended into the water. Words and power were one, power and words melding until her thoughts came to life.

Fire spurted beneath the water. There were no limits to her strength, and she felt the intoxication of her magic as a wine that coursed through her blood. It was joy and bliss and it gave life and purpose to her being. It would do anything for her, and she anything for it. It was alive.

Once again, she felt a stirring of unease and suppressed it. At her thought the fire turned scarlet and then green and then blue. She shifted between them in a frenetic rush, playing with her power, toying with the forces that moved and substanced the world. She reveled in it, and yet knew at the same time that there were those who would say that such an uncontrolled use of the power reflected an uncontrolled mind, a mind that was insane, a mind where the power controlled her and not her it.

She made the fire shiver with a thought and laughed. Fools! All of them were fools. I am sane and the rest of the world is wrong!

Her hands grew rigid and her fingers stabbed down. Fire plunged into the depths of the lake, down to the muddy bottom and the solid earth beneath. Nothing happened. The world became suddenly still. Then a great chill descended. The stars glittered above and frost glistened on the long needles of the pine trees.

Suddenly, the water of the lake seethed. It hissed and boiled and thrashed, growing angry. The water tossed and turned like a man gripped by a terrible nightmare. It writhed with forces seeking escape, forces that she had called into being. The water became fire, turning and shifting to her every thought.

A noise began. It was not the splash of water nor the cackle of fire. It was a desperate wailing. And there were words within it, angry words, swearing and curses. There was pleading and threats and screams and promises of dark deeds.

Then the faces appeared. The fiery water showed them all. Staring faces. Cruel faces. Kind and goodly faces. There were people and monsters and things born of other worlds. They tried to rise up into the air and escape the lake, but the water churned and pulled them down just as easily as it brought them up from the netherworlds that were their origin.

Ginsar laughed. Her fingers stabbed again and then clawed at the air. A swirling vortex formed far out in the lake. From this a figure rose, tall and splendid, robed in fiery water and crowned with white froth.

The sorcerers behind Ginsar fell to the ground. Power throbbed in the air, and the figure, mantled in awe and dread majesty, drew a shuddering breath and lifted high its arms. Then it bent, and lowering a hand into the churning water upon which it stood, drew up a lesser figure to stand in its shadow.

Together, the two figures glided over the water and came toward the shore, shadowy robes billowing in otherworldly air.

Ginsar let out a breath between clenched teeth, and it turned to a white plume in the frigid air. The summoning was complete. As the dead who were called forth approached, the white sand at the margin of lake and land turned red as though wetted by the blood of all who had ever died.

She shuddered and dropped to her knees. "Hail!" she cried in a trembling voice. "Hail, master and beloved!"

Away in the forest nothing moved. But the trunks of some of the trees, gripped by frost and frozen, burst with deafening cracks.

11. The Voice of the Past

Gil and Elrika followed the stairs. They led back up into the palace, but where they would finish was a mystery beyond guessing.

The timber was rickety, and dust covered everything in deep layers that had laid undisturbed for years beyond count. Gil doubted anybody had been this way in centuries. The dust seemed thick enough for that, but there was no way to tell for sure.

The stairs were narrow, and they were hemmed in by high balustrades of carved hardwood. The two of them walked together, forced close by the railings. Gil did not mind.

Elrika ran her hand over a balustrade. The dust peeled away revealing timber that was deep red with a fine grain.

"So much dust," she said, "but once this was an expensive staircase. It might be narrow, but the timber is far better than what was used in the servant's stairwells. And the craftsmanship is better too. All of this means something, you know."

"What do you think?" Gil asked.

She shot him a look. "You know what it means."

It was true. They had gained entry by lòhrengai, and not just lòhrengai but by the Seal of Carnhaina. This was a passage designed for the great queen, and possibly it was a secret. No, he decided. It *was* a secret, even in her time, and the secret had died with her, else the stairwell would have been in everyday use.

The walls around them turned from wood to stone. It seemed to Gil that although the stairs remained the same the passage that they took had been built at different times. That was possible, of course. Carnhaina had not founded the city. Her father had done that, and it may be that she had furthered the construction of some secret tunnel. None of that, though, explained its origin in the first place. What need had there been for a secret tunnel at all, whenever it was built?

Whatever the case, the fact that the walls were of stone gave Gil the idea that they were now somewhere in the actual outer wall of the palace. That made some sense, because it would be easier to keep the construction secret that way. On the other hand, it limited the number of places that the stairwell could lead.

Yet, evidently, it did lead to other places. From time to time they came to doorways. These, they did not open. At least if they kept to the main stairwell they could not get lost. Moreover, they both had a feeling that the stairs led somewhere important. They would keep on following them up and to whatever place that was.

They went ahead. The stairs grew slightly wider now, and were in better repair. The dust, however, remained just as thick.

"We must be high in the palace," Gil ventured.

"At the very top, I think," Elrika answered. "The stairs cannot go on much longer."

She was correct. Very soon after they came to a chamber. It was, at least it had been, well decorated. Old hangings rotted away on the walls. Gil's eyes were drawn to marks on the stone. Halathgar was there again, the same as in the entry chamber. The paint was bright blue this time, outlined in white.

Gil stepped ahead and wiped the dust off the image. The constellation shone brightly, and he did not even have to reach out with his mind to sense the lòhrengai about them.

"Here it is," he said. "Surely there is a room on the other side of these marks."

They paused. "What do you think it is?" she asked.

"I don't know. Perhaps a storeroom full of gold and treasure?"

"Maybe," she said. "Or perhaps a chamber where she worked her magic in secret."

That was possible too. But he felt that her magic, at least her great spells at any rate, were worked from the tower in which her tomb was eventually built.

He shrugged. There was only one way to find out. "Shall we?" he asked.

She nodded.

Gil put his hands to the constellation. The marks on his palms tingled. With a click and a rush of power, the door that he knew was there slid open.

They looked inside the next room. It was lavish, but still a small chamber – long but narrow. A couch, lush and soft, filled most of it. Dust covered it now, yet still the color of the fabric shone through. Royal blue.

The hangings on the wall were the same color. These were mostly intact, and they showed scenes of Cardoroth's history, and of the time even before the city was founded. Gil recognized images of the Camar race, his ancestors, camped in tents and villages by a great river. Beyond was a forest and within that a mighty city. That was Halathar, the home of the immortals who had befriended and taught many tribes of men. To them the various races of men owed much. But they had given

128

much also of themselves in service, in war and battle against the enemies of the Halathrin before they ventured further east to found cities such as Cardoroth.

There were other images too. One showed the fabled standing stones, a place of worship and ceremony that dated back to his earliest ancestors. It was a place from history that was not forgotten, but that had become legend. It was from a time that Gil's books called the *Age of Heroes*.

He looked around at the tapestries. There were other stories on the wall, drawn from the ancient past. The migration of all the Camar tribes was there, ever travelling from west to the east. But there was war also. Great battles against the enemies from the south were shown. There were elugs, that race of creatures like men, which some knew as goblins, and their hordes blackened the wall-hangings. Elùgroths led them, cloaked in shadow and pointing wych-wood staffs with the menace of sorcery.

And then other tapestries showed Cardoroth: red-walled, splendid, its wide and myriad streets filled with joyous people – among them Carnhaina herself. Suddenly the image of her filled Gil's vision: a great lady, holding in one hand a spear while the other was raised, palm down, in a gesture of benevolence. About her neck was a torc of gold, an ancient symbol of nobility and rule.

Gil took his eyes off her. There were other things in the room also, although they seemed matter-of-fact by comparison. The desk and chair drew his gaze more than anything, and he realized that this was a secret room for Carnhaina. She had sat on that very chair, placed her hands on that very desk, lit or extinguished the lamp that still rested upon it.

At that moment, he felt a sudden connection to her. She was not just an ethereal spirit, not just a presence in his dreams. She had been, once, a living and breathing person with dreams of her own. She was his grandmother, many times removed.

On the desk was a book, but there were many, many others in shelves along the back wall. This was a library, or a study, and he felt beyond doubt that it was hers. It was a place she came for solitude, away from her court and the incessant demands of leadership. Here, she pondered things and then issued commands. This was perhaps the heart of her realm rather than the throne room.

He glanced at Elrika, but she said nothing. This was not a time nor a place for speech. He moved to the table and glanced at the book upon it. It was open. It was, perhaps, the last book she was reading before she died, and it had been left thus, undisturbed, through the long centuries. Yet if so, strangely, it had not accumulated much dust. Nor had the top of the table.

With trembling hands, he reached out and picked up the book. It was heavy. Turning it over he studied the script. It was written in a fine but spidery hand. The language was old, but still readable. The speech of Cardoroth had not altered much in the centuries, and Gil had read other books nearly as old as this.

The book had been left open on the table, spine up, but he saw at once that it had been left on the first page. Glancing at its top he saw something that made him gasp. There, in that spidery writing, there, written almost certainly by Carnhaina, was his own name. *Gilcarist.*

It was like a blow to his stomach that took his breath away. He realized that he was looking at a letter. It was addressed to him, written by a person who had died nearly a millennium before his birth.

Elrika had seen it also. She backed a little away from him.

"Read it," she said. "It's for you."

Gil hesitated. It *was* for him, though how that could possibly be he did not know. What power of foresight had Carnhaina possessed? How great her skill in magic must have been? Yet still, he would not have been here without Elrika. So, he read the letter aloud.

"Hail, Gilcarist. Prince now, and mayhap king to be. When you read this, I am dead. Long years have passed. But know, though death has turned me to dust, still I have power. In death shall I guard my people even as in life I led them.

"One day, their governance may fall to you. But that is undecided, and even my arts have limits. I cannot see with certainty, and fate, as ever, is fickle. But long I knew you would come. By the time you read this, long will I have waited. For understand! Your coming is told in the stars. You are the Star-marked One. You are The Boy with Two Fates. The Guarded and the Hunted. The King Who Might Rule, or the Lòhren Who Might Teach. You are also the Boy Who Might Live, and the Boy Who Might Die. You are the Savior and the Destroyer. But to me, your foremother, you are my grandchild. You are Gilcarist, and I love you.

"Know, Gilcarist, that it is in your power to shape the destiny of your people. Know also that nothing is as it seems. Friends may be enemies, enemies friends. Or not. Trust few, but trust fully. Choose your companions wisely, for they will stand by you when the forces of the Dark seek your destruction. And they will. Remember that.

"We have met, or we will meet, or we will meet again. Until then, fare thee well. And know, O child, that in life I was stern. Even with my children. But I was proud of them, and I am proud of you. Good luck. You will need it, for the Dark conspires against you. Do not forget."

The letter ended. Gil ceased speaking. There was an immense hush in the room, and Elrika looked at him. There was awe in her eyes. Or perhaps fear.

12. Chaos Serves the Dark

The water of the lake calmed. The apparitions came to a standstill before her. They were near the shore, yet still above the water as though standing on a ledge of up thrust stone. But there was none.

Ginsar felt the cold of the earth burn her knees where she knelt, but she did not move. She had not the strength, nor the desire.

The taller of the two apparitions spoke, his voice a whisper of death in the frost-cold air.

"Why have you summoned me?"

"To learn, O Master."

"Then speak my name."

Ginsar knew this spirit's name, the name it bore in life. She knew also that to speak the name of a spirit was to give it greater power in the mortal world.

"Shurilgar," she answered without hesitation.

The shade drew itself up, Shurilgar that was, and the shadows that formed him took more substance.

"What would you know?" he asked.

"Will I succeed in contriving the downfall of Brand and the boy? Will I destroy them, and then kill them?"

Shurilgar stood like a ray of darkness spawned by a black moon. The shadows around his face were impenetrable. His voice, when he answered, seemed distant and empty as the void.

"I am no longer part of this battle. The dead have other concerns than the conflicts of this smallest of worlds." He paused. "Yet this much I will say. The fate of the boy remains undecided. The destiny of Brand is now set. He has made his choice, and he will now die. It is unalterable."

Ginsar cackled with glee. She knew better than to believe that Shurilgar was unconcerned with the outcome of her plotting, but his similitude of indifference did not matter. He played his own games, in death as in life, but none of that mattered. He had said that Brand would die, and the dead saw the future as the living could not.

She stifled her joy and looked back at the spirit. The long arm of Shurilgar, he who was and would always be her master, pointed slowly at her, and his voice was chill with anger.

"Beware! Brand's death is not an end. It is a beginning. If you be not careful, you shall snatch dry dust where you sought to scoop water."

The lake suddenly thrashed all about him, responsive to his mood. It hissed and spat. "Beware. Things are not as they seem. This much I am permitted to say, and no more. Beware!"

The lake stilled. Shurilgar drew in on himself. The shadows about him deepened.

"What else would you ask? Time grows short. Your summoning weakens."

Ginsar spoke quickly. "What of the city itself? It did not fall in the recent war, might it fall now, if Brand dies and the boy is friendless or dead also?"

Shurilgar replied, his voice remote and subdued. "You have brought forth the four riders. They are chaos. All now is possible. All. This may work to your favor. Chaos serves the Dark better than the Light. But beware. Not all ends can be seen, even by the dead. Chaos also serves the Light."

134

The dark spirit paused, lost in some recollection of the past or some glimpse of the future. "Remember that," he whispered. "But know also that the four riders, or the forces you have channeled into the bodies of those who once were men, call to others of the Dark. Your allies in the south were defeated. They will need time to recover, to grow again in strength. Your allies to the north gather. They shall flock to you, and an army you shall have."

Ginsar bared her teeth. "Then I shall conquer! With Brand dead, none will rally the city. None will have the strength to withstand me!"

The waters of the lake seethed and churned. They muttered angrily, impatient for release from the summoning that held them.

"Time is gone," Shurilgar said. His shadow form began to recede, gliding back toward the deeper water whence it had risen.

"Tell me!" Ginsar shouted over the growing distance and the splash and roil of the water. "Will I be queen of Cardoroth?"

Her master pointed at her once more, his long arm covered in the tattered shrouds of death.

"You shall triumph! Yet in the moment of your victory is the seed of failure. Beware!"

The dark form at her master's side cried out, just one voice now among the many that lifted up from the lake seeking life and freedom. But she *knew* his voice.

"Avenge me! Avenge me!"

Ginsar's blood burned with fire. "I shall, Felargin. I shall, my brother!"

The spirits sank beneath the waves. Her brother first and Shurilgar second, his long arm still pointing at her.

135

The lake swallowed them. It heaved and turned, and then grew slowly still. All noise ceased.

Ginsar staggered to her feet. Her strength was spent, yet a great joy bubbled within her. The dead did not lie. She would triumph! Yet still a single doubt nagged at her jubilance. What had Shurilgar meant by the seed of failure?

13. This is Home

"There's more," Elrika said. "Go on. Read some of it. It's for you."

Gil hesitated. The rest seemed to be a diary of some sort. It was too much to read at one sitting. Far too much, and it scared him. Yet it compelled him too. The words belonged to his far distant grandmother. They were written in her own hand...

He flicked through the book, noticing the spidery script alter from a firm and confident hand into a frailer one. Age and death had claimed her, despite her great power. Or perhaps she had let it do so, renouncing the longevity of lòhrens and sorcerers, not using magic to sustain her life as they did.

"There are dates at the top of each page," he said to Elrika. He did not tell her that the writing burned from the page into his eyes. Here were not just the thoughts of another person, but the history of another age. This was a kind of magic nothing to do with lòhrengai. It was a window through the wall of time and into another world.

One page caught his eye, and he read some of it out loud.

"I have it! Magic some call it. Lòhrengai. Sorcery. Witchery. What matter the name? It is the heart, body and mind of the user that gives it power and form. If these be unified, no spell is beyond reach, no power beyond summoning. When need is the greatest, do not let the unity slip away. Harden your will. Grasp it. Make the power your own, and then nothing is impossible."

137

Gil flicked to another page and read something new.

"Alas! Battle went against us this day. The Dark closed in. Hope was lost. All my power was as nothing. My armies were scattered before the winds of fate, and the great dark fell before my eyes. Yet one man saved us. A peasant. He withstood the rush – rallied his friends about him and the army after. Thus the battle turned. I do not even know his name, but today he was king."

The diary said nothing more of the conflict than that. Gil wondered what battle was being fought and what man had saved the day. But whatever had happened, and to whomever ... they were all dead now, their life-and-death struggles forgotten. It was a lesson to him, a reminder of mortality and that the passage of time would one day expunge all memory of him, too. But for a little while, he had a voice, and he would make sure the world heard it. He had things to say, and to do, before he was swept into oblivion.

Elrika caught his glance. "Maybe we should go back now," she said. "You've been gone a long time, and the Durlin will be looking for you."

Gil drew himself out of his reverie. "You're right. But we'll come back."

He took a long look around the room. Apart from the diary, there were shelves of unread books. This was his place. This was his home. This was where he would discover, or decide, just who he was.

14. The Gaze that Misses Nothing

Elrika moved toward the door that they had used to enter the chamber.

"Wait," Gil said. He stood where he was, reasoning something through. "This room," he told her, "must have been Carnhaina's study, her secret library. At least while she was in the palace rather than her tower. She would not have entered it from far below. The stairs were built as a means of escape or for secret meetings. For everyday use, she would have entered from somewhere at the top, from somewhere convenient to her personal rooms."

"What are you getting at?"

"I think there's another way out, or into, this room."

They looked about, but there were no more eyes, no more images of Halathgar.

Gil felt defeated. He knew his reasoning was sound, but reality had proven it wrong anyway. He was about to give up, and then something occurred to him.

"She was a lòhren," he said, "Or a sorceress. But the top rooms of the palace are well frequented. Some sort of hidden mechanism would have been used, as with the other doors. But it would be constructed of magic so that it could not be accidently discovered. And the risk was greater up here, up where her rooms were because that's where people would have expected to find such a thing."

"But if it's not marked," Elrika said, "and if you don't know the spell, then how can you find or open it?"

139

Gil looked at the books on the shelves. It was possible that the answer might be written in there somewhere, but there was no time to look for it. Nor, he supposed, was it likely that Carnhaina would have written such a thing down. So, reasoning it through, it would therefore more than likely have been something easy to recall, something familiar and every day to her, but something unseen to anyone else.

And then he knew. The other doors had been marked with a sign and opened at the touch of his lòhrengai, but that was not the only way to construct a spell.

"Halathgar," he said in a solemn voice. It was still Carnhaina's mark, but spoken rather than painted.

Nothing happened. "Halathgar!" he said again, with more force. Still, nothing happened.

What was he missing? The word alone was obviously not enough – he would need to invoke lòhrengai with it.

He closed his eyes and slowed his breathing, thinking of Brand's oft-repeated advice. *Let the magic come of its own, rather than try to bend it to your will.*

Light glimmered on his palms. He tried not to think too deeply about it, but just accepted that it had come at his need. He faced the wall opposite, and reaching forth he placed his hand on the stone. "Halathgar!" he commanded.

Light flared, a brilliant blue that filled the chamber. He felt a power respond to his own. It rose up, sought him out, assessed him and then withdrew. And then suddenly there was a grinding of stone and another door appeared.

Gil dropped his hands and the light faded. Together, he and Elrika walked through the door. The room beyond was a surprise. It was Brand's own bed chamber.

Once, it had been the king's, and Gil supposed it had always been so through the ages. Once, even Carnhaina had slept here.

There was no one about. The room was plush, even luxurious. It was so different from the way Brand normally was.

"Halathgar," Gil said, almost casually, and the door closed behind them.

They opened the door out, just an ordinary door this time, and a palace corridor was beyond. There was no one here, either. The servants had already made the bed in Brand's chamber and must have cleaned the other rooms on this floor as well.

They closed the door behind them and then hastened along the corridor. But almost straight away they heard someone walking, and then Brand himself turned a corner to face them. His expression seemed troubled, but instantly that look was gone, and then he held them both with his clear-eyed gaze that missed nothing.

"What have you two been doing?"

"Nothing!" they answered in unison.

Brand looked at them, a slight smile on his lips. Then it was gone, and Gil was not sure that it had ever been there at all.

"Shorty is looking for you. He's not happy that you gave his men the slip – again."

"I'm sorry," Gil said. He looked down at the floor.

"Don't apologize to me. Shorty is the one who deserves it. Or better still, the Durlin who were guarding you at the time that you ... disappeared."

"I'll find Shorty right now, and then the guards," Gil said. He was surprised at how calmly Brand was taking this, and there was no suggestion of punishment. With

141

Elrika close by his side, he began to walk away, but Brand called after them and they turned.

"So," he said. "You found it." This time he did not hide his smile.

Gil was shocked, but he should have known that Brand would have found the chamber himself. He was a lòhren, not just the regent.

"Yes. But how did you know that?"

Brand's smile broadened. "Look at your boots. They didn't get like that walking around the palace. Not through the normal corridors, anyway." And then he turned and was gone.

Gil slowly shook his head. "Nothing escapes him."

Elrika did not answer at first. She remained staring down the empty corridor in awe.

"He's a great man," she said softly. "I don't care what they say. He'll never betray you."

Gil looked at her in surprise. "But he didn't even say hello to you. How can you know something like that?"

She shrugged. "He didn't speak to me, but he looked into my eyes, and I looked back. Trust me Gil, whatever is going on he is the person to trust most in all the world."

15. Speak My Name, Boy

Gil dreamed again that night, but he knew straightaway that it was not the normal dream.

He stood upon a knoll, looking down over sweeps of green grass. A gusty wind blew hard from the west, and the scent of rain was in the air. Clouds reached out across the sky, shifting, changing, growing and disappearing under ever-altering buffets of air. The sun winked and shone from behind the gray clouds, covered at times while at others breaking forth with piercing rays.

He stood alone in a great wilderness, but he was not scared. Dusk settled about him, and he knew that between blinks of his eyes hours had passed, as was the way with dreams.

The wind died down, and night drew over the land. The clouds blew away, and stars sprang to life. Out of nowhere a campfire burned before him. It flickered comfortingly.

Gil looked out beyond the fire, and by the light of stars he saw what he had not seen before: a forest. A great sweep of trees, dark and brooding, marched along the horizon. They were pines. They were just like the trees that surrounded Lake Alithorin. The forest even had the same feel to it. And then he knew. It *was* the same forest.

Gil sat down near the fire and thought. Somehow, he had been caught out of time. He was on a grassy knoll where the city of Cardoroth would one day be founded, near a thousand years before he was born. The idea of it made his mind spin. It was also possible, he supposed, that he was in the future, at a point in time so far ahead that the city was gone and no trace of it remained. *Nothing*. Yet he trusted his first instinct better. He was in the past; that was how it felt.

He looked now into the fire, and it drew him in deep. Tongues of flame turned and twisted, and the hot air trembled. There was an image within all the movement, vague and shimmery. Then a voice, born on hot air and wisps of smoke, came to him.

"Do not be frightened," it whispered. The words twisted through the air like the tongues of flame.

"I'm not," he replied.

A swift laugh came in answer, carried on a flurry of ember-sparks and swirling smoke.

The voice spoke again, suddenly warm and rich. "Speak my name, boy. And I will come to you."

Gil knew who it was. Cardoroth called her the Forgotten Queen. Some named her the Witch Queen. But neither was her name.

"You are Carnhaina."

The fire flared. Sparks flew. In a billow of smoke the image gathered form and stepped out of the flame. A woman now stood before him, tall and majestic. She gazed down upon him, her eyes still sparking with the light of flame. But the flame was blue, and it burned with a cold light. Her red hair spilled like blood over her pale skin, and both hair and skin were brighter than he remembered. Nor was she the large woman that he had seen atop the tower. Here, youth flushed her features and there was a twinkle of merriment in her eyes. Yet still the same gold torc gleamed about her pale-skinned neck, and as always, in her right hand she grasped an

144

iron-headed spear. But he knew it was more than that. It was a lòhren-staff, and the power of magic played like running fire the length of its metal tip.

She smiled. "Only when you speak my name do I have the power to come. In the flesh."

He looked at her anew, and realized that she was as real as him, whatever that meant in a dream.

"Why have you come? Why am I here?"

"So many questions?"

He grinned back at her. "That's what Brand says. He also says that if you don't ask you don't get, and if you don't question you don't learn."

"A wise man is Brand. Wiser far than his years, for he is still young."

Gil stood up and bowed. When he straightened, he asked a very direct question.

"Will he betray me?"

"Do you think he will?" she replied immediately.

"Do you always answer a question with another question?"

He thought for a moment that he had overstepped the mark, but Carnhaina merely laughed.

"You have spirit, boy! Not many dare to banter thus with the dead."

He did not know what to say to that, and there was a momentary silence.

Carnhaina's mood changed. "This much I'll say, as I said once before. There is great danger. To you. To Cardoroth, and to Brand most of all. To save himself, he must lose."

Gil held her gaze. "That makes no sense."

"Ha! Mayhap it will in time. We shall see."

She pulled her mantle about herself, feeling a cold breeze that he did not.

"Sit," she said, and pointed with her spear to the grass. He did so, and to his surprise she sat down lithely and faced him.

They talked for a while, as grandmother to grandson. No longer was she a queen. She was proud of her line, she said. Proud most of all of Gil's grandfather. "But Gil," she said, "You may yet rise above them all. Cardoroth needs you, but before that … Brand will need you first."

"How so? I don't think he needs the help of anyone."

"Oh, you are wrong there. Brand is strong, but he will need to be. Few men have ever passed through such testings as has he in his life, and the testing has only begun. Even the strongest metal can shatter. Indeed, it *will* shatter if enough force is applied. And Brand is a man. That makes him both weaker and stronger, for while the *body* has limits, the *will* can endure beyond the constraints of the physical. Let us hope Brand proves that true."

Gil did not answer, and Carnhaina sighed. "You will understand better one day. For now, it is enough that you know how to get help when he needs it most."

"And how shall I know when he needs it most? And how shall I get it?"

"Hush, child. You will know. Oh, when Brand needs help, if things come to pass as I fear, and as I hope, then you will *know*. The how is much easier. I shall give you the means to summon me. But it will work once, and once only. Use it wisely."

She reached forth with her hand and traced her fingers along his temple. He felt the cold brush of death, of a void beyond the life he knew, dark and distant. But her touch seemed real also, born of flesh and blood. And there was love in it. Then he felt her palm press against his skin. Something passed from her to him, but he could not grasp what it was.

She leaned back wearily, and dropped her hand. "It is done," she said. "When the time comes, you will know what to do and have the power for it. In the meantime, have courage. Endure. Never give up hope."

She said the last with a keen look in her eye. A while she looked at him thus, and then, almost regretfully, she raised her hand again, fingers thrusting toward him.

"Sleep," she said.

Gil tried to keep his eyes open, but he could not. Weariness stole over him. The night and the fire faded. Last of all disappeared Carnhaina, her eyes gleaming like the twin stars of Halathgar, and then they too blinked out. As he drifted into sleep her whisper followed him. *Sleep. Sleep, and have courage.*

16. I Rule!

Brand sat on the lesser chair beside the throne of Cardoroth. That ornate symbol, carved of ancient wood, embossed with gold script, crusted with gems, dominated the room. He ignored it.

It was morning. The early light of the sun beamed through the stained-glass windows. The white marble of the floor glittered with light like the surface of a lake. Above, the vaulted ceiling rose to a dizzying height, grand and eloquent. It was all beautiful, but it did not take his mind off the troubles he faced.

A score of soldiers flanked him, standing poised and alert. Taingern and Shorty were among them. A soldier, ceremonially dressed, opened the great door to the throne room, and the delegation that had insisted on seeing Brand this morning came through. They did not look at the art of the grand room. They did not speak to each other. A dozen strong, grim faced, they strode purposefully toward him.

Brand knew these men, or some of them. The others, he knew of. Sandy had seen to that, and she was about somewhere, concealed in an alcove listening. Of that he was sure.

He knew what they would say. Sandy had told him, for there were few secrets in the city that she did not uncover. Few secrets, and few conspiracies. These men were aristocrats all, and even without her earlier warning he could have guessed their intentions. But it was nice to be forewarned anyway.

Their leader stepped to the front when they came to a stop. He did not bow.

"Do you know me, Brand?"

There was silence. Only the nervous shuffles of the soldiers broke it, and the faint clink of chainmail armor that they wore.

Brand ignored the lack of protocol at being addressed merely by name. He ignored the rudeness, and he allowed a faint smile to play across his face.

"I know you. You are Lord Dernbrael. Once, you commanded the right flank of Cardoroth's army when we fought enemies from the south. I know you, and your history. It's said that you are in league with the old king's half-brother, who has long sought to return from exile and claim the throne. Of course, that's only a preposterous rumor, and I don't believe it. This much I know, for I observed it first hand on that battlefield. You are a brave leader, for I saw you command with unflinching courage. I saw and watched while you stood on the hill and gave orders to your men who fought."

Dernbrael looked at him. There was puzzlement on his face as he tried to discern the meaning of what had been said to him. That puzzlement fled, and his face went red as he realized that he had been insulted twice under the guise of two compliments.

"The past is of no matter," Dernbrael said. "I come to speak of the future, and I will be heard."

Brand looked to the floor, as though in thought. "The death rattle of a thousand throats is what I hear. The cries of the dying, the shouts of the living and the roar of battle. I remember that still, hear it waking or sleeping. And I can picture you in my mind, a glorious figure on the hill, your cloak billowing out behind you, your sword, sheathed at your side … your pale armor glinting, free of dirt and blood. Yes, Dernbrael, I know you. Your

149

bravery earns you many rights. So speak. Speak, and be heard."

The soldiers stilled. Shorty and Taingern stiffened. Those two had been there that day, had fought in that same battle. They knew Brand had just called the man who stood before him a coward. They knew also the insult had been delivered as a calculated retribution for the lord's failure to meet protocol. What would happen next, nobody knew.

There was silence, deep and unbroken. Not even the great vaulted ceiling of the throne room cast back any whisper of sound, as it usually did.

Suddenly, Dernbrael laughed. "Thus do you offer me a reprimand for my own lack of courtesy. A wild man of the Duthenor some call you, but I perceive that you have a nimble mind and have learned refinement at our court. It is a place where words are edged like swords."

"So it is. And words can cut, but never yet have I seen them spill the guts of a soldier standing beside me, trying to hold the line."

Dernbrael looked at him coldly. "Are we done sparring?"

"Speak," Brand said. "And I will listen."

"Then this is what we have come to say." Dernbrael gestured at the nobles behind him. "You know it already, but let us clear the air. "Your rule is wrong. You are not one of us, not of Cardoroth. You do not understand, even after the years you have spent among us, our ways. And why should you? There is great history among the city's people, great traditions. You make decisions without thought of that, and it disturbs the people. There is unrest. If you were wise, you would go now while you have the thanks of Cardoroth's citizens. Leave it too late, and you will earn their enmity instead. Be wise, Brand. I urge you, be wise."

150

Brand leaned back into his chair. It was hard and uncomfortable. Momentarily, he glanced at the cushioned seat of the throne.

"Traditions, you say," he responded. "Traditions such as those that surround the position of Swordmaster. The Swordmaster that I dismissed. Perhaps I should have let him stay. After all, he was the son of the *last* Swordmaster appointed by the king. That is the sort of thing you mean, is it not?"

Dernbrael gave a curt nod. "That is exactly the sort of thing that I mean."

Brand rested his hands on the arms of the chair. "I see. A tradition had been established. It was not the place of an outsider to break it." Brand looked thoughtful, and then crossed his arms. "But does competence not mean anything? The man called himself a Swordmaster, but there are a hundred soldiers in the palace at this very moment who could best him with a blade. He was no Swordmaster. Worse, he was a fool. I dismissed him because he was not fit for the job, no matter who his father was, or who else he is related to. As it happens, I know he is your cousin. But you are as great a fool as he if you think that I will promote the aristocracy, or preserve their titles and duties, if there are others of less noble birth but greater ability to carry out those tasks. And you are a fool twice over if you think I will walk away from the regency. The king appointed me, and here I will stay until Gilcarist is ready to ascend the throne."

Dernbrael stiffened. "You dare call me a fool? The old king was the fool, appointing you! Old, did I say? Rather, I meant *senile*. Thus runs the whisper through the city. He was decrepit, and you are a mistake of his dotage. The people begin to see it. They begin to see

151

your true purpose and goal, and they will have none of it!"

Brand felt a white-hot anger well up inside him. The old king had been his friend, and he deserved a better remembrance than this.

He stood from his chair in one smooth motion, and his hand rested on the hilt of his Halathrin-wrought blade. It was time to show them his anger.

"The king was a better man by far than any of you. By his wit, and by his courage and determination, he saved this city from destruction several times. Many are our enemies. They are in the north and in the south. Better might it have been if he had failed, and the hosts of our opponents had poured in to overrun the city. Then, I would not have to deal with the likes of you!"

The nobles gathered before him grew pale. Some fidgeted. But Dernbrael was not put off.

"These are our demands," he said coolly. "Too long you promoted commoners above the nobility. The nobility will negotiate amongst themselves who is best to take the throne. That may take a while, but it will not be the boy; he is too young. As you say, Cardoroth has many enemies. We can ill-afford either a boy or a foreigner to rule. Until a king is chosen, I shall act as regent." Dernbrael took a step closer. He was not armed, but he showed no fear at coming within reach of Brand's own sword. "This you will do, or there will be civil war. Think not that it is only the nobles gathered before you who rebel. All of Cardoroth is against you."

Brand sat back in his chair and thought quickly. When he spoke, it was almost to himself. "All this because I promote commoners?" He let out a long sigh. "Bah. Commoners are many, and the nobility are few. Why should it surprise you that they get promoted?"

Dernbrael considered that, and Brand smiled inwardly. The man was a fool, and Brand now had time to think when instead he should have been backed into a corner and forced to make decisions quickly.

"It is not about numbers," Dernbrael said. "It is about rights, ancient rights and traditions."

"What you mean is that the nobility are born to rule, and the commoners are not."

Dernbrael lifted up his hands. "Such is life."

"Rubbish," Brand answered. "That's a pile of horse manure, and you know it." He stood up again. "You're so bent, Dernbrael, that I bet you can't even lie straight in bed at night."

Brand allowed himself another smile. He had had the time he needed to think. Now, he was deliberately speaking like a commoner in order to upset his enemy. Dernbrael would not like it. It would annoy him and the sudden change of tone would throw him off balance.

Brand pointed at him. "You would have the throne yourself, that much is obvious. And no doubt the nobility hate me, and plot against me. But just now you have committed treason. It was a mistake."

Dernbrael laughed. "Idiot. That alone should tell you that the power is mine, else I would not have dared it. If you leave now, you may leave with your life. If you stay, we will call a council of the nobility. It is in our power to do so. There is no doubt that the council will revoke your regency, and one of us will take your place. This is within the law."

Brand had reached the end of his patience, but he had thought things through and knew he was right.

"Maybe the council has the right to do that, and maybe they even would. Or maybe they wouldn't. The lawyers could debate it all for months, and the nobility may not see fit to place you on the throne, at any rate. But you're forgetting something."

Dernbrael smiled smugly. "I doubt it. But *do* tell."

Brand slowly drew his sword. "You call me a wild Duthenor, a tribesman, unfit to rule. Let me tell you then how a wild Duthenor tribesman thinks. I could kill you all now. Every one of you, and spill your blood in the throne room."

They shrank back. Even Dernbrael stepped away from him.

"Nothing could stop me," Brand continued, "for there is not a man among you. You speak of law? Then know this! Should I choose, I could rule by the power of the sword. The army is mine. I was one of them, remember? I shed my blood with them, as you never have, and they know it. Lawyers and councilors be dammed! The king made me regent, and regent I will be! Your demands are worth less to me than the dirt on your boots. Now leave, or you'll be taken out of here by bucket and mop. Have your council if you wish. It is nothing to me but leaves on the wind. I rule! And you cannot change it."

Even Shorty and Taingern went white at those words. The nobility stared at him, fearful that he would carry out his threat. But Dernbrael merely chuckled.

"Well. Then the rumor is true. I see it now. You would usurp the throne and set aside Gilcarist yourself."

Brand looked at him coldly. He sheathed his sword. "You know I could do so any time I want. But I haven't. Nor will I. Gilcarist will rule. He nears manhood now, and he learns well. He will take his place soon, and I will be free of the likes of you."

"So you say, but—"

154

"Enough! You are dismissed. You and your ragtag followers."

The nobles looked at him silently, and Dernbrael hesitated. But before any more words were spoken a soldier hastened through the room, his running steps loud on the marble floor and the echo of his coming thrown back down from the vaulted ceiling.

The room fell silent. The soldier came before Brand, short of breath and trembling.

My Lord," he said. "Three Durlin are slain. Gilcarist is missing."

The man did not speak quietly. All the nobles heard, and Dernbrael spoke into the silence that followed.

"So it begins."

17. Dark Rumors

Gil woke, and the memory of his dream, if dream it was, remained strong in his mind.

He felt a great sense of peace and belonging. But almost immediately those feelings, strong as they were, began to fade. Increasingly, he sensed that something was wrong. What had woken him? Had there been a noise?

He lay in bed, alert but still. He listened intently, but there was nothing out of place. Nevertheless, panic gripped him. There was no name for it. There was only a growing dread, without source or focus. But it was there.

He got up and dressed. Quickly, he belted a sword to his side. He did all this, his hands shaking badly, but there was still nothing out of place.

It was then that he heard a bump on the other side of his door. He stood motionless, his head cocked to the side, listening for more. A moment later the door burst open, torn off its hinges, and crimson fire flared within the opening and then winked out.

Three dark-cloaked figures rushed into the room. The light of dawn lit Gil's window, but these men from the corridor outside brought only darkness with them.

They came toward him. None of them carried a staff, but he knew they were elùgroths. Black-cloaked, their faces hidden by deep cowls and the skin of their hands pallid even in the dim light, they could be nothing else.

Gil tried to draw his sword, but he did not manage to free it completely from its sheath before a vice-like grip from one of those pallid hands clamped about his wrist. And then there were other hands grasping him and a fist smashing into his face. His head rocked back and pain flooded through him.

He struggled, but they were too many and too strong for him. They ripped the sword from his hand and discarded it on the floor. A knife was put to his back, and a face thrust up close before his eyes.

"Choose," an elùgroth said. "Live or die. Fight any more and your corpse will be left in this room."

Gil knew the man meant it. He went still, and he guessed this much at least; they were not assassins, else he would already be dead. They wanted him alive, and that gave him hope, though not much.

They moved out through the smoldering doorway. It was still quiet in the corridor, for likely the occupants of the rooms had been asleep, including the Durlin not set at guard at his door. It may be that they still slept, notwithstanding the noise.

The elùgroths hastened Gil forward, and then he saw the Durlin stationed outside his bedroom. All three were dead, strangled and burned by sorcery. The elùgroth who held a knife at his back made a gesture. The others worked quickly, dragging the bodies back into Gil's room. But there was another figure on the floor as well. It was an elùgroth, and Gil realized that the Durlin, though obviously taken by surprise, had still managed to fight back.

They closed the door and went forward. Another figure came into view, leaning against the wall. There was blood on his hand where he clamped it to his side. He too had been wounded by the Durlin, though not killed. Nevertheless, he looked badly injured. He muttered

157

under his breath in some harsh language that Gil had never heard before, and straightened as they approached, ready to join them.

Gil understood. The elùgroth had been releasing a sorcerous spell. The air stank of it, and it was no doubt intended to ensure the occupants of the adjacent rooms slept deeply. He was sure that it was this that had woken him, but he was keenly sensitive to the use of magic through his training. The others did not have that benefit.

It might be a long time before this attack was discovered, and Gil considered crying out for help. But the knife hovered at his back, and he knew these men would kill him and flee if they had to, even if that was not their purpose.

The palace was in shadow and darkness, and like shadows themselves they flitted through the corridors. The sorcerer who cast the spell stumbled ahead of them, but he continued to chant and Gil felt drowsiness steal over him. He fought it off, but when he was alert again they were already in the palace stables.

He drifted once more, but knew that he had been seated on a horse. The elùgroth rode behind him, one hand on the reins and the other with a knife still at his back.

Through the streets they raced in mad flight. But they were not elùgroths with him anymore. Now they were soldiers of Cardoroth, or so they seemed. Gil could not focus on them clearly.

The sun came up. Light glittered. It dazzled his eyes, and he realized that he was out of the city, come through the gate and that a road lay before him. Beyond, the western horizon was green.

He guessed where they were going. That strip of green was the pine forest that surrounded Lake Alithorin. He had heard dark rumors of that place. It was legendary, woven through the folklore of the city and bound with a heavy history of evil. Shadowy things dwelt there, neither man nor beast. Magic lurked beneath the trees, magic and death for the unwary. It was forbidden to him, but now he did not doubt that he would learn some of its secrets. But what then?

The elùgroths, if elùgroths they were, held him prisoner. But they were servants of someone else. For whom did they act? Were outside forces trying, as ever, to bring Cardoroth down? Or did his captors owe alliance to some traitor within the city?

The last thought disturbed Gil most of all. How had these men known which room he slept in? How had they navigated the palace so swiftly on their way out?

The sun rose higher. The horses sped beneath them. The elùgroth who had chanted in the city slumped on his mount's back. When at length he fell, the others did not slow. He was dead, or soon to be dead. The Durlin had claimed him, Gil thought with grim satisfaction. *Good for them.*

18. The King's Huntsman

Brand questioned the soldier who stood before him in the throne room.

"What's known so far?"

"Gilcarist is gone. His sword was found on the floor of his bedroom."

"And the Durlin?"

"Dead. They were in the room. And…" the man hesitated.

"Speak!" Brand said. "Speak freely but swiftly."

"It seemed as though sorcery was used. There were strangle-marks about their neck, but there were burns also. And the door was charred."

"Is there more?"

"There are reports of four strange men and a boy riding away from the palace. But they are unreliable."

"Why so?"

"Because some say they saw black-cloaked riders, others soldiers and some … Durlin, or at least riders in white surcoats."

There was a momentary silence. Not even Dernbrael spoke, but there was a sneer on his face.

"Which direction did the riders head toward?"

"On that, strangely, all witnesses agree. They went west."

Brand turned to Shorty and Taingern. "The enemy has him. They will have gone through the West Gate, the Arach Neben. The forest around Lake Alithorin is where they will head. Evil always finds a home there, and there

160

we shall find Gil. This much at least I can say. He is not dead. Otherwise, his body would have been left in the room. This is no assassination, and other plots are afoot." He turned his gaze to Dernbrael.

"We will speak later, if chance allows. And remember, I'm not from Cardoroth, as you earlier reminded me. I'm a barbarian. Should I discover that you were involved with this in any way, your aristocratic blood will not save you."

Dernbrael shrugged, but did not answer. He left, taking his group of nobles with him. None of them bowed as they left, but Brand was already issuing orders.

"Send for the Durlin," he said to Taingern. "All of them, whether on duty or not. We'll gather at the palace stables."

Taingern left, and Brand turned to Shorty. "Find Hruilgar, and bring him to the stables also."

"The king's old huntsman?"

"Yes. He still lives in the palace. Find him and bring him. We'll need a tracker, and none is better than that old man."

"What of the army, Brand? If the prince is held hostage, shall we not need soldiers also?"

"No. This is not an enemy of opposing soldiers that we face, as Cardoroth often has before. This is different. This is an enemy of sorcery. Quickly now! Do as I say."

Shorty left, and Brand looked around him. The throne room was silent, but word would get out swiftly of what had happened. He wondered what the people of the city would make of all this. But it was not really hard to guess.

He looked at the soldiers still flanking him. Their eyes were upon him, filled with doubt. He considered that.

161

These men were loyal to him, and the doubt in their eyes was not concern about his motives, but about the wisdom of chasing after Gil with only the Durlin and the old tracker instead of the army. No matter. He knew what he was doing.

Quickly, he went to the stables, detouring only briefly to retrieve something from his room. It was a long object, bundled in cloth and tied with two thin straps of leather. Then he went down to the stables and found the Durlin gathering.

They saddled their horses, and Brand chose his old black stallion. It was a reminder of his past, a time when he was a stranger to this city. It seemed long ago now, and the world had changed since then. So had Cardoroth, and so had he. Nothing was the same. Nor would it ever be again.

Taingern came, and with him the last of the Durlin. Only Shorty was absent, and when he arrived they would be twenty-seven: three short of their true number of thirty. Three would never ride again.

Shorty came soon after. With him was an old man, white-haired and silver-bearded. His face was ruddy and wrinkled from long years in the sun. Brand looked at him, surprised at how old he seemed and doubtful that he could make the journey. It had been at least a year since they had last met, and Brand wondered if he had miscalculated.

But the old man mounted the horse prepared for him without difficulty and sat astride it with the look of someone at ease.

Brand nudged his horse over. "Hruilgar," he said as greeting.

162

"Brand," the other replied. He had never been much for formality, and Brand liked that about him.

"Shorty has told you what's happened?"

"Yes," the old man answered. It was another good sign. The man wasted no time on useless speech.

"I think they've taken Gil into the forest. Once through the Arach Neben, you'll take the lead." Brand paused. "I'll rely on you most of all. We can do nothing unless we find the boy."

"If there's a trail, I can follow it," Hruilgar said simply.

Brand waited no longer. "Men," he said to the Durlin. "This will be dangerous. But our honor as Durlin is at stake, and our honor as men. We will find Gil. We are sworn to protect him. We will not give up. Speed now is our friend, rather than numbers. But mark my words, there will be sorcery at the end of our ride. Stay clear of it. There will be death also."

He almost said more, but even as he uttered those last words they triggered a premonition. As surely as he could see the men before him, he also saw glimpses of what was to come. The magic was both curse and blessing. He did not know which it was just now, but swift as the second sight came, just as swiftly it left.

The Durlin drew their swords when he stopped speaking. Their white surcoats gleamed, and they shouted the Durlin creed:

Tum del conar – El dar tum!
Death or infamy – I choose death!

Without another word, Brand nudged his horse into a gallop and the others followed. Through the streets they

163

raced, and the clatter of hooves on cobbles was loud. The citizens gave way, melting into alcoves and hugging the side of the road. Some cheered as they passed, and Brand knew that word of what had happened had already gotten out into the city. This was a dangerous thing, for rumor would spread with it, and, under the circumstances, rumor was not his friend. When he returned, if that would ever be, he might find the city turned against him. But if so, that was a problem for another day.

They rode ahead. The city was large, but they reached the Arach Neben swiftly and passed through the shadowy gate tunnel.

Brand shivered in the sunlight on the other side. This was where he had met the horseman. This was where he had met Death. And he knew now that he would meet him again.

He shrugged off the doubt that beset him and slowed down. There would be time now to spare the horses, for the old man would go at a slow pace to track. He must be careful not to miss any sign, especially if the riders they pursued left the road. Once they were in the forest, it would be slower still, but the tracking would be easier.

Hruilgar came to the fore. He led them now, his head low over his mount while his eyes scanned the ground.

Within moments the old man stopped. He pointed to the ground.

"Four riders," he said. "They passed this way not long ago. The one who leads them rides erratically. He is injured. See! One of the others carries a heavy burden, or two ride the same horse. Its tracks are deeper in the dirt."

"How fast do they ride?" Brand asked.

164

"Swiftly. The tracks are far apart. There is fear upon them. And well should there be – I have their trail now." The old man spat to the side of the road. "I'll not lose it. Not unless they use sorcery."

Hruilgar waited for no answer. He kicked his mount forward and the hunt began.

On they rode. The sun rose high in the sky and beat down. The red granite walls of Cardoroth grew smaller and smaller behind them. The green strip of forest ahead grew larger. Brand looked behind him. There were signs of old battle there. The wall was pock-marked from attacks. The ground was scarred by the encampment of a massive army. The enemy of the south had broken themselves on that wall. He remembered that army well. But this battle was different. He could not help but wonder if he would ever see those walls again. Or the green fields of the Duthenor that he yearned for.

There was no one else on the road. It was deserted, deserted and silent. The Durlin did not speak. Nor did Hruilgar, but it was clear that he followed the trail, and he did so with confidence. It surprised Brand when the tracker pulled his horse to a stop.

He nudged his mount forward and drew level with the old man.

"What is it?"

Hruilgar shifted uncomfortably in his saddle, and then lifted a thin arm to point ahead. He did not speak.

It took Brand a moment to realize what the tracker indicated, then he saw. There were crows ahead. Black dots from this far away, but he saw them hop and flutter on the ground. On the road. They had been attracted to something. And crows were carrion eaters.

He looked at the old man. The old man did not meet his gaze. They both knew that Gil could be out there.

"Be wary of a trap," he said to all the riders. He did not think there would be one, for he saw no obvious places for concealment. But the crows, and what they portended, might divert the Durlin's thoughts. He did not doubt the enemy might well look for such an opportunity.

The group cantered ahead. Dust rose from the sun-bleached road. Soon, the cawing of the crows grew loud. More flew in from the surrounding wild.

Something took shape on the road ahead. The crows tore and pecked at it. They fought and struggled amongst themselves. They paid no heed to the approaching riders.

Brand drew to a halt some thirty paces away. He studied the scene. A body lay there, bloating already in the sun. The crows tore at it. But it was muffled in dark clothes, and he could not tell if it was Gil. It could be an elùgroth. But if so, how? Had they fought among themselves?

He studied the surrounds. He saw no one else, no trap, nothing but the drying grass and the odd clump of trees. The old man pointed again, and Brand saw it. A lone horse standing beneath the shade of a distant tree. It had no rider, or none that was visible.

"First things first," Brand said without emotion. He nudged his horse forward toward the body. Shorty and Taingern came with him. The others held back.

The crows cawed madly and then fluttered away. Some flew and landed nearby. Others perched in the closest trees and watched with bloodied beaks and beady eyes.

Brand dismounted. The corpse lay face down, but a hand stretched out, clutched into a claw. It was a pallid hand, blue-veined and bony. It was the hand of an elùgroth, a sorcerer who lived by night rather than day, shunning the sun. Shorty and Taingern saw it also. Brand heard them both let out a sigh of relief.

"Why is there is no staff such as they usually carry?" Shorty asked.

"They relied more on stealth than sorcery," Brand answered. "But the lack of a staff does not mean that an elùgroth cannot conjure magic. They can, and they did."

He turned the corpse over with his boot. It was a middle-aged man, and one eye stared up at him. The other was a bloody socket. The crows had begun their work.

"Look," Shorty said. "There's blood."

Brand looked lower. Sure enough, the black cloak was caked with blood. Brand drew a knife and bent. He ripped at the material and exposed the flesh beneath. There was a wound there, small but deep. It had been a killing stroke by a long knife. But not immediately lethal.

"I think," Brand said, "that this was no fight amongst the elùgroths. The Durlin who guarded Gil fought. One elùgroth they killed on the spot, but this is a second. They did the best they could, even though they were outmatched."

He signaled Hruilgar to come over. If the old man was disturbed by the sight of death, he did not show it.

"Can you tell anything from the tracks?"

The old man rode slowly around the corpse, and then trotted ahead a little way before coming back.

"It's simple enough. The man fell from his saddle, and the others kept riding. They did not miss a stride."

167

Hruilgar spat again, his contempt for the riders obvious, but unspoken. "The man did not die straight away. He crawled for a little, perhaps tried to reach some shade, but he did not have the strength."

Brand stood. They had learned all they could here. The riderless horse might reveal more. He got on his own mount and they went back to the Durlin.

"Be wary," he said. "Keep your eyes open. The enemy hastens, and that means they fear us. As well they should. But they may also seek to ambush us. First, we will get that horse, and then we will ride again."

He led them off the road and toward the horse that stood beneath the tree. Soon, they came to it, and it was clear that there was no trap. There was nothing there but the horse, the tree and withered grass.

Brand gave a sign and one of the Durlin went over. Carefully, he approached the horse, whispering to it soothingly and taking hold of the reins that trailed on the ground. It was nervous, but he did not have much trouble.

"Unsaddle it," Brand said. "Remove the bit and set it free."

The Durlin did so and was about to return.

"Look in the saddlebags, son," Hruilgar called out.

The Durlin bent over and rummaged through their contents.

"Nothing," he said.

"Nothing at all? Not even food?"

"No. Nothing."

Hruilgar turned to Brand. "That's good."

"How so?"

"Because tracking is more about getting into the mind of what you follow than studying the physical trail it

168

leaves. That this sorcerer had no provisions means, likely enough, the others didn't either. That shows they did not intend to ride far, or that they would soon meet with others who waited for them."

Brand gave a slight nod. "The forest is their destination. And there *will* be others." He said no more. They turned back toward the road and made for it. He felt the eyes of the Durlin on him. They sensed that he knew more than he was saying. That was true, but he could not tell them. It would make no difference.

He closed his eyes momentarily against the harsh sun. But he did not see blackness. Instead, another vision of the future came. He rode beneath the shade of trees. A cave mouth opened ahead, and then he was inside. It was darker here. Cooler. Filled with a sense of doom. He recognized it; it was the feeling of death. It rose from the floor. It fell from the shadowy roof. It was in the very air he breathed. And it suffocated him.

He opened his eyes to the sun again, and shrugged off the vision. The second sight was not strong with him. It was not reliable. Other lòhrens were more gifted at it than he.

But he knew he was only trying to convince himself. The more he used the power, the more the visions came. But right or wrong, visions or no, he had a task to do and he would carry it out.

They took up the pursuit again a little way ahead of the dead elùgroth. The crumpled body receded behind them. The crows had gathered to feast again, and they paid the living riders no heed. Slowly, their croaks and caws faded into the distance.

Hruilgar was at the fore again. Brand wondered if they would need him after all. The elùgroths had made

169

no attempt to hide their passing, nor would they once they reached the forest.

They *intended* for him to follow. He knew that now, knew it for certain.

The group had not gone more than three miles when the old man slowed and studied the ground carefully.

"Tracks," he said. "There are many now. A dozen or more riders met them here. They were waiting."

"Keep going," Brand said.

The old man gave him a strange look, but said nothing. The tracker did not like the feel of things. He was one to trust his instincts, and Brand could not fault him on that.

They moved forward slowly now. Hruilgar was careful to make sure those they pursued did not leave the road in the confusion of all the tracks. Brand said nothing. But he knew they would not.

At length, the road petered out to a dusty track. Ahead was the fringe of the great pine forest that surrounded Lake Alithorin. No one had ever explored it. Not properly. Few of those who tried ever returned to Cardoroth.

Brand looked back over the distance they had travelled while Hruilgar once more studied the tracks. Cardoroth was still visible, red and hulking on the horizon. It was not a pretty city, but it had become his home. The wild barbarian who had first seen it years ago had died. He was a different man now. And he knew that his life was about to change yet again.

"They went into the forest," Hruilgar said. "All of them."

"We will follow," Brand replied. "Take us to their lair."

Slowly, they moved into the trees. Once more he felt the eyes of the men on him. He had said little, and his mood was grim. It was not like him, even under circumstances such as these, and they knew it. They knew something was wrong, but they did not know what. Not for sure.

It was not only dark beneath the tree canopy, but cooler. And quieter. It was quiet as the tomb. But Brand had been here before. And Shorty also. They knew what to expect, and the Durlin were brave men, not easily scared by folklore and superstition. But they knew also that trouble lay at the end of this ride. They rode in silence, alert, watchful, ready.

They rode into thicker forest, following a wispy trail into the gloom. And the murk welcomed them. Brand's mood was one with it. It was a dark place, a fitting place for dark deeds.

19. We Are Strong!

Gil became more alert as the morning wore on. Whatever sorcery the elùgroths had used to lull him, they had ceased to employ. Or, it may be, that the only one of them who had that power was the one who had died on the road. Could he make use of that? Were the others unskilled at sorcery? If so, he may have a chance to escape.

Escape! How he longed to do that, but sorcery or otherwise there seemed little chance of it now. Near the forest other sorcerers had joined the group. They all watched him closely. They all looked at him with hidden knowledge in their eyes. They all knew what their destination was and the plan for him. He, on the other hand, knew nothing. Nothing except that the leader for whom they had done all this was a woman. They whispered her name, and he saw adoration mingled with fear on their faces when they did so. She possessed great power, even if they did not. And the more he studied them the more he came to believe that. They were elùgroths, but they were not of the same kind or stature as those who had threatened Cardoroth in the recent war.

The morning wore away and they rode, single file, toward the sweeping expanse of Lake Alithorin. They followed a path so faint that Gil doubted anyone would have found it but them. Yet, if anyone followed, if anyone knew to follow ... or cared to do so ... the trail was now beaten and marked by their passage.

The path snaked back and forth, not seeming to head anywhere in particular, but it always drew them deeper into tall stands of pine. It grew dark beneath the tree canopy, and the air was dank and acrid with the smell of decomposition. Bright orange fungi flowered in lush growths on fallen trunks and long lengths of gray-green moss trailed from overhead branches.

The elùgroths slowed and dismounted, walking their horses forward. Gil was pulled down and prodded ahead also. Travel was difficult with his hands tied behind his back and twisted roots beneath his boots.

Gil looked around as best he could while they progressed. It was a different world here, inside the forest. It was an unnerving place, but he could not quite put his finger on what disturbed him.

Eventually, the trail widened just a little and climbed uphill, away from the lake. Even during the day fog drifted from the water and cast seeking fingers through the trees. Moisture clung in a film over the pine leaves and dripped from their needle-like ends.

Soon, the forest thinned and they faced rugged cliffs. The jagged overhang of the crags ensured the crannied rock-face was obscured by shadow. The path came to an end, and the riders spread out over the short grass of a meadow.

One of the elùgroths grabbed Gil roughly by the back of the neck and pointed at the cliff.

"Behold! You see the home of our Mistress. It is a place of treasures beyond your imagination. The wealth of kingdoms and the luster of gold lie within. And power such as you have never seen!"

Gil scrutinized the cliff-face. After a few moments, he saw a cave; the entrance was little more than a man-sized shadow. He wondered how deep it went and what lay within, but he knew that he would find out soon enough.

Most of the elùgroths began to walk their mounts further along the meadow. Three stayed with Gil, giving their mounts to others to tend. These three led him up to the cliff-face and to the cave.

A musty smell came from the opening, but Gil could see nothing within. They moved into the cave, and one of the elùgroths retrieved a lantern from the floor and lit it. By its swinging light, Gil saw something of what lay ahead.

The entrance was small and confined, but the cave soon widened into a large chamber with a sandy floor. There were tracks in the sand showing the passage of many booted feet over a long period of time. The cave continued, but at a downward slope.

The elùgroths hastened Gil forward, and he soon noticed that the walls grew damp as they descended. Beyond doubt, they were already below the water level of the nearby lake, and were going deeper still. The floor eventually opened up into a pit. Light rose from within, and there was a murmur of voices also. They descended, following a crude ramp of gravel and rock.

They came to the bottom. The floor here was of dirt, and there were signs of mud all about, but it had dried into hard crusts on the lower portions of the walls, pale and flaky.

Gil noticed also that the walls were no longer natural. They were formed of chiseled stone. He did not doubt that the floor, had he been able to see it under the patchwork of sand and dried mud, would have been constructed of flagstones.

Glancing about he saw that the walls were decorated with the remnants of tapestries, long since rotted and spider-haunted. At some time in the past the chamber had been fashioned deep below the surface, and later destroyed by flood.

Who, Gil wondered, had built this place? But it was of no concern to him now. Ahead, was a series of statues. They almost seemed to move in the swinging light of the lantern. There were sculptures of men and women, the features of both stern and aloof. The men had the appearance of prideful warriors, and the women were beautiful but cold as the stone of which they were made.

Beyond the statues was a dais. Upon it a throne. This was of wood, black and polished. It must have been above the reach of the waters that flooded the chamber. It was intact, the arms and legs carved with ornate scrollwork.

Behind the throne was a wall, covered by a great tapestry, ancient but still beautiful. But it was she who sat upon the throne that Gil looked at, and could not take his gaze off.

It was her. The woman from his dreams. Beautiful she seemed, and terrible. Colder was her glance than the lifeless gaze of the statues. Cruelness etched her high-cheeked face and the red curve of her lips. Anticipation, burning, smoldering, barely held in check, leaped and danced in her eyes like a cold flame. About her, cowed by her, made insignificant by her presence, dozens of elùgroths stood: mute, silent, mere shadows of her power and glory, acolytes to her beauty and darkness.

Gil came to a trembling stop. An elùgroth at his side prodded him on; there was still some way to walk before he came directly before her. *Her.* His enemy, in dreams and now in waking life, for he sensed enmity roil from her in waves. She hated him with a consuming passion.

He tried to think clearly, but his thoughts were despairing. She had power greater than any he had ever sensed. It hit him like a slap across the face. If the magic gave Brand power like this, he veiled it. Slowly, he

175

shuffled forward, and a chill filled his body, seeming to settle into his very bones. Think! What would Brand do?

But he knew that he did not have Brand's skill at combat, nor at magic. These opponents far outpowered him, even without *her*. So, then what? What could he do? Nothing? No, Brand would not do that ... then what was left? Very little, but he would do it. He would engage his captors, extract what information he could, and then wait for any chance that might turn things in his favor.

"Who is she?" Gil whispered to the nearest elùgroth.

A mocking smile crossed the man's face. "You will see."

"Brand will come for me, you know."

The smile widened, but the elùgroth did not reply.

Gil did not like the feel of that answer. Did they know that Brand would come, because he was a part of this? Or did they set a trap for him, and hoped that he would spring it?

It was time for a different approach. "You're all elùgroths, aren't you?"

"Yes."

"But you're not like the ones I heard of or saw during the war."

"No!" the man whispered harshly. "They serve in their way, and we in ours. But we of the north are different. Sparse, but we are strong!"

"Who is your leader? Who is *she*?"

"One who knows you, but you don't know her. Now, be silent."

Gil did not ask any more. He shuffled slowly forward, thinking on what had been said, and if he had learned anything. This much he guessed, whoever these elùgroths were, and he did not think they were powerful, they were all here now in this chamber. But it was not them that he, or Cardoroth, really had to worry about. It was her.

The dais was surrounded by burning torches. Smoke scented the air and shifted and moved across the shadowy ceiling. Before the throne, set upon a black-clothed table, stood a silver basin. He knew its purpose. It was a vessel used to scry, and that was a difficult task. Great power was needed, but also dark rites. Brand had once told him with distaste how it worked. Lòhrens did not employ the practice, but relied on visions instead.

He braced himself and raised his eyes to look at the lady again. This time she was much closer. She was all that he had seen and sensed before, but he noticed one new thing. There was not only power, and coldness and cruelty in her gaze as she looked back at him, but also madness.

Gil felt scared all over again.

20. He Comes!

The dark lady looked into Gil's eyes. "Do you know who I am?"

Her voice was deep and resonant. It did not seem to fit her tall and slim body. He realized that she used elùgai to enhance it, and that gave him insight into her personality. For all her power, she felt the need to impress. In that way, if no other, she was weaker than Brand.

"No," he replied simply.

She seemed annoyed at his answer. "Then learn!" The lady smiled at him suddenly, shifting from thought to thought and mood to mood too swiftly for him to follow. It was another sign of her madness. Gil was sure of it.

"I am older than I look," she said. "Old as the hills I am. I was born before Cardoroth, hovel that it is, was raised from the dust, stone by red stone."

Gil watched her closely. She seemed to be speaking more to herself than him, and he did not believe her claim, but with lòhrengai and elùgai, all things were possible.

She leaned forward and whispered, as though telling a secret to him alone, oblivious to the elùgroths at her left and right.

"In those days that are forgotten, I had a master. I have him still, though he is dead. Do you know *his* name?"

Gil tried to remain calm. He did not know what to expect from her, still less did he have any idea what she was talking about.

"No, lady, I do not."

"Then I shall tell you. Step closer."

Gil did not wish to. Nor did the elùgroths by his side push him. Nevertheless, under her gaze, he stepped forward.

"Good boy," she said, looking at him knowingly. "Listen then. This is a name that all Alithoras knows. Mighty he was. Mightiest of them all, save one. *That* name we do not speak, but my master was … my master is … Shurilgar."

It was a name that Gil had indeed heard. It was a name from legend, a name of infamy. Shurilgar. Shurilgar the Betrayer of Nations. The sorcerer had died long ago, so long that history and myth had become one. The Age of Heroes his books called it. But for all that the elùgroth had lived so long ago, still the whispered stories came down through the ages. His name was a byword for treachery, dark deeds and sorcery. And it was rumored that his acolytes survived him.

The sorceress flashed him a sudden smile, all white teeth and red lips.

"Ha! I see you know *that* name, as well you should. Now, you will discover mine, and you will learn to hold it in dread even as you fear my master."

She drew herself up from the throne and stood. Regal she seemed, and power glittered in her eyes. Her glance was as a spear cast by a fierce warrior, sharp and piercing, and Gil flinched before it.

"Kneel, boy! For I am Ginsar, Mistress of Sorcery and Queen of Darkness. Kneel, for even Death rides at my whim and bows in my presence.

Gil felt his legs weaken. He did not kneel, rather he stumbled to his knees. He knew that she used sorcery to awe him, but he could not resist her.

Tall she was, a slender thing yet filled with the strength of unbreakable steel, and the light of the torches seemed to flicker as a crown atop her head. Yet the shadows about her feet deepened and swirled like drifts of smoke. She was queenly, otherworldly, a thing of terrible beauty.

Her acolytes moaned and prostrated themselves. And yet, as swift as she had called up her power, she let it go. Once more she seemed as a normal woman, save for the flicker of madness in her eyes. She sat down and grinned at him.

"What is my name, boy?"

Gil struggled to his feet. "I heard you. Your name is Ginsar."

She smiled at him sweetly. "That is my name. You will not forget it. Ever." Her gaze fell away from him and became vacant, as if she saw something that no one else in the room could observe. But then she focused on him again, her eyes boring into him. "I have a brother also. Once, Felargin and I served the master. Perhaps you have heard of him?"

Gil shook his head. "No," he answered, and fear tightened his throat and made his voice waver.

"No matter," she said. Then she giggled. "I'm more famous than he is."

A cold anger began to burn in Gil. This woman was mad. And she had great power. But he would not cower before her. He was the son of kings.

"I have never heard of him. Nor have I heard of you." He did not raise his voice, but he spoke with clarity and confidence.

Once again, Ginsar's mood changed rapidly.

"Fool!" she screamed at him. "I am told that you have some power. Can you not sense it in me? Can you not feel that I hold your life like a strand of spider's web in my fingers? Pah! You are descended from a second-rate sorceress."

Gil straightened and a calm stillness settled over him. What would be would be, but he would not accept insults in silence.

"Carnhaina was a lòhren," he said, "not a sorceress."

The elùgroth to his side struck him across the face, but he ignored that and returned Ginsar's gaze.

She shrugged nonchalantly. "Lòhren. Elùgroth. How little you understand. There is not much that separates us." She pointed a long arm at him. "But what of you? Is your magic of the Light or the Dark?"

Gil stared at her, taken by surprise, and he did not answer.

"Ha!" she said. "We shall see!"

Suddenly, he felt the full force of her mind. He realized in that moment how gentle Brand had always been with him in their training. Her power was overwhelming. It was like being crushed under a mountain. Slowly, surely, against his will he felt the magic inside of him being grasped and squeezed. She forced it out of him, made it gleam in the air between them, silver,

181

blue and green. It was a shimmer of light, flickering colors as they each vied for control.

But she was mightier than he. His strength gave way before her. His will crumbled.

She reached into his mind and called forth an image. It was a memory of his grandfather, but she made it her own. The king of Cardoroth now stood between them. A crown was upon his head. He was old, his once-black hair turned silver with age, but leanness and strength were etched into his frame. He had something of the look of a wolf about him: patient, but fierce and bold when necessary. He shimmered with light, and then turned to smile at Gil. But it was his grandfather no more. Instead, the face shimmered and became Brand's. The crown flared with silvery light upon his head.

Tears streamed down Gil's face, but Brand gave him a mocking bow. He straightened, and uttered a single word. *Elùgrune*. And then the image stepped to the side so that Gil looked into Ginsar's eyes.

"Carnhaina was a fool," she said. "And your grandfather was a fool. So too is Brand. Only I have the true power. Nothing is beyond me."

Gil felt the cold anger inside him begin to burn. He would test her claim, if he could.

With a sudden determination, he wrenched control of the image from her. He made it turn, a blade appearing in its hand. It strode toward Ginsar, and surprise appeared on her face. But swift as that look came it left, and with a wave of her hand the image faded.

Gil staggered back, and Ginsar cackled. But he sensed that what he had done had startled her. She was not invulnerable. But then he remembered Death. It was not just she who was the enemy. It was also the powers she had loosed upon the world. Whatever weaknesses she had, she controlled forces beyond the strength of any man to fight.

Gil heaved for breath, exhausted by fear and drained by the use of lòhrengai. In the silence, an elùgroth scrambled down the ramp of ancient rubble and ran the length of the subterranean hall toward his mistress.

"He comes!" the elùgroth called, and there was fear in his voice. Hope rose in Gil. He knew who it was. Then he wondered if it was fear in the man's voice, or excitement.

Ginsar confirmed his growing suspicion. "Of course Brand comes. That is the plan, fool."

She turned her gaze back to Gil and smiled wickedly. "Do not take heart from this, boy. Brand brings someone with him. His name is Death."

21. Live, or Die

The elùgroths who ringed the dais stood still. Ginsar waited. She seemed calm and serene, but her breath came quick and her chest rose and fell rapidly.

Slowly, noise penetrated down to the chamber from the outside world, and a glimmer of light came with it. Then Gil saw them. There were Durlin, their white surcoats gleaming. Hruilgar was with them also. Of course, he was a tracker, and Brand would have needed him. But it was the man who came before them all who drew his eyes.

Brand led them. He came down the rocky slope of rubble, poised and balanced though loose stones and dirt shifted beneath his boots. To his side was sheathed the great sword that he had borne on many adventures. Gil had hefted that blade. He knew its history and its quality. And he knew the fighting skill of the man who carried it. There was none better.

In Brand's left hand was a long object, wrapped in cloth. Gil could not be sure what it was, but he guessed. His gaze shifted to the Durlin who filed down behind the regent. He regretted now that he felt stifled when they guarded him. He regretted that he had not understood them better. Now, he realized they could die if they tried to save him, just as had the three who had stood watch before his door in the palace.

Yet, he soon came to see that there were only the Durlin, and there was no sign of soldiers from Cardoroth. Why was that?

There was no sound but the rasp of boots on stone as Brand and his men walked down the long aisle of statues toward the dais.

The Durlin held their hands on the hilts of their swords, but they did not draw steel even though they now approached the elùgroths.

Brand, at their head, still held the cloth-bound object, but his right hand hung easily by his side. There was no emotion on his face. His features were the perfect mask of lòhren inscrutability. He never faltered in his step, either coming down the treacherous slope or walking the shadow-haunted hall between the statues. He seemed sure-footed and unconcerned by his surroundings. He seemed to know his way, as though he had been here before.

He brought the Durlin before the dais and stopped. His gaze was fixed on Ginsar, but once it flickered briefly to Gil. Gil could read nothing of what was to come in that look.

"Welcome to my realm," Ginsar said. Her voice was deep and resonant. "Have I not a beautiful throne room? Fairer by far than that hovel in Cardoroth."

Brand looked around momentarily, taking in the rubbish, the ruin and the debris of long-ago floods. A slight frown marked his face, and Gil knew that he had just realized that Ginsar was insane. But Brand said nothing of it.

"I've been here before," he said. "It's not much different."

Ginsar stood, and she took a grip of Gil's arm. Her fingers tightened into his flesh like steel pincers, and he realized that she was much stronger than she looked.

"Yes. You have been here before," she repeated. "But things will go harder for you this time than they did then."

"As I recall, they were not easy the first time."

Gil did not understand what they were talking about. Something else had happened in this chamber once, but he had no idea what it was.

Brand looked at Ginsar closely. "I was here that day, the day of which you speak, but you were not."

"No. No I was not. And lucky for you."

Brand considered her quietly for a moment, then spoke in his usual direct manner.

"What is your grudge against me? We have not met."

Ginsar laughed, but her eyes flared with the cold light that always burned in them.

"You," she said, stretching forth her long arm, "killed a man. You killed him, here in this underground sanctuary, just a little behind me in the great treasure chamber." She gestured imperiously with a finger to the tapestry-covered wall behind her, but did not take her gaze from him. "I'm sure you remember the way."

Brand looked at her a long time. "Now I know. A man died here. Others too. Good men, some of them. But the one you speak of was called Felargin. Yet he was a sorcerer, and he would have killed us."

"But you killed him instead!"

Brand shrugged. "He brought it on himself. He did a wicked thing, and he betrayed us. He would have given us over to a fate worse than death. I have no regret for my actions that day."

Brand, forthright as ever, returned her gaze steadily.

"Who was he to you?"

"My brother."

The chamber was silent. Ginsar and Brand held each other's gazes, unflinching. Gil shifted uneasily, but the grip of the sorceress tightened further on his arm and he stilled. At least there seemed no chance that the two of them had conspired together. It may be that Brand had never betrayed him at all.

At length, Brand spoke. "And this now is revenge? Your brother was evil. I wish that none of that had happened, but I did no wrong. The wrong was his, and now it is yours."

Gil feared an outburst from Ginsar, but instead she only smiled at Brand as though he said the very thing that she wanted him to.

"You know so well what is right and wrong? Then I will give you a choice. And in the choosing you shall reveal what manner of man you are." She squeezed Gil's arm even harder, but he refused to show any pain.

"I hate you," she continued. "And I hate the boy. He is descended from Carnhaina, and I hate *her* most of all. She destroyed my people, stole away our glory in battles long before either of you were born."

Ginsar looked at Brand and her gaze was fierce and exultant. This now was her moment, and Gil realized that it was what she had been waiting for all along.

"Know this!" she said, and the cold fire in her eyes now filled her voice. "Revenge is sweet upon my tongue, but even in victory I show you mercy. See! I will make you this offer. Leave, and become king of Cardoroth. Or stay and perish. So easy, Brand. Betray and live, or remain loyal and die."

"And the boy?"

"It is the same for him. One choice brings life, another death. But I give only you the power of choosing. Your life is his death, his life is yours."

She looked at him with glee, but Brand's expression did not change. Still, there was a sense of danger about him.

"I and the Durlin are not powerless here."

She laughed. "No, but that too is a choice. Should you try to rescue him I will still his beating heart. Even now my will is bent upon it."

Brand considered that. "And how do I know that you will keep this bargain, if we make it?"

Ginsar pursed her red lips. "I swear it upon he who was my master. My soul belongs to him. Let him claim it, let death take me. Let the dark magic that gives me life spin me into the void if I lie! But only this day, one of you may walk free. Tomorrow, well, that is different."

Brand's eyes bored into hers. There was no indication of what he was thinking.

"And the Durlin?"

She shrugged. "They are nothing to me. They can go."

Gil did not understand exactly what was happening. But he sensed another presence nearby. The realization came to him slowly. He looked around the chamber, but he saw nothing except shadows. Yet his instincts warned him that something was coming.

Ginsar tossed her hair impatiently. "Have you made your choice?"

"I have," Brand answered.

"Then I summon one who will extract its price from you. You, or the boy. And know, all gathered here, that he who comes cannot be defeated."

188

The shadows in the chamber thickened and cold seeped up from the ground on tendrils of twisting mist. The torches guttered, but the light in Ginsar's eyes burned all the brighter.

"Choose!" she yelled. And then her laugh came wild and free until the vast chamber echoed with the sound of it.

Eventually, silence returned. But in that quiet, another noise began. It came from without. Gil knew it was the thing that he had sensed before. But now, he could put a name to it. Everything was coming together. Everything was beginning to make sense. But nothing was right, nor ever would be again.

22. Grace

Death entered. He came upon a black horse, and his white robes shimmered about his body. His cowl, white also, shadowed his face. But Gil had seen the visage it hid. He had looked into those eyes from atop the Cardurleth when the horseman had come to the city gate. He had looked, and he wished that he had not.

The black horse snorted, and curls of fire reddened its flaring nostrils. Then, at its master's urging, it picked its way down the slope of rubble. Dust lifted into the air. The cold mist swirled and eddied. The earth itself seemed to groan with the rush and tumble of debris stirred by the horse's coming.

Death came to the bottom of the slope. His mount pranced slowly over the now-level ground, a puff of dust rising from each fall of its dark hooves. Those hooves were shod with metal, and the muffled clang of iron against stone throbbed through the chamber.

The horseman proceeded slowly. Down the aisle of statues he came, riding tall and still as a statue himself, though his mount shook its head and strained at the bit. He was close now, close enough that Gil could see the flies that swarmed and buzzed about him, close enough to smell putrification.

A sword was in Death's hand, sickle-shaped and wicked. The naked blade gleamed, and though the metal was black, unearthly lights glimmered along its length.

The great horse came to a rattling stop and snorted. It was a big animal, all wild and untamed, too big and too alive to be in this chamber.

With a heave, Death leapt from his mount and landed on the floor. The ground trembled. Mist curled up like steam beneath his black boots.

The strange blade hung loosely at his side. But very slowly he raised it up before his face. Then he licked its cold, gleaming length.

Ginsar looked at Brand and spoke, and her voice was crisp with urgency.

"Choose!" she commanded. "Fight what cannot be fought, and die. Or leave the boy in your stead, and return to Cardoroth as king!"

Gil felt cold as ice. In those words he heard the pronouncement of his doom. No man could fight Death and win. No man would dare, not even Brand.

He straightened. So be it. He could not blame Brand. But in the face of such cruel destiny, the pride of kings from which he was born stirred his blood to life. He would not cringe. He would not beg for mercy. He would not allow Ginsar that satisfaction.

Brand turned to look at the dark lady. Finally, there was an emotion on his face. It was resignation. After a long silence, he spoke.

"You are a fool," he said softly to Ginsar. "I made my choice long ago, and I will accept the consequences. You understand nothing, if you do not understand that."

He turned to the men of Cardoroth. "Durlin!" he said. "You will stay out of this. You cannot help, only die. Trust in me, for this is the way it was meant to be. I have known this for a while." He paused, gathering his thoughts. "Protect Gil when I am gone, that is your

191

charge. Do not fear, for the sorceress will keep her word. She has sworn by the magic that gives her life, and she must let you go, or die. And she is not ready for that, nor will ever be."

He looked at Taingern and Shorty. "That is my last command. Do not dishonor me by disobeying. Look now to Gil – he will need you after this."

Brand turned to face Death. He cast away the cloth that covered the object in his left hand. It was a staff. It was his lòhren's staff, so seldom seen. With his right hand he drew his Halathrin-wrought blade. This would be a contest of both magic and cold steel.

Gil felt a lump in his throat. He could not believe what was happening. Death and Carnhaina had both prophesied Brand would die unless he took the throne of Cardoroth. Those prophecies were no longer mere words; the proof of them was come to fruition within this chamber. And Brand had chosen death over betrayal. He would give his life so that Gil might live, and Gil felt a slow tide of shame creep over him at the doubts that he had harbored. But the blood of Carnhaina that ran through his veins began to sing.

The two combatants squared off. Death bowed, long and slow and deep.

"You know that you will die," Death said, and his voice seemed to rise from the earth itself.

"All men die," Brand answered simply.

The two of them faced each other. Death stood erect, a massive figure, broad of shoulder and seemingly solid and invulnerable as the earth. But he was no man; he was a force immutable as the passing of time. Brand was smaller, more vulnerable for all his poise, his head lowered but his breathing slow and steady.

192

Death struck first. Swift as thought his sickle-shaped sword sliced through the air. It hissed. The dark blade flared with cold light. Brand, barely seeming to move, raised his sword in answer. The two blades clashed. Steel screamed and sparks showered through the shadowy air.

The combatants gave no ground. They struck at each other after that again and again, moving, shifting, transforming from defense to attack and attack to defense in a seamless dance.

Dust fell from the high ceiling. Mist eddied over the floor. The echo of the battle was as ten men fighting, and it thrummed through the chamber, rolled through the isle of statues and vented through the mouth of the cave into the world beyond.

But for the two combatants the world had disappeared. All that existed was their enemy and the ebb and flow of battle, the chances of life and death.

Gil had never seen anything like it. He did not think anyone had. Here, in both adversaries, was great strength combined with blinding speed. Death was the stronger, but just as quick. Yet Brand had the greater skill.

The regent's blade cut, parried and stabbed. Ever it moved with swift and adroit skill, deflecting all attacks and delivering its own venomous strikes. And some of those struck true.

Death had been cut. He had been stabbed. The flies that formed a cloud about him hissed angrily. Yet no blood was drawn. He did not slow. He did not show pain. He did not change at all. Death, even as promised, could not be killed.

Yet Brand was slowing. His breathing was quicker. The skill a little less in his muscle-weary arms. Now, the combatants moved around the chamber somewhat more.

Gil realized that this was Brand's doing. There was no retreat, as such, but the extra movement meant fewer strokes and this gave him some opportunity to try to recover.

But Death, unrelenting, sensing his advantage, drove forward in attack. Brand retreated for the first time. Back he stepped into the row of statues. There, tiredness drew an error from him and he stumbled. It was only a slight failing; it merely put him partially off-balance, but Death pounced.

The great sword cut a glittering arc, all black metal and cold fire. It sizzled through the air like a flash of otherworldly lightning. Down it came at Brand's head.

Gil gasped. The world seemed to still. Only the sword moved, and then somehow Brand ducked beneath the blow.

Thunder rumbled through the chamber as the sword smashed into a statue. The sculpture tumbled and fell into a rumbling heap.

Brand, the staff held wide in one hand for balance, and the sword in the other, pivoted and slashed. His Halathrin blade slid full across the abdomen of his opponent. It was a killing blow.

Brand stepped back, his balance regained. Death straightened and turned to face him. The white robes were slit. A great gash was opened in his leathery flesh, and the stench of corruption filled the air. The flies buzzed, and in a cloud they swarmed about the tattered edges of the rent cloth.

But no blood flowed. Instead, maggots crawled through the opening and fell to writhe on the floor.

Brand took another step back. Gil felt Ginsar tremble with excitement at his side. And then Death moved again. Slowly, he reached up, took hold of the white cowl and tipped it back to reveal his face. Gil saw, even as he had once before from the Cardurleth, that the rider was no living man. Where a face should have been, there was a skull. Tufted hair sprouted from its dome in lank patches. Skin clung tight to bone around the jaw, but hung in loose folds over the sunken cheeks. Maggots squirmed in the eye sockets. Yet those eyes, bubbling pits of horror, still seemed to see and they fixed upon Brand with unwavering hatred.

"I am Death," the creature said in a hollow voice. "My purpose is to kill. I am the Great Dark. I am the Tomb that Welcomes and the Void that Awaits. You cannot kill me, for I am already dead."

Brand leaned upon his staff and the point of the sword in his hand trailed toward the ground.

"That may be," the regent said wearily. "Or it may not. From the Dark you were born. Back into the Dark you can be sent."

"You will learn," Death replied. "I cannot be killed. I have no weakness. None."

Brand did not answer, but the tip of his sword lifted slightly, and a faraway look came into his eyes. He had learned something. Gil was sure of it.

And then Brand took them all by surprise. He attacked, but not with the sword that was already moving. Instead, the staff lifted and thrust forward. Flame burst from it, silver white. It rushed through the air with a roar, and engulfed his opponent. The flies burned away in a spray of sparks. Flame seethed and twisted. Death staggered back, his arm brought up to shield his face. The whole cavern burned with light as though the midday sun had risen from the floor.

195

Brand did not relent. He prodded with the staff. The flames roared louder. Death fell to his knees and the fire burned around him. The dust on the floor turned to ash, and the flagstones beneath glowed red.

At length, Brand's arm trembled. The fire went out and he staggered and fell to his own knees. But there, before him, Death grinned.

Slowly, the creature stood. Wisps of smoke curled from his scorched skin. The tufts of hair were gone and more bone showed. But he seemed unharmed.

"I am Death. I have come. And all the world shall tremble at my feet."

The creature did not even look at Brand. He did not look at Ginsar. Instead, he seemed to be speaking to the world itself.

The Durlin edged forward. Brand raised his head to look at them, particularly Shorty and Taingern.

"No, my friends. Do not jeopardize things. I have already won freedom for Gil."

Brand forced himself to his feet. Death stepped toward him, his sickle-shaped blade raised high. Once more the clash of steel rang through the chamber. But it was no longer the match that it was. Brand was weary now, and yet Death was the same as he had begun.

Yet still Brand landed blows with his sword. And where fire had failed, he summoned cold and wind and darting lights to his opponent's eyes. But neither steel nor lòhrengai had effect.

Death struck blow after blow of his own. On he came, relentless, unyielding, insurmountable. Brand fought bravely, but this was a fight beyond mortal strength. He could not win. He knew that he could not win. Gil finally realized that he had known this from the beginning, yet still he had chosen to fight.

Brand staggered back. Death stalked him. The regent looked to Shorty and Taingern. He gave them the flicker of a sad smile. Then he fixed Death with his gaze. But when he spoke, it was more to his friends.

"You are a force not of this world. You were drawn into the shell of what once was a man, given life for one reason only … to kill me or the boy. Now, I am marked, and I must die. But she who brought you into this world draws on powers beyond the reach of her thought. She does not grasp that she cannot control them. But this I know. Your powers grow, and they will continue to grow as her control lessens. And though you think yourself invincible, there is one way you can be defeated, though it cost me my life."

Brand cast aside both sword and staff, and they rattled against the floor. He stood before his enemy, weaponless. Gil felt his arm grow numb where Ginsar gripped him, and as Brand spoke her fingers sank even deeper into his flesh.

"The magic that called you forth," Brand said, "has a weakness, as all spells must however strong they be. Yours is that you exist to overcome and kill your opponent, for that was the nature of the magic that drew you into this world. You must take life. Thus, you do not weaken no matter how much I fight for mine, for it fulfills your purpose to take it from me." Brand paused, and then spoke slowly. "Yet what if the struggle ceases? I think then that your foothold in this world will diminish, and you can be sent back whence you came."

Brand opened wide his arms. He advanced slowly on Death. "Come! I resist you no longer!"

197

Brand stepped forward. Death stood, uncertain. But when Brand was within reach Death thrust out with his sword. Or Brand fell upon it. The sickle-shaped blade went right through the regent, and a moment they stood thus.

Brand groaned. Death seemed puzzled, as though surprised that he had struck. And then Brand stiffened. With a shout, he flung himself forward, driving the blade further through his body.

Blood spurted from his back and sprayed over the floor. Yet his hands reached forth, somehow still strong, and they gripped Death's head. There they squeezed, and a silver light flickered at the fingertips.

Death tried to back away. Brand kept his grip. For several long moments they stood together, and then Death screamed and pulled himself free.

He ripped the curved sword from Brand's body, and the regent screamed also. But somehow he kept to his feet. There they faced each other. Death raised high the sword to strike again, but even as he did so, even as he prepared to land the final blow, the strength that was in him withered away.

The sickle-shaped blade fell to the floor with a clatter of steel. The sorcerous light that once infused it was gone. Instead, it glistened with Brand's lifeblood.

A cold wind blew, stirring up dust, tearing apart the mist that rose from the ground, and then it ran through the aisle of statues and moaned as it rushed from the cave mouth.

Death still stood, but he was changed. There was no life in him. The body, held together by sorcery alone, collapsed as the spell that bound it broke.

The once-mighty figure fell to the ground. A foul stench spread through the air. Bones rattled within the white robes and maggots wriggled over the floor.

A moment Brand stood. A moment he regarded the enemy that he had vanquished. And then he also toppled to the floor.

Into the now-silent chamber, Ginsar screamed. Gil ripped free from her grip and ran to Brand. He knelt beside him, and knew that Shorty and Taingern were close by.

Blood seeped from a corner of Brand's mouth. But his eyes were open and they focused on Gil.

"All things have a beginning," the regent whispered to him. "And all things end. As it is in nature … so it is with men." He coughed, and then winced with stabbing pain. "A man must learn to accept death … to face it with grace. Remember that, Gil…"

The regent's voice trailed off. With a sigh, he died, and the light vanished from his eyes. Gil trembled uncontrollably. But it seemed that the whole world around him had gone perfectly still, that it marked the passing of a unique greatness.

He began to sob, but he was roughly pulled away from Brand's body by an elùgroth. Ginsar was there suddenly, and she kicked Brand's corpse. New blood seeped from his wound, and his dagger tumbled from the sheath in his belt, the dagger once given to him by the old king. It lay there on the dirt-crusted floor, next to Brand's lifeless hand. On a finger of that same hand Gil saw the ring that Brand always wore, the very ring given to him by Carnhaina. And on both dagger and ring was the sign of Halathgar.

Ginsar bent down to Gil. "Look on him well, child. He is dead, and you will also die soon. Not today, but maybe tomorrow." She straightened and laughed gaily. "You will not know where I or my allies are, or how we shall strike. But strike we shall. You shall fall. Cardoroth shall fall, and Carnhaina's despairing howls will fill the void!"

She flicked her fingers at him contemptuously, and then strode toward the cave entrance. She paused only to grasp the reins of Death's horse as she passed. The elùgroths filed silently after her, a trail of shadows in her wake.

Gil bowed his head and wept. But soon he felt a hand on his shoulder. It was Taingern.

"They're gone," the Durlindrath said.

Gil looked up. The Durlin surrounded him and Brand's body. There were tears in Taingern's eyes, and also in Shorty's who stood next to him.

"Brand knew," Taingern said. "There was only one way to defeat the creature that the sorceress had called forth. All along he *knew*.

"But how did he do it?" Gil sobbed. "I don't understand."

Taingern knelt beside him. "Brand's every action showed it. And his last act was to voice it. Death cannot be defeated. It cannot be stopped nor banished. But it can be accepted. By acceptance, its power is reduced."

Taingern stood again. The Durlin drew closer. As one they raised their voices in the Durlin creed:

> *Tum del conar – El dar tum!*
> *Death or infamy – I choose death!*

The words drifted away to silence in the vast chamber. And then Shorty and Taingern spoke in unison: *We will not forget him*, they said.

The Durlin gave the ritual reply: *Long will we remember him*.

Gil sobbed anew. Those words were from the Durlin funeral ceremony. He could not believe this was happening. Brand was dead. He was dead, and though Carnhaina had promised she would help him when he needed it most, there had been no sign of her.

He could not stop sobbing. It racked his body and made him tremble. Tears filled his eyes and ran down his cheeks. He could not see clearly. But he could not take his eyes off Brand, and he knew that he would see what he saw now all the days of his life.

Through his blurred vision he saw once more the sign of Halathgar on the signet ring and the dagger. And the twin stars blinked and shimmered back at him, like eyes.

23. I Who Straddle Life and Death

The Durlin were silent now. Gil ceased to sob. He lifted his head and looked at Taingern and Shorty.

"Carnhaina came to me in a dream," he told them. "She warned me – she *warned* me that Brand would need help. She gave me the power to summon her. If only I had done that before!"

Shorty rested a hand on his shoulder. "Don't blame yourself, Gil. Brand knew what he was doing. Only by accepting his death did he weaken that thing, whoever or whatever it was. He had to die to win, and I don't think Carnhaina would have changed that. She warned him of it, after all."

That was true. And yet Gil had a feeling that things were not finished yet. If not before, was now the moment that Carnhaina had told him about? It was too late, and it did not make sense, but the more that he thought about it the more certain he grew that something remained undone.

He looked down again. Carnhaina had told him that he would know how to summon her when the time came. Once more his eyes were drawn to Brand's signet ring and dagger. Again the mark of Halathgar twinkled at him, and like eyes in the dark they watched him. He felt the marks on his palm itch, and finally he understood how to call her forth. In realizing this, he also knew that it was the moment to do so.

"I can do it," he whispered. "And I must."

Shorty and Taingern looked at him strangely. For a moment, they did nothing. Then they signaled the Durlin to stand back, but they did not move themselves.

Gil bent down. Gently, he removed Brand's signet ring. He clenched it tight to the palm of his left hand. In his right, he took a firm grip of the dagger.

Both items were once Carnhaina's. There was magic in them also; he sensed its presence readily enough. But that alone would not suffice to bridge the gap between life and death and summon Carnhaina's spirit to him. More would be needed to connect him to her, and he knew what.

The sign of Halathgar on the two objects touched the marks on his palms. There they tingled, and the magic within them stirred, expectantly. Even as Brand had once told him, it was alive.

He concentrated. The magic pulsed, and he coaxed it forth. The power inside him, the magic that he was born with, sparked to life also. It rose within him, stronger and surer than he had ever felt it. He almost panicked, but he drew the two powers together and mingled them inside himself. Then he gave it focus in the way that he must in order to summon Carnhaina.

He thought of her. He remembered her. Most of all, he opened himself to the way she made him feel. There were no words for that. There were no thoughts. He just allowed the emotions to wash over him, to become one with him and the magic that pulsed to life inside him.

And then there was more than thought and memory and emotion. She was here. He sensed her presence all about him.

He stood up and turned around. She was there, looking at him. But she was not as he had seen her on the tower of Halathgar. Now, she seemed real. There was different magic at work here. Stronger and more dangerous.

She stood, regal as always. The spear was in her hand, the point gleaming with a cold light like stars on a winter's night.

The Durlin edged forward. They did not know who she was, and there was fear on their faces, but it was clear they were prepared to protect Brand's body if they must.

"Leave him!" commanded the queen.

Taingern signaled everyone to step back, and they did so reluctantly.

Carnhaina knelt. With a pale hand, yet one that seemed real rather than ghostly, she touched Brand's cheek.

"Here is one," she said, "who gave much to Alithoras. All, in the end. A hero, and there are few like him. Even in the Age of Heroes, there were few like him…"

"Can you bring him back?" Gil asked. It was the first thought that crossed his mind, however foolish.

The queen used the spear to help her stand again. There was a vast silence after his words, and it seemed that the roof of the chamber pressed down. The Durlin watched, pale-faced and wide-eyed.

"I am Carnhaina. I am mighty in power and learned in lore that would shrivel most souls. Yet that, *that* is beyond even my strength."

Gil dropped his head, but the queen was not done.

"But know this, brave child. Ginsar, in her madness, has opened ways to other worlds. That is whence the Horsemen come. The walls of reality are sundered, and just now, I, who myself have been summoned to this land; I, who straddle life and death; I, one of the great powers of Alithoras, may yet have a chance to recall Brand's spirit and heal his body through the same ways that she herself has opened." Light flickered at the sharp tip of her spear. "Stand back!" she cried, and dust fell from the ceiling as her voice rang in the chamber. "Stand back!"

They all moved. Gil, frightened and in awe of her, staggered away, but Shorty and Taingern were at his side and steadied him. If they were as scared as he, they did not show it.

The queen lifted her arms. Thunder rumbled through the cavern. Dust and ancient plaster fell from the ceiling. The earth screamed as stone ground on stone, and water bubbled through widening gaps in the floor.

Gil's vision swam. When it cleared, it seemed to him that he stood in two places at once. The torch-lit chamber was still around him, but he also saw, as though etched over that, the ice-cracked stone of a high summit beneath his feet. Beyond was the shoulder of a rock-strewn mountain. A long and grassy slope tumbled away before him, leading toward a green valley; and he smelled trees. Pine trees, sharp and fresh.

Brand was there. He lay, dead, upon the floor of the chamber. But he stood in that other place, tall and powerful and alive. A light was in his eyes, and he gazed at Carnhaina who stood before him, her spear raised above her head.

She spoke. Brand answered. But Gil heard nothing of their words. After a moment, the regent lifted high his arms and looked to the sky.

The mountain lurched. The queen pointed at him with her spear and called lightning from the heavens. It struck Brand, searing him, running up and down his body. But he stood still and kept his arms up as though to embrace it.

Back in the chamber, Carnhaina was in the same position, but multicolored flame streamed from the tip of her spear. This was pointed at Brand. The flame enveloped him, and his body trembled.

Thrice she thrust the spear. Thrice Brand's body flinched under the influence of her magic. Gil saw also that atop the mountain she called forth lightning three times. The last was a searing bolt that sizzled through the air, struck Brand, and leaped to the stone near his feet. The rock split. Water gushed through the crack and hastened in a stream down the green slope and into the valley.

In the chamber, the flame flickered out. Brand lay still, but the blood on his clothing was burned away. His chest heaved, and then with a great gasp he gulped in air. His eyes flickered open.

"It is done!" Carnhaina proclaimed. She seemed very weak, and lowered the butt of her spear to the floor so that she could lean on it. "Listen!" she continued. "Ginsar has loosed forces upon the land that tear at reality. Because of her, a way was open for me to return Brand. In her madness, in her lust for revenge, she opened a portal and drew these forces in. She thinks to master them, but they will conquer her instead. And after, they will turn to this fresh world, to every blade of grass, every grain of sand, every day and every night, to every person; and they will make it all their own. That must not be! You must prevent it! You must close the opening that Ginsar has made."

Carnhaina trembled and shut her eyes. When she opened them, she stared straight at Gil.

"How can we close it?" he asked her.

The queen slowly shook her head. "I don't know. I have no idea."

Gil was staggered. He had thought that her knowledge and power was enormous. And so it was, but even such as she had limits.

"But know this," she said. "This quest I set you. It is for this that you were born. Seek the answer, and you will find it."

Her voice trailed away in weariness. Gil would have asked her more but she held up her hand.

"I am spent. Have faith that you will know what to do and how to do it … when the time is right. But you will need to be strong."

With a groan, she fell to her knees. She looked up at him, her eyes piercing bright, willing him to take up the quest, and then she wavered and was gone as though a light had been extinguished.

Gil looked at Brand. The regent still lay on the ground, but he was propped up on one elbow, watching. And those eyes, those intense eyes fixed on him, those same eyes that moments ago had stared at him without life. Now, there was a myriad of emotions in them, too deep and too complex for Gil to understand.

Around them all, the chamber began to rumble violently. The water that gushed through the cracked stone began to hiss and steam.

"Earthquake!" Hruilgar yelled.

All thought of the quest given to Gil was lost. He thought instead of the weight of the earth above him. Even as he did so sheets of plaster and loosened rock

207

began to fall. The earth shook beneath his feet and he stumbled. Brand tried to rise, but fell.

The Durlin moved with speed. While Gil was still caught by fear some of them drew around him and propelled him forward. Others gathered Brand into their arms and lifted him. Then they ran.

Hruilgar led the escape. Sweeping up a torch from the dais into his steady hand, he led them off. Through the aisle of statues he raced, but those statues shuddered and moved about him. Some tumbled to the floor. But nothing stopped either him or the Durlin. They hastened forward, bringing their charges with them, and they came to the slope of rubble.

This was harder. It moved and seethed as the earth shuddered. Yet still Hruilgar found a way up, and the Durlin followed him. Twice those carrying Brand fell, and twice other Durlin lent their strength until they were at the top.

The cave was dark. It shook and rumbled and air hissed through the entrance a little way ahead. They raced for it, striving toward the daylight that they could see and to the open air they knew was beyond.

Behind, the earth groaned and the slope of rubble collapsed into the chamber. A plume of dust rose, choking and thick.

Gil could barely breathe. He saw nothing through the dust-thickened air. Even the daylight at the entrance that moments ago had served as a signpost of escape was gone. All around him massive chunks of stone fell from the ceiling and tumbled to the floor. The sound of it was like drum strokes of doom in his ears.

He coughed and spluttered. The Durlin around him moved. But they moved slowly, as disorientated as he was, and he did not think they knew better than he where the mouth of the cave opened to the outside world.

It was then that he heard a horn. Over the tumult it lifted. A clear sound, a crisp sound. A sound called forth to save them, if they could but heed it in time. It was Hruilgar's hunting horn, and he had found the way out.

Thus ends *Prince of the Magic*. The Son of Sorcery series continues in *Sword of the Blood*, where Gil will learn more of the threat to Cardoroth and the quest bestowed upon him.

Amazon lists millions of titles, and I'm glad that you discovered this one. But if you'd like to know when I release a new book, instead of leaving it to chance, sign up for my newsletter. I'll send you an email on publication.

Yes please! – Go to www.homeofhighfantasy.com and sign up.

No thanks – I'll take my chances.

Encyclopedic Glossary

Note: the glossary of each book in this series is individualized for that book alone. Additionally, there is often historical material provided in its entries for people, artifacts and events that are not included in the main text.

Many races dwell in Alithoras. All have their own language, and though sometimes related to one another, the changes sparked by migration, isolation and various influences often render these tongues unintelligible to each other.

The ascendancy of Halathrin culture, combined with their widespread efforts to secure and maintain allies against elug incursions, has made their language the primary means of communication between diverse peoples.

For instance, a soldier of Cardoroth addressing a ship's captain from Camarelon would speak Halathrin, or a simplified version of it, even though their native speeches stem from the same ancestral language.

This glossary contains a range of names and terms. Many are of Halathrin origin, and their meaning is provided. The remainder derive from native tongues and are obscure, so meanings are only given intermittently.

Some variation exists within the Halathrin language, chiefly between the regions of Halathar and Alonin. The most obvious example is the latter's preference for a "dh" spelling instead of "th".

Often, Camar names and Halathrin elements are combined. This is especially so for the aristocracy. No other tribes of men had such long-term friendship with the immortal Halathrin, and though in this relationship they lost some of their natural culture, they gained nobility and knowledge in return.

List of abbreviations:

Azn. Azan

Cam. Camar

Comb. Combined

Cor. Corrupted form

Duth. Duthenor

Esg. Esgallien

Hal. Halathrin

Leth. Letharn

Prn. Pronounced

Age of Heroes: A period of Camar history, which has become mythical. Many tales are told of this time. Some are true, others are not. And yet, even the false ones usually contain elements of historical fact. Many were the heroes who walked abroad during this time, and they are remembered still, and honored still, by the Camar people. The old days are looked back on with pride, and the descendants of many heroes yet walk the streets of Cardoroth, though they be unaware of their heritage and the accomplishments of their forefathers.

Alithoras: *Hal.* "Silver land." The Halathrin name for the continent they settled after their exodus from their homeland. Refers to the extensive river and lake systems they found and their appreciation of the beauty of the land.

Anast Dennath: *Hal.* "Stone mountains." Mountain range in northern Alithoras. Contiguous with Auren Dennath.

Arach Neben: *Hal.* "West gate." The great wall surrounding Cardoroth has four gates. Each is named after a cardinal direction, and each also carries a token to represent a celestial object. Arach Neben bears a steel ornament of the Morning Star.

Arell: Rumored to be Brand's mistress. A name formerly common among the Camar people, but currently out of favor in Cardoroth. Its etymology is obscure, though it is speculated that it derives from the Halathrin stems "aran" and "ell" meaning noble and slender. Ell, in the Halathrin tongue, also refers to any type of timber that is pliable, for instance, hazel. This is cognate with our word wych-wood, meaning timber that is supple and pliable. As elùgroths use wych-wood staffs as instruments of sorcery, it is sometimes supposed that their name derives from this stem, rather than elù (shadowed). This is a viable philological theory. Nevertheless, as a matter of historical fact, it is wrong.

Aurellin: *Cor. Hal.* The first element means blue. The second appears to be native Camar. Queen of Cardoroth, wife to Gilhain and grandmother to Gilcarist.

Auren Dennath: *Comb. Duth.* and *Hal. Prn.* Our-ren dennath. "Blue mountains." Mountain range in northern Alithoras. Contiguous with Anast Dennath.

Brand: A Duthenor tribesman. Appointed by the former king of Cardoroth to serve as regent for Gilcarist. By birth, he is the rightful chieftain of the Duthenor people. However, a usurper overthrew his father, killing him and his wife. Brand, only a youth at the time, swore an oath of vengeance. That oath sleeps, but it is not forgotten, either by Brand or the usurper.

Camar: *Cam. Prn.* Kay-mar. A race of interrelated tribes that migrated in two main stages. The first brought them to the vicinity of Halathar; in the second, they separated and established cities along a broad sweep of eastern Alithoras.

Camarelon: *Cam. Prn.* Kam-arelon. A port city and capital of a Camar tribe. It was founded before Cardoroth as the waves of migrating people settled the more southerly lands first. Each new migration tended northward. It is perhaps the most representative of a traditional Camar realm.

Cardoroth: *Cor. Hal. Comb. Cam.* A Camar city, often called Red Cardoroth. Some say this alludes to the red granite commonly used in the construction of its buildings, others that it refers to a prophecy of destruction.

Cardurleth: *Hal.* "Car – red, dur – steadfast, leth – stone." The great wall that surrounds Cardoroth. Established soon after the city's founding and constructed with red granite. It looks displeasing to the eye, but the people of the city love it nonetheless. They believe it impregnable and say that no enemy shall ever breach it – except by treachery.

Careth Nien: *Hal. Prn.* Kareth nyen. "Great river." Largest river in Alithoras. Has its source in the mountains of Anast Dennath and runs southeast across the land before emptying into the sea. It was over this river (which sometimes freezes along its northern stretches) that the Camar and other tribes migrated into the eastern lands. Much later, Brand came to the city of Cardoroth by one of these ancient migratory routes.

Carnhaina: First element native *Cam.* Second *Hal.* "Heroine." An ancient queen of Cardoroth. Revered as a savior of her people, but to some degree also feared for she possessed powers of magic. Hated to this day by elùgroths, because she overthrew their power unexpectedly at a time when their dark influence was rising. According to dim legend, kept alive mostly within the royal family of Cardoroth, she guards the city even in death and will return in its darkest hour.

Chapterhouse: Special halls set aside in the palace of Cardoroth for the private meetings, teachings and military training of the Durlin.

Dernbrael: *Hal.* "Sharp tongued, or by some translations, cunning tongued." A lord of Cardoroth. Out of favor with the old king due to mistrust. It is said that he is in league with the traitor Hvargil, though this has never been proven. It is known, however, that Hvargil once saved his life when they were younger men. This occurred in a gambling den of ill-repute, and the details are obscure. Nevertheless, all accounts agree that Hvargil was wounded protecting his friend.

Durlin: *Hal.* "The steadfast." The original Durlin were the seven sons of the first king of Cardoroth. They guarded him against all enemies, of which there were many, and three died to protect him. Their tradition continued throughout Cardoroth's history, suspended only once, and briefly, some four hundred years ago when it was discovered that three members were secretly in the service of elùgroths. These were imprisoned, but committed suicide while waiting for the king's trial to commence. It is rumored that the king himself provided them with the knives that they used. It is said that he felt sorry for them and gave them this way out to avoid the shame a trial would bring to their families.

Durlin creed: These are the native Camar words, long remembered and much honored, uttered by the first Durlin to die while he defended his father, and king, from attack. Tum del conar – El dar tum! Death or infamy – I choose death!

Durlindrath: *Hal.* "Lord of the steadfast." The title given to the leader of the Durlin. For the first time in the history of Cardoroth, that esteemed position is held jointly by two people: Lornach and Taingern. Lornach also possesses the title of King's Champion. The latter honor is not held in quite such high esteem, yet it carries somewhat more power. As King's Champion, Lornach is authorized to act in the king's stead in matters of honor and treachery to the Crown.

Duthenor: *Duth. Prn.* Dooth-en-or. "The people." A single tribe, or sometimes a group of tribes melded into a larger people at times of war or disaster, who generally live a rustic and peaceful lifestyle. They are raisers of cattle and herders of sheep. However, when need demands they are fierce warriors – men and women alike.

Elrika: *Cam.* Daughter of the royal baker. Friend to Gilcarist, and highly skilled in swordcraft. Brand has given instructions to Lornach that she is to be taught all arts of the warrior to the full extent of her ability. He is to groom her as the first female Durlin in the history of the city.

Elùgrune: *Hal.* Literally "shadowed fortune," but has other meanings such as "ill fortune" and "born of the dark." In the first two senses it is often used to mean simply bad luck. In the third, it describes a person steeped in shadow and mystery and not to be trusted. Also, in some circles, the term is used for a mystic.

Elugs: *Hal.* "That which creeps in shadows." A cruel and superstitious race that inhabits the southern lands, especially the Graèglin Dennath.

Elùdrath: *Hal. Prn.* Eloo-drath. "Shadowed lord." A sorcerer. First and greatest among elùgroths. Believed by most to be dead.

Elùgai: *Hal. Prn.* Eloo-guy. "Shadowed force." The sorcery of an elùgroth.

Elùgroth: *Hal. Prn.* Eloo-groth. "Shadowed horror." A sorcerer. They often take names in the Halathrin tongue in mockery of the lòhren practice to do so.

Elu-haraken: *Hal.* "The shadowed wars." Long ago battles in a time that is become myth to the Camar tribes.

Esanda: No known etymology for this name. Likewise, Esanda herself is not originally from Cardoroth. The old king believed she was from the city of Esgallien, but he was not certain of this. Esanda herself refuses to answer any questions about her origins. Notwithstanding the personal mystery surrounding her, she was one of the old king's most trusted advisors and soon became so to Brand. She heads a ring of spies devoted to the protection of Cardoroth from its many enemies.

Esgallien: *Hal. Prn.* Ez-gally-en. "Es – rushing water, gal(en) – green, lien – to cross: place of the crossing onto the green plains." A city established in antiquity and named after a nearby ford of the Careth Nien.

Felargin: *Cam.* A sorcerer. Brother to Ginsar. Acolyte of Shurilgar, Betrayer of Nations. Steeped in evil and once lured Brand, Shorty and others under false pretenses into a quest. Only Brand and Shorty survived the betrayal. Felargin himself suffered the doom he had prepared for his victims, and it was a fate worse than death.

Fereck: *Cam.* The royal farrier. Emigrated a great distance from Esgallien but soon found employment in the palace of Cardoroth due to his great skill. A quiet and thoughtful man, and one from whom Brand sometimes seeks advice.

Foresight: Premonition of the future. Can occur at random as a single image or as a longer sequence of events. Can also be deliberately sought by entering the realm between life and death where the spirit is released from the body to travel through space and time. To achieve this, the body must be brought to the very threshold of death. The first method is uncontrollable and rare. The second exceedingly rare but controllable for those with the skill and willingness to endure the danger.

Forgotten Queen (the): An epithet of Queen Carnhaina. She was a person of immense power and presence, yet she made few friends in life, and her possession of magic made her mistrusted. For these reasons, memory of her accomplishments faded soon after her death and only snatches of her rule are remembered by the populace of Cardoroth. Yet the history books record a far fuller description of her queenship.

Gil: See Gilcarist.

Gilcarist: *Comb. Cam & Hal.* First element unknown, second "ice." Heir to the throne of Cardoroth and grandson of King Gilhain. According to Carnhaina, his coming was told in the stars. He is The Star-marked One, The Boy with Two Fates, The Guarded and the Hunted, The King Who Might Rule, The Lòhren Who Might Teach, The Boy Who Might Live and the Boy Who Might Die. He is also foretold as The Savior and the Destroyer. But these names meaning nothing to him, and he prefers to follow Brand's view that a man makes his own fate.

Gilhain: *Comb. Cam & Hal.* First element unknown, second "hero." King of Cardoroth before proclaiming Brand regent for the heir to the throne. Husband to Aurellin.

Ginsar: *Cam.* A sorceress. Sister to Felargin. Acolyte of Shurilgar, Betrayer of Nations. Steeped in evil and greatly skilled in the arts of elùgai, reaching a level of proficiency nearly as great as her master.

Goblins: See elugs.

Graèglin Dennath: *Hal. Prn.* Greg-lin dennath. "Mountains of ash." Chain of mountains in southern Alithoras. The landscape is one of jagged stone and boulder, relieved only by gaping fissures from which plumes of ashen smoke ascend, thus leading to its name. Believed to be impassable because of the danger of poisonous air flowing from cracks, and the ground unexpectedly giving way, swallowing any who dare to tread its forbidden paths. In other places swathes of molten stone run in rivers down its slopes.

Grothanon: *Hal.* "Horror desert." The flat salt plains south of the Graèglin Dennath.

Halathar: *Hal.* "Dwelling place of the people of Halath." The forest realm of the Halathrin.

Halathgar: *Hal.* "Bright star." Actually a constellation of two stars. Also known as the Lost Huntress.

Halathrin: *Hal.* "People of Halath." A race named after a mighty lord who led an exodus of his people to the continent of Alithoras in pursuit of justice, having sworn to redress a great evil. They are human, though of fairer form, greater skill and higher culture than ordinary men. They possess an inherent unity of body, mind and spirit enabling insight and endurance beyond other races of Alithoras. Reported to be immortal, but killed in great numbers during their conflicts with the evil they seek to destroy. Those conflicts are collectively known as the Elù-haraken: the Shadowed Wars.

Harath Neben: *Hal.* "North gate." This gate bears a token of two massive emeralds that represent the constellation of Halathgar. The gate is also known as "Hunter's Gate," for the north road out of the city leads to wild lands full of game.

Hruilgar: *Comb. Cam & Hal.* First element unknown (but thought to mean "wild"), second "star." The king's huntsman. Rumored to have learned his craft as a tracker in Esgallien and to have come northward at the same time as Sandy.

Hvargil: Prince of Cardoroth. Younger son of Carangil, former king of Cardoroth. Exiled by Carangil for treason after it was discovered he plotted with elùgroths to assassinate his older half-brother, Gilhain, and prevent him from one day ascending the throne. He gathered a band about him in exile of outlaws and discontents. Most came from Cardoroth but others were drawn from Camarelon. In confirmation of his treachery, he fought with an invading army against his own homeland in the recent war.

Immortals: See Halathrin.

Lake Alithorin: *Hal.* "Silver lake." A lake of northern Alithoras.

Lòhren: *Hal. Prn.* Ler-ren. "Knowledge giver – a counsellor." Other terms used by various nations include wizard, druid and sage.

Lòhren-fire: A defensive manifestation of lòhrengai. The color of the flame varies according to the skill and temperament of the lòhren.

Lòhrengai: *Hal. Prn.* Ler-ren-guy. "Lòhren force." Enchantment, spell or use of arcane power. A manipulation and transformation of the natural energy inherent in all things. Each use takes something from the user. Likewise, some part of the transformed energy infuses them. Lòhrens use it sparingly, elùgroths indiscriminately.

Lòrenta: *Hal. Prn.* Ler-rent-a. "Hills of knowledge." Uplands in northern Alithoras in which the stronghold of the lòhrens is established. It is to here that the old king and queen of Cardoroth traveled to spend the last years of the lives in peace after their service to the realm.

Lornach: *Cam.* A former Durlin and now joint Durlindrath. Friend to Brand and often called by his nickname of "Shorty."

Lost Huntress: See Halathgar.

Magic: Supernatural power. See lòhrengai and elùgai.

Nightborn: See elùgrune.

Otherworld: Camar term for a mingling of half-remembered history, myth and the spirit world. Sometimes used interchangeably with the term "Age of Heroes."

Sandy: See Esanda.

Sellic Neben: *Hal.* "East gate." This gate bears a representation, crafted of silver and pearl, of the moon rising over the sea.

Shadowed Lord: See Elùdrath.

Shorty: See Lornach.

Shurilgar: *Hal.* "Midnight star." An elùgroth. One of the most puissant sorcerers of antiquity. Known to legend as the Betrayer of Nations.

Sight: The ability to discern the intentions and even thoughts of another person. Not reliable, and yet effective at times.

Spirit walk: Similar in process to foresight. It is deliberately sought by entering the realm between life and death where the spirit is released from the body to travel through space. To achieve this, the body must be brought to the very threshold of death. This is exceedingly dangerous and only attempted by those of paramount skill.

Sorcerer: See Elùgroth.

Sorcery: See elùgai.

Surcoat: An outer garment. Often worn over chain mail. The Durlin surcoat is unadorned white, which is a tradition carried down from the order's inception.

Swordmaster: A title bestowed by the King of Cardoroth. It comes with obligations, the most well-known of which is the tuition of gifted youths in the art of sword fighting. In ancient times, it was held to be a high honor and there were often several appointed at one time. In the later days of Cardoroth, the tradition has diminished to more of an honorary role.

Taingern: *Cam*. A former Durlin. Friend to Brand, and now joint Durlindrath. Once, in company of Brand, saved the tomb of Carnhaina from defilement and robbery by an elùgroth.

Torc: A neck ring, either of multiple strands of gold twisted together or one thick strand. A symbol of authority and power in ancient Camar society. The most resplendent ever made once adorned Queen Carnhaina herself, and it was interred with her as was customary in Camar tradition.

Tower of Halathgar: In life, the place of study of Queen Carnhaina. In death, her resting place. Somewhat unusually, her sarcophagus rests on the tower's parapet beneath the stars.

Turlak: A youth of Cardoroth city and scion of a noble house. Favored pupil of the Swordmaster.

Unlach Neben: *Hal*. "South gate." This gate bears a representation of the sun, crafted of gold, beating down upon a desert land. Said by some to signify the homeland of the elugs, whence the gold of the sun was obtained by an adventurer of old.

Witch Queen: See Carnhaina

Wizard: See lòhren.

Wych-wood: A general description for a range of supple and springy timbers. Some hardy varieties are prevalent on the poisonous slopes of the Graèglin Dennath mountain range and are favored by elùgroths as instruments of sorcery.

SWORD OF THE BLOOD

BOOK TWO OF THE SON OF SORCERY SERIES

Robert Ryan

ISBN-13 978-0-9942054-8-3
(print edition)

Trotting Fox Press

1. Like a Tomb

Gil drew in a breath, but the dust-thickened air choked him. His strength was nearly gone, and hope had faded with it.

Nearby, the earth groaned and more rubble collapsed from the roof of the cave. It sounded like thunder in the confined space. All about him was mayhem. But what disturbed him most were the curses of the Durlin. They were strong men, and fearless, but they were no better off than he was. They were all going to die.

He could not see the Durlin, for the air was a swirling mass of dust that shifted and eddied like the currents of a river. But they were everywhere about him, groping in the dark and calling out.

Though he shielded his eyes from dust and grit with a trembling hand, he still saw nothing through the maelstrom – especially not the daylight at the entrance of the cave that moments ago had served as a signpost of escape. Forced to draw breath again, he coughed and sputtered while his eyes teared up.

But then the horn sounded once more. Hruilgar's horn. The king's huntsman had not deserted them, and though Gil could see nothing he knew from what direction that sound came, and he turned a little to his left and stumbled toward it, for the huntsman had been near the entrance before this chaos had begun. All about him he sensed movement as well. The Durlin were following the sweet sound of hope.

Someone bumped into him. Or he bumped into them. Then he felt a hand on his back, urging him on.

He nearly tripped on a fallen rock, but he regained his balance.

When the horn blew again it seemed that it was nearly in his ear, and then he saw the thin frame of Hruilgar and the old man's strong arm quickly reached out and pulled him forward.

There was sudden light, and a breeze on his face. He rushed forward, escaping the cave and then other hands, Durlin hands, were guiding him away from the entrance.

The sun was on his face. The air was fresh once more. He gulped it in and reveled in the relief of escape, in the sensation of open space and freedom.

Behind him the remainder of the Durlin staggered into the light. Taingern was among them, and he began counting men.

"We're all here!" he yelled.

Gil could scarce believe it. They had survived, all of them. His eyes fell on Hruilgar. It was this man who had saved them, but he had not come out unscathed. A rock must have struck him a hard blow, for blood matted the gray hair near his left temple and dripped down his cheek, the red rivulets cutting through the thick layer of grime that coated his face.

There was a noise above him, and Hruilgar looked up.

"Away!" the old man suddenly screamed.

The Durlin reacted instantly. Tired as they were, they wasted no time. The cliff face above the cave entrance began to seethe with treacherous movement, the rock and stone shifting like mud.

They all ran, and Gil ran with them. The earth heaved beneath his feet. The cave entrance seemed to cough and expel dusty air, and then the opening was covered by falling rock. It toppled in a grinding mass, bringing bushes and stunted pines with it. But quick as it began, it ceased just as swiftly.

The Durlin had reached safety some forty paces away, and there they paused. An eerie silence settled over the forest. The ground grew still again. No noise rumbled up from the earth, and the dust in the air silently drifted downward.

Gil looked around. The Durlin were studying the cliff face. Their eyes were grim, but there was a sense of victory in the way they stood. They had survived, and Gil felt it too. Death had been cheated, and life was sweet for all their exhaustion.

He looked at Brand. The regent lay on the ground where the Durlin had carefully placed him. He was conscious, but he seemed very weak. He was not the man that Gil knew, but time and rest would cure that. At least he hoped so.

Gil swore under his breath. Ginsar had a lot to answer for. She was the cause of all this. But the thought of her brought renewed fear. *Where was she?*

Shorty was obviously worried about the same thing. He set a perimeter of guards – the least injured of the Durlin, and they gazed into the shadowy pine forest with alert eyes. Ginsar was out there somewhere, and no matter her assurance of safety for the rest of the day, her promises were like daggers sheathed in an enemy's back.

They rested briefly. Taingern went among them speaking to the men and applying bandages where they were needed and offering words of encouragement. They had all been through much, and seen things beyond their understanding. From time to time their glances strayed to Brand, but they did not linger long before they shifted uneasily away.

The regent slept. Shorty and Taingern consulted with each other in whispered voices.

Gil sat quietly and thought. He had been taken into the cave by his captors in the late morning. It was now a little after noon. Neither Shorty nor Taingern would like to be here when night fell over the forest. No, they would not risk that. Therefore, the time for rest that they allowed would be short.

Laying back on the grass he closed his eyes and relaxed while he could. He thought of Carnhaina and the quest she had given him. Ginsar had opened a gateway to another world. Forces were loosed upon the land that would tear at reality. She had done this in her madness, in her lust for revenge, and though she thought she could master them they would conquer her instead. So Carnhaina had foretold. And then this world would fall, bit by bit, to the dark forces the sorceress had summoned. Worst of all, Carnhaina had said that *he* must prevent it. That he was born to close the opening that Ginsar had made.

That was all well and good. But she had no idea how he should go about it, and he had even less. It was disturbing to say the least. It was a responsibility that weighed him down. He could not give it to anyone else, but he did not know how to even begin discharging it himself.

"Let's go," Shorty said. His voice was crisp with command and Gil was glad of it. It would be better to be up and moving and to occupy his mind with something else for a while. Getting out of the forest would be the first step – all else could wait.

They began to walk. Shorty did not set a fast pace, for the ground was rough and trees grew thickly the moment they left the clearing. At this rate they would be stuck in the forest overnight. But surely when Brand and the Durlin had come to rescue him they had ridden? Where were the horses?

They went ahead. Soon, Gil realized, they approached the shores of Lake Alithorin. He heard the gentle lap of water and the calls of countless frogs. And then, descending into a concealed gully, he saw the horses and the one Durlin left to guard them. This man asked no questions. His sweeping gaze saw Gil and Brand, measured the state of the Durlin, their dust-covered faces, makeshift bandages and then he immediately began to untie his horse's reins where they were looped around a branch. The other Durlin went for theirs.

When they were all mounted, Brand sitting behind one of the smaller Durlin, Shorty spoke.

"We don't want to be in this forest at night," he said. "So, ride as swiftly as you can down the forest trail. Hruilgar will lead. But ride carefully. Let's go!"

The old huntsman nudged his horse into a trot, and the Durlin followed.

Gil was in their midst. Brand rode a little ahead. The regent sat in the saddle well enough, but he seemed disorientated. Certainly, he was not taking command as Gil knew he would have if he were well. There was something wrong with him, but that was small wonder. For a time, no matter how brief, he had been dead.

They followed Hruilgar back toward Cardoroth. The forest seemed quiet. The gloom amid the trunks grew deeper and the silence heavier as the afternoon wore on. But then, unexpectedly, a wolf howled.

The riders looked about them. The sound did not come again, but their pace quickened and their eyes kept careful watch of the forest.

The afternoon gave way to night. It fell swiftly amid the trees. The silence grew menacing, for now the men expected to hear the wolf again, or the call of others in the pack. But the silence deepened, laying over everything more sinisterly than any howl, and then when there finally was sound again, it was not the wolf at all.

They had come close to the edge of the forest, for the dim light of stars peeked between the thinning canopy, and the trunks of the trees grew further apart. But they were no longer alone. Somewhere ahead was the sound of trotting horses. Then there was a neigh swiftly followed by a muffled curse.

2. Heir to the Throne

The Durlin came to a halt. There was no time to move off the trail, nor any room to spread out in a defensive position. Hruilgar was in the lead, and though not a soldier he drew a long knife. Two Durlin drew their horses level and flanked him; no more would fit on the trail.

Ahead, there was movement. Then riders came into sight. It was a column some twenty strong, and they were armed men, yet they seemed to be surprised to find the Durlin.

The lead rider of the newcomers reined his horse in, coming to a swift stop. The riders behind him did the same.

Gil could not see clearly in the growing dark, but it seemed that they wore the livery of soldiers of Cardoroth. They should be friends, yet there was treachery afoot in the city and these men might owe allegiance to one of the lords who sought to overthrow Brand.

The lead rider was still. Then, slowly, he raised his hand and saluted the Durlin.

"Well met," he said, lowering his hand just as slowly. He was careful to give no indication of reaching for a weapon.

"What are you doing here?" one of the Durlin answered.

The soldier kept his hands still. "We seek the regent, for we have news for him." He hesitated. "We're loyal to him," he added.

Shorty nudged his horse forward and the Durlin on the left eased back to let him through.

"I know you, Drinbar," the Durlindrath said. "Speak freely captain – you're trusted here."

Most of the tension seemed to leave the newcomer, and the men behind him relaxed.

"It's good to see you Shorty. Very good indeed. I have a message for the regent."

The man's eyes flickered toward Brand in the middle of the Durlin.

"Brand is … ill-disposed at the moment," Shorty said.

Drinbar glanced nervously at the regent. "So it seems. I will deliver it to you."

He made to speak again, but Shorty held up his hand. "Brand is ill-disposed, but the heir to the throne is present. Deliver the message to him."

Gil felt the gaze of the captain turn to him, summing him up. He read uncertainty in the man's glance, but Shorty eased his mount back and Gil moved into the space he had left. He did not quite understand what was happening, for Shorty and Taingern were in charge here, but he knew what was expected of him.

"Thank you for coming. You may deliver the message to me."

Drinbar saluted, and his hesitation disappeared.

"Yes, my lord." He gestured back at his men. "We're glad that you've been rescued. But you should know that rumors are abuzz in the city. The nobles have called a council, and they gather from far and wide. Some say Brand is a traitor. Some say he is dead. Some say you're both dead. Frankly, no one knows what's happening. But worse, there are soldiers gathering with the nobles. And they seem to have formed allegiances. To be blunt, the city is in turmoil, and just now anything seems possible."

The man ceased speaking, aware that he may have said too much.

Gil felt everyone's gaze upon him, especially Shorty's and Taingern's. Behind them, Brand dozed in the saddle. This was a situation that Gil had never been in before, and he did not know what he should do. But, he decided to show none of his doubt. Certainly, the two Durlindraths could handle this far better than he could. He knew that. And *they* knew that. This, therefore, was a test for him. They wanted to know what he was made of. Brand was unwell, and someone had to fill the leadership void.

The soldiers ahead of him sat uneasily on their mounts while the silence grew. Gil wondered what Brand would do. Confusion and doubt, he had often said, were the enemy. Correct knowledge and determination, friends.

"Thank you," Gil said, at last knowing what to say. "This has been a time of doubt, but that no longer exists. There is no betrayal. Brand is my friend, and remains regent. He was badly … injured fighting to save me. So, take this message back. Fly with all speed, and we'll follow. Brand is alive. I'm alive. We return to the city, but Cardoroth's enemies gather outside. Plots are afoot, and worse. But Cardoroth, as ever, will endure. And spread the word. Brand remains regent, and I will be king one day, and the nobles who think otherwise are fools. Tell them I said so, and that treachery, schemes and plots against the throne will be punished."

The captain was silent, mulling over those words and measuring the strength of will behind them. A slow smile spread across his face, and then he saluted once more.

"As you wish, my lord! I'll tell them. Personally."

He gave a nod to Shorty and then turned his horse. Giving a command, his men did likewise and they began to gallop back in the direction from whence they came.

Gil noticed that Shorty and Taingern were looking at him.

"Well spoken," Shorty said. "But it'll take more than threats to control the nobility if they've really begun to vie for the throne."

Taingern looked at him solemnly. "Do you know what the word was for king in the ancient tongue?"

"No," answered Gil, surprised by the question.

"It was Gorfalac," Taingern informed him.

"What does that mean?"

"It signifies *sword of the blood*, and this you must become. The protector of the realm, the realm's defender."

The moment Gil heard the words, he knew they were true. He looked at Brand. The man had given all that he could, and then more. There would be no further help from him, at least for a while. What was needed now was that Gil himself put to use all that Brand had taught him over the years.

He looked at Brand one final time, but there seemed to be no recognition in the man's eyes.

"Let's go," Gil said.

He nudged his mount forward. His horse responded swiftly. It was Brand's black stallion, and it felt strange to be riding him, but appropriate also.

Gil did not look back, but he knew the others followed. It was but the first step of many that he now must take.

Darkness grew about them. Somewhere behind, the wolf howled again, and there was a sense of loss in that sound, a mournful cry into the heavens that could easily have been human.

It took very little time to reach the eave of the forest. The trees gave way suddenly, the sky opened above, but it was the view ahead that caught Gil's attention.

In the distance was the shadowed mass of Cardoroth. But there were lights within it, flickering and ruddy. There was trouble in Cardoroth as the captain had warned, for the ruddy light was fire. Parts of the city burned. It was worse than the captain had said, but he would not have known. The increasing dark had shown up what was happening better than he would have seen riding into the forest while daylight held.

The captain and his men were somewhere ahead of them on the road, but they had already disappeared into the gloom. Gil hoped they reached the city as soon as possible and spread the word of truth. Both he and Brand were alive. And they were returning. That should give pause to any nobles inciting trouble.

They rode on, slower than the soldiers for they were weary and had many injured men among them. Soon, the scent of smoke drifted to them, and Gil tasted bitterness in his mouth. There were enemies abroad, Ginsar among them, but there were enemies at home too.

3. Like a Rat Down a Hole

They galloped through the rising dark. The smell of smoke grew stronger. There was little talk as they rode, for they were weary and there would be no rest for them when they reached the city. Also, fear was on them, for there was trouble afoot in the kingdom – the kind that led to bloodshed. Already there would have been the flash of swords and the slaying of men. It would get worse swiftly unless order was returned.

Better and better did Gil understand why Shorty had pushed him forward into the role of leader. Leadership was needed now, more than anything, and there were few who could supply it. The role required more than ability; it required the respect of the people. It required a figurehead who could draw the populace together. As prince, that was him. No matter that others, such as Shorty and Taingern, were better skilled. The people would look to him first, as they had done to his forefathers for generations beyond count.

They approached the city, and the great wall of the Cardurleth that surrounded it bulked before them. The fires did not seem so bad as they drew near, or perhaps they were being put out. Gil felt a wave of relief, for if they had begun to spread they would soon reach a point where nothing could stand in their way and the city would be destroyed.

He studied what he could see quite carefully, and it seemed that fires burned now in isolated spots. Even those were rapidly diminishing. The populace must have worked well and swiftly to control them. For all the betrayal and treachery in the city, most of the people were fiercely proud and loyal. They loved their home and they fought for it.

The West Gate came into view, the Arach Neben in the old tongue. The road was white beneath the hooves of the horses, gleaming pale beneath the stars. The wall, though pockmarked by the ravages of war, seemed smooth and graceful in the dim light.

Gil shuddered. It was here that he had first seen the Rider called Death. It was not a good memory. Brand had walked through the gate to face him, but the gate was now closed and the ornament of the Morning Star that decorated it shone fitfully.

The riders drew up. Soldiers moved behind the thick gate-bars.

"Who comes to Cardoroth?" asked one of the soldiers, his figure dim and his voice sounding hollow in the gate-tunnel.

Gil paused a moment. He did not know for certain where the loyalty of these men lay, but he had the Durlin with him. Also, this was the very gate where Brand himself had once been a captain. The men knew him well.

He edged his mount forward. "Open, for I am Gil, Prince of Cardoroth, and the regent and the Durlin are with me."

There was a pause while the shadowy figure peered through the gate. Then there was a rough command and several men moved swiftly.

The gate swung open. A flickering torch was lit, and by its light Gil saw the present-day captain standing there with several men behind him.

The captain saluted, his gaze taking in the tattered Durlin and the quiet figure of Brand.

Gil returned the salute. "At ease, captain."

The man relaxed. "We're glad to see you. And Brand too." He seemed genuine, and Gil guessed that this was one of the men who had personally served under Brand in the past.

"What's been happening here?" Gil asked.

"We're not quite sure. We know there has been some fighting, and trouble among the nobles. But the fires are nearly out now and the city has grown quiet. I sent a man in to find out what was happening, but he hasn't returned yet."

Gil thought about that. But not for long. There was no way to know what was happening, but Brand had taught him never to show indecision. He did not know for sure what was going on in the city, yet there were only two ways to find out. Wait here until word reached him, or enter and find out for himself.

"Thank you, captain. We'll go through now."

The captain moved aside, and his men followed. They all gave a salute, but it was for Brand rather than Gil. But the regent sat slumped in his saddle, and there were concerned looks in the eyes of the soldiers as the Durlin rode past.

They entered the dark gate-tunnel. The clatter of hooves was loud. The confined space here always made Gil nervous, but it was worse now. It was a killing ground, and many were the slots in the wall from which arrows could be loosed.

He rode ahead. The Durlin rode with him. In moments, the tunnel gave way to a city street and the star-strewn heavens opened above.

"Where to?" Shorty asked.

"The palace," Gil said without hesitation.

They pressed forward, riding close and keeping their eyes open. At first, it was quiet, but as they turned a corner there were suddenly people on the street. They saw Gil and Brand, and recognized them swiftly.

The Durlin bunched closer, but there was no need to worry. A cheer went up from several in the crowd, and then they all joined in.

Suddenly there were more people. They saw Brand and the cheer grew into a chant.

Brand! Brand! Brand!

Gil felt a surge of pride. He looked at the regent, and Brand seemed to rally, sitting straighter in the saddle and looking around. He offered a little wave to the crowd, and the chanting swelled louder.

Taingern whispered in Gil's ear. "Brand always says he isn't well liked in Cardoroth, but he's been dealing with the nobles too long. The people love him."

Gil knew it was true.

They rode on, heading toward the palace. The scent of smoke was pungent in the air, but there were no fires to be seen, nor any burned buildings. Not on the main road at least.

They entered the palace grounds. Taingern and Shorty flanked him protectively now.

"There," Shorty said, nodding curtly to the left.

Gil looked in the direction that Shorty had indicated, but saw nothing.

"Look at the grass," Taingern instructed.

Gil saw it then. There were scuffle marks and bare earth had been exposed. Something glistened darkly too.

"Blood," Shorty confirmed.

They moved through the gardens slowly. There were more signs of fighting, and Gil sensed the Durlin growing tense all about him.

There was movement ahead near the palace doors. Someone rushed out, but Gil saw that it was Arell.

The healer moved swiftly. And there was fear on her face too. Gil knew then that the rumors were true: she was Brand's lover.

There was concern etched into her expression, and she had eyes only for Brand. Yet as she neared she looked at Gil also, and he saw her relief. But she went straight to the regent.

"Brand? Brand?" she said.

The regent looked at her, but gave no answer.

Arell's face was white, but she seemed professional and in control. She assisted while a Durlin helped Brand dismount, and then at Taingern's nod several Durlin dismounted and took the regent toward the chambers of healing. Arell supported him on one side, but he walked at a slow pace as though he were a man half asleep.

The rest of them dismounted also, and the remainder of the Durlin led the horses toward the stables. Shorty and Taingern stayed with Gil.

"Is it safe, do you think?"

"Of course," Shorty answered. "Otherwise Arell would have said something."

Gil cursed inwardly. He should have reasoned that through himself.

They entered the palace. There were soldiers on guard everywhere. They looked at Gil. Most glanced away quickly, but some few showed surprise. He guessed that word of his capture had spread wide, and that there were rumors of his death.

But he was not dead, nor was Brand. Somehow, they had survived an encounter with Death. But not without scars. Gil began to wonder if Brand would ever be the same man again.

"Where should we go first?" Gil asked.

"The throne room," Shorty answered. "There we'll find some answers to what's been going on in our absence."

"But what if nobody is there?"

Shorty shrugged. "Then we'll send for them. But this is an emergency. And word of our return will have come before us. Someone will be there."

"But why the throne room?"

"Because that's where orders are most often given from. It's a place of authority, and in an emergency people seek that out."

They walked through the corridors. For all that Shorty said it was safe, he and Taingern proceeded with care, their hands never far from their sword hilts and their eyes alert for any sign of danger.

It did not take long to reach the throne room. Soldiers stood without, and Gil saw tension ease from his two companions. These were men that they obviously knew and trusted.

The soldiers opened the great doors. Gil walked through with the Durlindraths. The marble floor was white and polished, and their steps echoed loudly around the room. It was especially the vaulted ceiling far above that cast the sound back and made it sound as though there were double the number of people.

An older lady was there; one whom Gil was sure that he had seen before, and yet not one that he knew.

The lady was by herself, but she seemed at ease. Moreover, neither Shorty nor Taingern seemed surprised. Gil began to wonder exactly who she was.

"It's good to see you," she said, addressing both the Durlindraths. Her eyes strayed momentarily to Gil, and he felt the keen intelligence of her mind, weighing him up and forming opinions swiftly. He was not sure he liked it, but he had the feeling that most of her judgements, whatever they were, were likely proved correct by time.

He saw an unspoken question pass between Shorty and the woman. Whatever it was, Shorty seemed to have received an answer, for he turned to Gil and spoke.

"I have the honor," he said, in a voice somewhat more formal than usual, "to introduce you to Esanda. She has no title, is not of the nobility, and yet she served in the highest capacity as a counselor to your grandfather and now, in turn, to Brand."

The old lady inclined her head ever so slightly. Gil studied her, and was amazed. He knew all the counselors. Every one of them. She was not among them. So, who was she?

"Pleased to meet you, madam," he said. If he was surprised and confused, he was not going to show it.

Esanda laughed. "Ah, Brand has taught you well indeed. You do not have a clue who I am, although I know you very well. But you refuse to be thrown off balance. Nor do you even ask who I am, and why I am not known at court."

Gil was beginning to get an idea, and random comments and bits of information that had previously seemed unconnected to fell into place.

"Brand has taught me well, but I fear I'm not a great student. Nevertheless, I can make some deductions."

"And what do you deduct?"

"Only this. If your presence and identity have been kept a secret, it is for a purpose. What purpose could that be? Well, one where the work you do can best be achieved anonymously. What work lends itself to this situation? I can only think of one answer. Madam, you are a spy. More than that, given that you advised my grandfather and now the regent, I should say you are *the* spy. There would be a network of them, but you are at its head, the holder of every secret in the realm. Even," he added with a rueful smile, "the ones a mischievous prince would prefer to have kept to himself."

Taingern chuckled. Shorty winked at him, but Esanda studied him with a long and appraising glance before she smiled.

"I'm impressed. Brand has indeed taught you well. There's a beauty in logic, and that was a masterpiece of sound reasoning. Moreover, everything you say is right." She paused. "It's pleasing to know that I don't work for dolts. That being the case, I don't need to warn you that you must keep your … guesses to yourself."

"Of course," Gil answered promptly. He understood that he had been entrusted with a state secret, and no force on earth would ever get him to utter a word of what he knew.

"Good. Now, we had better get down to business, and swiftly. Much is afoot."

Gil listened as she spoke. He remembered her now, a shadowy presence throughout his life, somehow always around but seldom ever seen.

She gave details of what had happened while they were out of the city.

"Dernbrael called a Council of Nobles as he had threatened to do. But it did not work out quite as he expected. There was much talk, and much talk against Brand. But for all of that, there were not that many who wanted to move openly against him."

Shorty grunted. "A bunch of cowards," he said. "Soft to the core like a rotten apple."

"True," Esanda agreed. "But there are some who are loyal to Brand. But more still fear him. Between that, and the fact that many of the noble houses think they may yet have a chance at the throne, Dernbrael did not get the support he anticipated."

245

"He probably didn't bribe them enough," Taingern said.

"That too," Esanda agreed. "Dernbrael has expensive tastes in many things, and a fondness for betting on slow horses as well. His wealth is greatly reduced these last few years, and that may also be spurring him along the course he's chosen. As king, he would find a way to redistribute treasury funds into his own name."

"But surely," Taingern said, "he didn't attempt to have himself crowned straightaway? He would seek the regency first, would he not?"

"His financial position may have driven him further than was wise," Esanda told them. "He went for the highest prize, grasped at it with both hands."

"And what happened?" asked Gil.

"He failed," Shorty said. "Or else we would have all been arrested when we returned."

Esanda gave a solemn nod. "Shorty is right. He failed. The vote went against him, because he tried to force the issue too soon. The nobles were not ready for that decision, not at all. Especially when Brand might still be alive, when he might return and make them regret it."

"Is he regent then?" asked Taingern. "But that cannot be, or we would still have been arrested."

Esanda grinned. "The man is a fool. He risked too much, pushed too hard for the crown, and that caused great divisiveness. When it failed, that mistrust and divisiveness remained. He lost the vote to be regent as well. One that he might otherwise have won."

"And the fires we saw in the city?" Gil asked. "How did that happen? Dernbrael must have been desperate."

"Ah, you see where this is going. Yes, he was desperate, for he saw the chance of a lifetime slipping between his fingers. He tried to force the issue, just him and the factions most closely aligned to him. He tried to take the palace, thinking that once he had that, and that once Brand was dead or discredited, he could rouse the people to support him, and at that point a vote of the council was redundant."

"But the soldiers stationed in the palace fought him off," stated Shorty.

"Indeed. He underestimated their loyalty to Brand. He came with a force of over a hundred, but it wasn't enough."

"And where is he now?" Gil asked.

"He's in hiding. Disappeared like smoke on the wind," Esanda answered.

Shorty clenched his fists. "More like a rat down a hole."

Esanda grinned at him. "Yes, that too. But there are only so many rat holes in Cardoroth, and sooner or later I'll find the one he's using."

Gil did not doubt this was true. One way or another, sooner or later, Dernbrael would show up. But that was a problem for another day. What to do now? That was the question. And as soon as he asked it of himself, he realized that the others had grown quiet. They were asking themselves the same thing.

He looked around at them. Their eyes were all upon him. And he knew that they were weighing him, scrutinizing him. Esanda's gaze was the sharpest of them all, but they must all have been wondering the same thing in their own ways.

They looked at him because he was the future of Cardoroth, if it were to have one. Only he could unite the people. It was his destiny, his responsibility. And right there in that moment he understood what leadership was. A king, a leader of any kind, served those he led. He did what he did for them, and them alone, rather than himself. He did it because it was right, and because it was his duty. Not because he wanted to.

Gil sighed. It seemed that he must sacrifice his dream of learning deeply about magic. When he spoke though, he was decisive and there was no regret in his voice.

"Right then," he said to Esanda. "I would like you to find Dernbrael. No matter what hole he has gone down, I would speak with him. I would tell him what I think of his treachery, for I am heir to the throne. Then I would see him brought to justice. There can be no tolerance of treason, not when the realm is at risk. And his capture and punishment will send a message to the other nobles. Their chance has passed. Whatever opportunity they had is gone. I *will* be king, whether I want it or not, whether *they* want it or not. I would willingly renounce my claim to the throne for Brand. I would follow him all the days of my life, but it's clear that he's unwell, and if he recovers I don't think he'll stay in Cardoroth much longer. He too has a destiny … and it calls him. Just as does mine."

He felt their gazes on him again. They were weighing him and judging him anew. And this time there was growing approval in their expressions.

4. Anticipate the Enemy

There was a glitter in Esanda's eyes.

"Truly, Brand has taught you well. But I see your grandparents in you also." She stood. "I'll work on it. Dernbrael will be found. Someone, somewhere, knows where he is. I hear every whisper in the city, eventually. Word will come to me. More importantly, we have a leader that the people of Cardoroth can follow." She gave him a slight bow and left the room.

Gil turned to Shorty. "How is Brand? You've known him longest … is he going to be alright?"

Shorty shook his head. "It's impossible to say, lad. There's something wrong, that's for sure. He's not as he was, or as he would want to be."

"No, he is not," Taingern said. "But we must have faith in Carnhaina. She would not have brought him back from death itself only for him to die soon after or fail to regain his strength."

"I think you're right," Gil agreed. "But what man could go through what Brand has and not be unchanged? Even damaged?"

"Brand is not as other men," Shorty said softly.

Gil agreed with that. But still, he remembered what he had seen on that mountain somewhere in the spirit world when Brand had died.

Carnhaina had spoken to the regent, but Gil had not heard the words. He wished he knew what they were. Brand had answered, and there was a look on his face that Gil could not begin to understand. Then Brand had

249

lifted high his arms and looked to the sky. The mountain on which they stood lurched. The queen pointed at him with her spear, and lightning flashed from the heavens. It struck the regent, searing him, running the length of his body. But he stood still and kept his arms up as though to embrace it. Thrice the lightning struck. And the last was a searing bolt that sizzled through the air, struck him, and leaped to the stone near his feet. The rock had split. Water gushed through the crack and hastened in a stream down the slope and into the valley. What had it all meant? Was any of it even real, or was it in their minds? But there was magic at work, mighty magic, for back in the chamber where Brand lay dead his chest heaved, and then with a great gasp he gulped in life-giving air.

Gil would never forget what he had seen. Brand would be changed, but Gil must put all that aside for now. He must think of the next step, of what was best for Cardoroth, as Brand would have wanted him to do. He must anticipate the enemy.

Gil considered the situation. There were two enemies. The first was internal, part of Cardoroth itself. The nobles were among that group, but they were not the only ones. There were dark forces within the city too. Forces in allegiance with Cardoroth's enemies.

For the moment, he could do nothing about Dernbrael. He trusted that Esanda would find him, and Gil guessed that the noble was not only in hiding, but in fear of his life. His plan had failed, and both Gil and Brand had returned to the city alive. Dernbrael would be desperate, but that also made him dangerous. Could he do anything besides hide? Had he any last strategies available to him?

Gil's thoughts shifted to the external enemies of Cardoroth. What would they do? What of the quest that Carnhaina had given him that would defeat them?

She had revealed that Ginsar had loosed forces upon the land that tore at reality. In her madness, in her lust for revenge against Brand, she opened a gateway and drew them in. Carnhaina had warned that however much she strove to master them, they would conquer her instead. And after, they would turn upon the world to make it all their own. How earnest Carnhaina had seemed! There was almost fear in her voice, and she had charged Gil with preventing that catastrophe. She had charged him with closing the gateway that Ginsar had made. But when he asked her how, she had said that she did not know, that he must discover for himself. But that it was for this that he had been born.

It all seemed too much. There were too many enemies, too many things that he did not know.

He turned to Shorty and Taingern. "How are we going to do this? Where should I even start?"

5. A Son of my Sons

Gil knew that the quest was what mattered most. Carnhaina's charge must be his priority, for if the forces of which she warned were unleashed upon Alithoras the entire land would be destroyed. Dernbrael was nothing compared to that. And yet, could he be sure there was no connection between them? It was possible that Ginsar was a link between them all, the single thread sewn through an entire tapestry.

One thing he knew for sure. He could not do everything at once, nor all by himself. He must delegate.

"Shorty, Taingern … listen to me." He spoke with resolve. "You know that I'm not yet ready to be king. I'm still young. But Brand is ill, and I have to step up to my responsibilities. The kingdom must have a leader who can unify. Brand did it, because, well, he's Brand. Now, as heir, it must be me. But I'll need your help."

"Lad," Shorty said. "You have it."

Taingern looked him in the eye. "Lord, we are at your service."

Gil felt a surge of loyalty wash over him. These were true men. Handpicked by Brand, and each of them had survived terrible dangers with their leader. They were men of courage and men of reliability. They were also smart men, and as Brand had often told him, it did not matter a whit that they were as chalk and cheese. When it mattered, they would both do the same thing: give their all.

"Right," Gil said. "Ginsar has opened a way between worlds and allowed these dangerous forces into Alithoras. Carnhaina has charged me with closing that gateway, with sending those forces back whence they came. I must concentrate on that. No one else in Cardoroth has any understanding of the magic as do I. I shall send word to Lòrenta and seek help from the lòhrens, but I fear that the problem will need solving before any help from that quarter can arrive."

"And what of Dernbrael?" Shorty asked.

"I have a feeling that Esanda always finds whatever she searches for. He'll turn up, and I can wait until then. In the meantime, we'll forget him." Gil had a thought while he spoke. "We could, of course, brand him as a traitor and issue orders for his arrest. But that will only send him deeper into hiding. Better to stay silent. Let him think that just maybe he might not be a priority. He may get careless then and give Esanda a better chance to discover him."

"And what of the nobles who sided with him?"

Gil thought about that. "There was nothing improper in the Council of Nobles itself, and they were free to cast their vote there and express opinions. Forget about them. But the nobles who gathered force afterward, who assisted Dernbrael to assault the palace, that is a different matter. That was treason, and more. The whole city could have burned. Get the City Watch onto them. Have them arrested, and held in prison. There need not be any trial until after the crisis with Ginsar is averted."

Shorty chuckled. "The captain of the City Watch was appointed by Brand. He was not a noble, and they will not like being arrested by him, not one bit."

"I think I can live with their discomfit," Gil said. "Oh, and that being the case, please tell the captain to arrest them in public places. That'll help spread word that treason isn't tolerated."

"More than that," Taingern added, "the people will like it that one of their own is arresting the nobles."

"Excellent," Gil said. "What else should we do?"

"I suggest increasing the guard around the palace," Shorty said. "The Durlin are tired, and we cannot be sure there won't be another attempt on your life."

"Agreed. And send out scouts into the wild as well. Cardoroth's enemies may attack after recent events, sensing turmoil in the city."

Shorty scratched his head. "I think that might be about it, at least for the moment."

"Not quite," Gil answered. "There's one thing more, but I must do it myself. Still, it's best that you know about it."

The two Durlindraths looked at him with interest.

"Carnhaina told me that she didn't know how the gateway between worlds could be closed. But I must discover it as she charged me to do, and I've been thinking."

He felt a wave of determination rise within him. He thought of what Brand had given for Cardoroth. He thought of his grandparents. They had never given up, even in the darkest of hours. He knew there would be a way to do what he must, and he would keep seeking until he found it. But there was a place to start.

"There's a secret chamber behind Brand's bedroom. It was built long ago, by Carnhaina herself. She used it as a library, or a study. I think it was a place where she would not be disturbed when she practiced magic."

He felt the eyes of the two men on him. They were listening carefully, wondering where this was going.

"In that room I've found a diary. At least, it's mostly a diary, but at times she addresses me directly."

Taingern raised an eyebrow. "Are you sure? She died long, long ago. It was another age."

"I'm sure," Gil said without hesitation. "It's hard to know just what her powers were, but certainly one of them was foresight. And that might be a good choice of words, for though I can give no rational explanation for it, that's where I feel I must start my quest. There'll be something there, some snippet of information."

Even as he spoke, he felt the truth of those words in his bones. It was not something that he had felt before, but Brand had spoken of it. For a warrior or for a lòhren, instincts often prompted action.

"Sounds to me like a good place to start," Shorty said.

"The reason I'm telling you," Gil explained, "is that I'm not sure how long it'll take. The diary is large and sometimes hard to understand. I could be there for many hours at a time, and I wouldn't like you to think that I'm shirking my responsibilities."

Taingern clapped him on the shoulder. "Don't be concerned. We know you take this seriously. Gil, you're no longer a child, and we know it. Do what you must do, and follow your instincts. Brand was always at his best when he was like that."

"And we'll send some Durlin with you," Shorty added. "You must go nowhere without them now."

Gil thought how much had changed in such a short period. Only days ago the thought of a guard chafed at him. Now, he wanted nothing more. This was going to be a dangerous period, and he longed for Brand to get

255

well and take over. But that might never happen. Anyway, he was close to manhood now, and he knew better than to wish for things. He must make them happen if he wanted them to happen at all. And all else he must accept with good grace.

They went to the great doors and Shorty opened them. Two Durlin waited without. They had changed their clothes and washed. The white surcoats that they wore, markers of their position as Durlin, gleamed. Gil felt dirty and wanted a wash and a change of clothes as well, but that could wait.

He left Shorty and Taingern then, moving up through the palace to higher floors. The Durlin walked with him, silent and watchful. He did not mind their presence; he was in fact reassured by it, and he cursed himself for being a foolish boy all those times they annoyed him in the past.

The Durlin walked a pace behind him most of the way. They seldom spoke, keeping their eyes and ears alert to their surroundings. This behavior was only changed when they approached a corner. At such a time, one Durlin went ahead first while the other stepped up to be level with Gil.

They reached Brand's room. The door was closed, but Gil knew that Brand was not there. Arell was caring for him down below in the chambers of healing.

He knocked on the door just to be sure, but there was no answer. Then one of the Durlin opened it and went through, Gil following.

The room was clean and tidy, and the bed was made. Suddenly, Gil felt loss wash over him. Brand may never be well enough to live life as he had done again. Perhaps he would be confined to the chambers of healing for the rest of his life. If so, it was Gil's fault. Or maybe not directly his fault, but something for which he knew he would always feel guilty. Not quite the same thing, but not a good feeling either.

He walked to the far wall. There he hesitated before turning back to the Durlin. "Don't be alarmed," he said. "And please, keep to yourself what you're about to see."

"Of course," one of them answered in a steady voice. But he could tell they did not like it. Their hands strayed to the hilts of their swords.

Gil held his right palm to the wall. Straightaway the sign of Halathgar, the two pale dots like eyes, began to tingle. Then he invoked lòhrengai. He felt it spring to life, stronger, more sure than it ever had before. Something had happened in his struggle with Ginsar, something had been woken inside him.

Light glimmered on his palm. He did not think too deeply about it, but just accepted that it had come at his need, just as he knew it always would.

"Halathgar!" he commanded.

Light flared, a dazzling blue that filled the chamber. He felt a power respond to his own. It rose up, sought him out, assessed him and recognized who he was. Then, satisfied, it withdrew. As it did so, stone ground on stone and a door appeared.

Gil lowered his hand. The blue light faded. He turned once more to the Durlin. He saw now that their hands gripped their sword hilts, but they still appeared calm.

He thought for a moment. "Best that you stay here," he said. "I'm safe in the room beyond."

"We should go with you everywhere," one of them replied.

"Not here, I think," Gil answered. "This was once the study of Carnhaina. It's small, and you will find it uncomfortable. Stay in this room and relax. I won't be more than an hour or so."

He stepped through the door. "Halathgar," he said once more, and the door slid closed with a grumble behind him.

He breathed in of the air. It smelled of secrets, of long-forgotten magic. But it was dim, and he summoned light to his hand and then, without thinking, cast it gently upward. It floated to the ceiling and stayed there. It was a strange light, bright and warm, but it had a shiver like starlight to it. Stranger still was that Brand had not taught him how to do that. But he had said that the magic had a life of its own, and that when it began to flow through him it would express itself in different ways from what Brand could do or teach. *None of us is the same, nor the magic we wield. Learn what you can do. Test yourself. You are the magic and the magic is you.*

He looked about the room. It was lavish though small, if somewhat long and narrow. A couch, lush and soft, filled most of it. Dust covered it now, but the color of the fabric shone through. Royal blue.

The hangings on the wall were the same color, and Gil studied them, breathing in their history, the history of his ancestors. The tent camps and villages by a great river. Beyond, the forest. And within the deeps of the trees a mighty city. Halathar, the home of the immortals who had befriended and taught many tribes of men. There were more images. One showed the legendary standing stones, a place of ceremony that dated back to his earliest ancestors. It was a place from history that was not forgotten, but that had become myth. It was part of the *Age of Heroes*.

Then he saw the migration of the Camar tribes as they traveled eastward. But there was war also. Massive battles against the enemies from the south were shown. There were elugs, which some called goblins, and their mighty armies were so vast as to darken the wall-hangings. Elùgroths commanded them, cloaked in shadow and pointing wych-wood staffs with the menace of sorcery.

Gil loved it all. It was the memory of another time, of an age before his. But the more things changed, the more they stayed the same. All this could come to pass again. Would come to pass, unless he fulfilled Carnhaina's charge.

His glance turned to the desk, and the book set upon it. Why was he drawn to this? Was it magic? Was it destiny? Why should he think there were any answers there for him? Then again, why would there not be? This was his connection to Carnhaina, to his great ancestor, and somewhere in his heritage was sure to lie the answers he sought. Why else would Ginsar wish him dead?

He sat down and opened the book at random. One place was as good as another to read, but he wished that Elrika was here as she had been last time. It was not the same without her. He missed her, and he had much to tell her. She was really the only person he could confide in, or *wanted* to confide in. Brand was like a father to him. Shorty and Taingern like uncles. But she was different. She was something else…

But the book called to him, and he began to read. He flicked through pages, waiting for something to trigger his instincts.

"Evil," Carnhaina wrote at one point. "What is it? Men call it Dark, and themselves Light. But does not a bright Light cause blindness? And does not the Dark offer nurture and comfort? Are each of these elements also not a part of man? Certainly, he is made of both, for all men and woman carry the seeds of each within them. Perhaps evil is a term for those who do not struggle. To give in to the Dark entirely might be evil. But evil sees it as a purity of spirit, as a person fulfilling their destiny. Am I evil because I understand the Dark? Some say that I am. Fools. I am neither Light nor Dark. I am Carnhaina, and that is enough for me."

Gil read, trying to grapple with the issues. He knew that Cardoroth's philosophers wrestled with them too. And they had answers, which he did not. Did that make them smarter than him? Or were they fools, thinking to unravel the secrets of humanity and understand the hearts of men, thinking they understood and all the while oblivious to their ignorance?

"Elùdrath!" Carnhaina wrote, and Gil sensed her enmity leap off the page. "He is evil, beyond doubt. Or at least my enemy, which is the same thing. It is from him that the Dark in this land spreads. He is its center, its origin. The Dark Lord! The Shadowed Lord! The master of elùgroths. To combat him the Halathrin ventured to this land, made their exodus leaving behind all that they knew in exchange for struggle and woe. Ah! A great people, but they have their flaws too. Who does not?"

Gil felt that he was reading history, as he was, but he was also in Carnhaina's mind. These were her words, her thoughts, her innermost musings.

"Shurilgar! May a thousand fires burn out his eyes. The Betrayer of Nations. His Darkness is strong, strong! And yet he is but a servant of Elùdrath. The wicked are mighty, but the Light has power too. But men? Most are fools. They forget. They fail to think. Shurilgar will come to a bad end, I can see that now, but it will not be by my hand. Elùdrath is different. He is beyond my sight. Men think him dead. But I feel in my bones it is not so. He lives! And his darkness will spread through the long ages to come."

The words sent a shiver up Gil's spine. Brand had once whispered something to him, something like that. *Why do the elugs attack us? Who controls them, drives their enmity?*

He turned the page, and then turned some more. Something stood out to him. The script was different, as though Carnhaina was older.

"In time, a son of my son's distant sons will be borne. Power shall be his. He will be marked with the sign of Halathgar. Evil will overshadow the land, and four Riders shall come, and death and destruction will be as their shadow, following in their wake wherever they go. Behold! The void shall be breached, for the Riders come not of this world. The gateways will open. The possible will be impossible. The impossible possible. But harken to my words – the powers that form and substance the world will seek balance. If evil is born, so too is good. It shall rise amid the shadows. Look for it. Seek it out. Revere it, for it is the key…"

261

The text cut off there, but there was a drawing. It was by Carnhaina's hand, and the image was of her tower, of the Tower of Halathgar. There was a trapdoor, and then a stairway leading underground. Gil remembered seeing that trapdoor. But what lay beneath it? The drawing did not say. The stairs petered out and at their end were two twinkling dots, like stars. It was the Seal of Halathgar. That was all. Was it a hint of something? But that did not make sense. Stars did not shine underground. Was the drawing even connected to the text? There seemed no connection between them at all, but the drawing *did* appear straight after it.

He flicked through some more pages, but there was nothing else that stood out to him. The next sections were about the administration of a kingdom. What taxes were raised, what effect they had on employment and how to balance the need to raise state revenue with the necessity of stimulating the economy.

Gil put the diary down. He began to have the feeling that this was not an ordinary book. It called to him to read it, but he was not sure if the pages were the same each time he picked it up. And as though it knew when he had read what he was intended to, it showed him boring material that discouraged him from reading more.

He leaned back in the chair. Perhaps he had read enough anyway, but whether that was the book or his own instinct, he was not so sure. His curiosity was raised though. He allowed his feelings to rise, to replace his rational thought. He did not seek an answer, did not ask himself any questions. He just let his feelings flow unchecked through him.

This was a meditation that Brand had taught him. He saw again the image of the tower, and his feelings swirled and surged. He acknowledged them but viewed them dispassionately, as though they belonged to someone else. What dominated? Unbidden, the answer came to him. Curiosity. He must go back to the Tower of Halathgar and discover what was beneath the trapdoor. Fear was entwined with curiosity though. He knew he might learn more there, and the magic within him stirred in response. He felt that it was right to return, but that it might come with some cost. There may be danger. Yes, there was definitely danger, but then cold fear shot through him. Was the danger ahead of him, or was it present now? His emotions surged again, and he began to think with the rational part of his mind.

The dispassionate feeling evaporated, and he lost the feel of the meditation. With a long breath he stood up. It was time to go. He took one last look at the room, knowing he would return here again and again. Then he invoked the magic and opened the door into Brand's room. Stepping through, he closed it behind him.

Straightaway, he sensed that something was wrong.

6. A Duthenor Warrior

Gil studied the room. He saw nothing that should not have been there. It was lavish, so unlike Brand, and yet it was the bedroom of kings and queens back into antiquity. Brand would have had little choice in the furnishings or historical decorations. They probably remained much the same generation after generation.

His gaze swept over it all. The bed was made, the rugs on the floor clean. Two cushions rested neatly on the couch, and there was no dust anywhere. The weapons that hung on the wall glittered. Even the dark walnut bookshelf was polished to a smooth shine. That at least was a personal mark Brand had made on the room: he loved to read.

Gil went still. He knew what was wrong. The Durlin were not there. They would not have left this place, not even for a moment. Unless, of course, they had merely decided to wait outside the regent's personal quarters.

The door to the corridor was closed. Did the Durlin close it after they entered the bedroom? He could not remember. And if they had gone out, why had they not left it open?

He stood motionless, and listened. He heard nothing. Quickly, he summoned the magic within him. With it he could detect if there were people outside the door, perhaps even recognize if they were the Durlin. He was about to cast it forth with his hands when sudden movement disturbed him.

Out from behind the couch leapt a man. It was not one of the Durlin. He moved quickly, a dagger in his hand, and his strides were swift and purposeful.

Assassin. The word rang like a bell in Gil's mind. But it was not the same man who had attacked him before. And beyond doubt this one intended to kill him. He saw determination glitter in the intruder's pale eyes.

The assassin lunged toward him. Gil lifted high his hands. He had not yet discovered how to summon lòhren-fire, the weapon of choice for lòhrens, but nevertheless a bright light flashed from his palms blinding the man.

Gil stepped to the side. He darted to the wall and drew a blade. If he had not already had the magic summoned, he would be dead. But now the magic was alive within him, and he held a blade of cold steel in his hand. It was a chance at life, and he was going to make the most of it.

The assassin hesitated, perhaps still blinded though more likely confused. Few knew that Gil studied the arts of a lòhren. Gil stepped forward, intending to take advantage of the situation. But the man reacted swifter than expected.

In a smooth and practiced motion, he hurled his dagger. Gil twisted to the side, but still the blade tore at his shoulder. Pain flared.

There was no hesitation now. The man drew his sword and advanced. He lunged forward in a killing blow. Gil stepped back, using his own blade to deflect the strike. He followed through with a riposte, his sword flicking deftly at his attacker's neck, but the man was too skilled to succumb. He deflected the counterattack with

265

ease and then drove forward in a flurry of swift and deadly strikes.

Gil held his own. The man was skilled, perhaps more skilled than he was. But there was fear on him, and it caused him to hurry. If he were caught, he would be sentenced to death. So he attacked with all he had. Gil, on the other hand, realized he need only defend. Time was in his favor. He could call for help, but there was a pride in him that refused to do that. Besides, the clang of blade on blade would soon be heard by someone.

He defended, being sure not to allow himself to be cornered. He tried to maneuver toward the door, but the attacker would have none of that.

"Die, you bastard!" the man said with intense force.

It was an eerie feeling for Gil to hear those words, to know that someone wished him dead with all his heart. And yet it gave him strength too. This man was becoming frustrated, and that meant Gil was doing well.

They moved to the other side of the room, past the bed. Blades flicked and ragged breaths were drawn. Gil realized something else. The man had spoken with an accent. He sounded like Brand, only his accent was far stronger. Brand, as he mastered all other things to which he turned his attention, had learned the dialect of Cardoroth to near-perfection. This man had not.

Gil felt the magic within him grow restless. It was time to use it again, to see if he could once more surprise his attacker.

They moved toward the couch, and the assassin's desperation grew. He had counted on a quick killing, not a drawn-out fight. Gil grinned at him, seeking to unbalance him, but the Duthenor was a professional. He merely pressed his attack forward just as he had been doing.

Gil saw something on the floor, and his grin vanished. There was a pool of blood, dark red and stark. It splashed across a beautifully-woven rug.

Then he saw the body. Horror washed over him. It was of a Durlin, and an arrow protruded from the back of his neck. But the assassin carried no bow … and Gil suddenly realized that the man had an accomplice. He would be outside, keeping guard so that the assassin remained undisturbed. But they would not have expected their quarry to disappear: they knew nothing of the secret library. How long had they been waiting? And where was the second Durlin? And what was to stop the accomplice from entering now to aid his comrade?

7. Cold as Ice

The attacker must have sensed uncertainty. Gil had been thrown off balance by the sight of the dead Durlin, and then by the realization that there were *two* assassins. The intruder came at him again in a desperate rush. Time was running out.

Steel clanged against steel, and gone was all pursuit of skill. This was an attack of brute strength, driven by cold fury and desperation, but still controlled by a professional warrior who did not panic.

Gil could not stand his ground. He gave way, yet he did so grudgingly, step by step, deflecting his opponent's powerful strikes rather than blocking them.

He saw the desperation of the man grow, and his confidence increased accordingly. Brand had taught him well. He had survived all that this warrior, this assassin, could throw at him, and he was still there. Young as he was, he had skill enough to withstand his enemy, and for the first time he believed that not only could he fend him off, but that he could defeat him.

The fear that had sunk into Gil's belly at the beginning of the fight was less now. And anger stirred. This man had killed a Durlin, was trying to kill him. He had endured enough of that lately. No more.

Gil slowed his retreat. The attacker, wearied by his onslaught, could no longer strike as swiftly or as powerfully as he had been doing. One moment he had dominated the fight, and the next the situation was reversed.

With dazzling speed Gil unleashed his own attack. He was mad, anger burning hotter and hotter within him, but he ignored it as Brand had trained him to do. He just let his skill take over, allowed his arms and body to move with freedom, allowed them to flow with the grace and deadliness of the techniques that he had long practiced.

The assassin stumbled. Glad was Gil then for Brand's training, for the anger within him rose up and sought to leap forward with a killing stroke, but his training held him back. Wariness and patience were weapons in the warrior's arsenal, as useful as sharpened steel. So it proved now. It was not a stumble, but a feint, and the assassin's blade twisted up in a disemboweling stroke even as his feet righted themselves. But his blade cut only the air.

Now was Gil's chance. His sword knocked aside his enemy's, and then drove forward taking the man in the neck. Blood spurted as one of the great arteries was severed, but the blade struck his spine too.

The man reeled back and convulsed. His eyes bulged; one hand clamped over his neck to stop the blood, but it sprayed through his fingers. A moment he stood thus, and then the life went out of him and he dropped to the floor. There he writhed for a few moments. His hand fell away from the wound, but the blood no longer spurted. His heart had ceased to beat.

Gil felt sick. He had killed him. He began to retch, but when he turned away from the sight the urge to vomit was less. A moment he stood there, the sweat all over his skin as cold as ice and the heaving breaths of air that he drew in like fire, but he forced himself to think and become calm.

What should he do now? Was the assassin's accomplice still on the other side of the door? Gil could almost feel his presence there. But that might just be fear giving life to his thoughts. He could cast forth his magic as he had intended before, but if the man was there it would not change anything.

It was time to act, and Gil did so. He swiftly grabbed a chair. It would serve as a shield from any arrow fired against him.

He took a deep breath and moved toward the door. It was better to take the initiative and confront whatever fate awaited him than stand still in fear and uncertainty.

8. You Shall be Rewarded

Ginsar bit her lip. A drop of blood slowly beaded there, and she tasted it upon her tongue. She looked at her hands, her long-fingered and beautiful hands. They were pale and trembling. Cold fear roiled in the pit of her stomach, and uncertainty gnawed at her. Was her premonition founded?

Soon, she would find out.

The acolyte walked toward her. His tread was slow and his head bowed. It was not a good sign. The coven made way for him, slipping aside like shadows to allow his passage.

But there was envy in their glances as they gave way, for he had been chosen above them all. Yet if he returned with ill-tidings or had failed in his mission, then he would suffer. This they knew also, for past experience had taught them that, and therefore yearning was in their gaze too. One less at the top of the order meant opportunity for them, as it had in times past.

Slow was the advance of the acolyte, and she smelled his fear. For once, it did not please her. She wanted news, and his tardiness was an irritant. Yes, one way or the other, he would suffer.

He came before her, and kneeled.

"Speak!" Ginsar commanded.

"Lady, I entered the city in disguise as you wished. I passed through the gate, and—"

"Fool!" Ginsar spat at him. "I do not need your prattling. Answer me this. Does Brand live?"

The man began to tremble. "Yes, Lady. I spoke with some who saw him return into the city with the boy."

So it was true.

Ginsar felt fury rise within her. How could this be? He was dead. She knew it. And yet in the hours that passed since she had seen his lifeless body her instincts warned her that somehow he lived. It was intolerable.

Carnhaina. Carnhaina! It was *her* doing. And there would be a purpose to it. And yet, was there not a way to gain from this? If Carnhaina had found a means of bringing back the dead, might Ginsar herself not do so? Could she return her Master and her brother into the world?

"What else?" she said, her voice cold and giving no sign of her thoughts.

"They say he is ill. Rumor is that his mind is broken."

"Rumor? I sent you to discover the truth, not rumor."

"Yes, Lady. But no one is sure of this."

"You are a fool. And the city is full of fools. Carnhaina has done this. Brand is not ill, nor is his mind broken. Not *him*."

She thought a moment. "What other rumors have you heard? Speak, and be heard!" She allowed anger to infuse her voice.

The acolyte groveled at her feet. The coven stepped back a pace, but their gazes intensified.

"The nobles rebelled, Lady. They tried to depose Brand, but their attempt failed. He is ... he is feared greatly. However, the boy now seems to rule. That is the word out of the palace. I have also learned—"

272

"Enough! It is all a ruse. Brand lives. Brand rules. Brand *still* schemes against me. Our enemy is not yet destroyed!"

Her fury ran free now, filling her voice and flashing from her eyes. And it burned her soul. *Shall such as Brand defy me?*

The acolytes backed further away, but they did not take their eyes off her. At her feet, the man trembled. He bobbed his head back and forth to the dirt, and inch by inch he began to withdraw. She stayed him with a touch of her boot, and he stilled as though the slightest movement could kill him. And it could.

Ginsar took pity on him. It was not his fault that he had brought unfortunate news. He had served her as best as he was able. Therefore, she would reward him. Yes, as indeed she would reward all her servants in the end. She would give every one of them what they deserved.

Her white teeth flashed in a sudden grin, and a throaty laugh followed. This disconcerted the coven even more. Mad, they thought her, but she would show them. And mad or not, they followed her for she gave them power. This was the lure that never failed, nor would it fail now. She would show them *power.*

She bent forward, and her long fingers ran through the hair of the man who prostrated himself before her. She breathed in of the air, dank and fetid as it was. She smelled the rank water that festered in the bottom of the grotto in which they had gathered.

The rocky sides of the steep-sided gully climbed about them. Ferns smothered it, hiding the treacherous paths down to this point. Above the sloping banks, tall pines grew and cast their shadows down as though from

273

a great height. Everywhere was mold and slime and fungus. Everything was damp. Ever the slow drip of water sounded, falling off leaf and stem and stone.

She breathed in of the air, and loved it. This was her natural haunt, a wild thing of magic at home where others dreaded to walk. And it was dark, dark as night even though the noonday sun shone on the world above. Oh yes. She shivered as she sensed it all. A dark place for dark magic, and she had the darkest at her command.

Tonight, she would invoke it.

Her hands ceased moving through the man's hair. "You shall be rewarded," she promised sweetly.

Slowly, the acolyte looked up.

Ginsar knelt and favored him with a kiss to the forehead. "You shall be rewarded, and will never need fear delivering bad news again."

She laid her hands firmly upon his head. A moment he looked at her, confused by what she had said, and then her hands stiffened.

The acolyte convulsed. His limbs thrashed and trembled. His fingers clawed the earth, ripping at dirt and stone. Foam appeared at his mouth and sprayed down to his chest. His eyes, filled with a wild fear, rolled in their sockets so that only the whites showed. But as swiftly as it all began, it ceased.

Ginsar withdrew her hands, and the man slumped to the ground and was still.

But he was not dead. One finger twitched ever so slightly. His eyes flickered behind the now-closed lids, and his chest rose and fell with breath.

With a fierce light in her gaze and a triumphant smile upon her face, Ginsar stood and looked around at the coven.

"He shall sleep until tonight," she told them. "And then you shall see the power that I have. You shall see, and the people of Cardoroth shall tremble in their sleep!"

9. A Glint in their Eye

Gil crept toward the door. He did not want to alert the assassin's accomplice that he was coming, but he could lose no time either. The accomplice would have heard the sword-fighting stop, but he would not know for certain who had won. Momentarily, there would be doubt. But the longer things went on the warier he would grow, because if the assassin had won he would swiftly make his escape.

With a chair in one hand, and the sword in his other, it would be hard to open the door. But he found that he could still use his sword hand to get a grip on the doorknob. There he paused, listening. All he heard though was the rush of blood in his own ears. There was nothing else.

He steadied himself for what was to come. This much at least he knew: he would not wait and cower. It was better to face his enemy, and if need be, sell his life dearly if it came to that.

He held high the chair and flung the door open. Swiftly, he dashed into the corridor, weaving as he moved rather than following a straight line and presenting an easy target.

His head snapped left and then right, but there was no one in the corridor. The accomplice had fled, no doubt hearing the fight within the room and fearing discovery.

Slowly, Gil put down the chair. He realized that his heart thudded in his chest and he felt dizzy. With a groan, he leaned back against the corridor wall. His heart slowed a little, but the dizziness did not improve. Then his body began to tremble.

Making sure once more that the corridor was truly empty, he slid his back down the wall until he was sitting. The trembling grew worse, and he gripped hard the hilt of the sword.

He knew he was lucky. Lucky to survive the first fight and lucky not to have to fight again. He breathed a long sigh of relief, but at just that moment he heard the rush of feet. There were several people at least. He staggered upright, still using the wall to support himself, and lifted his sword. If he were to die, he would die as a man.

Even as he fought to stay upright on trembling legs, the newcomers turned around the corridor to his left. They saw him straightaway, and they stopped. It was several Durlin, and Shorty and Taingern were at their head.

One look they gave him, assessing the situation in a glance. These were hard men. They saw the blood on his sword and knew he had survived an assassination attempt, survived it by himself. This was an achievement that took both courage and skill, and he saw recognition of that in their eyes. He was no longer a boy to them, and his pride soared.

The moment passed. In the next few seconds they were all around him and moving into the room to ensure no attackers were nearby.

"How did you know?" he asked Shorty.

The Durlindrath studied him a moment, making sure he was not wounded, then he answered.

"You have Elrika to thank for that. She ran into us, and hearing that you were safe and had returned from

277

the forest she wanted to see you. We told her where you were. But when she got here she saw a strange man at guard at the door, and she began to worry. She came and got us. And we knew there was something badly wrong."

At that moment there was the sound of more rushing steps. It was Elrika herself, and she had fetched a knife that she held before her. She saw them all and paused. Her face was grim and her eyes flashed, and then she saw Gil. She looked at him, and then ran over.

They hugged fiercely, and Gil saw out of the corner of his eye Shorty and Taingern exchange a glance. Shorty winked at his friend, and Taingern raised an eyebrow. Gil ignored it all.

One of the Durlin came out of the regent's bedroom. "There's an assassin in there. A warrior by the looks of him. He's dead. And so is Rhodeurl, slain by an arrow."

Once more he felt the eyes of the Durlin on him. He had survived when their highly-trained comrade had not, and they knew that he either had great luck or had fought with skill and courage.

A Durlin came out of the room next to the regent's. "Parviel was killed and his body hidden in there, an arrow in his back."

The words were simple enough, but Gil knew that the two Durlin had died for him. They had survived Ginsar and the collapse of the cave only for this. He felt grief wash over him, and with it came guilt.

"Retrieve the bodies," Taingern said softly, "and bring them to the chapterhouse. We'll commence the funerary rites. They were good men, and we'll honor them as best we can."

"What of the other man?" Gil asked. "We can't let the accomplice get away."

278

"He's gone, Gil. But one way or another we'll find him. That much I promise. He must have fled as soon as he saw Elrika, guessing that she was fetching help."

10. Then You Must Go

Shorty and Taingern looked at him speculatively, and Gil was not quite sure why. Elrika was no longer hugging him, but she was standing very close.

Taingern was the one who broached the subject. "This is the first time you've ever killed anybody. It can be a difficult thing to come to grips with. Let us know if you would like to talk things over."

Gil thought about the assassin lying dead in the room just beside them, and he shuddered. It could just as easily be him in there.

"That man came to kill me, and he *would* have if I didn't kill him instead. He got what he deserved, and his death was his own fault."

"Perfectly true," Taingern agreed. "You had no choice, and what you did was right. Even so, that does not always help. Especially the first time. You may still experience feelings of guilt. You may wonder if you could have disarmed him instead. Your mind will throw it back at you again and again, and in different ways. There's a logical side to this … and an emotional one. They don't always match."

Gil felt Elrika's hand in his own, and he sensed she was worried for him. "So what's the solution to that?" he asked.

"Ah, Gil. There *is* no solution. But what helps you deal with it is this. Accept both sides of things. Yes, you did what you had to do. And yes, it will throw up emotional turmoil in your mind. Accept that both are valid, and in time you will move on."

It was an interesting perspective, and Gil liked it. "You know, you sounded a lot like Brand just then."

Taingern looked away, his thoughts seemingly elsewhere, but he answered promptly.

"Who was it, do you think, that years ago gave me the same advice?"

Gil paid close attention to Taingern's advice. The Durlindrath had been through life-and-death struggles worse than this several times. He had struggled to live against someone who sought his death, and no one knew what that was like unless they had been there. And Taingern was right. It was fitting to fight for your life, there was nothing wrong with it, but surviving still came at a cost.

Elrika slid the knife she carried through her belt. "I wish I'd had a sword. I could have helped you."

Shorty glanced hard at her for a moment, but he seemed to be remembering something rather than looking at her.

"I think the two of you should stay close for a while," he said. "And I think, Elrika, that you should carry a sword. You're a skilled fighter, and it never hurts to be prepared."

Gil liked the sound of that, and he knew he could trust her as well. And she really was skilled with a blade.

"Here," he said. "Take this one. It has a good feel and balance. I think you'll like it."

With a sure grip Elrika took the blade, looking at it curiously. "It does feel good, but it's an expensive weapon, better than anything I've used before."

The two Durlindraths exchanged a look.

281

"It's a fine blade indeed," Shorty said. "A princely gift, and it has a history that I'm guessing neither of you know."

Gil shook his head. "I just grabbed it from the wall when I needed it."

"It was given," Shorty said, "by the first king of Cardoroth to one of his sons. See the three stars engraved at the top of the blade? That signifies it was given to the third son. There were seven sons, and seven blades were given."

The history of the first king was coming back to Gil now. He had heard of those seven sons before.

"There were seven sons," he said. "Seven princes. But they were more than that. They were the first Durlin. They protected their father, and when he was attacked three died defending him."

"Exactly so," Taingern said. "But there is more."

There *was* more, and Gil remembered it. He softly intoned the Durlin creed:

Tum del conar – El dar tum!
Death or infamy – I choose death!

He turned to Elrika, but she spoke first. "I too know the history of the Durlin. It was the third son who spoke those words. He was one of the three who died."

She gazed at the sword in her hand, holding it now with reverence. Then she offered the hilt to Gil. "I have to give it back. This is too good a sword … there's too much history that comes with it. I'm just a baker's daughter."

Shorty and Taingern exchanged another look, and they seemed to reach an agreement.

"Take the sword, Elrika," Taingern encouraged. "It was a well-given gift, and you've earned it. I do not think that he who once bore it would be displeased. Nor would Brand. He thinks you would make a good Durlin. And we agree."

Gil sensed that something else was going on here. Somewhere deep in his mind he also had a feeling that this was meant to happen.

Elrika took the sword. "Tum del conar – El dar tum," she whispered.

"Thank you," Gil said to Shorty and Taingern. He looked around at the other Durlin. "Thank you all."

The Durlin bowed formally to him, a gesture he had not seen before from them.

"Walk with me, please," he said to Elrika.

They moved away, and several of the Durlin followed, silent and inscrutable as always. Gil did not travel far, though. They came to his room, and once there the Durlin entered first and searched it thoroughly before allowing the two of them to go inside.

His room was not as grand as the regent's, but it was nice enough and he saw Elrika study it. He offered her a chair near the window, and took one himself.

"I have learned something," he said. "At least I think I have."

He proceeded to tell her what he had found in Carnhaina's diary. He spoke of the section where she mentioned the four Riders, the gateways and the powers that form and substance the world. He repeated what she had written about those powers seeking balance, that if evil is born, so too is good and that it shall rise amid the shadows. He spoke of how she had said to look for it, for it was the key.

"But she said in none of this *where* to look," Elrika guessed.

"No, not at all. But then there was a drawing, a drawing of the Tower of Halathgar and the trapdoor at its bottom. I felt strongly then that that was where I had to go. But now, the feeling has passed. I'm not sure anymore."

"Well," she answered, "you must go anyway. Trust to your original instinct."

"But it was just a drawing … just a feeling."

"Trust your feelings, Gil. They're usually good."

He looked at her, suddenly glad that in all the world he had found her for a friend. And maybe his instincts were good, as she said. At any rate, he had nothing else to act on. This was a start, but it nagged at him that he could be wasting precious time.

11. Before Cardoroth

Night had fallen. Stars gleamed in the shadow-draped sky. Among them, bright Halathgar. The two-star constellation shimmed in the void, like eyes through a silken veil.

Closer to earth, a breeze blew. It bent the tops of the tall pines. In the boughs of those same trees crows roosted, and they cawed and croaked restlessly.

Gil had seen it all before. He had been here previously, and now as then he felt odd, for this was an odd place. Even the pale marks on his hand itched, as though the light from Halathgar woke something within him.

And, just as before, the Tower of Halathgar rose into the night. It seemed mysterious, all curves and crenellations, lit by starlight yet still shadowed by the night. It was a place of secrets, a place where secrets were revealed, and a place of death, for the great queen herself rested in her sarcophagus upon the pinnacle.

The Tower of Halathgar was also a lodestone for rumor. Stories were legion. It was a focal point of legend, even a relic of the ancient past amid the modern city, surrounded by living, breathing people and the hustle of a large population, and yet it remained remote as though its thousand-year history formed an unbroachable barrier all about it.

"It's as ugly as a pig with the pox," Shorty stated.

Taingern did not answer. He looked at the tower, stony-faced and grim. Gil did not say anything either, but he recognized Shorty's reaction. It was the time-honored warrior's way of reliving tension – make a joke. He wondered what Elrika would have thought, but she was not allowed to come. She was not yet a Durlin.

They approached the tower. Two guards stood there, uniformed in the livery of soldiers of Cardoroth. They watched closely, hands near the hilt of their swords, as the group drew close to them, and then there was recognition in their eyes. They bowed to Gil and saluted Shorty and Taingern.

"We need to go inside," Taingern said.

"Of course," one of the guards answered.

Quickly, the door was unlocked and opened. The group passed through. One of the soldiers gave Shorty a burning torch.

"Good luck in there," he said.

"Thanks. We may need it."

The door was closed behind them. They stood still a while, waiting for their eyes to adjust. Gil felt his heart thud, just as it had last time he came here. Shorty and Taingern gave no sign of nerves, but Gil knew they felt them all the same. They would normally have spoken with the soldiers and made them feel appreciated, but outside conversation had been minimal. They had other things on their mind.

Gil looked around. Ahead, the spiral staircase commenced the long wind to the top of the tower. He knew what lay there upon the pinnacle beneath the starlit sky. The trapdoor was another matter though. What was below it? How long had it been since anyone had ventured through?

"There it is," Gil said.

The others did not answer. Nor did they make a move toward it. It was visible now, a single plank of ancient wood, dust covered but set neatly within the floor. A long-rusted iron ring stood out from its center.

"Let's get this over with," Shorty said after a moment.

Taingern grinned at him. "One more adventure," he answered. "And think of it. Even Brand has not gone where we go now. He would be jealous!"

"There's truth in that." Shorty lifted the torch higher so it threw better light at the trapdoor. Taingern bent and took a grip of the iron ring. With a heave, he lifted the plank.

Dust filled the air as the trapdoor came free. Taingern lifted it clear easily, for though it was made of hardwood it was thin and relatively light. He placed it down again beside the opening that was now revealed.

Shorty stepped closer. The light from the torch flickered and wavered. It did little to illuminate things, but they could see enough. A vertical shaft lay before them, disappearing into blackness. There were wooden stairs too. These were more like wide ladder treads than stairs, but they spiraled down, disappearing into the blackness.

"I'll go first and test out the timber," Shorty offered, handing the torch to Taingern. "I'm light and nimble."

It was true, Gil knew, but he was lighter still. Shorty was trying to protect him, which was strange because there were no assassins here. Then again, none of them knew what other dangers there might be.

With sure but careful movements Shorty lowered himself into the shaft. Then he rested his weight on each tread gradually, testing them out one by one.

"So far so good," he said. "They feel quite solid."

Down he went, until his head was now below the level of the trapdoor and he could see the staircase properly.

"It's all good. Very solid and soundly made. I think you can start to follow me down."

Taingern gestured with his hand. "You first, Gil."

It was yet another indication that his two protectors were nervous about what was down here. There would be one ahead of him and one behind in case of trouble. But Gil did not argue.

He moved down, quicker than Shorty had started for now they knew the stairway was sound. But he still moved carefully.

Below he could see Shorty, but the light was not strong. Still, the Durlindrath seemed to be moving quite quickly now, confident that the timber would not give way.

Light flickered and dust floated through the air as Taingern also entered the shaft. The smell of smoke from the torch grew stronger, but Gil was glad of it. This was not a place he wanted to be in the dark.

The shaft did not continue long. Soon, the ladder-like stairway brought them to a flat section of ground. They could not see much, but the shaft widened somewhat and plunged ahead, horizontally this time, into the dark.

They moved forward. The ground before them was covered deep by dust, but there were tracks there of at least one person.

"Did you explore ahead?" Taingern asked.

"No," Shorty answered. "They're not mine."

Gil was surprised, even alarmed. "Who else could have come here? Do you think they might be somewhere ahead?"

Shorty shook his head. "I don't think so. It's hard to tell, but those tracks could be weeks old. Maybe even years or centuries. Who can say? I get the feeling that nothing much changes down here, and there's no breeze to blow dust to cover any marks. For all I know, they might be the tracks of Carnhaina herself."

That was something that Gil had not realized. This place was ancient, and there was nothing to mark the passage of years or obliterate tracks. Perhaps, in a hundred years or so, someone would one day look at their own tracks and wonder who had made them and why.

They moved forward. It was hard to tell distances in the dim light, and their slow passage did not help. Gil felt a sense of timelessness as well, which was disorientating, but they had moved well away from the tower.

After perhaps a hundred feet they came to a door. It was made of wood, but either it was constructed of a different kind than the trapdoor or there was more moisture in the air here, because it was falling apart. Some of the boards that made it up had holes in them, and it sat at an angle on one hinge, part way open.

Very carefully, Shorty moved it. Several chunks of rotted timber fell away like moldy dust, but it stayed on the one hinge that supported it. Now, there was a big enough gap to pass through. Shorty did not hesitate.

The corridor widened from this point. Rugs covered the floor, or at least what was left of them. They were nearly rotted away. The walls were also covered. Tapestries hung there, and these were in better condition than the rugs. Some had fallen, and some were mold and lichen crusted, but many were still in fair condition.

289

The air was stale and unpleasant. It stank of rot. None of this stopped Shorty though. He moved forward, his head turning from side to side as he went, looking at the relics of the past or, more likely, checking for dangers.

Gil and Taingern followed. They did not speak, for this was not the kind of place for conversation. It was best to follow Shorty's example and move ahead slowly and cautiously.

They were further away from the tower now, perhaps somewhere under city buildings or beneath the tree-filled park near the tower.

Shorty slowed. "It's another door," he whispered.

This one was better preserved, though Gil could not understand why. It seemed to be made just as the previous one had been. The only difference was that this one had strange symbols carved into it.

"Do you recognize any of those marks?" Taingern asked.

"No, I've never seen them before."

"Does it look like it could be lòhrengai of some sort?"

"No, I don't think so. I've never heard of lòhrens using writing in their magic. At least, Brand never taught me anything like it. Some will speak in the Halathrin language when they invoke power … but this is not Halathrin script."

"No matter," Taingern said. "I just have a feeling that there is magic of some sort here, or at least there once was."

Gil had the same feeling. It might explain why the door was better preserved. Some power might still linger here. He could seek it out and find it with his own, but that might wake it from dormancy and it was best to leave things just as they were.

Shorty opened the door. The hinges still worked, but dust filled the air. As they moved through, Gil saw that within the carved symbols was the remnant of color. Once, they had been painted. Were they meant to stand out, perhaps as a warning of some kind?

They went into the chamber beyond. This was a square, and ancient benches lined the walls. People had gathered here for some purpose, or waited. The benches were once solid, but rot had set into them. Gil ran his finger along one, and chunks of timber disintegrated at his touch. Why had the door not rotted in the same way?

Ahead, another staircase began. They went to it and commenced to descend once more. Deeper into the earth they went, and it was hard to know just how far underground they now were. There was no noise save for what they made themselves, and this they tried not to do.

It was silent. The air itself seemed oppressive, though it was neither hot nor cold. There was no life here, not even insects seemed to survive in the century-old darkness. And then, without any warning, the surroundings changed.

Shorty paused. He looked around. "This is no longer a part of the tower," he said softly. "We're now in a natural tunnel."

"I think much of what we've passed through since coming down the trapdoor was built *before* the tower," Taingern suggested. He brushed off a layer of fine dust that had settled on his hand from the torch. "But this is older still."

It was an interesting thought, but one that Gil found disturbing. It raised a question for which he had no answer. The tower was old, dating back near to the foundation of the city. How then could there be man-made tunnels beneath it that were older? And if they were, who built them?

His mind moved back to the symbols on the door. He had never seen them before, nor their like. Perhaps that was because they had not been inscribed by his people at all, but by someone who lived here before the Camar settled these lands. If so, who were they? And why did they build these tunnels in the rock?

There were no answers, and they moved ahead. But they did not go far before Gil glimpsed something that disturbed him again.

"Look," he said, and pointed to the wall on their left.

Taingern moved the torch closer, and what Gil had glimpsed was revealed in full. There were more symbols there, this time carved into the stone.

"It's not like anything that I've seen before," Shorty said.

"Nor me," Taingern agreed.

Gil studied them closely. "I don't think it's the same as what was on the door. It looks different."

Taingern peered at the marks. "I think you're right. This is something else again."

"It's almost…" Gil hesitated, not quite sure if he were right. "It's almost like writing."

The torch gutted, and then it flared brighter. He saw more clearly now. "I'm sure of it. It's writing."

"It's not Camar though," Taingern said. "It's nothing like it."

"No," Gil answered. "But it's writing, and I think I now know who did it."

They turned to him, and in the flickering light he saw the curiosity in their eyes.

"Once," he said, "there was a race of people who held dominion over the land. It was long ago. None of the books I've ever read could say exactly when their empire began or when it ended, but it was long before the Camar came east. Long, long before that. Have you heard of them?"

Shorty nodded slowly. "I have. There are a few tales told about them by bards. It's hard to know what's true and what isn't."

"I too have heard of them," Taingern said. "Brand knows more than us, and he has spoken of them occasionally."

Gil was glad that they knew. His theory made sense, and it seemed possible, even likely, that Cardoroth was founded on the same place that some of the Letharn had chosen to live, that ancient race that once ruled much of Alithoras. But it did not answer the question of what this place was, and what they used it for.

"Best to keep going," Shorty said. "Letharn or not, these corridors lead somewhere, and it can't be much further."

They walked forward, and Shorty was proven correct within another twenty or so paces.

The torchlight fluttered once again. It went dark, and then as the light sprang up brighter a kind of portal was revealed, and a stele before it.

The portal was triangular in shape. Beyond was darkness. Before the portal the stele stood, squat and ugly. This was what drew Gil's attention. It was as tall as a man, but wider than it was high. Each of its four faces was inscribed with the same writing they had seen earlier.

He went over to look, and the others followed. The marks on the stone were easy to see here. They were a series of dots, slashes and half circles, obviously writing but different from anything he had ever seen before.

Gil was fascinated. The stele had an ancient and brooding presence. And though the script was clear, the stone was very, very old. It even showed signs of weathering, by rain or wind. Neither was possible in its present location. He walked around it to see what was on the other faces. All of them were inscribed, but on the one nearest the portal there were two sets of inscriptions: the top in the same script as the rest, and the bottom, much to Gil's surprise, in ancient Camar.

He could read it. He had learned this older version of Cardoroth's present language. He supposed that Shorty and Taingern could work their way through it as well, but not as fluently as he could. He read it out for them, his voice soft, but the hollow chamber took his words and hissed them back at him.

Attend! We are masters of the world. We possess the wealth of nations. Gold adorns our hands; priceless jewels our brows; bright are our swords. The world shudders when we march! But heed well that other powers are older and greater than we. Herein is one. He that is with power may invoke it. If he dares.

12. Filled with Terror

Night fell over the grotto and Ginsar grew excited. Moths flittered through the air, and the bats that hunted them wheeled and spun after their prey. But for all that death, for all that movement, it was silent. It seemed unnatural, and then even the moths and bats disappeared, taking their deadly game elsewhere. The grotto was still. At a signal from her, the acolytes stood and filed toward where she stood from their place of rest.

She waited. No words were spoken. None were needed. They had all seen this before.

She began to chant. It was soft at first, drawing forth the power that rested dormant within her, but also seeking out and joining to it the power that slumbered in the surrounding earth and air. Her voice became one with the night. It was a dark thing, full of the unexpected, imbued with the watchfulness of prey and the stealth of the hunter.

At her feet, the chosen acolyte stirred. He could not move nor speak, but his eyes rolled in their sockets. He too knew what was to come. There was horror in his eyes and the twist of his mouth, and tears streamed down his face. He saw his death in her gaze, and that he was powerless to prevent it fueled his terror.

Ginsar looked upon him, and his dread uplifted her. She fed upon it, making it one with her chanting and the dark night. Her heart swelled, and the power within her waxed greater.

Her chanting grew louder, filling the grotto and reverberating through the stone banks that bulked all about them in the dark. It snaked up the trunks of the tall pines, and their long leaves shivered in the starlight like a million daggers.

The acolytes drew closer, eager to see what was to come. Glee was on their faces and malice in their hearts. It could have been them, but it was *him* instead, and they liked that.

A cloud drifted across the sky, blocking out the stars and plunging the grotto into darkness so profound that it seemed impossible light could ever have existed. She snapped her fingers and one of the acolytes lit a torch that spluttered to life with ruddy light. The dark was good, but better still to see the transformation she would now work, and the sorcery that gave it life.

Ginsar's chanting rose to a crescendo, and then it ceased with the abruptness of a knife cut. In the sudden silence she reached out and placed a hand upon her chosen sacrifice. Then her hand slowly lifted, and the acolyte rose up before her as though pulled by an invisible rope.

Slowly, as though she had all eternity for the action, she reached to her side and drew a knife from her robe. It was a wicked looking blade, curved like a sickle moon and etched with runes that gleamed amid the dark with eldritch light. It felt good in her hand.

The acolyte's mouth worked soundlessly. Gently, she touched his head. In response, he tilted it back and exposed his throat. Almost lovingly, she caressed the flesh with the knife. A thin red line appeared. Then blood beaded and trickled down his pale skin.

The man's eyes bulged. There was pleading in them. She drank that in and cut deeper. Blood spurted now. Red, vivid, intoxicating to her as wine.

Ginsar shuddered. The knife slid a little deeper, and a crimson spray erupted from the pulsing artery. Slowly, she pushed the man down to the ground. He could not resist. There she had set a small basin of metal. It was dark and empty. Soon though, it filled with the acolyte's life-blood. Spasms jerked his body, and then he slumped fully to the ground. The blood ceased to spray as his heart stilled.

She ignored the dead body. What mattered now was the blood in the basin. She studied it, marveling at the sheen on its surface and the strange play of light that gleamed and glistened as the swirling fluid congealed.

13. A Past Age

Gil knew that it was time he took the lead. This was his quest, given him by Carnhaina herself, and he would follow it. Now, it led him toward the triangular portal, and he moved forward.

Shorty made to step in front of him, but Gil placed a hand on his shoulder.

"Not this time, my friend. The time has come for me to grow up."

Shorty hesitated. "So be it. But be careful. We don't know what's down there."

Beyond the portal Gil discovered a natural cave. There was nothing man-made about it at all. The floor dipped and rose, the walls were irregular and the flickering light of the torch cast many-angled shadows. From the domed roof grew stalactites, wet with moisture and gleaming yellow-white from the torch light. And here and there on the ground rose stalagmites like the arms of dead men spearing up from the earth.

The cave was eerie and disconcerting, but there was something else that disturbed Gil even more. The city was somewhere above them, no more than a hundred feet or so away, but this was another world and it was entirely remote and alien from anything he knew. And there was *power* here.

Now, he must cast forth his own and discover it. He must find its source, for that was why they had come. He signaled the others to stand still and then allowed the lòhrengai within him to stir, to reach out and seek what was in the cave.

His senses became far more acute, and he heard the drip of water from somewhere nearby and his eyes pierced the gloom beyond the reach of the torch light.

Straightaway, he found the source of power that filled the cave, and his eyes locked upon it. He could see it, yet he did not think the others could. He moved forward again, cautiously, and the two Durlindraths stayed close at his side.

In the center of the domed cave lay a small basin, about the size of a long stride. It had been delved into the stone by the hand of man, or at least someone at some time had taken what nature provided and evened out its shape.

The stone of the basin was dark, and its rounded lip polished to a gleam all about its perimeter. Within, lay a sheet of water, impossibly still as though caught out of time. Nothing moved within it, nor caused its surface to break. Yet reflected from its mirror-like surface was all the ceiling of the cave, the glint of long-pointed stalactites and the shadow-pocked surface of the cave roof. But from deep within, light stirred and ebbed, reacting to the flicker of torch light.

"It's a scry basin," whispered Gil to the others. They studied it, but did not answer.

Brand had once told him of them, and Gil had read of them also. They were a thing of ill-name, for sorcerers used them. Ginsar, he recalled, had one. But this was not of that kind. There was no sacrifice here, no blood nor residue of evil.

Gil looked up. Directly above the basin was a stalactite. It gleamed with moisture, and at its dagger-like

299

tip a single drop of water hung suspended. It was this that fed the basin, though it was impossible to say how often that drop fell. It might be poised there for hours or even days before it fell.

Gil sensed the age of the thing. Old, old as time. The basin had lain here since before the Camar, since before the Letharn. It had begun to fill when the world was young, and the power of magic that coursed through the earth was strong within it: ùhrengai, the primordial force whence the sorcery of elùgai and the enchantment of lòhrengai both sprung.

But that was not the only power that hung in the air. All about him Gil now sensed the remnants from once-mighty spells of a past age. The feel of the magic was not quite like his own, but he recognized it. It reminded him of Brand's staff, the one that the great lòhren Aranloth had given him.

Clearly, Carnhaina had discovered this place and she had used it. He felt the residue of her power also, somewhere between sorcery and enchantment. This was why her tower was built where it was, to allow access to the basin and to hide it.

And that sparked a question. Carnhaina had used it, but could he? Did he have the power? And if he did, what might he learn to give direction to his quest?

14. A Red Mist

The eyes of the dead acolyte glinted. Ginsar ignored them. With a flick of her knife she deepened the wound in his neck, and a last trickle of blood dribbled into the basin.

Ginsar breathed in of the night air. Life felt good, and power coursed through her. She suddenly laughed with the joy of it, and then sobered quickly. There was more work yet to do.

Gently, reverently, she removed the basin and allowed the corpse to settle to the ground. She sensed the eyes of the acolytes upon her, watching wide-eyed with anticipation. They knew what came next, for they had seen it before.

Ignoring the coven, she studied the basin. The life-blood within it had already begun to thicken. Carefully, she stirred it with the blade of her knife. But her deft movements were not random. She shaped runes with each cut and stroke of the blade. Letters formed, and then dissolved back into the blood. But the power she drew forth remained, and slowly grew.

In the grotto, the air began to turn cool. An icy breeze stirred, sucking heat from those gathered there, and they pulled their cloaks tightly about them. Above, the dim tops of the pine trees were still.

Ginsar began to mutter as her blade moved through the blood. Her words were harsh and guttural, and as she spoke them she heard in her mind her master utter them also. Shurilgar had taught her what to say, and his voice resonated now with her own.

She chanted louder now, no longer muttering but fiercely casting the words into the air. The blade in her hand grew hot to touch, and a sudden wind roared to life and flew through the grotto. Now, the tops of the pines began to lurch and sway. The wind howled among the trunks, and in the grotto the hollows between stones screeched and groaned.

And then there was more. There was a voice, and Ginsar felt the touch of something otherworldly on her mind.

"Come!" she commanded. "Come hither. You are called!"

Steam, red-tinged and ethereal, rose from the basin of blood. The wind took it and dashed it madly into the air. The voice answered, cold and remote.

"I come, Ginsar. I come, and your world shall tremble."

The blood in the basin thickened. The knife now stirred it with great difficulty. Steam continued to rise from it, but the wind no longer dashed it away. It formed around Ginsar like a cloak.

The wind died. The trees stilled. The moaning from the rocks ceased, and the steam churned. Mist-like, it swirled through the air, flowing around Ginsar, twining about her limbs and caressing her face.

She trembled at its touch, feeling the power that she summoned, breathing it in and exhaling it, becoming one with it.

The acolytes fell to the ground, awed by what she had done, fearful of the dread power that had come among them. Even Ginsar felt a twinge of panic, for she sensed the hunger of the spirit she had summoned. Her body would serve as host better than the one she had prepared for that purpose, and the spirit-thing sensed it too. It probed her, tested the strength of her sorcery and the vigor of her mind.

Her heart thrashed in her chest. Goosebumps formed on her skin, and the muscles of her body tensed like cords of iron. She flung the congealed blood from the basin down onto the dead acolyte.

Blood must follow blood, and the summoning must leave her and enter the corpse. She felt its resistance to the pull, and then with a last caress it left her and sped like an arrow into the dead acolyte.

The red mist clung to him. It knifed into his flesh, and his head jerked back. His body twitched and spasmed, then thrashed in wild convulsions.

Ginsar stepped back. The acolytes watched in horrified satisfaction. He who had once been their brother was changing.

The corpse screamed. Its skin tore where muscles bulged. Its eyes popped. Even bones cracked, jagged edges showing before knitting together again in an altered shape.

This was more than Ginsar had expected. The body before her was reshaping, changing and forming into something new. The previous Rider had not done this.

The body stilled. It lay hunched over on the ground. Then a hand reached out, and it levered itself upright. Slowly, it stood. The acolyte was gone, though the robes that once he had borne still clung, ragged and bloody, to the creature that now stood there.

Even Ginsar was horrified. This was more than she had sought, but it was *hers*. Hers to command and use as she pleased. Hers to send against her enemies.

A slow smile spread over her face. How her enemies would fear *this*. Ah, life was sweet. For all who opposed her must soon fall, and her power was growing. She felt it swirl within her now, coursing through her body like the red blood that thrummed in her heart.

15. Knives in his Back

Gil knelt beside the basin. Shorty and Taingern kept close. The water in the pool was still as glass, reflecting all that lay above, but showing nothing of what lay within. It was strange, for it must be only shallow, and he should be able to catch a glimpse of its bottom, but there was nothing. Perhaps it was deeper than it seemed.

He dismissed these thoughts from his mind. What mattered now was what he could do with it.

"Be careful," Taingern said.

Gil nodded, but did not answer. Careful of what? Certainly, there were dangers here. There were dangers wherever great power was concentrated. But he did not know enough about what this place was to know what the dangers were. He would have to find out, bit by bit, as he went. But that was a dangerous process in itself…

He cast his senses out, letting the lòhrengai within him expand, letting it go where it was drawn. But nothing happened. The tendrils of magic probed the basin, felt the age of the stone and the power within the water, and though they were drawn to it, they were rebuffed from the still surface as though it were made of stone.

This was something Gil had never encountered before. He thought a moment, unsure of his next step. Magic was a thing of the mind rather than the body, but that was not working here. Should he touch it?

Unsure, he reached out. Shorty and Taingern tensed beside him. With the deftest movement of a finger, he touched the surface of the water.

He felt nothing unusual. The water was cool to touch, and the reflections within it danced and shivered, but nothing else changed.

Tentatively, he allowed several fingers to break the surface. His lòhrengai reached out from them to plumb the water, but everything seemed muted and he could not detect any change or means by which the power of the pool might be summoned. Was it even a scry basin after all? It was possible that he was missing something obvious, but he could not think of anything.

Had he been wrong to touch the water? A scry basin showed images, and still water was necessary for that. But he had not been able to invoke its power when it was still, and its use as a conduit of visions came not just from the water but also from the power that resided in the soil, rock and air all through the cave.

He lowered his hand deeper into the basin. Strangely, he felt no bottom. Reaching down further, he slid in his arm until it was elbow deep.

He felt foolish, and he knew Shorty and Taingern were watching him, wondering what he was doing and if he had sufficient skill to invoke the magic that was bound to this place. He tried yet again to send tendrils of lòhrengai from his fingers, but his probing remained muted.

The water was different to his touch though. Once he was below the surface layer, it turned blood warm. It felt pleasant, and the mark on his palm tingled. Yet still, nothing happened. It was as though he were trying to run over ice. He could gain no traction, and nothing was

306

working. Everything he was doing was wrong, but why? His lòhrengai should be able to join with the existing lòhrengai that the ancient Letharn had created. He should be able to join with it, and then activate it. Why could he not do that simple thing?

The answer came to him, and he withdrew his arm from the water and looked up at his companions.

"I've been a fool. I knew I was missing something obvious."

"We all do, lad, from time to time. Have you worked out now how it works?"

"I have. I was trying to use lòhrengai to invoke the power here. But this isn't lòhrengai. It's ùhrengai, the primordial power from which both lòhrengai and elùgai derive. This scry basin was made before those terms meant anything. The power here is primitive. It's not invoked and turned toward a purpose ... it's unleashed, for want of a better word. Watch now, but be careful for I have no real control over what will happen."

Gil dipped his hand into the water once more. He did not bother to send out his lòhrengai into it, rather he felt the ùhrengai and allowed it to enter him.

He swirled his hand in the water, and he felt the primordial powers that formed and substanced the world gather into the vortex of the water. His senses ventured into it, not trying to control or bring order, but just to become one with it.

His palm tingled and the water grew heavy. He did not swirl it fast nor slow, but gradually increased the speed until the vortex increased. He was one with it, swirling with it, and then, slowly, the greater power that infused the whole cave began to ebb and flow, twisting through the air as though one with the water. And Gil was in the center of both forces, the conduit for powers ancient as the rocks of the earth itself.

He felt giddy, as though his mind also spun. But he did not fight it. He allowed it all into him, and he became the water, the air and the rock. He was here now in the present, but he felt that he was also falling, falling deep into the past as well. Everything was one, and he was one with everything.

The water in the basin seethed and steamed, and he withdrew his hand. Sparks dripped from his fingers. He ignored them, ignored the steam and watched the water carefully.

The steam subsided. It seemed now that the water was still and the cave swirled about him. He continued to watch, and in the water lights flickered and images formed.

Shorty and Taingern did not move, but the breath hissed from their mouths. A grotto appeared in the water, dark and gloom-filled. Tall pines shadowed it. The rock was slick with moisture and ferns grew from cracks and crevices.

The vision was black as midnight, but a sickly glow spread from its center. Ginsar stood there, tall and terrible. He would know her anywhere. About her were gathered her acolytes. They had prostrated themselves before their mistress, but one of their number rose from where he had lain at her feet.

The figure stood. His every movement was lithe and graceful. He seemed young and lively, though there was a broody darkness to his eyes that spoke of long years of discontent. Golden hair spilled down around his shoulders. He turned a little, looking around him, and Gil gasped.

Sticking from the man's back were knives. They were lodged deep, seeming a part of him, for they moved when he moved. And blood dripped from each wound, trickling down the back of his cloak.

Gil remembered Carnhaina's warning. This was not a man, but another Rider.

"Betrayal," he whispered.

Taingern and Shorty drew their blades, as though ready to strike. He held up a hand to them.

"Watch. And do not touch the water!"

Gil studied the Rider. There was as yet no horse, but he knew that would come. As though from a great distance, he began to sense more about the thing that had been summoned.

It now inhabited the body of one of the acolytes, but there was more than that. Gil felt also a sense of opening, a passageway between worlds. He could not see it, but he intuited it was there. It loomed like a gaping hole in something that was once solid, and he wondered that Ginsar evidenced no sense that it existed. That it had been created, she must know, but that it had failed to close completely she seemed unaware.

Carnhaina was right. Other things sought to enter beside the Rider that had been summoned. He felt their shadowy presence, and fear rose within him.

The water of the scry basin shimmered. It seemed that the darkness of the grotto grew, and then suddenly there was a shiver of light and he looked upon a different scene.

A face came into focus. An old face. A woman's face. Her nut-brown face crinkled in what might have been an irritated expression. Her rheumy eyes glanced around as though seeking something unseen. About her shoulders was a threadbare shawl, and her short, coarse hair was lank. The sun-beaten skin of her brow furrowed, and suddenly her glance focused on Gil. She was looking straight at him.

She grunted, though there was no sound, and a bony hand waved through the air. Even as she moved, the scry basin hissed and spat water. Gil caught a glimpse of another face, this one young and beautiful but strangely serene. Then the water returned to its glass-like state. The visions had ceased.

Shorty broke the silence. "The seer!" he hissed.

"Who was the man?" Taingern asked.

"The man," answered Gil, "was one of the Riders that Carnhaina foretold. Betrayal. She warned of his coming. But I don't know the others."

"The old lady was a seer," Shorty told him. "Brand has met her. She's famous, but very cantankerous. She lives outside the West Gate."

"And what of the young girl?" Gil said.

The others knew nothing of her, but it was her that intrigued Gil the most. How could such a young face appear so tranquil, so wise and at peace with the world? There was a mystery there, and he hoped to unravel it.

Shorty must have seen the curiosity on his face. "Time will tell, lad. It always does. One day you shall know who she is, but likely enough she will prove to be nothing like what you're expecting. It's always the way."

What Shorty said was true, and Gil knew it. "You're right. So, let's concentrate on what we *do* know. This much seems clear at any rate … Ginsar has summoned the second Rider. At least, if the basin showed the present rather than the future. He will come against us. And that is likely to be soon. What else have we learned?"

310

"The seer has a true gift," Taingern answered. "It may be that she can help us. We should seek her out."

"Oh, she has power alright," Gil said. "She knew she was being watched, and she didn't like it. Not only did she discern the magic of the scry basin, but she dispelled it with great casualness. Not even Ginsar did that."

As soon as Gil spoke though, another thought occurred to him. If the seer knew she was being watched, perhaps Ginsar had as well. She might have allowed him to see what she wanted him to, or even manipulated it in some way. He was not sure if that was possible, and he had no time to think about it.

"And the young lady?" asked Taingern. "What can we deduce about her?"

Gil turned his mind to the question. "Very little," Gil replied. "But the basin does not show images at random. The scry magic is one with the user's mind, and it shows what the user needs to see. Whoever she is, she will prove important by the end. And I think, one way or the other, the seer will lead us to her."

16. All things have their Opposite

They returned to the palace through the quiet streets. It was dark and subdued, for there seemed no revelers. Perhaps it was too late, because the night was nearly done. The gray of dawn had begun to slip through the streets even as did they.

By the time they reached the palace grounds, bright sunlight shone and the sky was brilliant blue. Gil marveled that it could dawn so fine a day when he knew what darkness lay ahead. Betrayal was coming, the second Rider, and evil would follow in his wake.

They were in the grounds now, the gardens all about them. The paving was clean beneath their boots, the grass well clipped and the shrubbery to their left in full flower. Here and there guards patrolled, and he knew that others were stationed in various towers, watching keenly day and night for intruders. Even so, Shorty and Taingern did not let their guard down. They stayed close as they proceeded, their eyes casually assessing everything they saw for signs of danger.

They drew near to the palace. Gil was preoccupied. What would Ginsar do? In what way would the Rider attack them? He did not know any of these things, and that worried him. How could he defend against the unknown? It was troubling, and it also gave him a glimpse into the lives of his grandparents. During their reign, it had been much the same, year after year and decade after decade. The nobility were fools, for they sought to be kings themselves. How swiftly they would tire of the burden!

There was movement in the shadow beneath some trees. Gil had just seen it, but the two Durlindraths who could not have seen it any sooner reacted faster than he would have believed possible. Their blades hissed from their sheaths and they sprang before him.

"You won't need those, boys," a voice said dismissively. "Put them away."

Neither Shorty nor Taingern moved. From beneath the trees a figure emerged into the sunlight. She shuffled forward, seemingly aged and arthritic, leaning on a walking stick. But Gil was not fooled. There was strength in her body yet. He saw it in her eyes.

"Put them down, I say."

The two Durlindraths lowered their weapons, but they did not sheath them.

"I know you, lady," Shorty said. "You are the seer."

"Bah! You know me not at all. And it's better that way. But yes, you can call me that if you like. I don't really care."

"How did you get into these grounds?" Taingern asked.

The old woman fixed him with a rheumy stare, but there was iron in her gaze.

"Who could stop me?"

"There are guards and watchmen everywhere."

"Whoop-de-do!" she cackled. "I walk where I will. At least, wherever these old legs will carry me."

She nimbly hopped on one foot and mimicked using the walking stick to keep her balance. Then she bowed to the Durlindrath. When she straightened, she gazed straight at Gil and all sense of humor was gone from her face.

"Hail, king to be. And well met."

"Greetings, lady." Gil offered her his most eloquent bow.

313

"Ha! I see that Brand has taught you manners. Good for you." She stared at him closely, and he felt that her gaze saw right through him. "And he has taught you more besides. That is clear too."

He knew exactly what she meant. Magic. Though how she could tell, he was not sure. He sensed none about her, but he was willing to bet she possessed great talent.

"You are correct, lady."

She grinned at him impishly. "I'm no lady. If you knew my story ... well, never mind. Call me lady if it pleases you."

"Who are you then?"

"Just an old, old woman."

"And is that all?"

"Is it not enough?"

"Of course," Gil said.

She grinned at him. "I'm a seer also."

"That much, lady, I knew."

She stepped closer to him, and then pinned him once more with her stare.

"Would you like to know your future?"

"Perhaps."

She clapped her hands together, somewhat like a child who is greatly pleased.

"Ah. You are *so* like Brand. He was reluctant too."

"And you told him his?"

"I told him some, but not all. Oh, he is a great one, he is. Yes. And fate has only just begun with him. But now, now is your moment, king to be."

She studied him carefully, and he felt uncomfortable but tried not to show it. She laughed, as though she understood his every thought.

"Then what would you tell me, lady?"

"What would you like to know?" she countered.

Gil was uncertain. He had never met anyone like her.

314

The old woman cackled. "You are not ready, boy. But you have seen much, and there is power in you. Oh yes! My eyes see what others don't. Yes, there is power in you boy. This much I will say. Seek Brand. He will tell you."

"Brand is … ill."

"He is not. He's fine. He withdraws, that is all. His time in Cardoroth is coming to an end. Seek him and learn."

"Is that all you would tell me? What of Carnhaina?"

"Ah. Her quest."

Gil knew then, beyond doubt, that she was a true seer. Very few knew of the quest, and she had no ordinary means to discover anything about it.

"Yes," he said.

"You will be savior. Or you will be destroyer. You will be the Light, or you will be the Dark."

"I will always be of the Light," he said quickly.

She slowly shook her head. "Foolish boy! Stupid. You know so little of the world, but you are learning."

He ignored that. "How shall I close the gateway between worlds that Carnhaina warned of? How shall I fulfill my quest?"

"Oh, you still have so *much* to learn. You? You cannot do it."

Gil straightened. "I must. And I will."

The old woman leaned on her walking stick, and looked at him as though she were seeing him for the first time.

"You know, I see your grandfather in you. Yes, I see it. But you're wrong. You can't do it. You don't have the power. No one does."

"Then you think the world is lost?"

"Did I say that, boy? Listen. You don't have the power. None in Alithoras does. But think of this. Brand has taught you that all things have their opposite, has he not? All forces, once set in motion, have a result. And consequences breed consequences. He will have told you these things, or something like them, yes?"

"He has," Gil agreed.

"He will also have said this. The powers that form and substance the world seek balance. Always. Ceaselessly."

"Yes," he said.

"Then think, boy!"

"On what?"

She raised her walking stick and pointed it at him. "Typical! The young can be so wise and stupid at the same time. They have so much energy, so much time, and are so quick to ask questions instead of think for themselves. Worse, when they are given answers, they believe them. Foolish!"

"I need your help, lady."

"Ha! I'm too old to help. Too old to care. The world can look after itself without me."

"I need you."

"Figure it out yourself, boy. Prove yourself worthy of Carnhaina's trust. But know this. War comes. Armies march. Cardoroth must fight once again if it is to live. Already I hear the battle crows caw."

She tapped a finger to her head, and pulled her shawl higher over her shoulders. Then she hobbled off into the shadows of the trees again. Gil took a few steps after her, but like smoke on the wind she had disappeared.

It was then that he understood. She had never been here at all, not in person at least.

He turned back to Taingern and Shorty. "What would she have me do?"

They studied the shadows where she had disappeared carefully, and then sheathed their blades.

"I have no idea," Taingern answered.

"Nor me," Shorty said.

One thing Gil knew. The seer had not come to him for no purpose. For all her bluster, she had offered help. In her own way perhaps, but help still. Somewhere in her words was the answer he needed.

17. Cardoroth Needs You

"What now?" Shorty asked.

Gil was not sure. The seer had not told him anything that he did not already know, and yet that only meant that the answers to his questions were within his reach, if he could but see clearly.

He realized that was not quite true. She had said that Brand was well. He was not, not at all. And yet what she said was possible. Perhaps he was withdrawing…

"We will see Brand," he said.

"A good place to start," Taingern agreed. "Always, he seems to be at the heart of everything."

They entered the palace. While they walked through the corridors, Gil had more time to think. Just as on the journey back from the forest, the two Durlindraths were letting him lead. He realized now that they wanted to let him feel the pressure of responsibility. That way they would see what he was made of. And he would discover it for himself, too. One day he would lead the realm, and this was their way of getting him used to it, of training him for the job.

He could not blame them. He *should* be tested. If he proved unworthy, then someone else should lead, for trouble was coming. But he would prove to them that he *was* worthy.

The thought occurred to him that in proving to the others that he was ready, he would prove it to himself. This was also part of their plan. And certainly, if he could fulfill the charge that Carnhaina had given him, he would be worthy to lead Cardoroth. Was she also testing him? Was that how life worked? Every step forward, every choice, a test?

They came to the area of the palace set aside for healing. This was Arell's domain, where she offered help to the population of the city, especially those who could not afford it or those that other healers within the city could not help.

They passed through the passageways. On either side of the corridors were rooms with beds. Some were empty, but there were sick people here too. They moved quietly so as not to disturb them. Brand, no doubt, would be close to Arell's office.

They entered the last corridor. A nurse passed by them, busy on some errand, but she smiled at Shorty. Taingern raised an eyebrow.

"You know her?"

Shorty shrugged. "I think she stitched a wound for me, once."

He hurried on, and they quickly came to the last room. It was full of people, the sickest of the sickest, for that way they would be close to Arell, but Brand was not among them.

"Let's try Arell's office," Shorty suggested.

There was one more room at the end of the corridor, but this one had a door. It was closed.

Gil stepped forward and knocked on it.

"Enter," came Arell's voice.

They walked inside. Arell and Brand were seated at a table. Gone was Brand's dazed look, and he seemed acutely alert. He was dressed in fine clothes, but he wore a chainmail hauberk and his Halathrin blade was sheathed at his side. He looked fit and ready to go, ready

319

for anything that life might throw at him. Yet there was a look in his eye that Gil could not interpret. The man had died and been brought back to life. It had changed him in some way, but Gil had no frame of reference to understand how.

The two of them looked at each other, and something passed between them. Gil knew that this man had died for him. He had died, not knowing that Carnhaina would bring him back to life.

"Time to talk," Brand said.

"Thank you," Gil answered. "We need to."

"Come, sit down then." Brand's gaze turned to the two Durlindraths, but it was Taingern who spoke.

"We'll wait outside, my friend."

Brand nodded. "Thank you. We'll not be long."

Gil pulled up a chair and Arell smiled at him. He saw worry in her eyes though, and he did not like it.

"You understand," Brand started, "that I had to pretend to be unwell. It was an opportunity to deceive Cardoroth's enemies, both those within the city and those without. But Ginsar, well, I don't think she'll fall for it. The nobles might."

"I understand," Gil said. "I should have realized it before now. Neither Shorty nor Taingern seemed overly worried. Did they know?"

"No, I didn't tell them. But they probably guessed. They've known me for a good while now, and understand how I think."

Arell poured Gil a glass of crushed juice, but she did not speak.

"My time in Cardoroth draws to an end," Brand told him. "I feel it in my bones. Everywhere I look, I see the signs. Soon, you will rule."

"I never wished it. I never wanted it. But I know that the responsibility is mine. I cannot pass it on to anyone else. It's a burden and an honor, and I hope that I'm up to it."

"You understand," Brand said. "And that pleases me. Even at your age you understand better than the nobles. They think that being king is all glory and wealth and triumph. They would learn a hard truth if their plots ever came to fruition."

"So they would."

Brand grinned at him. "They're mostly idiots. Never mind. We have more important things to discuss."

"Carnhaina's quest?"

"Indeed. And the seer."

"How do you know about the seer?"

"She saw me first, Gil. I knew what she would say to you. And it's true. There's a balance in all things. That is the key."

"Tell him," Arell said.

Gil saw the look on her face, and prepared himself for bad news.

Brand leaned forward in his chair. "The seer told me several things, but you don't need the gift of prophecy to see what will come next. War."

It was a bleak-sounding word, and one that sent a chill up Gil's spine.

"It's inevitable, then?" he asked.

"Yes. Ginsar, for all her thirst for revenge, for all her hatred of the both of us, serves a dark cause. There are those who would see Cardoroth topple, and all Alithoras with it. They would rule the land themselves and bring with them a reign of blood and sorcery."

"And my quest?"

321

"It's doubly important. Cardoroth depends on it, and Alithoras needs Cardoroth."

"How shall I fulfill it?" Gil asked.

"You've started well," Brand answered. "You've begun as all quests must ... by following your heart. But remember the advice of the seer. Balance is more inevitable than war, or peace, or life or death. It's the force at the heart of everything, for everything seeks balance and is always in motion to achieve it. It rules the world. Only people seek dominion and control to keep things just as they wish them. And of those who achieve it ... it is a transient thing."

Gil looked at his mentor. "I don't know what that means. I don't understand."

Brand sighed. "There are times, Gil, when I talk like an old man. Never mind. What does it all mean? It's just how life works. And magic. And love. In all things there is a balance. Think of it this way. If you ran fast for a mile what would happen?"

"I'd get tired."

"Exactly. And what would you do?"

"I would rest."

"And if at another time you were sick and confined to bed for several days, what would you do when you were better?"

"I'd want to get out of my room, to walk around and see and do things again."

"That is balance, Gil. And what if you lifted a heavy object above your head?"

"Then I would have moved its weight above me."

"Yes. The object would be above you, but would you also not be exerting more force on the ground than

322

before you lifted it? There are consequences to every deed, to every force."

Gil considered that. He thought he saw where Brand was leading him.

"Then if Ginsar has opened a gateway that should not have been opened, if she has allowed a force into the realm that should not be here, how would the world seek balance? Or how would the magics involved seek equilibrium?"

"How indeed," Brand said. "I don't know. But that's what you seek. And Carnhaina's diary is as good a place as any. Already, it has led you where you need to go – and the more you understand the better you'll be able to interpret her words."

"And what of you?" Gil asked.

A look of determination lit Brand's eyes. "I will lead Cardoroth to war. But not quite yet. And if we survive, then I shall leave. My homeland calls to me Gil, now more than ever."

"Cardoroth needs you," Gil said.

"Once, maybe. Now, perhaps. Later, there will be you. Lead her well, for the realm is grand and the people deserve a good future. You can give it to them."

"And if I'm not up to filling my grandfather's shoes? Or yours?"

"You won't know until you're in that situation. It will test you, but there's only one way to find out."

Gil thought very hard and very quickly. "If you wish," he offered, "I would renounce my claim to the throne and name you as king. I would do this not to avoid my responsibilities as I once would have, but to keep you here. I don't want to see you go where I can't follow."

323

Brand sat back and looked at him thoughtfully. "I appreciate that. You are … you are like a son to me. But I have taught you well, and you are ready now to fulfill your destiny. Mine rests elsewhere, but that does not mean that we won't meet again."

Gil felt the ache of loss already. But he knew that what Brand said was true, and no matter the outcome of their conflict with Ginsar, there was great sadness ahead.

18. Light and Hope

It was dim in Carnhaina's study. Every time Gil came here, he produced light through the lòhrengai at his command, but it never seemed as bright as it did elsewhere. He wondered if there was some remnant of magic that lingered long after her death that subdued other powers.

It was an interesting thought. This was her place, her private study, a room where she must have worked countless acts of magic. It was here that she had written her diary, and there was magic of a kind in that also. But none of these things seemed as interesting just at the moment as Elrika. She sat on the desk before him, watching him patiently as he read the diary.

He looked up at her. She seemed as she always did, but there was a serious expression on her face and the sword that now hung at her side gave her a dangerous look.

"Keep reading," she said. "You haven't found anything yet, but the answers will be there, somewhere."

"I think I need a break," he said. "Let's talk for a bit."

"Alright, then. What do you want to talk about?"

"I don't know. Nothing. Anything."

"You're so, so *male* sometimes."

"You say it like it's a bad thing," he answered. "But really, I don't know what I want to talk about. But I like hearing your voice."

She gazed at him strangely for a moment. "Well, for someone who doesn't know what to talk about, you know exactly how to say the right things."

He smiled at her. "Maybe you just bring out the best in me."

"Now," she said, "now you're going too far. But I have something I want to talk about. Or at least that I want to ask you."

"What's that?"

"What really happened in that cave in the forest? There are rumors flying through the palace. It's said that Brand died, and Carnhaina brought him back to life."

Gil's memory of those events returned, sharp and clear. He knew they would remain that way, no matter if he lived for a hundred years.

"It's true," he said. "I saw it. And you should know this too. Brand is loyal to me and to Cardoroth. I know what some people thought, but he *is* loyal. He *did* die, and he died to save me." A sheen of tears came to his eyes as he spoke.

She reached out and touched his hand. "You don't have to talk about this if you don't want to."

He rubbed his eyes. "I think it might be good for me to talk about it. I feel so guilty. He gave his life to save mine, because Ginsar gave him a choice. Save his own, or save mine. And he chose me."

"He fought the Rider?" Elrika asked.

"He did. And he knew he could not win, but he fought anyway. And though he could not win, he managed to kill the Rider even as he died himself."

"And then Carnhaina came?"

"She came, and she saved him. Ginsar had left, knowing her greatest opponent was dead. And then

Carnhaina ... I don't really know what she did or how she did it. It all happened so fast. But she said that because Ginsar in her madness had opened a gateway that should not have been opened, that it was possible. She said that the Horsemen come from another world, and that the walls of reality were sundered. She said that she had a chance to recall Brand's spirit and heal his body through the same way that Ginsar opened. And she did it. She returned Brand's spirit to his body, and healed his wounds."

Elrika stared at him. "Those were the rumors. It was hard to believe them, but I do now."

"It's all true, but it's also part of the problem. That's why the gateway has to be closed."

"Is Ginsar really mad? What was she like?"

"Mad?" Gil shivered. "She's insane. Worse, she's driven by a lust for revenge. One minute she's laughing, and then the next she fixes you with a stare that would freeze water. She's tall and beautiful, noble as a queen and dangerous as a snake in the grass."

"My, you can be quite descriptive!"

"Better a description than the real thing."

Elrika pursed her lips thoughtfully. "What do you think she plans now? You and Brand are still alive. That must infuriate her."

Gil stood up to stretch his legs. "Who can say? The next Rider will come, that's for sure. What will he do? I have no idea. Brand is preparing for war. That too is likely. I'm not sure what forces she has at her disposal, but there are elugs in the north and south of Alithoras. She must have some control over them, her and other elùgroths."

"I guess there are two wars really," Elrika said. "One will be a battle of swords. But the other is the important one. In the end, it won't matter who wins the first. The second, your quest, is the one that counts. If you can't close the gateway between worlds, then it's not just Cardoroth at stake, but all of Alithoras."

Gil sat down again. "You're right. And I'd better get back to this diary. Something in here will help. I'm sure of it."

He began to read again, flicking through the pages and looking for something of interest. As always, he had the feeling that the book showed him different things each time he looked at it, for he rarely seemed to see the same thing twice, but likewise he never seemed to reach its end. Magic. That's what it was. But it was of a kind beyond his understanding, and he wondered just how powerful Carnhaina had been. And why had she died after a normal span of life? The great masters lived longer than that. Aranloth, the greatest of the lòhrens, was said to be thousands of years old.

He kept turning the pages. Most of what he saw seemed to be random information. Some sections spoke of the balance of magic, but there was nothing there that he had not already discussed with Brand. One section was quite philosophical, and he read it out to Elrika.

"Light and Dark," Carnhaina had written. "Chaos and Order. Youth and Age. They are opposites, each on the furthest end of a spectrum. But only Man thinks of things in straight lines. In Nature, all is in motion. Everything goes through cycles, and one force leads to another. Thus it also is in human affairs, but the spans of our lives are too short to grasp this until age settles like a withering frost upon us. And this is worth considering.

In the world, frost gives rise to spring again. Night transforms into day. But for Man, does Death lead to Rebirth? What a thought! And one that the elderly mind is quick to ponder. But there are few answers, though I have learned some of them. But what use is knowledge? What will be will be, and the dreaded shall come to pass, as also the good in its turn. Yet these too are names given by Man. In Nature, there is neither good nor dread. There is just the Cycle. The wise man or woman, therefore, does not seek knowledge, but acceptance. For what good is knowledge without the grace to accede to the harmony of nature? It is a hard question, for it is a hard world. But the ancients learned this. The true leader waits. Inaction is a greater power than action, for action is the bluster of Man, trying to stamp his will on Nature. How foolish! How transitory! The wisest of leaders therefore does nothing, or almost nothing. But when they act, they act in accordance with the Cycle of Nature, and then all things are possible. So it is written, and thus has it proved to be during my long reign."

Gil closed the book. "She was a thinker," he said. "That's for sure."

"Did it make much sense to you?" Elrika asked.

"Not much," he admitted. "But I'll work on it."

Elrika slid off the desk. "Come for a walk then. We've been in here long enough."

Gil put the book down and stood. "I think you're right. There's a lot of what Carnhaina said bubbling away in my mind right now. Maybe a break will help something slip into place and I'll understand it better."

They left the hidden study and entered Brand's bedroom. There was still no sign of him, and Gil supposed that Brand intended to stay inconspicuous.

329

This would help lull his enemies into a false sense of security.

"Is that where my sword came from?" Elrika pointed to the wall. There were weapons hanging there, but an empty space was visible where something had been taken.

"That's it. Lucky for me that in the old days they thought weapons made good decorations."

"You're trying to make light of it, Gil. But you had to fight for your life in here. I'm very proud of you."

He felt a thrill run through him at her words, but at the same time he remembered the desperation of that situation. No training could adequately prepare someone for something like that, and having gone through it he would never be the same again. But it also gave him an edge. He had faced that, and survived. His skills were good and his courage held up. It gave him confidence.

19. The Sword and Crown

They walked onward. Gil could not help but picture the dead Durlin that he had found on the floor. And the second one that was killed and hidden in a room outside. Those men had died trying to protect him, and a slow anger began to build. One of the perpetrators was dead, killed by Gil's own hand, but the second was free. That man *would* be found. And he would be brought to justice.

Outside the bedroom his current Durlin guards were there. This time, there were four of them and he thanked them for waiting. They seemed a bit surprised.

They fell in behind him and Elrika as they walked the corridor, their movements graceful and smooth as every Durlin's always were. Their presence was quiet and unobtrusive, but he knew how quick they could be if necessary. And he also knew that potentially another attack could come at any moment. His hand was never far from his sword hilt, and he noticed that Elrika's gaze was sharp and alert. Shorty and Taingern had made her a kind of bodyguard herself, and though that disturbed Gil, he also liked the fact that she was going to be spending a lot more time with him.

They had no particular destination, and walked for the pleasure of it and each other's company. Despite the enormous pressure of the situation and the prospect of difficult times ahead, Gil felt that all was right with the world. It was not a feeling that he was used to, and not one that made sense for him to feel now of all times, but it settled over him nevertheless. And he liked it.

Elrika paused as they came to a corridor that had a balcony.

"Shall we have a look?" she said.

Gil opened the door. It was cleverly crafted to slide on tiny wooden wheels that fitted within a groove made by a metal track. This allowed for a doorway that when opened did not restrict space in either the corridor or the balcony itself.

"Oh!" Elrika said. "I've never been out on one of the balconies before that was this high up in the palace."

They looked out over the balustrade. They were on the western side of the building, and Gil's gaze flickered first to the dark smudge on the horizon that was the forest. Ginsar was somewhere in those dark tracts of trees, plotting and scheming for his death and the destruction of Cardoroth.

Closer, he saw the length of the white road that scarred the chalky soil around Cardoroth City. It ran from the horizon to the West Gate, whose towers he could see rising up from the city wall, or the Cardurleth as it was often called. Attacking armies had marched the length of that road in the past, and the litter of sieges lay abandoned in the pastures to either side. Tall grasses grew green there, their roots seeking nourishment from the soil and the legions of enemy dead that rested below the surface. So Brand had told him, and in a dark way this gave him hope. Cardoroth had survived bleak times before. Many of them. And this would be no different.

Down below was one of the city squares. There were soldiers there, rank after rank of them, performing a drill with sword and shield. It seemed to Gil that everywhere he saw the signs of the future. War was coming.

The noon sun shone from above. The swords glinted dully, but brighter was the contrast of the paving. Each square tile was neatly set, and the city square offered a perfectly smooth surface for such practice, but every second tile was a shade of pale brown beside one of a far darker hue. Light glimmered from the first, but the second was like a murky puddle of water that absorbed all light.

It was an old square, repaired many times over the years, but like much in the inner city of Cardoroth, tradition kept it as it was at the time of the founding. Had Carnhaina once stood on this very balcony and looked down at soldiers drilling? She probably had, and it was a sobering thought. Soon, he would be responsible for the welfare of an entire nation, just as she had been. But he was no legend. Even so, he determined that he would see her proud of him.

"There!" Elrika pointed. "Is that Shorty?"

Two men stood apart, watching the soldiers drill. One was very tall, and he wore the crimson cape of a general. The other was certainly short, but it was too far away to tell if it was Shorty.

"If it's him, he's not wearing the white surcoat of the Durlin," Gil said.

"It's him. No doubt about it," Elrika said. "I can tell just from the way he's standing. Let's go and see him."

Gil was not sure, and he had no idea what made Elrika positive. Both men seemed to be standing the same way to him, but he was happy to take her word for it.

They closed the balcony door behind them, and moved quickly through the palace until they exited at a servants' door down on ground level. Here, the noise of the drilling soldiers was much louder, and the stomp of their boots on the tiles was a rush of determined noise that matched the single-minded expression on their

333

faces. These men were new recruits, and they were training hard.

They skirted the square and came to the other side. Sure enough, it was Shorty. He saw them come, said something to the general and walked over to meet them.

"This lot has a way to go," he said, jerking his thumb toward the drilling soldiers. "But they'll get there."

"Drilling and fighting are different things," Gil said. "That's a lesson I learned recently. I guess they'll discover the same thing soon now."

Shorty gazed at the recruits thoughtfully. "Dark days are coming, true enough. But Cardoroth has seen such times before. Men such as these rise to the occasion. We all do. But it's true that drilling only takes you so far. A real fight is a different animal altogether. But tell me this, what else is drilling teaching them besides how to fight?"

Gil thought about that. It was true that fighting as a lone warrior was different than fighting as part of an army. But the essence of it all was the same. You had to defend against attack, and strike at your opponent's vulnerabilities. He knew that Shorty was trying to teach him something, but he could not see what it was.

"I'm not really sure," he answered. "It's teaching the men to trust in one another, to be part of a team."

"Aye lad, it's doing that. But it's also teaching them discipline. They learn to take orders from above. A simple thing, but they learn here to do it without question, and that adds *speed* to the process. In a battle, the ability to respond quickly to commands can make the difference between victory and defeat. When an opportunity comes, it must be taken. If not, the chance may be gone only moments later."

Gil thought about that. It was true. And it was a big difference from single combat. There was no chain of command there. No orders given and followed. It was lightening quick whereas an army was slow. Therefore, an army that was good at this, that became quick, held a decisive advantage.

"I get it now. I should have known that."

"You probably did. It would be in the books you study, but words on a page aren't real life. Some things you have to see to understand."

Shorty turned to Elrika. "Are you managing to keep him out of trouble?"

"I am. But who's going to keep *me* out of trouble?"

"A good answer!" Shorty laughed and winked at the Durlin guards. He looked again at the drilling soldiers. "This is thirsty work, standing out here in the sun. Let's say we get a drink. Have either of you palace-dwellers ever been to an inn before?"

They shook their heads, and Shorty grinned. "Well, let's fix that right now. There's a place close by that's friendly to soldiers. I've been there a time or two, and it's a nice place to spend a few hours."

He led them out of the square and down a few wide streets. Here and there a passerby recognized him and called out a greeting. Shorty responded to them all with a quick smile and a few words, though it became clear that they did not know him personally.

"Here it is," he said suddenly. "The *Sword and Crown Tavern*. Better known as just the *Sword*."

Gil saw the sign. It was a wooden panel hanging from two chains, and neatly painted upon it was the name Shorty had given and an image of a sword stuck into the ground at an angle. A golden crown perched at a rakish angle over the pommel, and a foaming mug of beer hooked by its handle on the sword hilt gave the impression of a drunk man standing there.

Shorty struck a similar pose to the image and Elrika giggled. Then he opened the door for them and they went through.

"I'll keep an eye on them," he said to the Durlin. "Best to wait out here so we don't draw attention to who they are. Sorry lads. No beer for you just yet!"

They went inside. It was neater than Gil had expected. Though the floor was made of timber it was covered by sawdust. This was to soak up spilled beer, or blood should a fight break out. At least so much Gil had picked up hearing soldiers talk. But neither seemed likely here. It was quite busy, but there were plenty of sturdy wooden tables and most folks were sitting down talking quietly with friends.

Shorty led them to an empty table and they sat down. A blonde waitress came over, her expression friendly.

"Welcome to the *Sword*. What can I get for you?"

"A tankard of beer for me," Shorty answered. "And I think perhaps two glasses of watered wine for my young friends."

The waitress turned to Gil and Elrika with a smile. "We have a fresh batch of white wine in. It's sweet and light, but don't drink too much. It has a harder kick than you'd think." She turned back to Shorty. "Anything to eat for lunch today?"

"Do you still make those meat pies here?"

"We surely do, sir. They're a crowd favorite and the cook has a batch just out of the oven now."

"Perfect," Shorty said. "Three of those thanks." He handed her some coins and she smiled and walked back to the bar.

"You're in for a treat," Shorty advised them. "Those meat pies are the best in the city. The beef is cooked nice and slow in a thick gravy, and the pastry is soft and buttery. They eat better here some days than at the palace."

Gil glanced at Elrika. He saw that she was excited, for she was being treated just as he was. Nor was this the sort of place that she was used to, and that added an element of interest. He was no more used to taverns than she was either, and that took his mind off his problems. He realized that perhaps it was for that exact purpose that Shorty had brought them here. For all his down-to-earth and ordinary ways, Shorty was one of the smartest and most intuitive men Gil had ever met. It was no surprise that Brand always spoke so highly of him.

The waitress brought over their drinks and gave Shorty some change. They drank quietly for a little while, savoring their surroundings. It was getting busier rapidly as more lunch-time patrons gathered. There were many waitresses now, all quick to clear used cutlery and bring fresh drinks. It was a well-run establishment, but when their pies arrived Gil's appreciation of the tavern increased further. Their aroma was fabulous and the taste even better.

Gil looked over at Elrika. Her father was the palace baker, but even she seemed impressed.

They finished their meal with little speech. All around them the conversations of the patrons grew louder, and were frequently punctuated by laughter.

Gil began to listen in to what was being said. Much of it was the ordinary talk of friends and family discussing everyday matters. But there was a darker undercurrent. He heard the word *war* repeated several times. There was discussion of Brand, and whether or not he was well, and if he would lead the army should some sort of attack against the city occur. Here and there, he heard the word *sorcery* as well. Though if this was in reference to Brand or the enemies of the city, he could not tell.

337

Gradually, a silence fell. It was strange after so much noise. People began to look out the tavern windows, and the three companions did so as well. They saw nothing, but there was a glimmer of light and a faint strand of music as though heard from far away. Something was happening, but Gil was not sure what. Yet it made him feel good somehow, and the talk of war and plots and the dark to come was momentarily forgotten.

20. A Flicker of Light

Night swept over Cardoroth.

The growing dark signaled the end of a shift for a company of soldiers stationed at the Harath Neben, the North Gate. This was what the people called Hunter's Gate, for the wild lands and woods beyond were rich in game. During the latter parts of the night, hunters would pass through regularly. There were the nobles and the wealthy looking for sport, or the poor and the downtrodden looking for cheap food. It was a boring time for the soldiers; they had seen it all before, and they had little interest in wild lands or in game. Better to be indoors, to find a lively inn where the beer flowed, the dice rolled and at least some of the female patrons were friendly – especially to those with coin.

Two soldiers, not really friends but sharing similar tastes, were headed away from the gate and walking an ill-lit street. It was in places like these that they found the entertainment they sought, and they were happy that for another week they were rostered for a day shift and the nights belonged to them.

"I heard a rumor the other day," one of them said. "Supposedly, Brand is dead."

"I heard that too," the second man replied. "It's not true though. One of my sister's friends works in the palace. She saw him return from the forest, all dirty and tired, but alive. And he brought back the prince with him. The Durlin were there too, and she says they were all covered in dust and grime."

"But," the first man insisted, "I heard the story from a sergeant who knows one of the Durlin themselves. He swore Brand was dead."

"Pah! Just stories. The city is always full of them. Few are true, and sergeants pass them on as readily as anyone else."

The first man considered that. "That might well be, but you have to admit that Brand is mixed up in some strange stuff. He's a warrior, but they say he's a lòhren too, a wielder of magic."

The second man laughed. "All those things, and king to be one day as well."

"No! Never that. He wouldn't do that to the young prince. Not that he couldn't if he had a mind to. But say what they will about him, Brand is loyal. He rescued that boy, didn't he?"

"That's true," the other said. "The real traitors are the nobles."

"Too right. That lot of troublemakers couldn't lie straight in bed at night, that's for sure. They're all crooked to the bone."

"Fools, the whole lot of them," the second man added. "They tried to usurp the throne themselves, and see where that got them? Brand has their measure. He's not a noble like them, and they hate his guts for it. But he's smarter than the whole bunch of them put together."

The first man hitched his sword belt a little higher, and felt for the hilt of the blade to be sure it was where it was supposed to be. This was just the sort of street where he may need it. When he was satisfied, he spoke again.

"The only problem with Brand is that he's too kindhearted. He should have killed the nobles aforehand.

A noble with his head on a spike in the palace gardens doesn't plot much treason."

The other man laughed. "That's something we can agree on. Those nobles have it all coming to them. And Brand may yet have a chance to give it to them."

They turned a corner and entered a narrower street. It was silent and dark. They did not like it, and their conversation faltered. This was no time to get waylaid. It was payday, and their moneybags were full of coin. It was one thing to waste their wages on gambling and cheap beer, but another to lose it at the points of a robber-gang's swords.

A cold wind rose, picking up dust and litter before channeling it down the street ahead of them. Then suddenly the air warmed. There was a scent in it also, sweet and fragrant like a meadow full of flowers in the spring.

"Do you hear that?" the first man asked.

"Hear what?"

"Music. A strange, lilting music."

They stopped to listen.

"I can't hear anything," the second man said.

"It's gone now. I don't know what it was, but for just a moment I was home. I don't mean home here in the city. I mean where I grew up on a farm way out beyond the gate. I could almost see the hills about me, the sweet scent of pine and the memory of long, cold nights while the hearth burned. And my mother, at that same hearth cooking breakfast while the sun rose and sent streaks of silver through the frosted grass." He shook his head as though to clear it. "It was the darnedest thing to remember."

"Strange," the other man said. "I smelled the sea. My da was a fisherman. We lived way, way to the east. A tiny village it was. We came here when I was very young.

Strange, I haven't thought of our old boat in years and years, but for a moment I felt it shifting under me."

The breeze died, and the dust and litter settled back down into place on the cobbled surface. But in the center of the street a shimmer of light briefly appeared before flickering away toward the corner and disappearing.

The two men looked at one another.

"What was that?"

"I don't know. But I feel different."

They paused for a moment, looking at each other as though embarrassed.

"I think I'll go home," the first man said.

The second looked down at the ground. "Me too. It's not a night to be out."

"See you tomorrow then. It'll be market day. That's always busy, but I think at lunch I'll go for a walk and buy my wife some of the perfume she likes."

The two men separated, one going back in the direction they had come from and the other forward. Both walked slowly, as though deep in thought.

Thrimgern pulled the great oak doors of his smithy closed. The day's work was done, and he was pleased. It was a profitable month, and the last order that he was working on was a big one.

It was a pity the order was for swords. At least he was able to charge a high price. The weapons were for a noble family, and prices were always inflated for them. His skill had something to do with it too. Not just any smith could make swords. Not quality ones anyway. But his best work, his love, was ornate doorknobs. Why did they not pay so well? The world was a strange place, but he would do what was needed to make his way in it.

Doorknobs. No, they weren't just doorknobs. They were the *best* doorknobs in Cardoroth. How he loved to craft them, to shape them out of a rough lump of metal, to transform them into the likeness of miniature animal heads that were so lifelike that people were hesitant to touch them for fear of being bitten. But the money was in *swords*.

No matter. He managed easily enough to pay the bills and keep his wife happy. She would be especially happy today when he told her about the price the noble family had agreed to pay. Or she would be happy once he had removed his leather apron and cleaned away the layers of soot and grime from his face and arms. The signs of a hard day's work to him – disgusting sloppiness to her.

He clipped the great lock into place through the heavy chain and secured the doors. Both lock and chain had been wrought by his grandfather many years ago. Strange that he should think of that now when he was so tired, but he had been there that day.

He remembered the chain being made, first by taking short iron rods heated to the working point, and then bending them back on themselves through a hole in the anvil. The rods were then hammered into a perfect loop over the anvil horn, red sparks flying from them. Many were made, and each two completed links were joined together by a third, this one bent and hammered through the others to form the link. And on it went until the great chain was fashioned. He looked at it now, and he could almost feel his grandfather there admiring the work as well, just as he had all those years ago.

Thrimgern smiled, lost in the memory, and then turned to walk to the house next door which was his home. Merril would nearly have dinner ready, and a glass of ale set down for him. She knew that smithying was thirsty work, and how much he enjoyed a quiet drink after a hard day of labor.

The front door was near when he felt a cooling breeze on his face. How sweet it was, easing away his tension and soothing his heat-reddened skin. He felt a change in the air, as though the weather was turning, and paused.

There was nobody in the street just now. But there was a light, a flickering light, and then momentarily he saw the slim figure of a woman, no a girl, young and fair. She smiled at him.

The sweat from his day's work stung his eyes. He rubbed them, but when he took his hands away she was gone.

It had been a long day. Wearily, he walked the last few paces to his home.

Grindar limped ahead, the grinding ache in his hip where the rheumatism often troubled him was bad tonight. That was the problem with getting old. All those aches and pains. And he was old as the hills and his body liked to let him know it. Still, he was able to light the street lamps and that kept food on the table. There were times when life had been worse.

He shuffled ahead, lifting up the protective dome of each lamp and lighting the candle wick. It was an easy enough job, but in truth he enjoyed still feeling useful.

The candle he was lighting flared to life, and the yellow light flickered over the leathery skin of his hands, all wrinkled like scrunched up parchment. At least he couldn't see his hair. That, he knew, was white and wispy. What was left of it, anyway. A far cry from the long raven-black hair he had once been proud of.

Time was nobody's friend, he mused, but what would be would be. It was not going to get him down. He shuffled ahead once more, his thin legs not much thicker than the poles upon which the lamps were set, but they got him around the city and that was enough.

He began to whistle as he walked. He did not care that no one else knew the tune. It was the price of getting older, but once that same tune had echoed through the streets about him. It was whistled. It was hummed. There were words that went with it too; merry words for merrier times. But they were all forgotten now, overwhelmed by the music of a different generation. No matter. *He* knew, and *he* remembered. That was enough.

He lit yet another candle, but just as the wick caught he saw a flicker of light from the corner of his eye. Turning, he saw a girl on the street behind him. What a vision she was! And just looking at her he felt younger. She was the most beautiful girl he had ever seen.

She smiled at him, and his heart fluttered in his chest. Her eyes seemed so bright, and her smile was like a summer's day, but there was sadness in her glance and the wisdom that came with deep sorrow. Oh, he knew that look, but he had never seen it on a girl like her before. She had seen a thing or two in her time, that was certain. But who was she?

She smiled again, and her face seemed to him brighter than the light from a thousand candles. Then she walked away, but before she turned the corner she looked back and their eyes met one last time. He felt a sudden stab of sorrow. She was too good for this world, and the good did not last.

She disappeared around the corner. He missed her already, but he felt a touch of youth course through his body, and there was strength in his limbs as he had not felt for many a year. Better still, his eyes saw clearly as they had not done for a very long time, and he whistled again for the sheer joy that bubbled up inside him.

He felt like he was young again, and he almost went to follow her, but his years had brought him not just white hair but a measure of wisdom too. No joy would come from chasing after the impossible.

With a sigh he walked ahead to the next lamp, a wistful smile on his face. That girl *was* too good for this world. But she would try to do good while she was here, that much he felt with certainty, but it could not last for long. Nothing ever did.

He went about his work, and his thoughts turned from the strange girl to his first and his only true sweetheart. Oh, that was very, very long ago. But he remembered her well.

21. The Oath

Gil, Elrika and Shorty made their way back to the palace. The Durlin guards trailed closely. No one said much, for it had been a strange afternoon and they were thoughtful.

Ahead, a troupe of singers came into view. They were dressed in flowing robes and ancient costumes. Their voices rose in unison, giving voice to an old ballad about a hero of the Camar before they came to Cardoroth. There was a piper with them, and the sound of his music rose sweetly into the air.

Gil and the others moved a little to the side to allow the troupe room to pass. One carried a cloth bag, and it was in this that listeners threw a coin if they liked what they heard. Shorty did so, but just as he reached out there was sudden movement from elsewhere in the line of singers.

One of the men, his cloak flowing behind him, detached from the group and lunged toward Gil. He was fast, and steel flashed in his hands. Shorty yelled and had begun to react, but Gil knew that he would not be able to intervene in time.

Gil reached for his sword, but he also would be too slow. They had been caught off-guard, and panic surged through him.

The assassin was close now, bridging the gap swiftly, and the dagger in his hand thrust forward in a deadly strike. But from near to Gil, Elrika moved. She was faster than them all. One moment her blade seemed poised in mid-air, and the next it darted forward in a deadly thrust.

Elrika's bodyweight was behind her thrust, even as they had both practiced so many times in the training yard, and the blade barely slowed as it slid through the attacker's clothing, through fat and muscle into the vital organs of his torso. And then, also as they had practiced, she angled the point of the blade upward at the end of the movement, and drove the tip behind the ribs and up toward the heart.

The man turned and twisted. With a grunt he staggered to the side and wrenched the blade from Elrika's grip. She cried out in surprise or pain, and the man that she had struck turned upon her.

He reached out with both hands, one still holding the dagger and the other clawing at the air. But he slowed and swayed where he stood, her sword still in his belly, and a froth of red blood at his lips. He tried to yell, but the blood flowed thicker in his mouth and he made only a horrible gurgling sound while red froth sprayed into the air.

Elrika held up her hands, but her face was spattered red. She stepped back, and the assassin fell to his knees. He fixed her with a stare of hatred, and then fell face forward to the ground. One leg kicked for a moment, and then he stilled.

The assassin's dagger lay dropped on the cobbles near the dead man's hand. Gil had seen its like before. It was a Duthenor blade. But now he knew that it was not at Brand's doing. These were Brand's enemies, enemies from his faraway homeland. They were still trying to mark Brand as a murderer. But why?

Gil turned to Elrika. She stood there, perfectly still. Her face was splattered with blood and her eyes were wide with fright. He reached out, intending to touch her shoulder, but she slumped against his body and hugged him fiercely.

"It's all right," Gil said. And he hugged her back.

The Durlin were all around them now, but there was no further threat. The singing troupe was in shock, and Gil knew they had nothing to do with it. The assassin had merely used them as cover to get close.

Shorty knelt by the body and examined it. Then he stood with something in his hand.

"We won't learn much from him. He's dressed in ordinary Cardoroth style, but the dagger is of Duthenor design. As is this."

He held up a brooch. It was of a snake looped in a circle and swallowing its own tail.

"I've never seen anything like it," Gil said.

"It's not a Camar motif. It, like the dagger, are of Duthenor design."

"They don't really care about me," Gil said. "All they want to do is get Brand in trouble, perhaps even executed as a traitor."

Shorty pocketed the brooch. "True enough."

"What shall we do about it?"

The Durlindrath scratched his head. "There's not much we can do. There's a vipers' nest of enemies somewhere in the city. But it's not our job to find them. We have other tasks. Sandy is looking for them, and we have to trust in her, and believe me – there's no secret she can't uncover given enough time."

"And then?"

"Then Brand will deal with them. Some at least are his countrymen, so it'll be fitting for him to decide their fate. He's their rightful chieftain, after all."

"No doubt," Gil answered. "But what then?"

"Ah, you have guessed. By sending these men the usurper who rules the Duthenor has woken Brand's

349

dormant oath. He swore a long time ago to avenge his murdered parents and reclaim the chieftainship. That day is now fast approaching. Soon, he'll leave Cardoroth and the usurper will wish that he'd left Brand alone."

"Can Brand do it though?" He gestured to the body of the assassin. "He has enemies beyond just one usurper."

"Don't judge the Duthenor by what you've seen. These men serve the usurper, and may come from a neighboring tribe anyway. Most Duthenor are like Brand, and they would have him as their chieftain with great joy, if only they had the choice."

"But if he goes, he cannot leave as regent, nor take an army with him."

"No, he'll go as a lone warrior, even as he came to us years ago. Don't fear for him though. See what he achieved coming to Cardoroth? A lone barbarian from the wilderness? Now, he's a greater warrior than he was then, and a lòhren too. No, don't fear for him. Fear for his enemies!"

Shorty turned to Elrika, and the fierce expression on his face softened. "You did well, today. Very well. I'm proud of you."

Elrika nodded slowly, but did not answer him.

"We'll work on your wrist strength next. But for today, you've earned the right to walk proud among any group of warriors in the city." He hesitated, trying to assess her emotional state. "You did what you had to do, Elrika. And think on this. If you had not done so, Gil would be the one lying there on the ground now."

Elrika bit her lip and nodded once more, but still she did not speak.

They turned to go, the Durlin close all about them. Gil led Elrika forward, still holding her hand, and he saw Shorty mouth to him away from her sight. *Talk to her.*

He would do so. But he knew she was not ready just yet. For the moment, she just wanted to hold his hand while she came to grips with what had happened. Then, she would want to talk.

He thought of the other things Shorty had said while they walked back to the palace. It was all true, and Gil had heard some of it himself from Brand's mouth. But one thing Shorty had not said. Would Brand really go alone? Certainly he would not take soldiers with him, or anything like that, but Gil had a feeling that he would not be *totally* alone.

22. Balance

It was late in the evening of the next day, and Gil sat with Elrika in Carnhaina's study once more. Here, where it was just the two of them, in this place of the palace that was theirs alone, she had opened up to him about killing the assassin.

"How is it," she had asked, "that I regret killing him even though it was necessary to save you?"

Gil had no easy answer for that. "I think that sometimes life forces things on us, gives us choices where there are no perfect outcomes. Had you not acted, I would have been killed and you would have felt guilty. If you attempted to disarm him, he may have killed us both because it was only by the decisive strike that you made that you got through his defenses. That man was committed to his cause. Neither a blow to arm or leg would have stopped him."

"I know Gil. I know, but I still feel bad. It was horrible."

He remembered the blood on her face and the look in her eye. Small wonder that she felt as she did. He was still grappling with the fact that he also had recently killed, and he had as yet found no answers for himself. But he understood just now how she felt, and perhaps it was enough to discuss it, to share their feelings and accept that there may be no answers to their questions.

They had talked for a good while. Then he had read from Carnhaina's diary. Once more they spoke, but there were no answers to any of their questions. But he felt the bond between them grow. They had been through a lot together, and their friendship was deeper, stronger, more enduring than it had been before.

"Have you heard the rumor going around the palace?" she asked him.

"Another one? What's Brand supposed to have done now?"

"Not Brand," she said. "And not just the palace. This one is about a girl."

Gil had in fact heard people in the palace talking about a girl.

"The beautiful one? The one with a light in her eyes that comes and then disappears?"

Elrika frowned at him. "You don't believe?" she asked.

"I don't know. There've been lots of rumors lately. None of them very close to the truth. Perhaps in these dark times people are searching for something good."

"Maybe," she said. "But this one feels different. And there are people, even here in the palace, who swear they have seen her themselves."

Gil had not heard that. But then people spoke to Elrika often. For the most part, he spent his days alone even though he was surrounded.

"Do you think it means something? Could it relate to something Ginsar has done? This girl doesn't sound at all like one of the Riders she's summoned though."

"No, I don't think it's anything to do with Ginsar. Not by the stories I've heard."

Gil leaned back and considered things. "Here's an idea," he said. "This girl appears about the same time as the Riders. But if she's nothing to do with Ginsar, who is she? I keep reading about balance and harmony. Brand has spoken of it. The seer talked about it. Is it possible that this girl came through the gate that Ginsar opened

353

for the Riders? Has she come through with them, but is really their opposite?"

Elrika pursed her lips. She seemed to be thinking hard, but all she did was shake her head.

"Who can say? Maybe all that is possible. Maybe. But we just don't know. Nothing seems to be simple anymore."

Gil knew what she meant. Nothing had been simple for a while now, nor was that likely to change anytime soon.

"You're right. We just don't know. But that only means one thing."

She looked at him carefully, sensing the determination in his voice. "You're going to try to track her down?"

"Exactly," he said. "That will be the surest way of finding answers, one way or the other."

"Have you considered that it could be a trap?"

That surprised him. He had considered no such thing, but it was entirely possible.

"You're a pretty valuable person to have around," he said.

She winked at him, something that he thought she had picked up from Shorty, but it was a relief to see a lighthearted expression on her face.

"We'll have to be careful," he said. "But truly, I don't think this girl, if she even exists, is part of one of Ginsar's plots. I've seen one of her Riders in person, and the other in a vision. There are two more yet to come. I don't think she's one of them. She seems precisely the opposite, and the more I think on it the more I believe that she may have something to do with the balance that everyone keeps talking about."

"But you'll be careful anyway?"

"Of course. I've been wrong before, so I don't intend to take anything at face value."

Elrika seemed satisfied with that. "And how will you try to find her? It's a big city."

That was something that he had been thinking about. It would not be easy, but the first inkling of an idea began to form in his mind.

23. I've Found Them!

Brand sat on his accustomed chair next to the ornate throne of Cardoroth. Everything was the same as it always had been. The throne room. Cardoroth. The world. But *he* was different. He had died, however briefly, and nothing could be the same after that.

At one moment he thought how empty everything was, how futile. For all endeavors eventually failed, and all that lived became dust. The next, he appreciated the beauty of life, that each moment was golden and that there was joy in the simplest of things: sun on his face, a cold glass of water, the smile of a passing stranger. Both life and death seemed masks over the same thing, but his mind could not quite perceive the single face beneath.

"What are you thinking?" Taingern asked.

"Nothing. Everything. It does not matter."

Taingern raised an eyebrow, but he did not reply.

A Durlin opened the great door to the throne room and entered. "One of your counselors is here to see you, my lord."

Brand did not need to ask which one. He knew, for he saw the puzzlement on the guard's face. No one knew who this counselor was, what she did or how she did it. And that was the way it was supposed to be.

"Let her in," Brand said.

Sandy came through quickly. She was old, but she moved well and showed little sign of her age. Of course, Brand could not be sure exactly how old she was, for she kept her personal life private. The irony of this, given what she did for the realm, amused him.

She swept the room with her gaze, seemingly to ensure there was no one else there. Then she glanced behind her to check that the Durlin had left and closed the door. She offered no greeting nor any small talk. As always, she was straight to the point.

"I've found them."

Brand always liked her directness. Just now, he liked even more the news she brought. He did not have to ask who *they* were.

"Where?" he said simply.

"They're based close by – a house near the palace."

She gave no emphasis to those last words, but Brand intuited what she meant. It was a house of the nobles, the house of a traitor who would conspire, and hide, foreign assassins.

"How many are there?"

"Five," she said, holding up one hand.

"Will they be there tonight?"

"If they follow their normal routine, yes. But later. They drink a great deal, according to my informant."

Brand grinned. "The Duthenor are like that, sometimes. But even so, they may be good fighters. Are the traitor nobles with them?"

"No. I'm still looking for them."

Brand turned to Taingern, and the Durlindrath anticipated his wishes. "Not the city watch, then? You want some Durlin?"

"Yes. Ten of them, I think. You and Shorty shall lead them. Besides that, another ten soldiers – make them the best as recommended by the captains of the four gates. That way the whole city will be represented."

357

"And?"

Taingern knew what he was thinking, as he usually did. Brand grinned at him. "I'll be going too."

To his credit, Taingern did not try to dissuade him from that.

"Also," Brand added. "We'll go in plain clothes. No Durlin surcoats, no soldiers' uniforms. Tell the men this may be hard. The Duthenor will not go easily. And I want them, or at least some of them alive. I need answers."

"As you wish. What time shall we leave?"

"We'll assemble here, in the throne room. Make it the hour before midnight. It won't take long to get to this house, and the late hour should give the Duthenor time to grow tired and careless."

"They keep a good watch," Sandy said. "But they don't think they're discovered, and that will work in our favor."

By that, Brand knew, they were somewhat reckless. Sandy always understated things. But reckless Duthenor were dangerous. He should know, after all.

24. Who are You?

Gil knew what he was going to do, and there was no point in waiting. It was already late at night, but there were some things that could not be put off until the next day.

"I can seek out this girl," he told Elrika. "And I can do it with lòhrengai. At least, I can make the attempt."

They left Carnhaina's study, and the Durlin went with them. If they wondered what he was doing this late at night, they did not ask.

Up they went, right up to the top of one of the palace towers. It was a long climb, and Gil's legs burned. He noticed that neither Elrika nor the Durlin showed any sign of discomfort. That the Durlin were strong and fit was no surprise, but Elrika stuck with him every step of the way, and that impressed him. She had courage, she had skill with a blade and she evidently had endurance too. With the right training, what might she achieve? Small wonder that Shorty and Taingern were giving it to her.

They reached the top of the tower and walked out to the crenelated fortification that ringed the open circle at the top.

The dark was still and cool about them, the stars twinkling above in the late-night sky. Below, the city was a mass of shadows and bright-lit streets. Further away he saw the Tower of Halathgar. That was where Carnhaina had worked much of her magic, but he realized that she

359

would have done so in lots of places, maybe even including where he stood now.

And magic he must work too, of a kind he had not attempted before. But the power was coming to him more easily of late. He felt confident, but not certain of the outcome.

They gave him a little space, and he stepped right up to the crenellations. Slowly, he composed himself. He breathed deeply of the air, drawing in the night, feeling the shimmering sky above him and the flickering city streets below. He became one with them, and he felt the lòhrengai within him flutter to life.

Down below there was movement. A group of men strode with purpose along a street, and one led them, his stride both swift and poised. That man seemed familiar to Gil, and at his thought the lòhrengai he had summoned leaped down to the city below. It was Brand. What was he doing? Where was he going this late at night?

Gil withdrew. He did not wish to disturb or distract the regent, which surely he would do if he probed any further with lòhrengai. Whatever questions Brand's presence late at night on the street below raised, they were questions for tomorrow. Right now Gil had a task to accomplish, and he felt a sense of growing urgency.

He cleared his mind, and opened himself to the pulse of the city below. His thought began to encompass it, reaching out all the way to the Cardurleth that circled the vast maze of streets and buildings and parks. At the same time, he sought his center, that place within himself that was the wellspring of peace and fear, hope and detachment, imagination and logic.

The marks on his palms tingled. All around him he felt acutely aware of life within the city, and he felt another kind of power also. This was one that he had not felt before, and it emanated from the dark sky. Each star, though incredibly remote, shimmered in his mind. And the constellation of Halathgar most of all. It was something that he had not experienced before, and was another sign that Brand had been right. The power within him grew as he used it rather than increased by being taught.

He accepted this new feeling, and then ignored it. His task now was simple, and he focused upon it. He reached back into his memory, recalling all that had been said of this girl that he sought, and then he cast those thoughts and images and feelings across the city. *Where are you? Come to me! Reveal yourself!*

All at once he felt something change. What he had expected, if it worked at all, was that he would sense her presence in some faraway part of the city, perhaps brush against her mind and get some understanding of who she was, where she was and what she was doing. But he got more than that.

The girl was very close by. And swiftly, almost as though she had been waiting for such a call from him, she came. There was a rush of light and a dazzlement of stars. He grew momentarily giddy, and then his mind cleared again.

"She comes!" he said, and he felt those around him stiffen in surprise.

And then she was there. She stood upon the very air beyond the parapet. Ephemeral. Beautiful. Remote. A sense of peace and goodwill radiated from her like warmth from the sun.

Gil suddenly thought of Brand. The regent and the girl were similar in some way that was not immediately apparent, but nevertheless striking.

"Who summons me?" she asked, and her voice was both light as a whisper and strong as steel.

Gil answered. "I have sought you out. I am—"

"I know who you are. I have read it in your eyes. You are more than you would say, but you don't know it yet."

Gil was at a loss. "What does that mean?"

"Time will show you. I see this, for I see what is, and what is yet to be."

"Who are you?"

"I? I am Life. And Trust. And Peace. I am also that which was before and will come after Time. You would call it Possibility."

This meant little to Gil. "But who *are* you?"

"I am your savior, and yet also, perhaps, your greatest sorrow."

"Lady. I'm confused. I really don't understand anything you're saying."

She gazed upon him, and there was a look in her eyes that may have been sorrow, but Gil could read her face no more than he could understand her words.

"Alas," she said. "You shall learn all soon enough."

"But—"

"No more!" She raised a slender arm before her to stop him. "There is not much time. Listen! I have been seeking you. Forces are loose in the world. They should not be. Not in *this* world. You must send them back whence they came."

"This I know," Gil answered, glad that what she said was at last clear. "I was charged with doing exactly that. But I don't know how."

362

The girl sighed, and it seemed that starlight shimmered through her body.

"You will learn. But you will wish that you had not. Yet first, you must know this."

25. Not in Cardoroth

Brand led the men. Gone was all pretense at being ill: he walked with purpose and acute watchfulness. His guise was no longer needed, though perhaps it had been fruitful. His enemies would not be expecting decisive action from him. Yet, wary as always, he was careful not to assume that it was so just because he wished it.

Even as he had ordered, there were ten Durlin and ten of the finest soldiers in Cardoroth. All were men of proven loyalty. He had briefed them personally when they had assembled in the throne room. He had told them to avoid bloodshed – if possible. But he warned them of the temperament of most Duthenor, and that the tribesmen were likely to fight no matter the odds against them. The men had merely looked at him, showing neither eagerness for trouble nor fear at its prospect. He was proud of them then, for they were *warriors*.

"Let's go," he had said. "Luck to us all."

Now, they walked through the streets of Cardoroth to the address Sandy had provided. It was not far, and he led them swiftly for he wanted no rumor of their march to proceed them.

His sword was belted at his side, as normal. But he carried something else. It was concealed within a sack and slung by a strap over his shoulder. If Taingern and Shorty knew what it was, they did not say. The men had no way of even guessing, and he sensed their curiosity.

They would have to wait a little longer to find out what it was though.

They were nearly there. It felt good, even exhilarating, to lead men on a mission. He was not regent now, or at least so it felt. Nor was he a lòhren. He was … he was just a simple man as he had been years ago when he had first arrived in Cardoroth. Once, he had been a mere captain, and he envied himself that time in his life. The world was full of promise then. But no matter what he wished for, he could never go back to that. Or could he? It was an intriguing thought, but he brushed it aside. Now, he had a job to do. Thinking about the future could come later.

They turned a corner. The street they were now in was luxurious, even for the center of Cardoroth. A white wall marked the perimeter of a manor house. The grounds were large, but he could see little of them because of the wall. That was one of its purposes. It was also topped by intricately designed metal spikes to keep trespassers away. No matter. He did not intend to seek entry just yet. Sandy had given him a detailed description of the estate, and he had a vague memory of it himself. He had walked and ridden past it on occasion.

They came to a gate in the wall. There was one guard visible, but Sandy believed there was a second. The first was placed to watch for intruders, the second to seek help on any sign of trouble.

Brand was not going to do anything to give the impression trouble was coming. He led the men onward, and they had been warned not to look at the gate or show any sign of interest. Shorty began to sing, a bawdy song he had learned in a tavern long ago. To the guard, they would seem a mere band of revelers returning home.

There was a purpose in what they did though. Brand had eased back into the group. He was instantly recognizable, and he used the men around him to shield himself from view. He could have come by himself, hooded to disguise his face. But hoods were not commonly worn except in bad weather and he would have roused suspicion.

In the midst of the men, he fell in beside Taingern and Shorty who might also have been recognized. Quickly, Brand summoned lòhrengai, feeling it thrum through him. He let it drift out of his body and ease toward the guard. He sensed the first sitting in a chair in the shadows of the gate, and then he discovered the second. This one was stationed nearby in a little alcove in the wall. But there was a third with him.

Brand could not read minds, a talent that he sometimes wished to possess. But he allowed his lòhrengai to settle over the men. He sensed that the first guard was curious but not alarmed. The other men were simply bored. That was the feeling he worked with.

The men Brand led had walked past the gate now, and there was little time left. He took the feelings of boredom and intensified them. It was not a type of magic that he had attempted before, but all things were possible. He eased into their minds and gave them thoughts of sleep, of closing their eyes momentarily for just a few moments of rest. He thought of sleep rolling over them in a comforting wave, and of their tiredness because of their long hours of work.

His sense of the men faded as he walked further ahead.

"Did you do it?" Shorty asked.

Brand flashed him a grin. "They'll not hear us or see us now, but we'd better be quick. I don't think they'll sleep for long."

"That's a handy little trick."

Brand shrugged. "It's late at night and I think they had been drinking. I wouldn't want to try it during the day."

They continued on. The gate was now well behind them, swallowed up by the dark, and the white wall rose up close to their side. It was slightly different here though. This was an older section and not in as good repair. There were still metal spikes atop it though, even if not as well-made as the newer ones.

Brand gave a signal. The chosen soldier stepped forward and knelt before the wall. A second soldier, thin and agile, nimbly climbed up to stand on his shoulders. Slowly, the first stood.

From his high vantage point the second soldier drew out a short rope from beneath his cloak. Swiftly he tied this to the top portion of a metal stake. He let the end of the rope fall, and then quietly dropped down to the ground again.

Brand kept an eye on the street. There was no one coming either way. So far so good.

A group of men took hold of the rope and eased away the slack. Then carefully, they used their combined strength to pull. There was little noise. The metal stake began to bend, but then unexpectedly brick and mortar gave way.

There was a pop of dust, a grinding noise and then the stake broke free. It was more than what was intended, for bending it near flat would have done.

367

Brand made to move, for he saw the metal stake flying through the air. If it clattered against the cobbles it would make enough noise to attract attention. But Taingern was closer. He had no chance of catching it, but he dived and speared out one arm before him. The bar struck it, and then bounced to the side. But when it hit the cobbles it made less noise than it otherwise would have.

Taingern rolled to his feet. Quickly, they went ahead with the rest of their plan. They were slightly slowed though, for the rope needed to be retied to the adjacent spike.

When this was done, they clambered up one at a time, slipped through the gap between spikes and dropped to the ground below. The last man drew up the rope behind him to hide it from sight, but he allowed it to dangle down over the inside of the wall. This was an escape route, if they needed one, but that was unlikely. Brand confidently took the lead again.

He wove a path through the manor grounds. Always he sought the deepest shadows, and ground that was maintained as well-clipped grass rather than garden beds where twigs or leaves could make noise beneath booted feet. This kind of stealth was not his talent, but he had done it before even if he did not have the skills of an army scout.

It was enough though. They moved through the grounds undetected. It did not seem to take long and they stood within the night-shadow of an oak grove looking out at the hulking shape of the manor house.

There Brand paused. He was not about to rush through the last hundred feet or so. It was all clear ground, and the possibility existed of being seen through windows. There was another risk too. Were the grounds patrolled? This was something that Sandy had not been able to discover.

Brand waited. The men waited silently behind him. No one moved. Everyone peered into the gloom, looking for signs of guards. There was nothing.

There was now no reason not to bridge the gap from their place of concealment to the house. Yet Brand still hesitated. He felt a sense of unease, but he did not know why. Yet, he had learned to trust his instincts.

He waited. They saw nothing. Slowly, he sensed the mood of the men around him change. *Why were they waiting?* He could give no answer. But a time came in any endeavor that a choice must be made: to proceed or to halt. He made his choice.

With a quick gesture he signaled it was time to move. He adjusted the sack that was slung over his shoulder, and then led the men forward. They did not run, for fast movement caught the eye. Instead, they walked slowly. And all the while they peered about them, looking for signs of guards or casual observers from the house. They saw nothing, but this did not still Brand's unease.

Brand did not like the feeling of being out in the open, no matter that it was dark. His hand strayed toward his sword hilt, but he did not touch it. The men would be looking at him as much as anywhere else, and if he showed signs of nervousness it would increase their own.

They reached the manor house without incident. There they gathered close to the deeper shadows of the wall to aid concealment. Nothing moved. Nothing stirred. All was silent. Yet even so, Brand did not like it.

There was nothing to be gained by prevarication. The confidence of the men would diminish though should Brand hesitate as he had before. Therefore, he went ahead straightaway with the plan he, Taingern and Shorty had developed.

Moving silently as a whisper, he eased himself along the wall, the men following him, until he neared a window. Carefully, he brought himself to a point where he could peer in from the bottom corner.

Now, he must be patient, and the men would understand that. He strained both eyes and ears to sense if anyone was in the room beyond. He did not think so. It was silent in there, and though he could see little there was no movement. To be sure, he summoned lòhrengai again, and let trailers of his thought drift into the room. Still, there was nothing.

Brand put the palm of his hand to the glass. He had explained to the men this part of the plan, and they had accepted he could do it. But he knew they were warriors and trusted in swords and steel more than magic. They would be uneasy with what he was about to do.

It did not matter. This was necessary to enter the house in silence, which was their aim. If they could surprise the conspirators within, bloodshed might be avoided.

He summoned the lòhrengai, and it blossomed in his palm. The glass was cold to touch, and he took that energy and concentrated it. Within moments the glass frosted up, strange patterns forming over it, swirls of white and silver that danced beneath his hand.

The glass was near to breaking, but if it did so it would shatter with noise. That was not what he wanted. He eased back a little, seeking now for something else.

There was harmony in all things. That was the balance of nature, and the seed of everything's opposite was contained within itself. He therefore sought out what warmth was left in the glass, and he drew it to his fingertips. There he gathered it, concentrated it, focused it in a small place.

With a sudden stab-like motion of his fingers, he released the heat in a surge. There was a pop, slight and barely audible. Several times he stabbed with his fingers and then a circular section of glass no bigger than his hand melted away and dripped down the glass.

A crack sprang through the rest of the frosted glass and Brand quickly cooled it. Then he waited a few moments, slowly withdrawing his power. The glass remained unbroken, but there was now a neat hole in it. He slipped his hand through and found the latch. Carefully, he lifted it and then eased the window open.

Brand felt the gazes of the men upon him. He did not like it, for he did not like to be different. Once, he was a warrior just as they, and distrusted magic. Now, he was a lòhren, and magic was another weapon at his disposal like knife, sword or bow. But the men, apart from Taingern and Shorty, were not likely to see it that way.

It did no good to think like that, and Brand shrugged the thoughts aside. He drew his sword, and nimbly went through the window into the dark. The men followed him.

26. Mother of Stars

Gil watched as the girl stepped forward. One moment she was in the air before him, and the next she stood upon the fortification before lightly jumping down to the flag-stone base of the parapet.

It was a strange sight, and Gil wondered what powers she possessed. All the more so, because while she had seemed ethereal before now she was as solid as he was. She was real and not a vision. The night-breeze ruffled her white gown, and he could smell the scent of her hair.

He looked at her in wonderment. When she stepped close to speak to him her voice was soft but resonant, and he felt the warmth of her body even from a pace away.

"One is here," she stated. "One of the Horsemen. His name is Betrayal. But pay no heed to names. They are mere noises in the wind, for Death was Betrayal too. And Betrayal can be Death. The power of the Horsemen is not in their names. Nevertheless, Betrayal is in this city. Close. Very close."

Gil had a sinking feeling in his stomach. Elrika shuffled beside him.

"Where?" he asked.

The girl's arm stretched out, slim and toned, left bare to the shoulder by her white gown. Her eyes glittered with determination, but there was sorrow behind them too, even if hidden, and Gil saw it and wondered why.

"Behold!" she said with force. "Though the four Riders came before me I must follow, for the Mother of

Stars seeks always for balance. Last I came, not summoned but drawn, and my powers still grow. Down there waits one of the Riders, and the man who defeated Death goes thither, but he does not know why. It is a trap, and he will die. This time, the true death."

Gil did not hesitate. "Not if I can help it!"

He knew what man she spoke of. Brand! And he had seen where the regent had gone. At least, he knew roughly, and the girl had said he was close, so he would not be hard to find.

He ran, and Erika and the Durlin ran also. They had heard the warning, and they intended to do something about it just as he did.

Down through the palace they raced, and the strange girl was with them. Who she was, or what, Gil did not care at the moment. All that mattered was reaching Brand and helping him. But nevertheless he knew that there was much more about her to learn, and that she had spoken only a little of all that she could tell.

The long corridors swept them by: doors, wall-hangings, startled servants all left behind in a dazzling rush. Gil raced as close as he could to a full sprint. Brand had been there when he needed him most. He *must* be there to return the favor.

Gil was fast. He had always been fast, and he led the others. The Durlin were close behind him, and just behind them he heard the separate footfalls of Elrika and the girl. That they kept up surprised him, but Elrika was full of surprises. He was not sure he *wanted* her to keep up though. Where they were headed was going to be dangerous.

They burst through the front door of the palace, and hurtled out into the gardens. Now, they could really run,

373

free of constraints and corners and a slippery surface beneath their boots.

Gil increased his pace, though his breath was already coming in great heaves of his chest. *Please! Please!* He thought as his feet pounded the ground. *Let me reach Brand in time!*

27. Neither Sword nor Helm

It was dark in the room that Brand and his men had entered. Dark and silent, for nowhere they heard any noise nor indication of anyone's presence. Yet Sandy had assured them that the conspirators they sought were here. This should have been pleasing, because it meant they slept, yet it only stirred Brand's sense of unease all the more.

One thing was visible though: a dim light ahead. Brand took it to be coming from an inner courtyard of the house. He had been told that one existed, and it seemed a likely place for the Duthenor to gather and share a drink. Such was the custom in Cardoroth. But if there was a light, where were the men? They would not leave a lantern burning for no purpose. Yet if they were there, sharing a drink, why could he not hear their talk?

Brand did not like it. But there was no going back now. He had come to find these renegade Duthenor, these conspirators that had tried to kill Gil and who sought to bring him down, and that he would do.

He moved ahead, one small step at a time, and the men followed his lead. He tried to remember what he could of houses such as these. Most rooms would border the inner courtyard. The center of the house was a paved and gardened area, often open to the sky. It was the heart of the house, where all occupants could gather in private and away from the hustle of the city. Here they would regularly eat, drink, tell stories or just talk. Often there were fruit trees in pots and vegetables as well as intricate ornamental gardens that looked tranquil and beautiful through the day but whose flowers released a range of perfumes at night. They were beautiful places, but not tonight. Tonight, every shadow was potential death.

Brand made a choice. There were many rooms in the house, but it made sense to head for the light first. That was where people were likely to be. So, he kept going in the direction he was headed, one slow step at a time, sensing the men behind him doing the same.

If he wanted to, he could cast out tendrils of lòhrengai to test where the occupants of the house were in the same way that he had done on the street with the guards. But that worked better out in the open. In a building, where there were likely to be several people all in fairly close proximity, it would not work well. Anyway, he preferred to do things the simple way, the way he had for most of his life.

He passed out of the first room and into a corridor. This, he did not like, for the men would be strung out and it would be difficult to bring their weapons to bear if that was necessary. But he could see the tiles of the courtyard ahead now, and that meant they were close to their destination.

Brand eased ahead, moving even more carefully now. The corridor gave way to the courtyard, and he felt space open up around him and a greater movement of air. The light was coming from the other side, perhaps forty or fifty paces away, and it was too dim to see much. The garden beds and tables and benches did not help.

He kept going, and he sensed the men behind him leave the corridor also and begin to spread out. They would be ready now for whatever was to come.

Beneath his boots were intricately decorated tiles. They were of varicolored geometrical designs, typical of such a house. There would be frescos on the walls as well, but all he could see of these were vague glints of color in the shadows. And there were too many of those. The courtyard was large, the shadows were thick and the conspirators could be anywhere. And still there was no noise nor sense of life within the house.

He paused then, uncertain as to what to do. This was not like him, and that worried him also. But his instincts flared to life. Something was wrong, and he had not survived the troubles of his past by ignoring his gut feelings. But what to do about them?

He felt the unease of the men behind him. Twice now he had come to a halt for no reason that they could see. Shorty and Taingern trusted him implicitly. The Durlin also. It was the soldiers that worried him the most. Whatever was done here would spread around the city. He could not afford to appear hesitant or undecided. Even worse, he could not appear to lack courage. These were fatal flaws in a leader, and soon, very soon now if he was not mistaken, Cardoroth would need a leader to guide them through battle and war.

Brand drew his sword. It slid slowly, almost silently out of its sheath. The hilt felt good in his hands, and the balance of the Halathrin-wrought blade was marvelous to feel.

The sword had been his father's, and before that belonged to a long line of Duthenor chieftains. The thought of all those ancestors, their blood in his veins, gave him a surge of pride. They were all dead now, but their names lived on. If he had come here only to die, then he would not go without a fight. He would leave a name after him fit to be spoken alongside that of his ancestors.

The blade glimmered palely before him, picking up the dim light from the other side of the courtyard. Behind him, he heard the whisper of many other blades being drawn.

Brand stepped ahead. He was ready now for what would come next, and he knew it would not be pleasant. But he would not be surprised. Nor would the men he led. If nothing else, his momentary hesitation had made them nervous, and nervous men were wary.

The light grew brighter. It flickered and shimmered, and Brand realized it came from a hearth. In many courtyards such as this, feasts were cooked out in the open when the weather was good. Afterwards, the household would gather by the dying embers to sip wine and talk.

He drew closer. The light flickered and flared, and he smelled the smoke now as the breeze changed direction. A moment later the light steadied, smoke drifted a little to the side, and a man was revealed.

The figure stood still, waiting. His pose was casual, yet he looked poised and ready to move in a heartbeat. That alone signaled he was a warrior, and the long sword at his side served only as confirmation.

Brand did not move. There was no need yet, nor was he about to go running into something that he did not understand. The man had seen him and was not surprised. He knew that men had come into his house to arrest him, for he was undoubtedly one of the Duthenor conspirators. It was obvious by the way he stood and the way he wore his sword, if not by his tall frame and pale hair. Yet why was he not surprised? Had he heard them

378

approach? Or had he somehow learned of the raid in advance?

The mysterious figure stirred. "We meet at last, Brand. Outlaw and hunted man."

The words did not disturb Brand. He would expect as much from one of the usurper's servants. But the situation *did* disturb him. Greatly. There was something terribly wrong about all of this, but he did not yet know what.

"Well met," Brand answered. "Thrall of a usurper."

The man merely shrugged. "I'm not that. No more than you're a typical outlaw. But this much is true. You're a hunted man, and have been for many long years. But the hunt is up. Did you ever think the king would forgive you for what you did?"

Brand remembered slipping into the usurper's house as a mere youth, the house that had been his own father's and that he had grown up in, and taking back his father's sword while the usurper slept.

"A king, is he? The title of chieftain is no longer enough, then?"

"It never was. But the time for words has passed. You will die now, as surely as you should have died all those years ago."

The man gestured. Out of the shadows behind him stepped the remaining Duthenor. There were only a few of them, but they looked like hard men used to fighting and confident of winning.

Their leader spoke again. But Brand searched the shadows with his gaze. The Duthenor were badly outnumbered. But they showed no fear. Why?

"You will die now, Duthenor that was and chieftain that never could be. And the hope that you sparked to

379

life long ago back at home, the very hope that people carry in their hearts because you yet live, will die with you. And the rebellious spirit that they show, thinking that one day you might return, will wither to ash and dust."

Brand considered those words. They were true. Yet the opposite was also true. How greatly the usurper would fear the rise of the Duthenor if the rightful heir returned, not as the youth that long ago escaped the hunt, but as a grown man ready and able to fight.

"If just my life gave them hope," Brand said, "then imagine what they will do when I return to my homeland, as one day soon I shall."

Slowly, Brand reached into the hessian pouch that he carried slung over his shoulder. He dropped the bag, and revealed its contents. In his hand he held a helm. This he placed upon his head. Long it had been since last he wore it, but it fitted well and pride surged again within him. It gleamed with a silver light amid the shadowy courtyard, and the patterns etched within the metal caught the ruddy light of the fire and cast it back like the promise of blood yet to flow.

Brand straightened to his full height. He looked into the eyes of the leader who stood opposite him. For the first time, he read doubt there.

The Duthenor the man led seemed uneasy also. They shifted nervously on their feet, peering at this new development.

"The Helm of the Duthenor!" one hissed.

"Indeed it is," Brand said. "The mark of the Duthenor chieftains of old, and worn only by the rightful chieftain. And that is me. And I will reclaim what is mine, and the master you all serve shall be thrown from the hall that he stole, the hall in which he murdered my parents. This I have sworn, and I swear again that it shall be so."

There was silence. Doubt grew among the enemy, and Brand sensed his own men ready themselves for a fight. But that would not come yet.

The enemy leader regained his composure. "A pretty trinket. And I will not dispute that it is the real helm. How ever did you come by it? It has been lost to our people for hundreds of years."

Brand smiled. "A pretty trinket? A cheap name for something crafted by the immortal Halathrin and worth more than all the gold in this city."

"How then did you acquire it?"

"I was willing to pay the greatest price of all."

"And what was that?"

"My life," Brand said.

The man smiled at him. "I see that you did not make good your end of the deal though."

"It was close, but I bargained better than the seller expected." Brand raised the tip of his sword. "It was not easy."

"And who was the seller?"

"You have heard of him. Shurilgar the Sorcerer. Shurilgar the Betrayer of Nations."

There was silence again. Brand did not mind talking, for all the while he was trying to work out what else was in the shadows behind his enemies.

"That is a lie," the Duthenor leader said at last. "Shurilgar is dead. All men know it."

"I don't lie," Brand said. "Shurilgar is dead, but yet still his spirit endures in Alithoras. And it is dangerous

381

beyond your reckoning. So, enough of this. Fight, or give yourselves up."

The man seemed disturbed. This was all more than he had bargained for, and he must have sensed the men behind him wavering. But he had a surprise of his own prepared, and decided to play it now.

"You defeated a legendary opponent, if a dead one, to claim the helm. But," he said, allowing a note of triumph into his voice, "neither sword nor helm will save you from this!"

The man gestured toward the shadows behind him. "Come forth!"

In the darkness, there was movement. A figure began to take form as it came forward. Brand's heart sank. He knew that the Duthenor had some last card yet to play, but he had not expected this. But he should have.

There was a clatter of hooves. The figure was mounted, and a sense of menace came with it. It was one of the Riders. His steed was gray, its hooves shod by iron that echoed dully from the four walls of the courtyard. It snorted, and its ears flicked in agitation.

The Rider upon him seemed a tottery old man. His back was hunched, his eyes were red and rheumy. There was palsy in his gnarled hands, and the skin that covered them was thin, hanging in flaps from little more than bone. Yet there was power in his gaze, power that took the breath away.

Brand sensed the blood magic that formed the Rider, and his instincts as a lòhren flared to life. The uneasiness that had long gripped him was finally given visible form, and yet something was still wrong. Carnhaina had said the second Rider would be War. Yet this, surely, was Time. But Brand had no leisure to consider such things.

The horse came to a standstill, only its ears still moving. Its eyes were bleak pools of shadow that no light seemed to bring to life. The Rider upon him bore no weapon, but his rheumy gaze gleamed with fierce malevolence.

"Well met, Brand," the Rider croaked. His voice was soft, but horrible to hear. It was like a whisper coming up from the deep soil of a grave.

Brand lifted high his sword. "You do not belong here. Go back whence you came!"

The ancient figure laughed. His lips drew back tightly, exposing rotting teeth and blackened gums pockmarked with sores.

"Fool. I belong everywhere. And with you especially. I have been with you all the days of your life."

Brand forced himself to step forward. His Halathrin-wrought blade rose higher still. The fire in the hearth had burned to low embers, and the room was colored by its ruddy light. The smell of smoke was stronger now, for the breeze had stilled.

Time sat astride his mount and watched Brand with an expression of infinite patience. Then he shook his head.

"A fool until the end. You cannot defeat me. All men succumb to me, in time."

"Then I shall give you none!"

Brand leaped forward. The Rider's head wobbled on his neck, and a tremor ran through one arm. But his rheumy eyes narrowed and gleamed.

Brand stumbled and fell. His sword clattered to the floor, and the Helm of the Duthenor rolled from his head.

There was a momentary silence. Taingern stepped forward. Shorty came with him.

"And do you also seek the same fate?"

The two Durlindraths did not falter. "Where Brand goes, we go," Taingern said.

They continued forward. Nothing happened until they reached Brand. From there, they prepared themselves to attack, but just as Brand had been struck down, so were they. They fell as though struck by an invisible force.

The soft laugh of the Rider filled the room.

28. Now is the Time

Gil ran as he had never run before. The others were still with him. It had been a mad rush through the streets, and though not far their speed had been great. But there was a price paid for speed: they were already tired and he knew a fight was yet to come.

He halted suddenly. There he stood upon the dark street, for his senses had caught what he was looking for. In moments, the others caught up. He spared them a quick glance. Would they be enough for what was to come? The four Durlin were skilled in combat, and equal to at least double their number of ordinary warriors. Elrika was skilled as well, and she had no lack of courage. The strange girl, the only one of them seemingly unruffled by the run, stood there and gazed at him. She was a mystery too deep for him to fathom, and he had no idea of what she might be capable. That she was here to help seemed plain enough, but the manner of that help was something that he would only discover when it was needed.

"Where's Brand?" Elrika asked.

Gil did not answer. He had sensed the regent's presence, or rather the feel of his lòhrengai. Gil summoned his own. It came in a swift rush, flowing up through him and pouring out with a life of its own. The magic was getting stronger each time he summoned it, and Gil was not sure that was a good thing.

Straightaway, the lòhrengai speared with a blue light toward a gate set within a perimeter wall of a noble's mansion. Gil sensed something of what Brand had done here. It was a small magic, but more subtle than anything that Gil could do. The traces of it lingered, and then further away, somewhere within the grounds of the manor, he sensed Brand's power again. This he could identify: heat and cold, the basic forces that lòhrengai often took and manipulated.

Gil thrust his hand out and pointed to the gate. "In there!" he cried.

The Durlin were quicker than he was. They raced to the gate and wrenched it open. There was a guard there in a chair, and he rose as the gate clanged. The man drew his sword and yelled. Gil heard footsteps pound toward them.

"Stand aside!" ordered one of the Durlin.

"Get out!" shout the guard in reply. The man wove his sword before him and the other two guards drew theirs with a hiss, their blades leaping into their hands.

Gil stepped forward. "I'm Prince Gilcarist. Do you recognize me? Brand is inside, and I'm going to see him. Whatever your orders are, I now revoke them. Stand aside!"

The guard studied him. "I know who you are, princeling. But I don't care. My master said not to let anyone in, and that's an end to it. Be off with you."

Gil felt anger rise. These men were not Duthenor, but Camar. But their lord was one of the nobles, no doubt one who plotted for the throne, Gil's throne, and the attitude of the nobles flowed down to their men. Yet still, he did not wish to see them harmed. But matters were taken out of his control.

"You've been instructed by your prince to stand aside," the Durlin spoke again. "Do it, or die. There is no more time to talk."

The guard spat. "That's what I think of you and the prince. Be off with you!"

The Durlin did not hesitate. There were four of them and only three guards. The guards did not have a chance, but probably did not even realize it. They had never seen the Durlin in action, but Gil had. His stomach churned with the thought of the violence about to be unleashed.

Without hesitation the Durlin acted. Their swords hissed from their sheaths and they bridged the gap between themselves and the guards with astonishing speed. Steel struck steel, but it was not a fight.

The Durlin were swift and skilled, while the guards were only average fighters. But the Durlin did not kill. Within moments they had disarmed the guards, sending their swords flying. One man fell to his knees, blood spurting from his hand, and the other two men backed away. But although the Durlin did not kill, they were not prepared to leave enemies behind them. The kneeling guard was struck with the pommel of a sword to his head. He collapsed like a toppled tree. The other two suffered a swift succession of kicks and elbows to body and head. They fell to the ground and did not move.

Gil was amazed. He knew the skill the Durlin had, but he also knew their rule. If ever they were forced to draw a blade, they must be prepared to kill. There was no safe way to merely try to disarm someone, but still they had risked it. They were good men, and their skill was only a part of it.

They sheathed their swords. "Let's go!"

387

This time, Gil and the others followed the Durlin. They knew where Brand was now, for the house was visible ahead through the night-time shadows. It hulked against the horizon, dark and forbidding.

Gil followed swiftly, wondering what lay ahead. He had no doubt the Durlin could deal with any physical threat, but there was likely to be magic also. And if Brand was in danger, then that magic would be very great. The question that ran through Gil's mind even as he raced ahead was what could *he* do to help?

The manor grounds were dark. Many of the nobles' homes had lanterns set on poles along the carriageway that led to the building. That was not so here, although Gil soon saw the poles existed but no lanterns were lit. He wondered whose house this was, and why Brand had come here with many men. The answer that came to him was one that he did not like. Sandy had discovered the hideout of either the rebel nobles or the Duthenor assassins.

They sped down the driveway. It was constructed of gravel to ensure that carriage wheels did not bog in wet weather. This meant that as they ran the sound they made was loud. But the Durlin made no attempt to move off the gravel, and Gil understood why. Brand may have come here in secrecy, but what mattered now was speed. Away from the driveway, there were gardens that would slow them down.

The house loomed ahead of them. They were close now, but the place seemed dark and quiet. No lights showed, and it seemed as though no one was even home.

Gil sent out tendrils of lòhrengai, seeking sign of Brand again. Perhaps he was not in the house but somewhere in the grounds. His mind swept the area, and his gaze also. He sensed nothing with the magic and saw only the shadowy outlines of trees and bushes and an expanse of well-clipped lawns.

He turned his magic toward the house. It was dark, relieved only by beds of bushes with night-scented blossoms that shone silver-white in the dim light.

The gardens would be beautiful by day, and the house also. And yet with a sudden stab Gil sensed evil within. Something was there, and it had summoned magic of its own. It was the Rider the girl had warned of, and Brand was already there.

"Hurry!" Gil shouted.

They had come now to the very front of the house. The gravel carriageway turned toward stables and sheds to the side. But a tiled path led straight to the front door. This the Durlin took, and the others followed close behind.

They came to a door set within a marble portico. The Durlin tried to open it, but it was locked. There was no way to force it, for it was made of solid oak.

One of the Durlin thought of something. He went swiftly to one of the nearby gardens and lifted up a large rock from the line of them that formed an edge to a flower bed. This he brought back and flung into the window of the room next to the door. There was a shrieking clatter of ruined glass and shards flew everywhere. He stepped forward then, his sword drawn, and kicked in the remaining glass.

"Careful!" he warned as he stepped through into the house.

The other Durlin were close behind. Gil stepped through next, followed by Elrika and the strange girl. It was dark inside, and Gil drew his sword also.

389

It was quiet again after the sudden noise. There was no movement nor sign of life. For all that Gil wanted to race ahead and find Brand, now was no time to be hasty. He could not help the regent if he were killed in the attempt. So, he followed the lead of the Durlin, who were far more experienced than he was.

The Durlin fanned out. Three went slowly ahead, swords drawn and creeping forward step by agonizing step. The fourth formed a rearguard.

Gil went forward with Elrika beside him. He could see her face in the dim light: pale, scared but determined. She may not yet have the skill of a Durlin, but one day he knew she would. She was gifted. And if she did not have that skill now, she was still dangerous. He would not like to cross swords with her.

The strange girl was just a little to his side and behind him. Could he trust her? He had no way of knowing, but his instincts told him that he could. She seemed to move without sound or fear, nor did she carry any weapon that he could see. For all that she had first appeared as an ethereal vision, she was solid now and there was no sign that that was going to change. Perhaps, even as she had said, she was seeking him, and having found him she would now remain with him. Perhaps, having become flesh and blood, she could not return to her former state.

The Durlin led them out of the room and into a corridor. This was not wide, and they drew close together. Gil could tell they did not like it. If they were attacked, they had no room to maneuver. As a consequence, their pace quickened.

Within moments a dim light showed at the end of the passage. It was faint, and the smell of smoke was in the air. Gil did not like that. Was the house on fire? He realized though that this was not the case. The corridor was headed toward a courtyard. It was natural that a fire would be set there in a hearth, and it explained the light also.

The Durlin paused. They had heard something, and then Gil heard it too. Voices.

There was nothing to do besides go forward, and this the Durlin did. Their white surcoats made them more visible in the dark, but that could not be helped. If they were worried about arrows or daggers flung from the dark, they did not show it. The possibility would have occurred to them though, and this was why they now held their blades vertically in front of their bodies. This position increased the surface area of the weapon before them, protecting them a little more than if the blade were held point forward. Brand had taught him that once, but he had forgotten.

Gil raised his sword in the same way. Slowly, the courtyard emerged into his view. There were figures there waiting for them. He could make little out except that there were two groups and that the presence of evil that he had sensed before suddenly increased.

In a few more paces he saw what he had wished never to see again. Brand was there, but the regent was on his knees. Shorty and Taingern lay stricken beside him. And beyond, now visible, was the nightmare figure of a Rider. It was not the one the scry basin had shown him, but the jolt of the creature's presence rocked him. It did not matter which it was, for each was as bad as the other. Each was a blight upon the earth, a presence in this world that should not be here and that sought the destruction of all that he held dear.

391

Gil gritted his teeth. One thing was certain: Brand was not dead, and he had arrived in time to help. But what could he, or the Durlin, do that Brand and his men had not already tried?

Through the shadowy light Gil sensed the eyes of the Horseman upon him. He looked up and held that awful gaze. But the evil that he sensed before was as nothing. Now, he felt a wave of hatred wash over him like a withering wind.

He understood how Brand and the Durlindraths had been felled. There was magic in the air, and Gil was only on the outer edge of it. Closer, he sensed that the force was stronger by far. There was hope in that too, for strong as this magic was, it had limits. And distance was one. But that thought was not overly comforting. He could not hope to defeat the Rider without getting close. But if Brand had fallen, how could he, so much lesser in the powers of body and magic, expect to approach and take the fight to the enemy?

Gil tore his eyes away from the Horseman, and the sense of being overpowered reduced. He glanced at his companions. They were rooted to the spot as was he, unable to move.

But one figure did move. Brand reached forth with a trembling hand and gripped the hilt of his sword that lay on the tiles before him. Slowly, he rose until he stood upon trembling legs. There he swayed, a picture of defiance in the face of all odds.

The Rider spoke, and his ancient voice was a croak of amusement.

"Ah, but this is glorious. So few, so very few defy me. But listen, mortal, and understand. None defy me for long."

Brand did not answer. He took a tottering step forward. But even as he did so Gil saw that it made him weaker. It confirmed that the magic of the Rider was stronger the closer it was brought to bear.

The Duthenor around the Rider laughed. Brand responded to this with a mighty effort, standing straighter and taking yet another step. But his arm that carried the sword trembled as though the blade were made of lead instead of Halathrin steel.

Gil was amazed. There was no give in Brand, and he would fight to the end. But this did not appear to be a battle he could win. He had not found a weakness in the enemy's power to exploit. Nor could Gil see one either. What arrogance had driven him to come here? He could not help. He was powerless. And yet he *must* find a way. For Brand, he would do anything.

The tribesmen taunted the regent. "Go ahead," they said. "Move closer. Each step is death, and we shall tell the tale of your fall at home. Every Duthenor, young or old, will hear it. We shall tell how you fell, how you died, helpless before your enemy."

Brand glanced at them. His gaze was colder than ice, and they fell silent.

He turned his eyes back to the Rider.

"Come, face me then. If I cannot walk to you, walk to me."

The Rider studied him a moment, as though assessing if he were capable of any harm. Then he nudged his horse forward, and a new wave of malice filled the room. It smashed into Gil like a wave, and he crumbled to his knees.

But somehow, despite it all, Brand remained standing. The Rider dismounted, his frail-seeming figure all tottery

393

and feeble. He hobbled closer to Brand on foot, and peered at him as though he were a man studying mud that had dried on his boots and deciding how best to dislodge it.

Contemptuously, he slapped Brand's sword away. It clattered to the floor. Then he placed a hand upon Brand's head. The regent looked as though he was going to throw a punch, but the strength left his body. Instead, he collapsed to his knees once more.

"Yes, mortal," hissed the Rider. "Bow to me."

The regent could not stand, yet he lifted his head high and gazed at the Rider. There was determination in that gaze, and the will to succeed that had seen him survive countless fights. Yet his arms hung loose by his side and the only fight that he had left within him was in his eyes.

Gil reached out with his mind. He sensed Brand's heart flutter. It raced and thrummed unnaturally. He would die soon, and there was no Carnhaina here to save him this time. Gil could not bear it. He turned his mind toward the Rider, and he sensed the inevitability of time. It radiated from the figure in waves, but they were concentrated on Brand rather than the others in the room.

Even so, Gil felt the last dregs of his own strength drain from him. It slipped away like the wind stripping autumn leaves from a tree. Yet this magic was no spell. Not in the sense that Gil understood it. Instead, it stemmed from the very nature of the Rider, and its origin was from another world, and ever so faintly Gil sensed that the Rider was still connected to that world through the gateway that had been opened and through which he had been summoned.

He considered that. Each Rider was an embodiment of a great force, but the Riders were not really the things themselves. Brand, far more adept at lòhrengai than he, must have sensed these things also. But could that knowledge be turned to an advantage?

The Rider leaned in closer, placing both hands upon the regent's head now, and slowly they slid down Brand's face until the fingers, knobbed and deformed by arthritis, were at his temples. But the thumbs were near Brand's eyes, and they moved toward them.

"Beg, Brand of the Duthenor. Beg, Regent of Cardoroth. Beg, and perhaps I will spare your sight."

Brand gave no answer. But his eyes flashed with defiance.

Gil burned with fury. He sensed no weakness in the Rider, no way to exploit his understanding of where his power came from. But he would do anything to help. He prepared to act, to hurl his own power at the Rider, though he knew it would do no good.

The Rider pushed back Brand's head. His fingers stiffened and his thumbs went rigid as they pressed toward Brand's eyes.

Gil sensed the glee of the Rider, though it was lessened by Brand's defiance. He also felt the regent's fear. Above it all was a pall of horror that hung in the room thicker than smoke from the dying fire. His senses were alert, the lòhrengai within him ready to lash out and attack. It rose, furious like a wild animal that is caged but about to break free.

No! The command rang through Gil's mind. It was the strange girl, and her voice was as thunder in his head. *Not that way. Forget the Rider. Think of Brand!*

395

The lòhrengai in Gil roiled and seethed, trying to break free. He could not restrain it much longer, and that scared him. It was growing within him, and he was not sure he could control it.

He wanted to scream. If he could not unleash his lòhrengai upon the Rider, what then could he do? He tried to move forward to intervene physically, but he had not the strength to do so. The power of the Rider held him in place.

Now! yelled the girl within his mind. *Now!*

At last, Gil understood. He had not the skill with lòhrengai nor the strength of body to help Brand. But Brand had both. Gil had thought he would do anything for Brand, and so he would. But at last he knew what that should be.

He dismissed the Rider from his thoughts and focused only on the regent. He reached out to touch his mind. For a fleeting moment, for just a single instant in time, they became one. Their thoughts and memories merged. Above it all he felt the indomitable will of Brand, the determination of someone who would never give up. And in that moment he pulsed to him through their link the last of his own strength. It flowed from his body into Brand's. It flowed from his mind too. And lòhrengai went with it.

Gil fell forward to the floor. He tried to get back to his knees, but he had nothing left to give. Yet his eyes remained open, and he watched.

Brand reached out. Suddenly filled with strength, his arms snaked forward and caught hold of the Rider's head. The Rider released his own grip and tried to step back, sudden fear in his eyes, but Brand's grip was like iron. His hands twisted with a jerk. There was a sickening crack, and the Rider went limp. His head sagged loosely as Brand let him go and he fell to the tiled floors. Even as he hit the ground his horse screamed and reared up. But it too, joined by blood magic to the Rider, died. It fell writhing to the floor beside its master, and then lay still.

There was utter silence. A cold wind blew and green flame licked around the corpses. The stench of death filled the air, and Rider and mount disappeared in a waft of greasy smoke.

Once more, Gil tried to rise. But the world spun and darkness closed in. His heart fluttered rapidly, and then the great dark swallowed him.

29. I have Many Names

Brand ignored the Duthenor. He turned and ran to Gil. He knew what the boy had done for him, and what he had risked to give aid. He knew what the price of such a gift might be.

Gil lay there, unmoving. Brand reached down and felt for a pulse. It was there, but it was erratic and thready. Nor was his color good. He was pale, and a sheen of sweat glistened over his sickly skin.

All about him the Durlin and soldiers were moving. They had their swords drawn, and it appeared that the Duthenor were going to fight even though the odds were against them.

"Enough!" Brand said. He stood and pointed at the Duthenor. "Today, you have served a great evil. If you would repent that, put down your swords and wait on my justice."

The Duthenor looked uncertain. They knew they could die in the name of justice. They knew also that they *would* die if they fought. And beneath it all, there was undeniable truth in the statement that they had served evil.

One by one, they placed their swords on the tiled floor. Their leader was the last to do so, and he did not like it. He had the most to lose and the least expectation of leniency.

The men of Cardoroth surrounded them. Brand paid them no more heed. He knelt again beside Gil. Once more he felt for the boy's pulse. It was worse than before.

He felt a hand on his shoulder, its touch soft and gentle. A girl stood beside him, dressed in white. She was dazzlingly beautiful, but her eyes were sad.

He studied her a moment. That she had come with Gil he knew, but he did not know who she was. He knew that there was a strangeness about her though.

Elrika was there also. She knelt and took Gil's hands. There were tears in her eyes.

Brand looked back to the strange girl. Something about her disturbed him. She seemed in some way to be similar to the Riders, and yet he knew that she was not. "Who *are* you?"

She took her hand from his shoulder. "I have many names. I am light and shadow, day and night, heat and cold, love and hate." She paused for a moment, and then added. "Need I say more to one who has seen the heart of both good and evil?"

"No. You are balance. At least, that is your function here. You have been drawn into this world in the wake of the Riders. Nature always seeks harmony. But you, just like the Riders, aren't really here. Not yet, anyway. You are all shadows, the image of things drawn into this world while the reality remains in your own."

Her eyes widened slightly. "You are very perceptive. But the Riders would come to this world in truth, whereas I would not. And you can guess, therefore, how this must all end?"

Brand understood. She was connected to the Riders, and they to her, by the gateway through which they entered his world. They could not be separated. At least, not in Alithoras.

"Sadly, I do."

She looked upon him with wise eyes, and he felt the sorrow behind them. "But the boy does not. Nor should he. And there is balance in that … even as there was balance in you offering your life for his in the past and he doing the same for you just now."

"And yet I lived, and it seems that he will not."

"No, Brand. He will not die. Not this day, at least."

She knelt down beside him. Once more she rested her hand upon his shoulder, but now her other hand also touched Gil's face. She closed her eyes, and Brand marveled at her. He knew her fate should she succeed in her quest. The Riders must be returned to her world, and he knew now that there was only one way to do that. Not even death sufficed, for the gateway remained open and they could come through again. She was a creature of such sweetness, of such strength. But above it all was the determination to fulfill her purpose … no matter the cost.

He felt the warmth of her touch. He sensed her power. And then he perceived what she was doing. She was drawing back from him the strength that Gil had given.

The prince gasped. He rolled his head from side to side, and then his eyes flicked open. His gaze settled on Brand. A moment they looked at each other, and then Elrika had her arms about the boy, hugging him fiercely.

The lady beside him took her hands away from both of them, and straightened. Brand stood up beside her.

"Thank you, lady," he said.

She nodded gravely, but did not reply.

Brand turned to the Duthenor. Their weapons had been collected and placed in a pile on the floor. The men stood within a tight circle, the Durlin and the soldiers of Cardoroth surrounding them with drawn swords.

The leader gazed at Brand with a sullen expression.

"Let's get this over with."

Brand looked at him coolly. "Get what over with?"

"I'm in no mood to talk. Just kill us quickly."

Brand returned his look, ice cold hatred in exchange for sullenness. Then without speaking he walked across the tiled floor and retrieved his sword and helm. The Helm of the Duthenor he placed once more upon his head, but the sword he kept drawn. A little while he gazed at the leader of the group of traitors who served the usurper and who had also tried to assassinate Gil. If any men deserved death, it was these.

At length, he spoke. "You will not die. Not today. But you will leave the city, and never return. Should you do so, then surely your life will be forfeit."

The men looked at him. He could see that they did not believe it.

"Go!" he commanded. "Return to your master. Tell him this. His plot has failed. Tell him that I will soon return. And justice will come with me. He shall wish then that he were never born."

They looked at him, baffled by his lenience. "Go!" he commanded once more. "And take your swords with you."

This time, the Duthenor moved. They could not quite believe what was happening, and nor could Brand's own men. Yet the Camar allowed them through to their weapons.

The Duthenor retrieved their blades from the floor, but the leader hesitated.

"Pick it up," Brand said. "But don't even think of using it."

The man reached for his blade. A moment he held it, and then he slammed it home in its sheath. His men sheathed theirs also.

"One last thing," Brand said. "I am the rightful chieftain of the Duthenor. You serve a usurper. But think well on this. You serve a traitor. It will not end well for you. He is doomed, and so will you be, while you serve him. This grace to depart in freedom that I have now given you is done as Regent of Cardoroth. Should I need to judge you one day as Chieftain of the Duthenor, I will be harsher."

The leader looked at him. "You seek to turn us to your cause?"

Brand shook his head. "No. You would need to change greatly before I would have you serve me. You are not good men. Yet neither are you truly evil. Go home. Pass on my message. Then, you shall stand at a crossroads. Serve the usurper and die. Leave him, and your destiny will be far richer."

The leader stared at Brand. "I knew you of old, though you don't remember me. You were never a prophet. Nor a seer. These are just words."

"I was never Regent of Cardoroth before," Brand replied. "Nor a lòhren. Now I am both. I have grown, and so may yet you. And I *do* remember you. Your name is Rathbold. Once upon a time you were apprenticed to the village blacksmith. But he dismissed you and you took up a life of outlawry in the forest."

The leader was surprised by this, but he said nothing. Instead, he gave a single curt nod and led his men from the courtyard.

Shorty came over to Brand as the Duthenor filed out. "They'll not change," he said.

The strange girl heard his words. Her gaze had been on the Duthenor as they left, but she had been watching them as though she saw with a sight beyond that of eyes.

"No, they will not," she agreed. "But one will, and he will do great good in the world that otherwise would not have happened." She curtsied to Brand as she spoke.

Shorty gave her a careful look, unsure who she was or what she was doing there but recognizing that Brand knew these things.

"But still," he continued. "To see them just walk out of here after what they've done. That's not right."

"No," Brand agreed. "It isn't. But it will send word swifter than an arrow to my people that I'm coming home. That word will spread wherever those men go. The rumor will catch like wildfire. And the usurper will begin to know fear. In the end, the release of these men will help topple a cruel tyrant. So, although justice is not served in Cardoroth, it will have a better chance of prospering in the lands of the Duthenor."

Shorty thought about that. Then he shook his head. "You always look at the bigger picture. But for myself, I would have killed them. Anyway, how do you know they'll not find another hideout in Cardoroth and keep plotting against you?"

Brand shrugged. "They might do that. But if I'm any judge of men, especially Duthenor men, they won't. They know that to stay is to die, and they would rather live."

"Brand is right," the strange girl said. "And also, the leader has lost the confidence of his men. He might have wished to stay, but the men have had enough."

403

Shorty looked at her again, his expression curious. "It is a pleasure to meet you, lady. But who are you?"

She smiled at him. "A friend, Lornach. But if I need a name, then please call me … call me Lady. I like that."

Shorty bowed. "Then, the White Lady you are."

There was a commotion nearby. Despite Elrika's protests, Gil had stood up. His legs seemed wobbly, and his skin was pale. But there was a smile on his face.

"We did it," he said.

"That we did," Brand answered. Then he hugged him.

They separated and looked at each other. "You've grown, Gil. You're ready to come into your own."

"Let's not talk about that just yet. Today is a day for celebration. We've defeated a Rider. At least you have, with a little help. And there are only two more to go before it's all over."

Brand looked at the White Lady, and he saw the truth in her eyes.

"It is not that simple," she said to Gil. "Two Riders are defeated. But they may yet come again, for the gateway remains open. And there are two left undefeated, Betrayal and War. Nor is that all. War is not just a name, but also his function. Even as we speak an army gathers against you, and War shall lead it."

Gil let out a sigh. "An army? And it's ready to march upon us?"

"Verily," the White Lady answered.

Gil turned to Brand. "You're still regent, assuming that you want to remain so. What do you suggest we do?"

"I have something yet to offer Cardoroth," Brand answered. "My day of departure is coming, but it won't be for a little while yet. I suggest two things. You must close the gateway, and I must prepare a strategy to defeat the army that comes against us. But I suspect, Gil, that the two are linked. Neither the gateway will be closed nor the enemy defeated until a great battle has been fought."

The White Lady nodded, but did not offer any information. Brand knew there was much she could say though. Yet perhaps she was right. Some things were better off unknown until the end.

He looked back at Gil. The boy that he once had tutored was gone. A young man now stood before him.

"One last thing, Gil. You will be king one day very soon. Though I remain regent for a while longer, the truth is that you now command. At least, I shall defer to your will should we disagree."

Gil heard those words, and even as he did so Brand saw the weight of responsibility settle over his shoulders. It was a weight that could crush. He hoped the prince was strong enough to bear it. For all that had happened so far was but a shadow of what was yet to come. And it was coming soon.

Thus ends *Sword of the Blood*. The Son of Sorcery series continues in *Light of the Realm*, where Gil will face the gathering threat to Cardoroth and attempt to fulfil the quest bestowed upon him.

Amazon lists millions of titles, and I'm glad that you discovered this one. But if you'd like to know when I release a new book, instead of leaving it to chance, sign up for my newsletter. I'll send you an email on publication.

Yes please! – Go to www.homeofhighfantasy.com and sign up.

No thanks – I'll take my chances.

Encyclopedic Glossary

Note: the glossary of each book in this series is individualized for that book alone. Additionally, there is often historical material provided in its entries for people, artifacts and events that are not included in the main text.

Many races dwell in Alithoras. All have their own language, and though sometimes related to one another, the changes sparked by migration, isolation and various influences often render these tongues unintelligible to each other.

The ascendancy of Halathrin culture, combined with their widespread efforts to secure and maintain allies against elug incursions, has made their language the primary means of communication between diverse peoples.

For instance, a soldier of Cardoroth addressing a ship's captain from Camarelon would speak Halathrin, or a simplified version of it, even though their native speeches stem from the same ancestral language.

This glossary contains a range of names and terms. Many are of Halathrin origin, and their meaning is provided. The remainder derive from native tongues and are obscure, so meanings are only given intermittently.

Often, Camar names and Halathrin elements are combined. This is especially so for the aristocracy. No other tribes of men had such long-term friendship with the immortal Halathrin, and though in this relationship they lost some of their natural culture, they gained nobility and knowledge in return.

List of abbreviations:

Azn. Azan

Cam. Camar

Comb. Combined

Cor. Corrupted form

Duth. Duthenor

Hal. Halathrin

Leth. Letharn

Prn. Pronounced

Age of Heroes: A period of Camar history that has become mythical. Many tales are told of this time. Some are true while others are not. Yet, even the false ones usually contain elements of historical fact. Many were the heroes who walked abroad during this time, and they are remembered and honored still by the Camar people. The old days are looked back on with pride, and the descendants of many heroes walk the streets of

Cardoroth unaware of their heritage and the accomplishments of their forefathers.

Alithoras: *Hal.* "Silver land." The Halathrin name for the continent they settled after their exodus from their homeland. Refers to the extensive river and lake systems they found and their wonder at the beauty of the land.

Anast Dennath: *Hal.* "Stone mountains." Mountain range in northern Alithoras. Source of the river known as the Careth Nien that forms a natural barrier between the lands of the Camar people and the Duthenor and related tribes.

Arach Neben: *Hal.* "West gate." The defensive wall surrounding Cardoroth has four gates. Each is named after a cardinal direction, and each carries a token to represent a celestial object. Arach Neben bears a steel ornament of the Morning Star.

Aranloth: *Hal.* "Noble might." A lòhren. Founder and head of the lòhren order. A great friend of Gilcarist's grandparents.

Arell: Rumored to be Brand's lover. A name formerly common among the Camar people, but nowadays out of favor in Cardoroth. Its etymology is obscure, though it is speculated that it derives from the Halathrin stems "aran" and "ell" meaning noble and slender. Ell, in the Halathrin tongue, also refers to any type of timber that is pliable, for instance, hazel. This is cognate with our word wych-wood, meaning timber that is supple and pliable. As elùgroths use wych-wood staffs as instruments of sorcery, it is sometimes supposed their name derives from this stem, rather than elù (shadowed). This is a plausible philological theory. Nevertheless, as a matter of historical fact, it is wrong.

Aurellin: *Cor. Hal.* The first element means blue. The second is native Camar. Formerly Queen of Cardoroth, wife to Gilhain and grandmother to Gilcarist.

Betrayal: One of the Riders, also called Horsemen, summoned into Alithoras by Ginsar. He represents and instigates betrayal. Yet, in truth, the Riders are spirit-beings from another world. They have been given form and nature within Alithoras by Ginsar. The form provided by her is part of the blood sorcery that binds them to her will. In their own world, they do not bear these names or natures. Yet they are creatures wholly of evil, and though bound by Ginsar they seek to break that bond. Even if defeated, the bond from the summoning persists and the Riders are capable of rising again, even though they are considered dead.

Brand: A Duthenor tribesman. Appointed by the former king of Cardoroth to serve as regent for Gilcarist. By birth, he is the rightful chieftain of the Duthenor people. However, a usurper overthrew his father, killing both him and his wife. Brand, only a youth at the time, swore an oath of vengeance. That oath sleeps, but it is not forgotten, either by Brand or the usurper.

Camar: *Cam. Prn.* Kay-mar. A race of interrelated tribes that migrated in two main stages. The first brought them to the vicinity of Halathar, homeland of the immortal Halathrin; in the second, they separated and established cities along a broad stretch of eastern Alithoras.

Cardoroth: *Cor. Hal. Comb. Cam.* A Camar city, often called Red Cardoroth. Some say this alludes to the red granite commonly used in the construction of its buildings, others that it refers to a prophecy of destruction.

Cardurleth: *Hal.* "Car – red, dur – steadfast, leth – stone." The defensive wall that surrounds Cardoroth. Established soon after the city's founding and constructed of red granite. It looks displeasing to the eye, but the people of the city love it nonetheless. They believe it impregnable and hold that no enemy shall ever breach it – except by treachery.

Careth Nien: *Hal. Prn.* Kareth nyen. "Great river." Largest river in Alithoras. Has its source in the mountains of Anast Dennath and runs southeast across the land before emptying into the sea. It was over this river (which sometimes freezes along its northern stretches) that the Camar and other tribes migrated into the eastern lands. Much later, Brand came to the city of Cardoroth by one of these ancient migratory routes.

Carnhaina: First element native *Cam.* Second *Hal.* "Heroine." An ancient queen of Cardoroth. Revered as a savior of her people, but to some degree also feared for she possessed powers of magic. Hated to this day by elùgroths because she overthrew their power unexpectedly at a time when their dark influence was rising. According to legend, kept alive mostly within the royal family of Cardoroth, she guards the city even in death and will return in its darkest hour.

Chapterhouse: Special halls set aside in the palace of Cardoroth for the private meetings, teachings and military training of the Durlin.

Death: One of the Riders, also called Horsemen, summoned into Alithoras by Ginsar. He represents and instigates Death. Yet, in truth, the Riders are spirit-beings from another world. They have been given form and nature within Alithoras by Ginsar. The form provided by her is part of the blood sorcery that binds them to her will. In their own world, they do not bear these names or natures. Yet they are creatures wholly of evil, and though bound by Ginsar they seek to break that bond. Even if defeated, the bond from the summoning persists and the Riders are capable of rising again, even though they are considered dead.

Dernbrael: *Hal.* "Sharp tongued." By some translations, "cunning tongued." A lord of Cardoroth. Out of favor with the old king due to mistrust. Attempted to usurp the throne from Gilcarist, and now in hiding after his scheme failed. It is said that he is in league with the traitor Hvargil, though this has never been proven. It is known, however, that Hvargil once saved his life when they were younger men. This occurred in a gambling den of ill-repute, and the details are obscure. Nevertheless, all accounts agree that Hvargil was wounded protecting his friend.

Drinbar: A captain in Cardoroth's army. Loyal to Brand and Gil. His father was once a Durlin who guarded King Gilhain.

Durlin: *Hal.* "The steadfast." The original Durlin were the seven sons of the first king of Cardoroth. They guarded him against all enemies, of which there were many, and three died to protect him. Their tradition continued throughout Cardoroth's history, suspended only once, and briefly, some four hundred years ago when it was discovered that three members were secretly in the service of elùgroths. These were imprisoned, but committed suicide while waiting for the king's trial to commence. It is rumored that the king himself provided them with the knives that they used. It is said that he felt sorry for them and gave them this way out to avoid the shame a trial would bring to their families.

Durlin creed: These are the native Camar words, long remembered and greatly honored, that were uttered by the first Durlin to die while he defended his father, who was also the king, from attack. Tum del conar – El dar tum! Death or infamy – I choose death!

Durlindrath: *Hal.* "Lord of the steadfast." The title given to the leader of the Durlin. For the first time in the history of Cardoroth, that position is held jointly by two people: Lornach and Taingern. Lornach also possesses the title of King's Champion. The latter honor is not held in quite such high esteem, yet it carries somewhat more power. As King's Champion, Lornach is authorized to act in the king's stead in matters of honor and treachery to the Crown.

Duthenor: *Duth. Prn.* Dooth-en-or. "The people." A single tribe, or sometimes a group of closely related tribes melded into a larger people at times of war or disaster, who generally live a rustic and peaceful lifestyle.

413

They are breeders of cattle and herders of sheep. However, when need demands they are bold warriors – men and women alike. Currently ruled by a usurper who murdered Brand's parents. Brand has sworn an oath to overthrow the tyrant and avenge his parents.

Elrika: *Cam.* Daughter of the royal baker. Friend to Gilcarist, and greatly skilled in weapons fighting, especially the long sword. Brand has given instructions to Lornach that she is to be taught all arts of the warrior to the full extent of her ability. He is grooming her to be the first female Durlin in the history of the city.

Elùgrune: *Hal.* Literally "shadowed fortune," but is also translated into "ill fortune" and "born of the dark." In the first two senses it means bad luck. In the third, it connotes a person steeped in shadow and mystery and not to be trusted. In some circles, the term has an additional meaning of "mystic".

Elugs: *Hal.* "That which creeps in shadows." An evil and superstitious race that dwells in the south of Alithoras, especially the Graèglin Dennath Mountains. They also inhabit portions of the northern mountains of Alithoras, and have traditionally fallen under the sway of elùgroths centered in the region of Cardoroth.

Elùdrath: *Hal. Prn.* Eloo-drath. "Shadowed lord." A sorcerer. First and greatest among elùgroths. Believed by most to be dead, but rumored by some to yet live.

Elùgai: *Hal. Prn.* Eloo-guy. "Shadowed force." The sorcery of an elùgroth.

414

Elùgroth: *Hal. Prn.* Eloo-groth. "Shadowed horror." A sorcerer. They often take names in the Halathrin tongue in mockery of the lòhren practice to do so.

Esanda: No known etymology for this name. Likewise, Esanda herself is not native to Cardoroth. King Gilhain believed she was from the city of Esgallien, but he was not certain of this. Esanda refuses to answer questions concerning her origins. Regardless of the personal mystery attached to her, she was one of Gilhain's most trusted advisors and soon became so to Brand. She leads a ring of spies utterly devoted to the protection of Cardoroth from the many dark forces that would bring it down.

Esgallien: *Hal. Prn.* Ez-gally-en. "Es – rushing water, gal(en) – green, lien – to cross: place of the crossing onto the green plains." A city founded in antiquity and named after a nearby ford of the Careth Nien. Reports indicate it has fallen to elugs.

Felargin: *Cam.* A sorcerer, and brother to Ginsar. Acolyte of Shurilgar the elùgroth. Steeped in evil and once lured Brand, Lornach and other adventurers under false pretenses into a quest. Only Brand and Shorty survived the betrayal. Felargin, however, fell victim to the trap he had prepared for the others. Brand was responsible for his death.

Foresight: Premonition of the future. Can occur at random but is also deliberately sought by entering the shadow world between life and death where the spirit is released from the body to travel through space and time. To achieve this, the body must be brought to the threshold of death. The first method is uncontrollable and rare. The second exceedingly rare but somewhat controllable for those with the skill and the courage, or the desperate need, to risk the danger.

Forgotten Queen (the): An epithet of Queen Carnhaina. She was a person of immense power and presence, yet she made few friends in life, and her possession of magic caused her to be mistrusted. For these reasons, memory of her accomplishments faded soon after her passing and only small remnants of her rule are remembered by the populace of Cardoroth.

Gil: See Gilcarist.

Gilcarist: *Comb. Cam & Hal.* First element unknown, second "ice." Heir to the throne of Cardoroth and grandson of King Gilhain. According to Carnhaina, his coming was told in the stars. He is also foretold by her as The Savior and The Destroyer. The prophecies mean little to him, for he believes in Brand's view that a man makes his own fate.

Gilhain: *Comb. Cam & Hal.* First element unknown, second "hero." King of Cardoroth before proclaiming Brand regent for Gilcarist, the underage heir to the throne. Husband to Aurellin.

Ginsar: *Cam.* A sorceress. Sister to Felargin. Acolyte of Shurilgar the elùgroth. Steeped in evil and greatly skilled in the arts of elùgai, reaching a level of proficiency nearly as great as her master. Rumored to be insane.

Goblins: See elugs.

Gorfalac: Cam. "Sword of the realm." An epithet for king. It literally signifies *sword of the blood*, and was a term in much use during the ancient days when the Camar migrated and danger surrounded them. The king was seen as protector of the people, and his courage and willingness to fight for them was his inherited duty.

Graèglin Dennath: *Hal. Prn.* Greg-lin dennath. "Mountains of ash." Chain of mountains in southern Alithoras. The landscape is one of jagged stone and boulder, relieved only by gaping fissures from which plumes of ashen smoke ascend, thus leading to its name. Believed to be impassable because of the danger of poisonous air flowing from cracks, and the ground unexpectedly giving way, swallowing any who dare to tread its forbidden paths. In other places swathes of molten stone run in rivers down its slopes.

Grindar: *Cam.* A lamplighter in Cardoroth. Once a soldier serving Gilcarist's great grandfather.

Halathar: *Hal.* "Dwelling place of the people of Halath." The forest realm of the immortal Halathrin.

Halathgar: *Hal.* "Bright star." Actually a constellation of two stars. Also called the Lost Huntress.

Halathrin: *Hal.* "People of Halath." A race named after an honored lord who led an exodus of his people to the land of Alithoras in pursuit of justice, having sworn to defeat a great evil. They are human, though of fairer form, greater skill and higher culture than ordinary men. They possess a unity of body, mind and spirit that enables insight and endurance beyond the native races of Alithoras. Said to be immortal, but killed in great numbers during their conflicts in ancient times with the evil they sought to destroy. Those conflicts are collectively known as the Shadowed Wars.

Harath Neben: *Hal.* "North gate." This gate bears a token of two massive emeralds representing the constellation of Halathgar. The gate is also called "Hunter's Gate," for the north road out of the city leads to wild lands of plentiful game.

Hruilgar: *Comb. Cam & Hal.* First element unknown (but thought to mean "wild"), second "star." The old king's huntsman. Rumored to have learned his craft as a tracker in Esgallien and to have journeyed north to Cardoroth at the same time as Esanda.

Hvargil: Prince of Cardoroth. Younger son of Carangil, former king of Cardoroth. Exiled by Carangil for treason after it was discovered he plotted with elùgroths to assassinate his older half-brother, Gilhain, and prevent him from ascending the throne. He gathered a band about him in exile of outlaws and discontents. Most came from Cardoroth but others were drawn from the southern Camar cities. He fought with the invading army of elugs against Cardoroth in the previous war.

Immortals: See Halathrin.

Lake Alithorin: *Hal.* "Silver lake." A mysterious lake of northern Alithoras.

Letharn: *Hal.* "Stone Raisers. Builders." A race of people that in antiquity conquered most of Alithoras. Now, only faint traces of their civilization endure.

Lòhren: *Hal. Prn.* Ler-ren. "Knowledge giver – a counselor." Other terms used by various nations include wizard, druid and sage.

Lòhren-fire: A combat manifestation of lòhrengai. The color of flame varies according to the temperament of the lòhren.

Lòhrengai: *Hal. Prn.* Ler-ren-guy. "Lòhren force." Enchantment, spell or use of mystic power. A manipulation and transformation of the natural energy inherent in all things. Each use takes something from the user. Likewise, some part of the transformed energy infuses them. Lòhrens use it sparingly, elùgroths indiscriminately.

Lòrenta: *Hal. Prn.* Ler-rent-a. "Hills of knowledge." Uplands in northern Alithoras where the stronghold of the lòhrens is established. It is to here that the old king and queen of Cardoroth traveled to spend their remaining years.

Lornach: *Cam.* A former Durlin and now joint Durlindrath. Also holds the title of King's Champion. Friend to Brand, and often called by his nickname of "Shorty."

Lost Huntress: See Halathgar.

Magic: Mystic power. See lòhrengai and elùgai.

Merril: *Cam.* Wife to Thrimgern the blacksmith. A popular name in Cardoroth. Once considered a man's name, but used by a female archer of outstanding skill some two hundred years ago who achieved fame by surviving a skirmish with elugs north of the city while

419

hunting and consequently has become a common female name.

Mother of Stars: A term of obscure origin, often used in mystic societies. It has various interpretations, but the most commonly accepted is that it signifies "the universe".

Nightborn: See elùgrune.

Otherworld: Camar term for a mingling of half-remembered history, myth and the spirit world. Sometimes used interchangeably with the term "Age of Heroes."

Parviel: *Cam.* A Durlin. Slain by Duthenor conspirators while guarding Gilcarist. Said to have been the best knife fighter among the Durlin.

Rathbold: *Duth.* A former outlaw in the lands of the Duthenor. He offered his service to the usurper, and was pardoned. He rose to prominence in the usurper's eyes due to his complete lack of scruples and his willingness to carry out any task. Eventually, became one of his most trusted advisors.

Rhodeurl: *Cam.* A Durlin. Slain by Duthenor conspirators while guarding Gilcarist. Said to have descended from a noble family who emigrated from the southern Camar cities to Cardoroth. The "rhod" element of his name is common in the south but not in Cardoroth. A man of great wealth who put it aside to pursue the skills of a Durlin.

Sandy: See Esanda.

Seal of Halathgar: A representation of the Constellation of Halathgar. Also known as the Seal of Carnhaina, for the Great Queen took it as her personal emblem.

Sellic Neben: *Hal.* "East gate." This gate bears a representation, crafted of silver and pearl, of the moon rising over the sea.

Shadowed Lord: See Elùdrath.

Shorty: See Lornach.

Shurilgar: *Hal.* "Midnight star." An elùgroth. One of the most puissant sorcerers of antiquity. Known to legend as the Betrayer of Nations.

Sight: The ability to discern the intentions or thoughts of another person. Not reliable, and yet effective at times.

Sorcerer: See Elùgroth.

Sorcery: See elùgai.

Stele: A vertical stone slab engraved with inscriptions or symbols. Used by most cultures in Alithoras. Sometimes constructed of wood, but these do not generally endure.

Surcoat: An outer garment usually worn over chainmail. The Durlin surcoat is unadorned white, which is a tradition carried down from the order's inception.

Sword and Crown Tavern: A tavern in Cardoroth. Owned by Esanda and used by her as a safe-house to hide discovered informants and to gather intelligence. Frequented by high-ranking military officers and nobles.

Their conversations are often heard by the barmaids, who are skilled operatives reporting to Esanda.

Taingern: *Cam.* A former Durlin. Friend to Brand, and now joint Durlindrath. Once, in company of Brand, saved the tomb of Carnhaina from defilement and robbery by an elùgroth.

Thrimgern: A blacksmith of high skill.

Time: One of the Riders, also called Horsemen, summoned into Alithoras by Ginsar. He represents Time – specifically as manifested by the aging process. Yet, in truth, the Riders are spirit-beings from another world. They have been given form and nature within Alithoras by Ginsar. The form provided by her is part of the blood sorcery that binds them to her will. In their own world, they do not bear these names or natures. Yet they are creatures wholly of evil, and though bound by Ginsar they seek to break that bond. Even if defeated, the bond from the summoning persists and the Riders are capable of rising again, even though they are considered dead.

Tower of Halathgar: In life, a place of study of Queen Carnhaina. In death, her resting place. Unusually, her sarcophagus rests on the tower's parapet beneath the stars.

Unlach Neben: *Hal.* "South gate." This gate bears a representation of the sun, crafted of gold, beating down upon an arid land. Said to signify the southern homeland of the elugs, whence the gold of the sun was obtained by an adventurer of old.

Ùhrengai: *Hal. Prn.* Er-ren-guy. "Original force." The primordial force that existed before substance or time.

War: One of the Riders, also called Horsemen, summoned into Alithoras by Ginsar. He represents conflict and battle. Yet, in truth, the Riders are spirit-beings from another world. They have been given form and nature within Alithoras by Ginsar. The form provided by her is part of the blood sorcery that binds them to her will. In their own world, they do not bear these names or natures. Yet they are creatures wholly of evil, and though bound by Ginsar they seek to break that bond. Even if defeated, the bond from the summoning persists and the Riders are capable of rising again, even though they are considered dead.

White Lady: A being of spirit drawn into Alithoras as an unintended consequence of Ginsar's summoning of the Riders.

Witch Queen: See Carnhaina

Wizard: See lòhren.

Wych-wood: A general description for a range of supple and springy timbers. Some hardy varieties are prevalent on the poisonous slopes of the Graèglin Dennath Mountains, and are favored by elùgroths as instruments of sorcery.

LIGHT OF THE REALM

BOOK THREE OF THE SON OF SORCERY SERIES

Robert Ryan

ISBN-13 978-0-9942054-9-0
(print edition)

Trotting Fox Press

1. Stillness in the Storm

Gil drew his sword, and the hiss of steel as it slid from the leather scabbard was the whisper of death in his ear. Now that he had drawn the blade, he must use it. That was the first rule of fighting. Avoid drawing to the last, but having drawn be prepared to kill. Or be killed.

He was now caught in a fight to the death. It was not of his choosing. It was neither his plan nor his purpose. But none of that mattered. His opponent had set this in motion, and having begun it must end in blood.

The day was bright and sunny. The sky suddenly blue beyond compare. The touch of air against his skin was a caress, and everything seemed alive and vibrant. He knew this was because he might die, and his mind was suddenly aware of all the things he could lose. But beyond that loomed the threat of the great dark, of the unknown, of death and oblivion. It stabbed fear through him. He felt that too, felt the tightening of his muscles and the churning of his stomach, felt it all with unsurpassed clarity.

He did not like it. But all that he felt, his opponent felt also, and that helped to steady him. He was not going to die here today, not if he could help it.

His opponent made a move. It was a feint, a mere ripple of motion intended to make Gil react. And he did, stepping smoothly to the side.

The dance had begun. This early period in a fight was a chance to observe how the enemy moved, which foot they favored, how they advanced and retreated. It was an

425

opportunity to appraise the enemy and discover a weakness, and one always existed.

There would be no rushed battle here. This was a duel, and one between accomplished swordsmen. No chances would be taken and no gambles on surprise or trickery considered. Not until they each had the measure of the other, not until one had the upper hand and the other was forced to try luck rather than rely on skill.

His opponent glided forward on practiced footwork, the tip of his sword thrusting. Gil rocked back, allowing his rear foot to hold his weight while his own sword deflected the strike. In the same motion, he sent a slashing riposte toward his adversary's throat.

The man parried it with ease, and the sound of steel on steel rang loudly. Gil did not mind. This too was part of the testing. He had learned that his opponent favored blocking rather than deflection.

They circled each other now. Eyes focused, concentration intense. Each step assessed, every movement of waist and limb studied for telltale signs of an impending strike.

Gil noticed the man watched his eyes. This was a tactic used for intimidation. And well might his opponent do so, for he was older, stronger and more experienced. Gil, in his turn, ignored it and kept his gaze at the center of the man's chest. From here, he could best see his enemy's feet and shoulder, which were often the first part of the body to move before a thrust or slash.

His enemy nimbly altered his footwork and began to circle in the opposite direction. Gil flowed smoothly with the change, knowing that if he had not done so the man would have attacked seeking to strike while he was off balance.

The cottage came into view behind his enemy, and the ploughed field beyond it. The building, though tidy and bordered by a colorful flower bed, was small and only had thatch roofing. It was not the kind of place that a member of the nobility would have much time for, and it must have discomfited Dernbrael that he had been forced into hiding here after his treacherous plot to usurp the throne failed. Gil had felt the man's shame on his discovery, but was there a way to use that emotion against him now that this duel had begun?

Dernbrael dropped low and slashed his blade at Gil's knees. Gil shuffled back, avoiding the dangerous strike, and not falling for the trap. Had he dodged and then leapt in to land a powerful overhand strike while his enemy was in a seemingly vulnerable position, he would have driven himself onto the follow-up strike – a disemboweling flick of the wrist.

Dernbrael stepped back and grinned. "Brand taught you well. He'll not be to blame for your death. But think on this, boy. You *will* die. And you have no heir. Your line will end with you, and Cardoroth will have a new king." He pointed with his sword. "It will all be for the best. You are *elùgrune,* boy. Nightborn. A thing of evil and no good can come from your life."

Gil felt a rush of blood to his face, and the pale marks on his palms itched, but he did not answer. He was not experienced, but he knew when he was being goaded. He would *not* react rashly, even if he felt the barb. He forced a grin instead, and held his blade steady before him.

Dernbrael attacked anyway, launching a vicious overhand strike intended to split Gil's skull. This time Gil blocked, for there was no safe way to deflect such a blow as that. Steel cracked against steel. The jolt of impact rocked him, and he was forced into a clumsy step backward. Straightaway Dernbrael followed through, trying a slashing technique for the throat.

Gil neither blocked nor deflected it. He sidestepped and began to circle again. He was patient, perhaps more patient than his opponent, and there was no rush. Dernbrael would have expected a counter attack, for a man attacked usually retaliated in kind. But Brand had taught him better than that.

The cottage and field were now behind Gil. Ahead of him, to the rear of his enemy, stood the ten Durlin guards and the fifty soldiers that had come with him out of the city to arrest Dernbrael. This fight was unnecessary, and he could end it now by a mere signal to his men. That was tempting, for the fear of death was upon him, but he had agreed to Dernbrael's demand to duel for a reason.

The rogue noble launched another attack. This was no mere testing strike, no probe of defenses: it was a sustained drive of blow after blow, each potentially deadly and all executed with skill and burning ferocity.

Gil swayed and stepped. He used movement as his first protection, evading rather than deflecting or parrying. But it was not enough. The enemy had his measure now, had learned his method of fighting and drove his blistering offense with precision. Gil was forced to not just deflect but also to block. This was not to his advantage because the other man was stronger, but almost as though Dernbrael could read his mind each jab and slash arrived just that little bit too fast for him, and always at the angle that was hardest to deal with.

Panic rose in Gil. His body grew tense and that ate away at the nimbleness of his footwork. His sword arm stiffened too, and this made his defense slower and more vulnerable.

But the other man was older, and his breathing began to quicken now. He slashed once more, a backhanded riposte that nearly tore away Gil's throat, and then stepped back.

They did not speak. The two of them gazed at each other. There was hatred in Dernbrael's eyes, but there was confidence too. It annoyed Gil, for the man thought he was the better swordsman. He believed it was just a matter of time and then, and then who knew? Did he think that having killed the heir to the throne he could survive being arrested? Did he believe he was still a chance of winning a trial, proving his innocence and then even being crowned king by the nobles? It was foolish, and yet with Gil dead and the threat of war on the horizon … anything was possible.

Gil nearly withdrew. Why had he agreed to this duel? But that was fear clouding his thoughts. He knew exactly why he had accepted the challenge.

When he had come with his men and called Dernbrael out of the cottage, hatred had flared on both sides. This was something personal between them, something more than justice and ambition. That alone was enough to stir up a fight, but there was more.

War loomed, sooner or later. Brand remained regent, but the time would come when he was not there. Then the people would look to their king, a young king, inexperienced and newly crowned. He would be vulnerable then. The plotting of the nobles would not cease. The morale of the people would erode. It was better to send a message now, to establish his reputation. And Dernbrael had given him that opportunity by challenging him to a duel. In this, Gil could show himself as an energetic leader of strength and courage. One able to personally fight his enemies. He was no callow youth, but a leader worthy of a long line of warriors.

Dernbrael had caught his breath. "So, boy. How did you find me here?"

Gil ignored being called a boy. It was another attempt to goad him. Nor was he going to be caught off guard. He stepped back, ensuring the other man could not launch into an attack while they spoke. Even as he did so, he read a flicker of annoyance on the other man's face at this precaution.

It was a pleasing reaction, for it showed that Dernbrael could himself be thrown off balance mentally. Gil noted it, and allowed himself a faint grin while he replied to the question.

"It does not matter," he said. "You are found, and you will be dealt with."

He knew that not giving a proper answer would annoy Dernbrael. It would only be natural for him to speculate if he had been betrayed by someone he trusted, and that would upset him. Goading worked both ways.

Dernbrael shrugged with seeming nonchalance, and then hurled himself into another attack. Gil had provoked it, even guessed that it would come, and he remained calm. This time he was better able to maneuver, using skill and footwork to avoid the deadly assault and deflecting the blade when he could not. Sometimes he was forced to block, but that was to be expected. They fought with long swords, and they were not weapons of great finesse.

All the while he obtained a better feel for his opponent. How the man moved. How he thought. But not as much as he wished. Dernbrael was experienced. He followed no set pattern. He attacked wherever he sensed there may be a weakness, and he probed it with relentlessness. Gil realized that even that was a pattern though. The rogue noble liked to attack. He liked to

430

dominate. He was a man of confidence and authority. The question was, how could this be turned against him?

Gil became even more defensive. He relaxed, sinking deep into his own mind. There was only the movement of swords and the rhythm of his footwork. Neither fear nor hope existed. His mind did not get in the way of his training, and the skills his body had learned blossomed. Muscles and reflexes were faster and surer than the conscious mind. That was what Brand had taught him. *Stillness in the storm*, the regent had called it. That state where the mind floated above the turmoil of the body and allowed it to move efficiently, unhindered by distress or desire.

Gil's patience provoked the intended result. Dernbrael, frustrated at not being able to exert control over the situation and engender fear, attacked once more. But this time he did so with wild hatred burning in his eyes.

The man moved swiftly. He slashed at Gil's throat and the blade hissed through the air only inches from delivering a death wound. Gil swayed back, and Dernbrael followed up with a brutal backhanded jab at his head.

Gil retreated. Dernbrael followed, pressing home his attack with a series of lightning-fast techniques. If he had been fast before, he was faster now. Anger drove him, and caution was lessened.

The rogue noble slashed again, but having missed he kicked out, nearly striking Gil in the groin. Gil stepped back and then to the side, narrowly avoiding another overhand strike.

With an agile pivot of his feet, Dernbrael thrust the tip of his blade at Gil's stomach. It was too fast, too

431

unexpected for Gil to avoid, but he smashed down his own sword just in time. The two blades screeched as metal hammered into metal and sparks flew.

Dernbrael flicked his wrists and his blade slashed unopposed towards Gil's throat. But Gil was already moving, anticipating the technique and stepping to the side just in time. He was barely aware of anything except this life-and-death struggle, but he sensed the unease of the Durlin watching.

Dernbrael did not follow him this time. He stepped back, seeking another rest. Only his eyes still held their fury and gave Gil warning. Even as the man moved back he swiftly drew a dagger from a hidden arm-sheath and flung it.

Gil dodged to the side, but the dagger struck him with a sickening thump. Pain shot through him, and his left shoulder felt as though it were on fire, but it had only been a glancing blow and the dagger dropped to the ground.

It was not enough to break Gil's concentration. He remained alert, his sword held high before him and poised to defend or strike. His readiness forestalled the follow-up attack that Dernbrael had planned on, and hatred and frustration twisted his face.

Gil glanced at the dagger on the ground, and then he looked Dernbrael in the eyes.

"Ah yes, of course. A Duthenor dagger. I'm not sure throwing it in a duel fits well with the chivalry of the nobles. But no matter. More to the point, where are your allies now?"

Dernbrael ignored the questioning of his honor. "They know how to take care of themselves. They'll appear when Brand least expects it ... and he will surely die. The Duthenor have an ally beside me."

Gil nodded slowly, breathing deep of the fresh air that smelled of the ploughed field behind the cottage. He would use this moment of rest to purpose.

"The ally you speak of would be one of the Horsemen?" he said casually.

It was with satisfaction that he saw understanding in Dernbrael's eyes. He knew of the Horseman and his presence in the city, had probably even arranged for his covert entry. This took his treason to a higher level.

Gil went on. "But you should know this. Since you have been hiding like a rat down a hole, things have changed in the city. The Duthenor assassins were discovered. Brand dealt with them. And the Horseman, in case you were wondering, is dead also."

For the first time, Dernbrael showed uncertainty. This was news to him, and in a single moment he sensed all his plans and his last hope crashing down around him.

It was Gil's opportunity, and he grasped it. Shifting from defense to offense, he leapt forward, his blade gleaming in his hand. Swords flashed and the clang of steel on steel shattered the air. Dernbrael fell back, unprepared and surprised, yet still a master swordsman.

The sound of riders swiftly approaching broke through Gil's concentration. He had no idea if they were friends or enemies, but he had no chance to look.

Dernbrael unleashed a powerful beheading stroke. Gil anticipated it by the surge of anger that flared in the other man's eyes. Angry men struck for the head. He slipped under the wicked blow and drove his own blade upward. The point slid through cloth and flesh, and then Gil angled it upward to reach the heart and lungs.

433

Dernbrael stiffened and cried out. Then, knowing himself dead, and driven by hatred, he forced himself forward. He was too close to use his blade, but he smashed the pommel into Gil's head.

Gil felt a roar of pain. The world went dark and spun in circles. His knees wobbled, and he nearly fainted, but the blow had not quite struck him cleanly and he did not pass out. Instead, he gathered himself and then surged forward, kicking Dernbrael from him and keeping a tight grip on his sword. But even as he moved he felt that the weight of Dernbrael was a dead weight.

The nobleman sprawled to the ground. Blood and froth foamed at his mouth, but he no longer drew breath.

Gil swayed where he stood, his sword slick with the dead man's blood. "So is justice done," he said. "And as you fell, so too shall all who betray Cardoroth."

One of the Durlin came to him. He drew a white cloth from an inner pocket of his surcoat and handed it over. Gil dabbed it at the side of his head, feeling the pain there begin to throb. Looking at the cloth, he saw it was stained by blood.

"Keep holding it firmly in place," the Durlin advised. "It'll stop the bleeding."

Gil did so. He had not realized how badly he had been hit and how much blood there was. But the pain kept growing the more that he thought about it.

He turned to the riders who had come. There were two of them. He saw first that they possessed quality mounts. They were sleek animals, well cared for, fit and of the finest breeding. When he looked higher, taking in those who rode them, he understood why. These were messengers. They wore the gray cloaks customary to the army, but they were pinned with brooches that signaled their role as messengers: a hawk with wings half folded as though stooping through the sky toward prey. It signified speed, the kind that the mounts of the messengers by necessity must possess.

The two riders dismounted and approached Gil. Two Durlin separated from their companions and walked beside them.

"What is the watchword, gentlemen," Gil asked.

"Conhain," answered the man on the left. Then both men saluted. Gil returned it. The protocol had been fulfilled, and these men were as they appeared and not misinformants.

"Your Royal Highness," the man on the left spoke again. "The regent has sent us."

"What news?" Gil asked.

"This, sir. The scouts you sent out have returned. They bring word of an army. It is still many leagues to the north, but the regent believes its destination is Cardoroth. The army is large. Some thirty thousand, though it may yet increase. The regent bids you to return to the city as swiftly as your … your business here is taken care of."

The man's eyes strayed to Dernbrael's corpse. No doubt he would have known him as the rebel noble had been a general in the army.

Gil nodded. He pointed to a wooden trough by the side of the cabin. "Best water your horses. Then return to Brand. Tell him the traitor Dernbrael is dead, and that I will return close behind you."

The two messengers saluted, gathered the reins of their horses and led them to the trough.

Gil looked down once more on Dernbrael's corpse. How could Cardoroth survive? There were enemies from within who plotted for their own benefit. There were traitors who conspired with outside forces. And there was now a vast army set to march upon the city and destroy it.

He took the cloth from his head. It was covered in congealed blood. The risk he had taken was extreme, and yet the soldiers would spread the story. That was something at least, some gain from today's events. His reputation was begun, and it must now continue to grow. More than ever the people needed to believe in him. Brand remained regent, and there was none better to lead them into war. But Brand could be killed. It was time that Gil stood up and showed himself as the king-to-be. If the morale of the people faltered, the enemy would overrun them. He gazed at Dernbrael's lifeless body. Blood had spilled from his wound onto the dirt, and flies crawled over his skin. If Cardoroth did not hold strong, such a fate awaited the entire city.

2. Born of the Dark

Gil hastened back to Cardoroth. The messengers were some half an hour ahead of him, but the news they had brought was on his mind. The much-feared war had at last eventuated. All he knew, all he loved, was in jeopardy.

His head still ached. It had taken some while to still the bleeding, and also to bandage his shoulder wound. It had taken just as long to find a blanket in which to wrap the body of Dernbrael, and then strap it over a horse. The rebel noble would come home too, but not as the king he had dreamed of to the last. He would return as a traitor, his body handed over to his family for burial. In this way he could serve Gil. It would help fuel word of what happened to traitors and spread the story of Gil's fight.

It was all something to think about. It could have been Gil himself there, tied to a horse and seeping blood into a blanket.

He breathed in of the country air as his horse trotted ahead. Ploughed fields lined each side of the road, and there were cottages much like the one in which Dernbrael had hidden. There were people too, unaware of what had happened or who these passing riders were. But many of them waved. Country friendliness at its best, and something that would not happen in the city. For all that it was a rougher life here, perhaps it was better. The sun shone, the wind blew and rain fell. Survival could be a struggle, as it was anywhere, but these people were untroubled by schemes and treachery and assassins.

Gil sighed. They did not have reputations to build and wars to win either. That was his job, and one that he did not like. But it was his duty, and he would no more shirk it than a farmer would shirk hitching his horses to the plough and working a hard day under a hot sun.

"You're still bleeding," the Durlin to his side said.

"It could be worse," Gil replied. He did not ask where he was bleeding from. He had felt blood wet both the bandage to his head and the one to his shoulder ever since he had started to ride. The constant motion was not good for wounds. But ahead, the South Gate to the city was just visible, and soon he could wash and change the blood-soaked bandages.

The road widened and they drew near. The South Gate was clearly visible now. The old name for it was Unlach Neben. And it truly was an old gate, as each of the four main gates were. It was said they were the original gates, constructed when the city wall was built. Gil believed it. He knew also that no enemy in the long history of the realm had ever forced their way though. He hoped it remained that way.

The gold representation of the sun upon it gleamed brightly. It was said to signify the sun beating down upon a faraway desert land. This was supposed to be the homeland of the elugs, whence the gold of the sun was obtained by an adventurer of old. Whether that was true or not, Gil had never learned.

Even as the glint of gold drew his gaze, something else distracted him. The air shimmered on the road before the gate. It seemed like a heat mirage, and yet Gil felt the sudden prickle of his skin and knew it was not. It was sorcery, and he raised his hand, fist clenched.

"Halt!" he commanded, and the column of riders drew to a swift stop.

Out of the shimmery air stepped a tall figure. Thin she was, black-haired and beautiful. As always, she had the bearing of a queen. All she needed was a crown and scepter.

Instead, she carried a wych-wood staff. It was Ginsar, and Gil felt the prickles on his skin turn to needles of ice.

The Durlin nudged their horses to gather close around him, and drew their swords. They had seen her before and knew who she was.

Ginsar tilted her head as though curious. "Why so scared?"

"We know you, witch," one of the Durlin answered. "Stay back!"

She studied him a moment. "And if I choose not to?" she answered, taking a slow step forward.

"Don't be alarmed," Gil said. "She can do no harm. This is an image only, and the true Ginsar is hiding in some dark grotto in the forest about the lake."

Ginsar turned her gaze to him, and her expressive eyes sparkled.

"My, haven't *you* grown. And however did you know? The casting of an image, and therefore the discernment of one, is beyond your skill. You surprise me."

"I know, Ginsar. That is enough."

She gazed at him speculatively a moment longer. "It's of no matter."

Gil sat straight in the saddle. "Speak," he said, "and then begone. I don't have all day to prattle with crazy ladies."

439

The witch's eyes flashed. "Crazy, is it? Well, perhaps I am." Her face softened and she laughed. "But I know a thing or two. Was not the great Shurilgar my master? Have I not lived since the birth of Cardoroth itself? I am old, though in truth I do not appear so."

She held the backs of her hands up to her face, studied them a moment, and then winked at him.

"I am old, and steeped in wisdom that you would not fathom in a hundred years from now. And I know secrets. Oh yes, plenty of them. It would pay you to show respect."

Gil shrugged. He did not know what she intended here, but she had not come without purpose. Only by talking to her could he discover it. And perhaps, by talking, she would reveal more to him of her plans than she intended.

"Then speak, Ginsar. And say what you will. Then I will ride on and you will return to your shadow-haunted forest."

"So sure of yourself? You have another option, you know."

"And what's that?"

"Come to the shadow-haunted forest yourself. It's beautiful there, and there are secrets within it that would make your heart sing. Truly, I'm not lying to you."

Gil frowned, surprised by her words. "I think you really are crazy. Why would I go there?"

"Because it is where you belong. What better reason could there be?"

Gil shook his head. "No. I don't belong there at all."

"Again, always so sure of yourself. But you don't know what I know, nor do you see what I see. You are far more *shadow-haunted*, as you put it, than you admit to yourself. Did you not find it easy enough to kill Dernbrael?"

The words hung in the air, and Gil had no answer. How did she know Dernbrael was dead, let alone how? Her scry basin, perhaps. Or maybe she was linked to Dernbrael by sorcery. She may have met him. That made sense. Likely, she even encouraged his ambition for the throne and fomented his treason. Such a link might have enabled her to watch over him with some degree of regularity. Otherwise the scry-magic was unpredictable. It rarely showed what the user wanted, and then only glimpses.

Gil had no answers to any of the questions his whirling mind posed, but he knew he had to reply.

"He was a traitor. He challenged *me*, and he died. It's that simple."

"Simple, is it now? Well, if you want simplicity, try this. The man died, but he need not have. His challenge was of no consequence. You could have overcome him. You had the men. No, Prince Gilcarist. You are elùgrune. Born of the dark. You *wanted* to kill him. Come to me, where you belong."

Gil understood her purpose now. At least, it seemed likely enough what it was. There were many people listening to what she said, and her words would spread through the city. It would cause distrust of him, and that would serve her during the war.

"I'm not elùgrune. I would die for my people. And this conversation is ended."

He reached out with his mind and felt the warmth in the air. There had been no heat mirage before, but now he made one. So strong was his reaction to her words that the air about the image of Ginsar crackled like a leaf thrown on flame and disappeared. Light flashed and thunder rumbled as though welling from the earth.

Gil hated using lòhrengai in public. Few knew he possessed the use of magic, but that number had

441

increased rapidly lately. Now, the whole city would know. Perhaps that had been part of Ginsar's plan as well, but there was nothing he could do about it.

He signaled the column forward again, and nudged his horse into a trot. He did not need to look around to know the eyes of the men were upon him. Ginsar had seen to that. If it were not enough that she had called him elùgrune, he had proved it to them himself.

The Durlin had already known he was skilled with lòhrengai. The soldiers did not. He had revealed it to them now, and that would feed rumor into the city until it blazed with the story. The witch had goaded him as Dernbrael had tried. She, however, had gotten under his skin and succeeded. He knew how, too. It was the way that she suggested he had wanted, even enjoyed killing the rogue noble. The tactic had worked because he knew, deep in his heart, that there was an element of truth to it.

He fumed quietly, trying to show none of his anger at the witch or himself. He rode to where her image had been and passed through it without hesitation. He noticed though that the soldiers did not do so. They guided their mounts to the side of the road and avoided the spot. Only the Durlin stayed with him, but they were tight-lipped and tense.

Soon, they reached the gate and passed through, the hooves of the horses loud in the gate-tunnel. He was home again. He was in Cardoroth, the city he was born in and born to rule. And his own words came back to him. *I would die for my people.*

He considered the statement. He had spoken them in anger, said them to prove that Ginsar was wrong. Were they true though? He had no way to know. Brand had proven that it was so for him. So had Shorty and Taingern. Many others had in the long history of the nation. He believed he meant it, but he was old enough to know that some things were beyond the reach of thought until circumstances arose to prove the answer one way or the other.

But those circumstances were coming. War was coming, and the Horsemen with it. Battle and sorcery. He would be tested as he never had been before. Soon, he would know the truth.

3. A Taste of Kingship

A Durlin opened the door, and Gil nodded his thanks as he entered the War Room of Cardoroth city. He had not yet washed or changed his clothes, and he felt uncomfortable walking into such a formal room covered by the dust of travel and with bloodstained bandages. But the regent had said to come swiftly, and there would be reason for that.

His steps echoed loudly. The marble floor, white and polished, was a surface that caused his boots to make a cracking sound each time the heels touched it. And the vaulted ceiling that rose to a dizzying height seemed to swallow the sound and then throw it back down at those below. The War Room was next to the Throne Room, and they shared many architectural similarities.

They were different though, too. Here, a long table of polished walnut ran dozens of feet down the length of the room. On the walls, all over them in fact, were maps. Some were very old. Some inaccurate, for they detailed far away regions more myth than reality. No one from Cardoroth had ever been to those places to verify their existence. Some were copies of maps drawn by the Halathrin. These were treasured, for the immortals had traveled widely when first they came to Alithoras, and they were extraordinary mapmakers. The majority of them, however, were of the surrounds of Cardoroth and these were the ones that would prove most useful now.

This was a room that Gil had rarely seen before. But as he stepped toward the table he had a sudden memory of his grandfather leaning over it and looking at a map that had been retrieved from the wall and spread out for study. Gil felt a stab of nostalgia. He missed him.

He stepped ahead, taking in who stood there now. Brand was at the head of the table. As always, Shorty and Taingern were nearby. Esanda was there also, and he remembered that it was she who had discovered Dernbrael's hiding place. Withholding that information in the duel had been useful. It would have irked his opponent no end not being able to find out how he had been found.

There were several other men too. Three generals and each had an adjutant. Gil approached the table and Brand's eyes flicked to him.

There was momentary concern in the man's eyes, but he covered it swiftly. Despite the blood and bandages, he realized that Gil was obviously not seriously injured. He did raise an eyebrow when he spoke though.

"I had thought there would be little trouble with fifty soldiers and the Durlin. Clearly, I was wrong. What of Dernbrael?"

Gil pulled up a chair and sat down. "To cut a long story short, he's dead."

Brand leaned back in his own chair, his expression thoughtful. "So be it. Probably for the best, I suppose."

One of the generals frowned. "You killed him? Without a trial? I cannot believe you would do such a thing."

"This is general Garling," Brand said by way of introduction.

"I think we've met, but it was some years ago. For what it's worth, I had no intention of killing Dernbrael. But he challenged me to a duel. He forced me into the fight, and so the fault is his. Had he not done so, he would still be alive."

Garling seemed less than happy with the explanation. His face reddened and he shook his head slowly. "I still cannot believe it. You did not have to accept the challenge."

"I think I did," Gil said quietly.

One of the other generals spoke. Druigbar, Gil thought his name was.

"No matter what you thought, it's a bad look. Very bad indeed. Dernbrael was a noble, no matter what crime he was accused of. He was entitled to a trial. What you have done has the appearance of an unauthorized execution."

"I agree," the third general said. Lothgern his name was, and Gil remembered that he had been sitting in the very same chair as he now was all those years ago when Gil had come in here to see his grandfather.

Gil was about to reply, but Esanda spoke first. "The nobles may see it that way, even though the man's guilt was clear. But the nobles don't count at the moment. Only the people of the realm do, and especially the soldiers. There are far graver issues to discuss."

"With respect, I *am* a noble," Lothgern said curtly. "All the generals are. And what we think counts."

Gil felt tension fill the room. But, it occurred to him that it had been like that since he entered, since before they knew about Dernbrael's death.

Esanda leaned forward and held the general's gaze. "No, you are not. You are a general in the army. Winning the battle to come is your one and only concern. In that effort, the lowliest soldier and the commanders of the army are equal, striving toward that single purpose. Nothing else counts."

None of the generals liked this, and Gil could see their tempers rising. They were about to debate the point, but Brand interrupted.

"Enough. Esanda is correct. War is coming, and we must be of one purpose. Now, nothing matters but surviving. And we have decisions to make, and swiftly if we are to give ourselves the best chance. Little time remains."

"I thought we had made those decisions," Druigbar said.

Brand sat back in his chair. It was a seemingly relaxed gesture, but Gil knew him well enough to detect his frustration.

"No," the regent said, his voice matter-of-fact. "You gave your advice, and I made my suggestion. Nothing was decided."

Brand looked across the table at Gil. "Very quickly, this is the state of affairs. I tell you this now because you will be king one day, and though that hasn't happened yet, you should still have a voice in all this."

Brand rubbed his chin and gathered his thoughts. "You sent out scouts recently. They have returned, and they bring news with them. Elugs are gathering at the point where the Alith Nien spills out from the mountains of Auren Dennath. They are some thirty thousand strong, and likely to grow. With them are hundreds of Lethrin, what my people call trolls. Elùgroths have also been seen. Not Ginsar herself, as yet, but no doubt they serve her." Brand paused. "Do you follow this situation so far?"

"I do," Gil replied.

"Very well then," Brand continued. "The army is camped about one hundred and fifty miles away. That is a five day march. They will come to Cardoroth. They are not river-faring people, and no craft were seen. Therefore, the enemy will not come by water. This leaves two routes. Down the Halathrin road to the west of the river. This is a path they could travel swiftly, but it is the longer way. Or down the east side of the river, into the hills north of Cardoroth. Or, perhaps, they could split their army and do both. That is the situation we face."

Gil considered what Brand had said. He had been very brief, but all the important facts were there, including Ginsar's tactical options. The Lethrin, even in small numbers, were a great concern because they possessed enormous strength and were very hard to kill. The elugs, goblins as some people called them, were not as dangerous. But in numbers such as that, it was an enormous challenge to Cardoroth.

"We know how large the army is now, but how large could it yet grow?" Gil asked.

"That, we just don't know," Brand replied. "The mountains are full of elugs. But I suspect it will not increase much further. The scouts reported that while new elugs came down to join the army every day, that number was diminishing."

"And what fighting force can we muster? Last I heard we had twenty thousand soldiers."

Garling answered him. "It's now twenty-five thousand. Mostly foot soldiers, but we have fine cavalry also."

Gil pondered that. "And what of our food and water supplies to withstand a siege?"

"Quite adequate," Garling said. "We have masses of stored grain, for the last few seasons have been good. And our water supply has always been good. There are many deep wells within the city. They have never run dry."

"So much for us," Gil said. "But what about Ginsar? Which route will she use to reach us, and how well supplied is her army?"

Garling spoke quickly. "The elugs are not great war-makers in terms of logistics and supplies. They could not

mount a long siege. Perhaps no longer than a month."
He paused, looking at Brand. "As for their route, they
will come down via the Halathrin road. It was built for
quick-marching armies and there is no chance of ambush
along its length. It's the safest, surest route and they will
take it."

The other two generals were quick to agree to this,
but Gil realized that this was the point of contention he
had sensed earlier.

He looked at Brand. "And what route do *you* think
they will take?"

"Ah, that is the question. For myself, I believe they'll
come down the other way, through the hills north of the
city."

"And why do you think that?"

"Because it offers the best chance of secrecy. They
have great numbers, but they would still prefer to catch
us by surprise, if they can. Every day of secrecy counts.
They need not march to the Cardurleth itself. If they can
get within a day or two before we discover them, it's still
a great advantage."

Gil thought about that. It was true. They were never a
chance of taking the city by storm. There was always
going to be a battle. But surprise gave the advantage of
being proactive to them and the disadvantage of being
reactive to Cardoroth.

"There is another reason," Brand said.

"What's that?"

"The elug tribes have no love for flat and open
country. They prefer hills and trees for cover. It's the
type of landscape that they're used to."

Gil mulled that over as well. Much of all of this was
guesswork, but that was all they would have to go on
until it was too late to make a difference.

He studied the generals. He knew their type. They were cautious men, promoted because of the influence of their families. They may or may not be skilled at warfare. Sadly, promotion through the ranks of government or army officials seldom related to ability.

"Do you think the enemy may split their force and come both ways?" he asked.

"No," Garling answered. "There is no advantage in it."

"On that, we concur," Brand said. "But the reason they will see no advantage in it is because they will hope to surprise us, but surprise or not, they will expect us to wait within the city and use the Cardurleth as our defense."

"They will expect that," Druigbar said, "because it's the sensible course of action. Why should we not sit secure behind our wall?"

"Well," Brand answered, "normally you would be right. But what sort of security does the Cardurleth offer against sorcery?"

Gil could sense they were close now to the real point of difference between views. And he thought he knew what it was.

"Please go on, Brand. What do you think Ginsar will do?"

"It's not possible to know anything for certain. But this is likely. She will rely on numbers first – her army is large. Then she will turn to the Horsemen. We have seen Death and Age already. Betrayal and War are yet to come."

"We don't know that for certain," Lothgern said quietly.

Brand turned his blue eyes upon the general, and there was no doubt in them. "I do. They will come, but even they are not the greatest threat."

Brand paused. Gil knew what he was going to say next. It was his quest to solve this problem, but he had not done so yet. He had found the White Lady, and he knew that she was the key. But she could not, or would not, reveal to him what he must do.

"The Riders," Brand continued, "are summoned from another world. Ginsar has opened a gateway between the two. In the end, it is this that poses the greatest peril. There are forces within that other world that would seek dominion of ours. They are greater by far than Ginsar. Already we are in peril of that, but should Ginsar be forced to increase the strength of the Horsemen in order to defeat us, it may open that gateway so wide that nothing could prevent their entry. The Horsemen would lead a wave of conquest across our world, and nothing could stop them."

Garling cleared his throat. "I don't know much about magic, but I fail to see how this has any real bearing on our decision."

"It's simple enough," Brand said. "The Cardurleth will keep us safe. But the enemy learned that last time. Why come again for the same purpose? I think Ginsar has a plan. It will involve the Horsemen, and their strength grows each time we meet them. She draws it into them from the other world. Where they ride, terror will follow. She will draw *more* from the other world, feeding them power. Increased in strength, and with an army, Cardoroth will fall. She will only give them enough power for them to win. But to win, she may give them greater power than she can then control. In the end, they will control her. This must be prevented at all costs."

"I see what Brand is getting at," Gil said. "The proposal is that we strike first. That we go out and meet them before Ginsar increases their power. In that way, just maybe we can prevail too quickly for Ginsar to increase their strength."

"Yes," Brand said.

The generals all seemed to object at once. Gil listened to them carefully. Their main argument was that there was just no evidence to prove any of it.

"I hear you," Gil said at length. "I hear you, but this much is true beyond doubt. The Horsemen exist. Ginsar summoned them from another world. That gateway remains open. Until it is closed, anything is possible. She can increase their strength. Perhaps even bring back the two Horsemen that have been vanquished. And Alithoras is in great danger every moment that gateway remains open. Most of all, Ginsar is insane. She would perhaps destroy the world just to beat us."

The generals remained unconvinced. For some while they spoke of the strength of the Cardurleth and the history of the city. It had never fallen to an enemy. "We believe," Garling said, "in swords and spears and arrows. And most of all, we believe in the Cardurleth and the courage of the men to hold it."

They had made up their mind, and nothing was going to change it. But Gil had been asked for his view, and he was still weighing up everything that was being discussed.

"You speak little of Ginsar," he said to the generals. "And I realize that you're familiar with battle and fighting much more so than magic. But please accept that what Brand and I say about her and the gateway is true. That being the case, do you still recommend the same defensive strategy?"

Garling leaned forward earnestly, resting his hands on the table as he spoke. "The Cardurleth is our strongest defense, no matter what. Stay here. Man the wall. Trust in our soldiers to do what they are trained for."

"And if Brand is right? That by going out to meet the enemy unexpectedly we have a chance of joining battle before Ginsar has strengthened the Horsemen? Perhaps our best and only chance to stand against the force she might otherwise unleash upon us?"

"He is *not* right," Garling said adamantly. "Nor is he right about the route the enemy will take to reach us. And if we march off into the wilderness, then we will leave Cardoroth undefended."

"That isn't so," Brand replied. "We could leave enough soldiers here to defend the Cardurleth. And our scouts will tell us soon enough if we are right or wrong about the route our enemies will take. If so, we can still return to Cardoroth in time."

Gil turned to Taingern and Shorty. "What do you two say?"

"I agree with Brand," Shorty said simply.

"And you, Taingern?"

The Durlindrath sighed. "Everything is a risk. But weighing it up, I agree with Brand too. I have seen Ginsar. She's insane and consumed by hate. She'll do what it takes, draw whatever power is necessary from the other world, to win. Sometimes offense is the best course of defense. That is the case now."

It was quite a dilemma, and Gil felt it keenly. Nothing was certain, and no strategy could be counted on to deliver perfect results. Whatever choice was made, there was risk of failure.

Brand sat calmly, though Gil guessed he did not feel that way. Nor was there any sign of anxiety when he spoke.

"Well, Gil, you have heard the arguments, for and against. I am regent. I could command, but I will not. You are a man now, and Cardoroth is your future and

453

not mine. You must decide in this case. I will fulfill your wishes in this."

It was not what Gil was expecting. He had thought his opinion had been sought rather than a decision. But he recognized what Brand was doing. Even now, he was teaching him, allowing him a voice in the future of Cardoroth, giving him a feel of the awesome responsibility that came with leadership.

He felt the gazes of everybody upon him, waiting upon his choice. It was a taste of kingship, a taste of what it would be like to be responsible for a nation. It was too much responsibility, but it must be borne anyway. It was his duty, and it must be gotten used to.

But what choice should he make? The wrong one would lead to ruin.

4. Dust and Ash

Gil sat in thought. The large room was silent. The high-vaulted ceiling above, though airy and spacious, seemed to press down and squeeze the breath from him.

It would be easy to side with Brand, for whom he would do anything. He owed him so much that he almost felt he should. But Brand would not want that. He would want him to arrive at the best decision that he could given the information he had, and make the choice that seemed right for Cardoroth. That was where his loyalty must lie.

Carefully, he considered all the arguments. One or the other would prove correct in the end. But which?

He thought he knew.

"Very well," he said. "This much is certain. *If* Brand is right, the course of action the generals advise would see Cardoroth fall, and then no doubt Ginsar would move on to other realms. Or the Horsemen would in their own right. But Brand may be wrong. Yet, if so, our army could *still* return to Cardoroth in time to defend it."

He looked around at those in the room, meeting their gaze one by one. "And if Brand is right," he continued, "then a battle will be fought at a time and place of our own choosing. But his plan still allows us, if necessary, if circumstances are unfavorable, the option to make a tactical retreat to the city. Therefore there is nothing to be lost by following his suggestion and perhaps everything to be gained. So, that's what we'll do."

The generals glanced at each other, their expressions sullen.

"Make it so," Brand said to them. "The army is ready. We will march tomorrow, according to the ideas we discussed before Gil arrived."

The nobles and their adjutants stood. They gave the customary salutes without speaking, and then they stalked from the room.

"Not a happy bunch," Shorty said brightly after they had gone.

"They don't get paid to be happy," Esanda answered with a scowl. "They get paid to do their job."

Gil let out a long breath. "There's something else that you should know," he said.

Brand's gaze settled on him. "What? Did Dernbrael reveal anything of interest?"

"No. It wasn't Dernbrael. It was Ginsar. She appeared before us as we came back to the city. It was near the gate. But it was only an image that she cast, not her real self."

"And what did she say?" Brand asked.

"A few things, and none of them good. But what worries me is that she knew what had happened with Dernbrael. Perhaps she had a personal connection with him, and because of that link could use her scry basin to keep watch on him. I don't know. But what if she is able to use the scry basin to see us march tomorrow?"

Brand thought about that, drumming his fingers on the table. It was a rare sign of anxiousness.

"As you say, I think she had a personal connection to Dernbrael. He had likely fallen under her sway, and that made it easier. Scry magic is unpredictable. And hers all the more so. Do you understand why?"

Gil nodded. "It's not like it was for me under the Tower of Halathgar. In her case, she uses blood. That's said to give powerful results, but with even less control. Blood magic is a force of chaos."

"Exactly," Brand agreed. "It's a one in a thousand chance that she'll see us in time for it to make any difference."

"It's much more likely," Esanda commented, "that spies in the city will send her word. We must count on that happening, but again it's unlikely for that news to reach her in time for her to act on it."

"We can only do what we can do," Brand said. "It will have to be enough. But the seer warned me of the possibility of Ginsar using her scry basin on me or the army. She said I would sense it when it happened. I have not … not yet. And if I do, I will try to repel her."

Gil ran a hand through his hair and sighed. "There's just so much that we don't know."

"That's true," Brand answered. "But there's much that we do. For instance, we know that the elùgroths around Cardoroth have long had a hold over the elugs that dwell in the mountains north of us. Ginsar can summon them to war. But how well will they fight? They aren't well organized like the ones from the south. We have an advantage over them there."

"We know also," Shorty added, "that we gave the southern elugs, those from the Graèglin Dennath mountains, a bloody nose last time they attacked. And our scouts report no sign of them, so that allows us greater freedom to march from the city."

"We know this too," Brand said. "We'll do our best to protect Cardoroth. If we fail, it will fall. But then someone else will be next. So we must *not* fail. If we do, then the Dark will hold the south as well as the north of Alithoras, and everyone in between will be squeezed in a death grip. And as I say, we must not let that happen. We *will* not."

Gil laughed, and Brand raised an eyebrow.

"You make winning sound like an act of faith."

457

Brand grinned at him. "Ah, but it is. I'm not oblivious to all that could go wrong. But yes, it's an act of faith. The thought comes first and the deed follows."

It was an attitude that Gil had never been quite able to achieve. He understood that the *will* to win was a strong factor in doing so, that belief gave rise to action and that the power of the mind was greater by far than most people realized. He knew also that self-doubt was more disabling than any enemy blow. He knew all this, but even so the responsibility that they *must* win was a terrible burden. And it gave rise to the thought that they might not. Brand seemed able to ignore that. Gil could not. Failure meant that the world he knew would be turned to dust and ash. How could he put that from his mind?

5. When the Time is Right

Gil left the War Room with a troubled mind after the meeting. So much was happening so fast. But above it all, beyond strategies and preparations for war, one thing remained clear. He had been set a quest by the spirit of Carnhaina. She had charged him to close the gateway between worlds that Ginsar had opened.

He had not done so. Nor had he even discovered *how* to do so. The White Lady, however, knew what he must do. He was sure of it, but all she would say to him was that he would know what to do when the time was right.

It was time to talk to her again. With war imminent, she might reveal whatever it was that she knew. Brand had allotted her a room in the palace, quite close in fact to Gil's and the one he had given Elrika. Yet despite their proximity he seldom saw her. It was almost as though she avoided him.

He got there swiftly, walking so fast that his two Durlin guards struggled to keep up with him. Briskly, he knocked on the door.

"Come in, Gil," the White Lady said.

A shiver went up his spine. She had known it was him without looking. He decided to ignore that though. With her, it was best to just accept who she was and what she was like. To ask her questions only seemed to encourage her reticence.

"I won't be long," he told the guards.

He opened the door and stepped into her room. She was seated in a chair near the window, gazing out with a faraway look on her face. But when he entered she turned her gaze on him and smiled.

Not for the first time, Gil was amazed at the radiance of her expression and the warmth that emanated from her. She was kindness and goodness personified. But there was always something sad about her as well, and this lent her a heartbreaking beauty.

He smiled back. Brand was the only person that she really talked to, and he had a feeling that the regent understood more of her purpose than anyone else. But looking at her now, he trusted her. She was here to help, and if she would not tell him what he wanted to know, he would not, could not, hold it against her. There must be a reason. Still, he intended to press her hard for answers.

"Please have a seat," she said.

Gil pulled up a chair opposite her, and looked out the window at the city below. It was a thriving place. People filled the streets and went about their daily tasks. Did they know yet that war threatened everything they loved?

"You have come," the White Lady said softly, "to learn what you must do to close the gateway between worlds."

"Perhaps I've come just to talk to you," he answered. "You spend too much time in here by yourself."

She smiled at him once more, and there was that look again: beauty and kindness tinged with a sadness that cut deep.

"I am not of this world, Gil. I should not be here. Nor the Horsemen."

"That may be, but still you are entitled to happiness. This room is not a prison. You are free to go where you will, see what you want and enjoy Cardoroth."

She gazed out the window. "Tomorrow I will. The army will march, will it not? I will be with it."

"How do you know that, lady?"

"I know many things, Gil. I know that the enemy prepares to march against us. I know that Brand is right and that they will come down through the hills and seek to surprise us."

Gil studied her. She seemed as any young woman. Here, in her apartment, she was barefoot, one leg pulled up beneath her on the chair, and wearing a simple white dress. But there was far more to her than he knew. She held secrets within secrets and possessed power beyond his understanding.

"How is it that you know these things?"

"We all have our gifts. Everyone does, even the Horsemen. Mine, at least in this world, is to see what could be, what should be and to make the latter happen."

"What could be and what should be are far from the same thing."

"Further than you know."

Gil looked at her. There was softly spoken determination in her voice. The mystery of *what* she was drew him. But the thought of *who* she was, as a person, was stronger still.

"What is your world like, lady?"

"Ah, Gil. There's so much I could tell you. But I mustn't. The gateway should not exist. Our worlds are separate, and should stay that way. It's best that you know little."

Gil sighed. "Is that why you keep to yourself so much?"

She looked away. "It's one of the reasons. There is another." She glanced back at him. "The future will come soon enough, Gil. In the meantime, have confidence in Cardoroth. She is a strong city, filled with strong people. Ginsar and the Horsemen are as shadows. There is no joy in them. Only lust for power. And the darkness consumes them so much that they cannot see their danger. That will serve us well."

"You are speaking, I think, of how the gateway will be closed," Gil ventured.

"Yes. But please, don't ask me any more."

"I will know what to do when the time is right?"

"Yes."

"Then lady, I will leave it at that. I trust you."

She smiled at him again, and this time it was dazzling. All felt right in the world. "Thank you." She looked out the window a moment later, her expression wistful now. "You will have to make choices when the time comes. And if I tell you more now you may refuse then."

"Will they be so bad?"

She did not look at him. "You will see. But in the meantime, ponder this."

She stood and strolled to the wall nearby. Gill followed her.

There was a painting there, and she gestured at it. "Tell me what you see?"

He looked at the painting. He had seen it before, and others much like it.

"I see Carnhaina, the great queen who once ruled here. She appears much younger than she is normally depicted. She's tall and thin. With her I see her father and mother, the first king and queen of Cardoroth. That must be her younger sister there too. And I see all her brothers."

Gil fell silent. He had realized something that he had overlooked before.

"You have noticed something?" The White Lady asked.

"I suppose so. Carnhaina is famous. So too are the first Durlin. Some of them died to protect the king against assassins. I just never thought of it before, but those same Durlin were Carnhaina's brothers."

"That is so, Gil." She hesitated, as though waiting for him to say more, and then went on. "Carnhaina never had it easy. She had to make choices too, some of them dark. But she was able. You are her heir, and you will do as well as she."

Gil inclined his head. "Thank you for your confidence in me."

"And thank you for yours in me. But I think you should see someone else now."

"Who is that?"

"Elrika. She's not best pleased with you."

"Why not? What did I do?"

"Speak to her, Gil, and find out."

With a hand on his shoulder, she guided him to the door. She seemed so frail and small, but he knew there was strength in her. One day soon she would reveal her true powers.

"I'll be with the army tomorrow, when it marches," she said.

"It would be safer for you here, you know."

"I wasn't born into this world to be safe," she answered.

He said his goodbye and moved along the corridor to Elrika's room. He had barely finished knocking when the door opened. Elrika stood there, dressed in trousers and tunic with the Durlin sword at her side.

"Ah, it's you."

"Can I come in?"

"Why ask? You don't seem to consult me about anything else."

Gil hesitated. "We can fight here in the corridor if you prefer. But it won't be as comfortable."

She arched her eyebrows at him. "You've learned more from Brand than you know."

"I'll take that as a compliment."

"I suppose it is," she said. "Come in then."

He moved inside her apartment but she did not offer him a chair, nor did she sit herself.

For a moment she stared at him, taking in his bandages. "Well?" she said eventually.

"Well what?"

"I heard what happened with Dernbrael." She looked at his blood-stained dressings again. "It was quite the fight, apparently."

"It wasn't easy," he said. "For many reasons, it wasn't easy at all."

Her gaze softened, slightly. "I know that. What I don't know is why you didn't take me with you."

"There's only one reason for that. I didn't want to take you into danger. I had soldiers and Durlin with me, but I didn't know for sure that he was by himself or if he had warriors with him."

She put her hands on her hips. "Fool. How would you feel if I went into danger and didn't take you with me?"

He had no real answer for that, but he knew he would not like it. "I would feel … I don't know. I would want to help but be unable to do so."

She studied him a moment. "Exactly," she said in a softer voice. "And will you ever do that to me again?"

"I'm sorry. I didn't see it that way before. And no, I won't."

She relented then. "You could have been hurt."

"Actually, I *was* hurt."

"I meant killed. And I wouldn't have been able to do anything to stop it."

He knew what she had meant, and he knew that he would feel the same way in her position.

"Anyway," she said. "The worst didn't happen. So let's forget about it. Have a seat and tell me about it."

They sat down around a small table and he told her of how Esanda had found Dernbrael and what unfolded after that, including Ginsar's appearance.

"I still don't see why you accepted his challenge to duel," she said toward the end of his explanation.

"It was a matter of honor, partly. And what sort of king will the people think me if they also wonder if I'm a coward?"

"You worry too much about what other people think. But anyway, I can't help feeling that it was personal too. Dernbrael was trying to usurp your throne. And he tried to kill both you and Brand. That's as personal as it gets, and I think you reacted in that vein."

"Ginsar said I *wanted* to kill him. She said there was a dark side to me. Just like her."

Elrika reached out and touched his hand. "There's a dark side to all of us, but mostly we keep it under control. You did so with Dernbrael. It was *he* that sought the duel."

"Yes, but I was the one that agreed to it."

"You had reasons. They're probably even good ones."

"I suppose so. But after it was all over … I enjoyed it too."

She looked at him carefully. "Listen to me, Gil. You are *not* like Ginsar. You're nothing like her at all. Could you become so? Maybe. But so could we all. That is the lesson here. Just don't let that happen."

Gil smiled at her. She was not necessarily right, but she was trying to make him feel better. "You're a good friend."

"You just remember it! Now, you'd better get cleaned up. And let Arell change those bandages."

"I will. But there's one more thing to tell you yet."

"I'm listening."

He could tell that she was still upset with him, but he put that aside. "Cardoroth is now at war. Ginsar is gathering an army of elugs from the mountains of Auren Dennath. They will soon march on us."

Elrika took the news calmly. She had been expecting it no doubt. Most people in the city did, in a vague sort of way. But it was a different thing to have your fears confirmed no matter how much you had been anticipating them.

"Are we ready for them?"

"I think so. As ready as we can be. Especially Brand. I think he's been planning for this a long time. He managed to surprise our generals too, so let's hope he can surprise Ginsar as well."

"What's his plan?"

"We're not going to wait behind the walls. We're going out to meet them, to strike first before Ginsar is ready. And before she opens the gateway between worlds any wider."

She thought about that for a moment. "Good," she said. "Best to get this over with."

"In the end, the only way to truly win this is to close the gateway."

Elrika pursed her lips. "The White Lady still won't tell you what she knows?"

"Nothing," Gil said. "She won't tell me anything at all. But I feel that I already know, at least that the answer is within my grasp, but I just can't quite see it."

"It doesn't matter Gil. Trust yourself. The answer will come eventually. And trust the White Lady. There's no harm in her. Whatever she does, whatever she says, or doesn't as the case may be, she has our best interests at heart."

Gil knew she was right. He made ready to leave, for he had to see Arell and then rest. Tomorrow would be a long day. But she placed a hand on his arm as he stood.

"Is there anything else you need to say?"

There was a glint in her eyes, and he knew this was important to her.

"Will you ride with me tomorrow when the army marches?"

"You know I will. But you may have to give me some lessons on the way. I haven't ridden much before."

"Of course. And I'll make sure you have a quiet horse."

They hugged, and he left her then. He felt rather strange, because while he would do anything to protect her he also wanted her with him. But at the same time, if something happened to her he would never forgive himself.

6. I Accept your Gift

Ginsar breathed deep of the air. It was fresh and cool and clean. She did not like it. Better by far were the pungent smells of the forest, and the shadows and sense of secrecy that went with it. But her coming here had been worth it.

The mountains of Auren Dennath climbed as a wall before her. All pine-clad slopes, twisting valleys and high ridges. It was blue too. Everything was blue from a distance except the snow-scattered ridges and the high peaks, capped by white.

She did not like the mountains. Nor the river that chattered away beside her, fed by the snows above and gushing down into the rest of Alithoras. The Alith Nien it was called in the old tongue. The Silver River. And it flowed into Alithoras, the Silver Land. She shook her head. A pox on the old tongue! Beauty was not found in nature, nor in people. It was found in power only. And *that* she had exercised in the last few days.

She had walked those blue mountains in ages past, knew the trails and the hidden valleys, knew the caves and grottoes where elugs dwelt. It had not been hard to find them again in the last few days, to draw them once more under her sway. It had been harder with the Lethrin who preferred the rocky heights, but they too were coming to war.

She cast a grim gaze over her acolytes. They liked this place no more than she. They sat and talked quietly by the river, away from her. At least down here the river slowed. It was loud and rushing no more. And this bend within it was a nice and secluded spot. The sandy shore was annoying though. But it did not run any great length. It soon gave way to a shelf of rock, and then a tree-clad hill rose to the side offering them shelter from prying eyes and something of the seclusion of the forest to which they were used.

It was sunny though, bright light everywhere. The acolytes hated that. But they were weak, even if useful at times. And she would have a special use for two of them soon. It was true though that the dark was better, but she could put up with the sunlight. Her army was coming to her, gathering nearby, and soon they would march.

Movement caught her gaze and disturbed her thoughts. One of the acolytes approached.

"He comes, Mistress."

It was just as well. She did not like this waiting. She turned her gaze up toward the hill. For a moment, she saw nothing. Then the black-clad form of her most powerful acolyte appeared from behind a stand of trees. With him were three elugs and a single Lethrin.

The small group scrambled down the steep slope. There was a trail there, of sorts, but it was a tangled mess of tree roots and loose rock. The acolyte descended clumsily. The elugs negotiated the slope with ease, though little grace. The Lethrin however, who should have fared the worse because of his size, moved with incredible nimbleness and balance.

The Lethrin, ahead now of all the others, leaped down the last of the trail to the rock shelf like a mountain deer. There he waited for the others, and his dark eyes found Ginsar and studied her.

She felt the strength of his will through that gaze. All the Lethrin were strong of body. Some of mind too, but here was a paramount individual. She could use that. Yes, he would be most fitting for what she had in mind, and the plan that she had nurtured for some while would be altered. And for the better. She smiled, but the creature gazed back at her implacably. Better and better.

The others joined him and the acolyte took the lead again. They approached her, and her heart quickened. Soon now her plan would come to fruition and her army would march.

The small group drew to a stop before her. The acolyte bowed, and the elugs followed his lead. The Lethrin merely inclined his head, the dark gaze of his deep-set eyes never leaving her own.

She turned to the acolyte. "The army is now gathered?"

"Yes, Mistress."

"And what are the final numbers?"

"We have thirty-five thousand elugs. Most of them are armed with swords, but some carry maces and timber clubs."

"And the Lethrin?"

The acolyte began to answer, but the Lethrin interrupted.

"We are one thousand strong, Ginsar. Our numbers may be few, but we are strong."

Ginsar was surprised. Most men trembled at the thought of even talking to her, and very few dared call her by her name.

She looked into his eyes. "I accept your gift."

The Lethrin gazed back, puzzled but undaunted. "What gift?"

She smiled at him. "The strength of your people. Even one … just one, is gift enough."

He did not answer that, and she read uncertainty in his expression. But she knew exactly what she meant, and he would understand soon enough.

After a moment, he inclined his head once more. But his expression remained perplexed.

She kept her face neutral, but in her heart she felt a surging thrill and the joy of life buoyed her spirit.

"Are you ready to kill?" she asked him.

"Yes."

"Are you ready to make war?"

"Yes."

"Then together we shall make war such as the race of man has never seen before!"

7. Leave the War to Us!

Gil sat on a roan mare. Elrika rode beside him on a quiet gray. Brand was nearby, and all the Durlin too, sitting proudly on their mounts and looking relaxed and yet ready to move into action at any moment. It was the look of the elite warrior, and Gil admired it.

The White Lady sat quietly on her mount, a pure white. Gil had never seen the horse before, and he was not sure where it had come from. But it was a fitting mount for her, even if unusual with its pink nose and blue eyes.

Elrika seemed calm, but he knew there were nerves beneath the surface. Yet no one had said anything about her presence, although the eyes of the Durlin strayed sometimes to her sword, the blade of that long-ago first Durlin. Gil realized why they did not say anything. It was because they respected her. She was not as skilled as they, but she was young. One day she would surpass some of them in skill, perhaps all of them. They had seen her use a blade, and they knew talent when they saw it. They accepted her as Gil's unofficial guard, and her place in the army too.

Dawn streaked the sky. Gil looked behind him. Cardoroth was awash with color, the low-glinting rays of the sun striking flashes of red from the strange stone of the city buildings. It was his home. It would always be his home. But he rode away now to protect it, if he could.

They had begun to pass through the city streets when it was still dark and the people mostly asleep. It had been quiet, but the smell of hearth-fires and baking bread was strong in the air. This was the last group to pass through. The army had gone ahead of them, moving in regiment after regiment through the night.

"Do you think moving the army under cover of dark worked?" Gil asked Taingern as the Durlindrath neared him.

"It's hard to hide the movement of an entire army. But it had to be tried. Likely a lot of people noticed something was happening, though not necessarily what and on how big a scale."

Shorty joined the conversation. "People would have noticed, but they would have noticed a lot more if the army marched during the day with fanfares and parades. Although the men would have missed all those well-wishers and the shouts of friends and the familiar faces of their families to see them off. But it couldn't be helped. Brand was right to march as secretly as possible."

"When will the city be told?" Gil asked.

"Brand left instructions," Taingern said. "No announcement will be made until two days after we've gone."

Shorty laughed. "And then they'll be told that the army marched along the old Halathrin road, and that going to the North Gate was a ruse."

"Hopefully all these things will throw the spies off our track," Taingern said.

"Most of them anyway," Shorty agreed. "But some in the city will have noticed what's going on and made guesses. They may try to follow us, and then get word to the enemy."

Soon after, they came to the North Gate, the Harath Neben as it was properly known. Gil studied the two massive emeralds representing the constellation of Halathgar. The gate was also called Hunter's Gate, for

473

the north road, out where the army now was, lead to wild lands of plentiful game. Gil had been through it before, but had not ever gone far into the lands beyond.

They rode on. Sunlight bathed the forested hills ahead. Behind, the city streets remained gray shadows. The road they followed ran straight at first, and then it began to swing to and fro as it climbed toward higher ground. Within half an hour they crested a hill and drew rein.

Brand sat upon his beloved black stallion, an old horse that had been his mount before he was the regent or even the Durlindrath. His hand was always reaching out to stroke its neck, but now he held the reins in a tight fist and Gil saw an emotion on his face that he had seldom seen before. Fury.

Below, gathered on a large expanse of grassland within a valley, was the army.

Gil glanced at Shorty. "What's the matter?"

"Brand instructed the generals to take the army into the hills and well beyond the city. They have not done so."

The regent nudged the stallion forward, and the group set off again. Brand had regained control of his emotion, but the look on his face was still cold and bleak.

As they moved down the slope Gil studied the army. He had never seen that many people in one place before. Twenty-five thousand men, their helms glinting, standards and flags sparking myriad colors into the air and the hope of a nation about them like an aura. This was what stood between the forces of evil and the people of Cardoroth. And he felt a sudden surge of pride that he was going to be a part of it.

The riders negotiated the slope down to the floor of the valley and passed through the outer perimeter of sentries and into the army.

Brand was in the lead, his black stallion moving with grace as though it knew it was making an entrance. Upon the regent's head was the Helm of the Duthenor, glittering silver in the early light. He sat tall and proud in the saddle, not like a regent but like a warrior-king of old.

The Halathrin blade, sheathed at his side, was no ornament and the soldiers knew it. Brand was the finest fighter in Cardoroth, if not Alithoras. There was no one they wanted with them more than him, for once upon a time he had been one of them. A soldier, a fighter. He had earned a place as a captain after a deed of unsurpassed bravery. And then surpassed it anyway to become Durlindrath.

All about him soldiers waved and yelled out to him and cheered. Brand acknowledged them, and here and there he even called to some by name. He knew these men, had served with them before his rise to power. He was, and always would be, one of them. That was why they respected him. He knew them. He cared about them. And there was a lesson in that. One that he had been teaching Gil for a long time, and one that Gil thought he had understood but now knew he was only just beginning to learn.

Thus they passed through the army, and it took much time to reach the front. Gil realized that it would have been much faster to have skirted round it than to pass through it. But Brand did nothing without reason. Why then had he done this? To help lift the morale of the men? That seemed likely enough. But also perhaps to gauge it in the first place. That seemed likely too. Or maybe to reinforce his bond with the soldiers? At some point he may fall out with the generals, especially if they disobeyed him, and he would want the support of the men. All of these seemed good reasons for what he had done. Perhaps *all* of them were right.

Unease settled over Gil. That there was a fundamental difference in view between the generals and Brand was apparent. That was no good thing, because in war the leadership of an army must send clear and unified messages to the soldiers. Doubt and discord were deadly. And Brand would certainly wish to lead the army himself, yet the generals were more experienced, and historically generals led Cardoroth's armies. The old king had been an exception. He was not the only one, but he was a rarity. This meant the generals would seek to wrest power back. The question was, what would Brand do?

At length the riders came through to the front. Brand angled his black stallion then toward where the generals were talking with their adjutants. Nearby, soldiers were saddling the generals' horses.

The anger that was in Brand resurfaced, though Gil knew he was holding it in check now, but some crept through into his voice when he spoke.

"Why have the men not marched well away from the city as I asked?"

Garling turned his gaze to the regent, and there was no give there.

"The men were tired from the long night of activity. They needed rest, and I ordered them to establish a camp here."

Brand did not back down. "You've given them a rest, and thereby increased the chances of them dying. They will not thank you."

"How so?" Garling answered. "What risk is there in this?"

"There are spies in the city. They will seek to follow us. Even now they may be in the forest, ahead of us. Nor was the gate closed as I asked."

Garling shook his head. "You imagine dangers and grow them in your mind. There may be spies. But marching from the city and closing the gate would not have stopped them."

"Perhaps not, but it would have reduced their numbers. Everything we can do to hinder them should be done."

"I considered these issues, and I made my choice."

"And the other generals?"

Druigbar answered. "We agreed with Garling. He is the most senior and most respected officer in the army."

"That, in short, is the answer to all your questions," Garling said to Brand. "We are the military experts here. We know what we are doing, and we insist that you leave the war to us. Do not interfere any further."

It went quiet. Gil knew that his earlier musings were correct. This was a power struggle, and the generals had deliberately ignored Brand's orders to force a confrontation and establish their authority at the outset.

The tension hung in the air, and Gil knew that Brand could not tolerate this. But Brand surprised him. The regent merely inclined his head.

"As you say, you are the experts. Carry on."

Garling signaled for a horn to be sounded, and the signal was given for the army to march. Brand fell back behind the generals as the army moved forward at a steady pace.

Shorty chuckled softly. "You're playing a dangerous game, Brand."

Brand gave a slight shrug, but did not comment.

"What game?" Gil asked.

"He doesn't trust the generals," Shorty said quietly. "The old king, your grandfather, was the great strategist. These men, they mostly just executed his decisions. In themselves, they're not really tested and proven." He lowered his voice still further. "Worse than that, Sandy suspects they were in league with Dernbrael, but she's not positive of the information she has. And given what we now know of Dernbrael, that means they might be in league with Ginsar. We just don't know."

That was a shock to Gil, and even Shorty seemed solemn as he spoke the words.

"So what is the game that Brand is playing?"

"Like I say," Shorty answered, "a dangerous one. It's hangman's noose. And he's giving them enough rope."

8. I have Obeyed!

Night fell, and a blanket of stars smothered the sky. The dark was to Ginsar's liking, and she became more alert, more focused, more alive.

In the distance she heard the rumblings of her army. It was massive. It would crush Cardoroth. And then who knew where it would sweep her?

She put that last thought aside. First things came first. Brand was her great enemy. It would not do to forget that, to take her mind off that battle until it was won. He had a way of surprising her, and she must not let that happen again.

The smell of smoke from thousands of cooking fires filled the air. Now that night had fallen, the ruddy glow from the army's camp lit the horizon. Ginsar liked that. Fire was better than starlight.

Tomorrow she would join the army and lead it. Cardoroth awaited them. But before that, she still had two tasks to accomplish. She was not looking forward to the first. It always drained her, and it was dangerous. But the second would be her reward for the first.

She pulled her black cloak closer about her, and drew the dark hood over her head. Slowly, silently, she summoned her power. Elùgai crept through her body, seeping out from her very bones and tingling her skin. She wrapped it about herself, cocooned herself in its embrace. The magic took on the darkness of the night. It became one with the shadows. It was the whisper of the wind in the tree tops and the bubble and lap of the river nearby.

Now that no one could see or hear her, Ginsar rose and slipped from the camp of her acolytes unnoticed. She had business of her own to attend to and questions that needed answers.

She moved toward the river and followed it downstream. It was better to be alone, away from the furtive glances of her followers and their incessant talk. Soon they were swallowed up by the night behind her. Even the distant noises of the army became more muted. At last, she was alone and one with the dark about her.

She let the elùgai that concealed her slip away. Great though her power was, she must still conserve it. It would be tested tonight, and also in the days to follow.

It grew darker. Clouds scudded across the sky. All that she could hear now was the soft murmur of the river. It ran slower here and widened out.

She came to another bend. Trees began to grow thickly, and she slipped within them like just another shadow of the night. It was black and sky-less here, the canopy of leaves a dome above her. It reminded her of a tomb, and well it might for in a way it soon would be.

Taking her time, for even her sharp eyes strained to penetrate the gloom, she moved toward the bank of the river. When she found it, she liked what she saw. It was suitable for her purpose.

The trees were willows now, and here by the edge of the river there was no shelf of rock nor margin of sand. It was an earth bank, and the hanging branches of the trees dangled out over the water.

Probing with her mind, she sensed that the river had gouged out the soil beneath the bank so that while she stood upon ground she stood over water too. That also was fitting for her purpose, because she must invoke that feeling with her magic: the feeling of different worlds in the same place, the melding of one reality with another,

480

the summoning of a spirit long dead into the realm of the living.

In the distance, an owl hooted. A sense of menace settled over the little wood in which she stood. It reminded her of home, and that comforted her. What she would attempt now was not easy. It never was, but she sensed that this time would be even harder.

She looked out over the dimly visible water. It was sluggish, barely moving, but here and there a ripple of water shimmered and gleamed in the inky blackness.

Ginsar remembered her childhood. He that she would now summon came to her first then. Her family did not like him. But she knew better. Her sister learned from him, but she pulled away at the end. But Ginsar kept going and the secrets of the universe, one by one, became hers. Yet he, the paramount elùgroth ever to walk Alithoras, was dead.

But not to her. Even dead, she could speak to him, and she would do so now to learn of the future.

She stepped forward to the very edge of the bank on which she stood. It was now the middle of the night, that crux of time where the night was neither young nor yet old. It was a moment in between, a transition of what was into what would be.

The willows moved behind her, their whip-like branches trailing like long and skeletal fingers probing the dark air. The water before her began to toss restlessly. A glimmer of starlight lit the river, but it touched only the surface. The murk below was impenetrable. Except to her magic, and she summoned it now, drew it in from the world about her.

Ginsar stood to her full height. Out, out her mind spread, casting tendrils of thought over the water. And then she plumbed the murky depths, becoming one with it, feeling its currents and then sinking lower until her mind perceived the mud-slicked bottom.

Unease gripped her once more. It always did at this point, but fortune favored the fearless and she stood even straighter. She turned her magic to what must come next, and mouthed words of power that filled the air and then sank like daggers of thought into the water. Words, magic and thought were one, and they came up against the forces of nature that held the world together.

Fire spurted beneath the water. Her sense of unease redoubled, but she suppressed it. She made a stabbing motion with her hands, and the fire plunged into the depths of the river, deep down to the muddy bottom and the solid earth beneath.

The world grew still. A great chill descended. The stars glittered through gaps in the scudding clouds, and frost began to glisten on the narrow leaves of the willows.

Something stirred in the water. The river began to seethe. A hiss of steam escaped the surface, and then the water boiled and thrashed angrily. It writhed with forces seeking escape, forces that she had called into being. The river twisted like a live thing seeking to throw itself out of the two banks that hemmed it in.

The noise began now, as she knew it would, as it always did. It was not the splash of water nor the hiss of steam. It was desolate wailing. And on the edge of her understanding were words – bitter, angry, pleading. Above it all was a sense of threat, that she too would join the maelstrom of lost voices one day.

Then the faces began. The fire-lit water showed them all. Staring faces. Cruel faces. Kind faces. They tried to rise into the air and escape the water, but the river threw up a plume of water that slapped them all back down to the netherworld.

Ginsar stabbed again with her hands, and then she clawed at the air. A heaving vortex grew in the middle of the river. From this a figure rose, tall and majestic, robed in fiery water and crowned by white froth.

Power thickened the air, and the figure, mantled in awe and dread grandeur, drew breath and lifted high its arms. "I have come," it boomed.

The water of the river stilled its thrashing.

"Welcome, Master." Ginsar said. But her throat was dry and her words raspy. The chill about her was like ice and her breath steamed. She forced air into her lungs and spoke again. "I have summoned you because—"

"I know why you have called me. The dead see many things. In death, there is no time. What was, what is and what yet may be are all one. Speak, and I will answer. Perhaps."

This was not quite what Ginsar expected. Had she performed the ritual wrongly, made some slight error? No, she knew she had not. What then was different? She must think on that later. Maybe she was different herself.

Her unease heightened, but she forced her words out with strength this time.

"Fate hastens. War looms. The fall of Cardoroth draws nigh. What plan has Brand set in motion to try to avert the disaster?"

The shade of her Master, the long-dead spirit of Shurilgar, tilted his cowled head. She saw no eyes, nor any face, but she sensed the force of his will.

"Brand is now beyond your reach. Your chance to destroy him has come and gone. You failed, and the opportunity will not come again."

Shurilgar's voice carried over the water to her, flew into her mind like arrows. They made her heart flutter in her chest and stabbed at her like little daggers of fear. But her Master was not finished.

"Beware! Brand is less your enemy than you think. You have others, and, perhaps, greater. But know this also. Though Brand will not fall to you, Cardoroth yet may. Or it may not. Should you draw too deep of the world from which you summoned the Horsemen, then they shall consume you. But if you do not draw enough then you shall surely fail. Again."

Ginsar felt the cold seep into her bones, and this time the judgement of her Master was plain. And it stung her.

"I control the Horsemen. They do my bidding. Mine is the greater strength, and I do not fear them. What else should I know of my enemies?"

Shurilgar spoke again. His voice was the whisper of death, and there was a glimmer of cold eyes within the shadow of his cowl.

"Pride is a friend to some, and an enemy to others. But you should fear also the girl-child for she will stymie you, and the quiet-one who shall have his day in the sun. Yet in the end, all will hinge on the princeling. He is the key, and the past will rise to call him, and the Pale Lady shall fall at his feet, and in dying save him."

Ginsar locked those words into her memory. They made no sense, for the dead spoke in riddles. But there would be truth in them nonetheless, once she unraveled their meaning.

"And what else, O Master?"

An otherworldly breeze ruffled Shurilgar's hood, yet no such breeze touched Ginsar.

"Time slips away," he said. "Brand is not the great foe that you imagine, but he is implacable. You seek to defeat him, but all the while he plans and moves to defeat you."

Ginsar considered that. She did not yet know what the other warnings meant, but this at least seemed clear enough. Brand sought to bring the war to her instead of the other way around.

Shurilgar continued. "All hangs in the balance, child of the Dark. What was will be again, and truths long hidden will surface. They may help your cause, or hinder them."

"Then help me, O Master. Reach forth and lend me of your strength."

"The dead do not help the living."

"That is not so! Carnhaina helps Gil. Do you love me less than she loves him?"

The water of the river churned, and it seemed that the current turned and flowed upstream. Fish leapt above the surface as though trying to escape the river, but then sank without trace.

Ginsar knew she had gone too far. Summoning the dead required a perfect balance of ritual and magic. She had disrupted that. Perhaps from the beginning, but she had tipped the balance now. To invoke emotion in a spirit was a dangerous, dangerous thing to do.

Shurilgar towered above her as an angry image. Strange lights gleamed and flitted below the river surface. The water lapped the bank and tore at the solid ground. His shadow grew massive, and then he strode across the water toward her.

His hand shot out. The river heaved. His cold fingers gripped her throat, or a lash of water struck her. She felt it being forced down and into her lungs. Or maybe it was the spirit-hand of Shurilgar choking her, depriving her of air.

She tasted death. Cold, lifeless, dark and dim with the memory of the light that was.

Shurilgar spoke, and she felt the breath of his voice upon her face, unless it was instead some stirring of a breeze through the ice-cold air.

485

"There, princess, I have obeyed! I have obeyed! I have given you a gift. It is inside you and will help ere the end."

He cast her back and she stumbled and fell. His shadow withdrew, growing smaller, fainter as it reached the center of the lake. There it descended.

He was gone. A plume of water geysered high into the air and then collapsed again. The stench of the muddy river bottom floated through the air.

Ginsar was colder than ice. She knew she was on the threshold of death. She could not stand, for there was no strength in her legs and her mind swam. But she had use of magic, and she invoked it now.

Elùgai flared to life. It glittered at her fingers and she cast it at the willow trees. At first only the leaves caught, but then she drew deep of herself and sent a bolt of sorcery at the nearest trunk. There was a boom of thunder and the earth trembled. When that subsided, and the smoke began to clear, she saw that the trunk had started to burn, and soon a roaring fire engulfed it. This spread from branch to branch and tree to tree until the entire grove was afire.

Gradually, warmth and life returned. Never before had she been so close to death, but having survived, a wild thrill ran through her. She dared things none other did. She had power that no one else had. She would achieve that which had proven beyond her innumerable predecessors – the subjugation of all Alithoras!

She rose to her feet, and weakness washed over her. But it would pass. She knew that she had gone too far, but it would serve her well. She had angered the dead, which most would say was unwise. But Shurilgar had given her a gift in the end. He had done something, though she knew not what.

She took a few deep breaths, loving the smell of smoke about her. The warmth was seeping through to her bones, and that was a feeling of unsurpassed bliss. Never had she been so cold before.

Wrapping her cloak tightly about her, she retraced her steps back toward the camp. She could not tell what Shurilgar had done, but she felt different. No matter. His gift would reveal itself in time.

9. A Dangerous Path

The road the army followed was of ancient construction. Gil marveled at how well it had survived the millennia, for it must have been built by the Letharn during that long-ago time when their empire spanned much of Alithoras.

Yet it was not paved, but rather made of hardened earth that now grew grass. Over the long years since the demise of the Letharn others had turned it to their own purposes, keeping it relatively clear of shrubs and trees. Now, it was mostly used by hunters and woodcutters from Cardoroth.

Gil could not help but wonder why the Letharn had built it. It led to Cardoroth, but so far as he knew there were no towns or ruins or signs of habitation in this place when his ancestors founded the city. Had the Letharn come, perhaps, merely for the scry basin beneath the Tower of Halathgar that was subsequently built over it? It was possible, though he felt there was something more. Whatever that something was, it appeared to be lost in the deeps of time.

The road, according to Brand, deteriorated through the hills. This was because it saw less use. Nor was it especially wide, allowing the men to only march four abreast. This was a concern, for later, especially when they penetrated deep into the well-forested hills, the army would be strung out and vulnerable to attack. But this could not be helped, nor was it unprecedented. Still, Gil could see why the generals did not like the idea. They had mentioned it at the very start of the march, and

Garling had dropped back to ride next to Brand to point it out again.

"It is exactly as we feared," the general said. "The road deteriorates swiftly, and the army will be in greater jeopardy the further we proceed."

"This is no surprise, Garling. We knew this in Cardoroth. But the swifter we travel the less our risk. Ginsar must know where we are in order to attack us."

"Perhaps so, but we should not have come here. We should return."

Brand shook his head. "It's too late now. For better or worse we're committed. To turn back would shatter the morale of the men, and they would have no respect for the army leadership. Nothing would lose us the battle with Ginsar swifter than that."

"What you say may be true, but there are limits. We don't know how much this road deteriorates. We don't know if the army can even traverse it all the way. Our maps become less accurate half way through the hills."

Brand raised an eyebrow. "You and the other generals have never been here yourselves?"

"No," Garling said.

Gil could see that Brand was surprised. The generals, more than anyone else, should be familiar with the countryside surrounding Cardoroth in all directions.

"Well, I have," Brand told the general. "The road is narrow, but it does not get narrower than it is here, nor does it deteriorate much more than this. It runs all the way through the hills and comes out the other side. There is danger in its narrowness, and in the concealment offered by hill and tree, but the remedy to that is swift marching and preparedness. The scouts will scour the area around us night and day."

"It's not the same," Garling argued. "No matter how good the scouts are they may miss something. There's just too much concealment available for our enemies."

"No, the risk cannot be entirely eliminated."

Garling did not seem best pleased, but he argued no further. "Very well, I'll send out the scouts."

Brand seemed dumbstruck. "You mean that you haven't already?"

"No. We're still close to home."

"Well, if it were me, I'd send them out now. Every one of them. And not just ahead and to our flanks but behind also."

"Their numbers are limited," Garling said. "Why behind us too? Ginsar can only be ahead of us, assuming she comes this way at all."

"Because we may be followed from the city. And then word sent ahead of us by swift rider."

Again, Garling did not argue the point, but he did not seem entirely convinced. He nudged his mount ahead and rode up to the other two generals. Brand never took his gaze off him, and the regent seemed less than happy.

The army moved deeper into the hills. There was a brooding sense about them, a feeling of an ancient land that seldom saw the movements of people and tolerated it less. The wilderness often felt that way to Gil, but it was a feeling only. It came from spending too much time walking city streets and sleeping in beds and having decorated ceilings keep off the rain at night.

Every hour the generals called a halt and the men rested briefly. They were setting a good pace, but there was a long way to go. Frequently, Brand dismounted and walked his horse. When he did so, the Durlin did likewise. Gil followed suit, but he was not sure what purpose it served. Then he understood. Partly, it was to rest the horse. Partly, it was to obtain exercise. And it

490

was also to stay limber and combat ready. Brand did not expect trouble yet, but it was in his nature to always be prepared for it.

The trees grew more thickly, and there was little evidence of logging. Mostly there were oaks, and the trunks were gnarled and the height of the tree stunted by virtue of the rocky soil of the hills. There were other broadleaf trees too, and here and there taller pines. It was the kind of place that Gil might eventually like if he spent enough time here. Evidently, the hunters who came to this region did. Certainly, there was a sense of peacefulness and tranquility that did not exist in the city.

So the day passed. Little happened, save for the grind of the march. Well before dusk they stopped. It took time to establish a camp, dig latrines, start fires, erect tents and cook food. All of this needed to be done while daylight lasted.

Gil picketed his horse when they stopped and rubbed the roan down. Looking back, he saw that many small camps were established, and the army stretched out at least a mile behind him. It was one thing to talk about the vulnerability of an army forced to march in this fashion, but another to see it. An attacking enemy could cause great destruction. But even as he watched, sentries moved out from the long line of the army, and closer to the camp armed men stood forward to form a protective guard.

When they were done with their horses Brand approached.

"Come with me," he said, signaling both Gil and Elrika.

They moved out of their own camp, but Gil noticed soldiers coming up to form a guard at the front of the army. This was in addition to the protection already offered by a contingent of cavalry that formed a vanguard.

"Where are we going?" Elrika asked.

"I have to see someone. And it'll be educational for you both to come along. Best pull up your hoods."

Gil grinned. That was so like Brand. He rarely answered a direct question, preferring instead for people to draw their own conclusions. He had no doubt that whatever lay ahead would be interesting though, and educational. Brand, though sometimes enigmatic, did nothing to no purpose.

They melted into the army, merging with the throng of people. Brand had left his helm with the Durlin, and he seemed just an ordinary soldier. Gil and Elrika passed as the same, though less assured of themselves.

It was a long walk, for evidently they were heading to the rear of the army. And that was some considerable distance. Nor was it an easy walk, for everywhere there were moving people and cooking fires and groups of boisterous soldiers talking. They had to weave in and out of the great mass.

Eventually, they came to their destination. At the rear was the main concentration of cavalry, and also wagons full of supplies and food. These were all heavily guarded.

At the very back was a group of scouts. Brand saw them and swung in their direction. Even as Gil watched, some men went out to the flanks of the army and disappeared into the trees. Others were returning.

Brand approached a small fire where a lone man sat, his bow beside him. His companions had just left him.

"Is there a seat here for a few hungry soldiers?" Brand asked.

"By all means," the lone man replied. But even as he spoke his gaze was fixed hard on Brand's face, trying to see beneath the hood. Brand pulled it back, revealing himself for a moment, and then he pulled the hood back up.

"Well met, old friend," the regent said.

The lone man stuck out his hand, and Brand took it in the warrior's grip. "It's good to see you."

"And you," the man answered. "But I take it you're just a soldier tonight?"

"Exactly so," Brand said. "Just a soldier. And here are two more."

They all shook hands. "This is Tainrik," Brand advised.

The man had a firm handgrip and an easy smile. Gil liked him, but he followed Brand's lead and offered no name. The man guessed it anyway.

"I'm in privileged company tonight," he said. "Forgive me for not bowing, but I guess you don't wish that."

"You always were clever," Brand smiled.

"I don't think so. If I were clever I'd be away from all this and somewhere in the woods hunting deer and building a supply of food to last me the winter."

"Ah, but you'd be bored then."

"Maybe. Maybe not. Can I offer you all some food?"

"That would be nice. It's been a long day."

Tainrik collected some wooden bowls and spoons from a central area and returned to the fire. An iron pot was set against the coals to the side of the flames. From this he spooned out what looked to be stew.

"No palace meals here, I'm afraid. Just dried meat and vegetables."

"We've eaten worse," Brand said. "And a day of marching whets the appetite like nothing else."

Gil took the bowl handed to him and thanked the man. The food did not look appealing, yet when he tasted it he found it flavorful.

493

They ate in companionable silence for a while. All about them men were doing the same though some groups were quite loud. Tainrik was a quiet man, however.

He was obviously a scout judging from his clothing and sword. These were different from standard army issue. Just as scouts were a different breed of men. According to what Gil had heard they tended to be loners, more at home wandering the wild lands than in company. He believed it, but he also sensed there was much more to this man than what he seemed on the surface. If nothing else, Brand's friendship with him proved it. The regent had a way of finding extraordinary people.

Brand scraped the last bit of food from his bowl. "So, what orders do the scouts have?"

Tainrik shrugged. "Just the usual. Wander around. Check things out. Then return and report what was seen to our commanders."

"And what if you discover people following us from the city?"

"Ah, I see. We were told to leave them alone unless they presented any hostile intent."

Brand shook his head in disgust. "Those orders aren't good enough. If we're being followed, the scouts should get help and bring those men in. I want to know who they are and why they're following us. These people could just be curious. But more likely they're spies. We couldn't ask for a better chance to discover who our enemies are."

Gil put down his bowl. "How could the generals not realize that?"

Brand hesitated. "Perhaps they did. They may not *want* the spies caught. It's possible."

Gil felt suddenly afraid. If they could not trust their own generals, who could they trust?

"You know your history, lad. It's been done before. Generals have betrayed their kings and their people."

Gil knew it was so. It was a discomfiting thought.

Brand stood, and everyone else got up too. He shook Tainrik's hand. "I'm sorry I can't stay longer. I have much to do tonight."

Tainrik shook the regent's hand warmly. "It's no problem. I can have a look out there," he gestured vaguely to the rear, "but what exactly do you want me to do?" He gestured in the direction of Cardoroth.

"Don't disobey your orders. But if you find we're being followed, bring word to me. I'll sort it out with the generals after that."

They shook hands, and then Tainrik turned to Gil. He hesitated, and Gil thrust out his own hand. "Be careful out there."

"Always," the man answered.

Elrika gave him her hand, but before he even gripped it he spoke. "A pleasure, my lady. I hear you're very good with that sword. Best stay close to your friend. Not all our enemies are out there." He pointed out into the forest once more.

"That's my intention," Elrika said. "I'll be ready if they come."

"I know it," Tainrik replied. He bent down and retrieved his bow.

"You always did keep your ear to the ground," Brand said. "Nothing much escapes you."

Tainrik winked at him. "I'll tell you what I find out there behind us. It shouldn't take long."

With a grin and a wave he strode off. In moments, he had slipped into the trees and disappeared into the night. They watched him go, wondering what it would be like

495

out there. If the army was being followed, would he find the spies? That would be dangerous. But he seemed sure of his skills and confident, and that would lessen his risk.

"How did he know who I was?" Elrika asked.

Brand flashed her a smile. "Your fame grows, young lady. You saved Gil's life. The Durlin saw it, and word has spread. Tainrik is a quiet man, but a good one. He knew who you were from the beginning. Like I say, he keeps his ear to the ground."

They moved off themselves. "Going back will take much longer than coming here," Brand said. But he did not say why.

10. Into the Dark

Tainrik eased into the dark of the trees. The forest grew thick about him, but he was in no hurry to venture further into it.

A pause would allow him to grow accustomed to the dim light. It would let him become attuned to the different environment, and a different way of moving. Most of all, he had to change his thought patterns. In the wilderness, he must think less like a man and more like an animal, for the wild was a perilous place. And the most dangerous predators hunted on two legs.

For all the dangers, this was where he loved to be. Alone. Just him and the forest. There was peace and quiet here, and things followed laws and behaviors that he understood. Once you knew it, it was predictable. The city was not like that. People were not like that. And for all its peril, the forest was a safer place than the city. If you knew what you were doing.

He eased forward a hundred paces or so, and came to a stop again. He looked about him. He smelled the air. He listened to the forest noises. There was nothing out of place. Everything was as it should be, and best of all there were no people. And treasure of treasures, out here he had no supervisor. He moved when he wanted to move. He made his own choices. He was his own master. What could be better than that?

The feel of forest seeped into him, and he became one with it. Just another creature beneath its canopy, another still shadow in the dark. But he was a man, and that meant he was a hunter. And it was time for the hunt to begin.

He moved ahead, treading softly on doe-skin boots. They were quieter than regular boots, and more comfortable. The sword at his side was thin and light. Walking with it would not tire him. The bow, also small and light, was his weapon of choice. Though if he needed it, that meant that his primary skill of stealth had failed. The knives he carried were throwing knives. They too were meant for use only if stealth and arrow had let him down.

That had never happened. Yet.

He thought as he moved ahead. The forest was good for that. The senses remained alert, but the mind was free to ponder. He was no warrior. He was what he always wanted to be. A scout. And who would want to be anything else? Growing up he had heard of the fabled Raithlin scouts of Esgallien. Stories of them were legion, and he had devoured them all.

There was no one in Cardoroth who could match the Raithlin. No one even got close. He knew he did not himself, and he was the best that Cardoroth had produced. Not that he was in charge of the other scouts. Probably he did not want to be anyway. It would prevent him doing what he loved the most, which was getting out into the wild. Their leader knew little about scouting, and he stayed in the city, or the army at present, and filtered reports.

Tainrik smiled in the dark. Typical of the army, or any government institution, to put someone in charge who did not understand the issues and that had never done the work. But in this case, he did not mind. What they had done for him though was make him a captain. It was a reward for his services, and it meant greater pay for doing the same job. He was not sure, would never know for certain, but he suspected Brand had arranged that for him. Another reason to like the man.

He had done a loop through the forest, adjusting to the environment, but now he had come back to where he wanted to be. He glimpsed the road the army was following through a gap in the trees. Now that he knew exactly where it was again, he must avoid it. He moved further back into the trees and followed a parallel course. Should spies be following the army, they would not be traveling the road where they could be seen. They would be near it like him, but not on it.

Now, he must put himself in their minds. How would they be thinking? What would they do? In this way he would best be able to find them, assuming they were there at all.

This much he knew. They would hang back. It was too dangerous to follow closely to the army, and it could easily be followed from a distance. It could not hide. The chance of discovery was higher up close because there were more scouts per square mile. The further away they were, their chances of discovery lessened exponentially.

But what was *too* far away? They would need to be in striking distance if they wished to observe what was happening, if they intended sabotage, or if they intended to send word ahead of them to allies. Time was precious. Therefore, the optimum distance to trail the army was in a range of two to five miles. If it were him, he would do so at two miles, but then he was skilled at staying hidden. Were any potential spies similarly skilled? There was no answer to that, but he must assume they might be. Or if not, that they were reckless, or bold enough, to do so anyway.

He was not yet far enough behind the army to be within the likely range. He slowed though, taking greater

499

care to move silently, and even within the dark to move from areas of deepest shadow to deepest shadow.

He must keep putting himself in their mind. That was the paramount skill of trackers. Following a trail required great expertise, but there were times that no discernable trail existed. Yet trackers could still follow their target. This was because they empathized with their quarry, understood what they would do and why.

Tainrik drew to a stop. Doing so would enable him to hear, and to smell better. It also made his movement through the forest less predictable. He never moved at the same speed nor the exact same direction for long.

Would any followers light a fire? He smelled no trace of smoke. Nor did he see the flicker of light. Of course, he would have to be close to see it. But the question was, would they light one?

No one liked eating cold food. Especially night after night. But the fear of discovery would motivate them to take less risk. Nor was it so cold, even at night, that they needed one for warmth. Yet again, if they were skilled in the wild, there were ways to conceal not only the light from a fire but also the smoke.

If they were some distance from the army, and had located a hollow, they might be confident that a fire would not be seen and the chances of someone stumbling across it by accident were very low. But what about the smell of smoke? They might risk that. It took great skill to detect the origin of a smell at night. In still air, as it was now, the smell would be faint but spread out over a large distance. And the smell could be minimized too. Old and dry timber burned cleanly.

The night began to pass. He walked forward again, keenly alert to all his senses. It was quiet. Nevertheless, a sense of unease settled over him. It was nothing more than a whisper of doubt at first, but it grew. Nor could he identify its source. He had learned to pay attention to his instincts though, and it gave him pause for thought. What should he do next?

He moved slowly now, no more than a few soft paces at a time before stopping near a tree trunk and assessing the night again. Something was disturbing him, and that he did not know what it was annoyed him. Worse, it was dangerous.

He stepped forward again, only to go perfectly still, his foot hovering above the ground. Slowly, he drew breath, turning his head gently one way and then the other. Then he had it. Smoke. He knew now what disturbed him, and for all that his body was still his heart raced in his chest.

He realized that he had been smelling the smoke for some while. It was so faint, its build up so gradual, that he had not consciously noticed. Then he heard a noise.

Gently, he lowered his foot to the ground and pulled his bowstring from a small pocket in his tunic. The noise was not close, and he risked stringing the bow. It was not good for the weapon to be strung for long periods, but now was the time to do it before it was too late.

He had not quite finished when he identified the noise. Horses. Coming close. There were riders on the road, perhaps a dozen of them.

His bow strung, he moved quietly again. It was not far to a vantage point where he could see the road the army had traveled earlier that day. Peering through foliage and trunks he saw the riders. They were a cavalry unit from Cardoroth's army. No doubt they were patrolling the road.

They rode on and the sound of the hooves diminished. But the riders had not lit any fire. The smoke was not of their doing, and it had been too faint for them to detect. Whoever had started it was still out there. Somewhere.

Not only was the person, or persons, who had lit the fire still out there, but now they would be doubly alert. The sound of the riders would have woken even a sleeping man, and no man in the forest, traveling in the wake of an army, slept deeply.

It was time to remain still and work his way through the problem. He must do something next, but what? Retreat was not an option. Brand would need to know more than this. Whoever was out there could be mere hunters or foresters.

The wind was coming from the east, but the movement of air was so slow as to barely exist. But it was enough. He was on the west side of the road, and he knew what he would likely have to do next but did not like it.

Carefully, he moved through the trees. He was trying to sense if the smell of smoke increased or diminished by heading south. It did not, and that meant that the smoke was coming from either east or west. Given the wind direction, it must be east.

He moved to the verge of the trees and studied the open road. He would have to cross it. It was dark, but he would be seen if anyone watched. Probably, whoever had lit the fire was well back from the road, but there could be more than one person. Or whoever it was could have slipped out toward the road to study the riders as they went through. He could not know, and he could not wait. The night would not last forever, and what he would have to do after crossing would take time.

There was no movement nor any sound. There was no sign of another human presence, so he stepped out of the trees and onto the road. Movement attracted the eye, so it was best to go slowly. Yet the longer he was in the open, the greater the chance of his being observed. So, he opted for a normal walk, neither fast nor slow.

Soundlessly, he crossed. But the moment he reached the cover of trees on the other side he came to a stop and listened.

The forest did not change. There was no noise or indication of movement that he could detect, no sense that anyone had seen him and fled, or headed in his direction. So far so good.

Patience was his friend now, and hastiness could get him killed. Slowly, he moved east into the breeze. He moved for some time, easing through the forest soundlessly and slipping from one shadow to the next. In time, the smell of smoke disappeared. He had overshot the camp and the breeze was taking the smoke away from him. This was confirmation that crossing the road had been correct, but it gave no indication of whether the fire was to the north or south.

There was no way to know, but he felt that the forest was thicker to the north, that it offered better concealment in that direction. If so, that would be where he would have established his camp.

He turned back, but was careful not to retrace his earlier steps. In a little while, he scented smoke again, and then turned north.

Soon, the smell of smoke became stronger, stronger than it had been at any time since he first smelled it. His choice had been correct. He slowed down even more. He noticed too that the ground became rougher and started to slope downward. That meant that there was probably some kind of hollow or gulley ahead. A likely spot to conceal a camp.

Tainrik came to a stop. His heart pounded in his chest and a cold sweat began to slick his skin. This was it. Somewhere ahead was the camp.

503

Was there just one man there? Were there several? Were they spies or foresters or hunters?

There was no way to know. But it was his job to find out. He ran his fingers over his bow, feeling that the string was properly attached. He adjusted the quiver on his back and counted his arrows. Twenty-one. He felt the hilt of his sword for reassurance, and then, with great care, he began to move again.

He would need all the skill he possessed, all the patience he could muster, and perhaps a bit of luck.

11. I Choose Infamy

It had taken a long time for Brand to return to the front of the army. After a little while, he had removed his hood so that he was recognized. Many spoke with him, and it seemed to Gil that he knew half the army by name. Even those he did not know, he soon turned into friends.

More than that, Gil knew, they were turned into his own friends also, for Gil had removed his own hood. Brand had winked at him when he did it, and he knew that this was the purpose for which he had been brought. He might be the Prince of Cardoroth, but he would not be seen as remote and aloof like the generals. Brand was making him one with the soldiers, as was he.

Gil relished it. These were good men, if boisterous and irreverent. But that was just how soldiers dealt with fear, and Gil enjoyed it. Here, among them, he was no prince but just a soldier. And that was a title they respected more than any royal designation.

Elrika took down her own hood too, and Gil was surprised how well she got on with the soldiers. She did naturally what he had learned from Brand.

But it was a long night, and though Gil had slept soundly, it seemed that he had barely closed his eyes before the dawn came and the army commenced to march again.

Gil walked his roan beside Brand, and he noticed that the regent seemed preoccupied.

"Is something the matter?" he asked. "You seem troubled."

Brand cast a glance back over the army that trailed behind.

"No, nothing is the matter. I've had no word yet from Tainrik is all, but it's probably too early to expect anything."

Gil understood then. Brand had sent a man into possible danger, and he did not like doing so. That it was necessary was obvious, but that did not make it more agreeable.

The morning passed. Clouds drifted in from the east, growing thicker hour by hour. The army reflected Brand's mood and became subdued, for the possibility of rain was not a good prospect. Nothing was hated more by an army on a long march, except arriving at its destination and facing battle.

The mood turned worse, for the threat of the clouds was delivered. It began to drizzle, very light but unceasing. Quickly, everything became wet, from the slippery grass the men must now tread to all their clothes and equipment.

"It's going to get worse soon," Shorty said.

He was proved correct. Soon it rained in earnest. Sheets fell in waves, turning the ground to mud.

Garling approached Brand, the other two generals behind him. "We're going to call a halt," he said.

Brand seemed furious, but he hid it well. "Halting the men in rain is no improvement on walking through it," he said.

Garling stiffened, but Taingern intervened. "Neither marching nor camping is pleasant in the rain. But there's another consideration."

"What's that?" Garling asked crisply.

Taingern seemed oblivious to his tone. "I used to hunt these parts. The terrain changes rapidly here, and the road traverses ridges and gulleys before it climbs

506

higher in the hills and reaches a plateau. Your suggestion, general, is wise. But if the rain keeps up, which it looks like it might, we could be cut off from going forward or back, perhaps for a day or two. Yet the plateau isn't that far away. If we reached it, then we can camp, and the ground would be less muddy too."

Garling considered that. He looked like he was going to disagree, then he shrugged and nudged his horse forward.

The march continued, and Gil saw that Shorty gave his friend a sly look.

"I never knew you were big on hunting?"

Taingern looked at him, the faintest grin on his face. "There's lots of things you don't know about me."

"Aye. You're right. Until now I didn't know you could lie with a straight face. No wonder I keep losing to you when we play dice."

Taingern grinned in earnest. "I'm good with maps too, and I studied them well before we left Cardoroth. Turned out to be a good idea."

"A *very* good one," Brand said. "Thank you. But what you said about getting cut off was right."

"I know," Taingern said. "And Garling realized it too. But he would not have changed his decision on your word."

"No, that he would not. Thank you again."

They went onward, but Gil could see that Brand remained agitated. That was not like him. He always gave an air of calm confidence.

"Something is troubling you, Brand. What is it?"

The regent sighed and seemed to relax a little. "Everything we are doing is dangerous. But not acting is dangerous too. I know these hills and these forests, though my memory is dim. Armies can hide here. I don't think Ginsar's army is yet close. But each day that grows less certain. And hers is not the only army. Hvargil is somewhere outside Cardoroth. He doesn't have a proper army, but even a few hundred outlaws could pose problems in such a place as this. Severe problems. And it's often postulated that his hideout may be somewhere in these very hills."

Gil considered that. The generals may be loyal, though possibly incompetent. But if not loyal, then they may be aligned with the group of nobles that Dernbrael led. Or they may be in league with Ginsar. And now, possibly, they could conspire with Hvargil. There were too many mysteries, too many unknowns, and each was dangerous. No wonder Brand seemed anxious.

Gil considered what chance Hvargil would have of claiming the throne. It was an impossible question. He was hated by many as a traitor. But he was brother to the last king Cardoroth had. He was popular too among many of the nobles. It was all a tangled web and there were no answers. But Brand was right. To do something, anything was dangerous. Yet doing nothing was far more dangerous still. And should they defeat Ginsar, the other problems would fall away.

They moved up a steep slope, and the rain eased momentarily. Gil remained deep in thought, but he listened when Elrika asked a question.

"Brand, would you tell me something of the history of the sword Gil gave me? I know the basics, but I feel that I should learn more."

The regent guided his black stallion a little closer to her gray. "Ah, I think I know what you mean. It was like that for me too. I own a sword that great men carried before me. I knew the history as well, but I wanted to know the *people* who carried it. Is that not how it is with you?"

508

She looked at him earnestly. "That's exactly how it is."

"Then I shall tell you what I know, but it was long ago and, in truth, very little is remembered. Most of what I can tell you will only be the dry facts, but you will glean something of the true person who carried the sword from them."

The regent paused a moment, finding the right place to begin. Then he spoke softly, using not his voice of command and authority, but his storyteller's voice.

"Long ago, the first king of Cardoroth had many enemies. It was much then as it is today. His seven sons were the first bodyguards, the first Durlin. They were strong men, and athletic, and ever they excelled at sports and the arts of the warrior. They were tall men and lithe, and in all this they took after their father."

The regent's gaze fell to Gil. "But magic was also a part of their lineage. This came from their mother, and their mother's mother before, and on into the deeps of time that the Camar now call the Age of Heroes. It mostly bore seed in the female descendants, but not always. Whether all the seven brothers possessed magic, I do not know. But one did, and the sisters. The older sister was Carnhaina, she who afterward became the famous queen of Cardoroth. The younger sister, Ginhaina, possessed it also. In the mysteries of magic they had a tutor. What name he used, I do not know, but his true name was Shurilgar, even that same Shurilgar who was known as the Betrayer of Nations and was a sorcerer of unsurpassed power."

Brand paused. The rain increased and began to whip at them, and the horses dropped their heads and plodded on.

"Shurilgar subverted them. The sisters fell to his charms, or lusted for his knowledge, and a brother also.

509

Shurilgar nurtured a plot to kill the king and raise Carnhaina as queen of Cardoroth, but when Carnhaina discovered it she repented. She disavowed him, and warned the king. But Shurilgar, seeing his plans wither before him, was not willing to pluck dry fruit from the vine of his ambition. He came for the king, gathering with him Ginhaina and the tainted brother, Felhain. With them were other traitors."

Gil's horse slipped on the wet grass, then righted itself. Gil barely paid any attention, he was transfixed by the story, for this was a version of it that he had not heard before.

"A mighty battle was fought," Brand continued. "There was sorcery and the flashing of swords. Blood flowed in the palace, even in the king's own room where he and the queen were brought to bay. Yet Carnhaina and her loyal brothers were there. If not for her, then they would have perished. Yet before it was all done, and Shurilgar defeated and fled, three of those brothers were killed."

Brand pulled his cloak tightly about him. A chill wind rose now with the rain, and it cut through them all. But Brand showed no sign of discomfort. He kept speaking.

"There in that room was first uttered the Durlin creed:

Tum del conar – El dar tum!
Death or infamy – I choose death!

What is not known is this. The motto was inspired by the fact that it was the betraying brother who had given him his death wound. That brother was said to have answered his father's condemnation with these words.

Tum del conar – El dar conar!

Down through time the first brother's courage, loyalty and words are remembered. Of the traitor, only the Durlin keep record of what was spoken in their secret histories. And now you know it. We keep it alive to honor the first, to respect that each man and woman makes their own choices, and sometimes live and die by them. That first brother was a hero. He was a great man, and every day the Durlin strive to honor his memory and live up to his example."

Brand gestured at the sword belted at Elrika's side. "That blade was his. It hung on the wall in the room where all this happened so long ago. His hands touched it. He fought his enemies with it. And I think he would be proud to know that it is now yours. For you are like him: courageous and loyal."

Brand ceased speaking. The wind whipped about them and the rain angled sideways. No one said anything else.

Gil looked at Elrika. He could see her working through what Brand had said. He could almost hear her own doubt, wondering if she were worthy of the sword and Brand's comments. He knew she was, but did she?

Brand guessed what she was thinking also. He reached out, placing a hand on her shoulder.

"We all doubt our worth at times. But we do what we must anyway."

Suddenly the regent shuddered, and a strange look passed over his face while his eyes grew distant. Then he was himself again.

Brand looked back and forth between her and Gil. "You two, stay close to each other."

Elrika seemed confused, but Gil nodded. Brand had seen a vision, perhaps some glimpse of the future. Use of

511

the magic tended to bring such a thing to the surface, but he knew Brand would not speak of it. Not yet anyway. Perhaps later.

The White Lady had been listening intently, and she spoke, directing her words at Elrika.

"Do not fear. You will acquit yourself well. This Brand knows, as do I." She looked then at Gil. "So will you, even if you do not like what you must do. Sometimes there are no right choices, but we do what we must anyway."

The White Lady's pale face was wetted by rain, but Gil thought he saw tears in her eyes too. But he could not be sure. Whatever vision it was of the future that Brand had just seen, she knew already, had long known it.

12. The Game is Up

Tainrik eased forward into the hollow. Immediately, the smell of smoke grew stronger. He could not see anything yet, but the fire must be close. Once again, he tried to reason how many people could be here, but there was no answer to that. The only way he could find out was to get closer.

This much was true though. He must assume it likely that it was a small group of men, and that there would be a lookout guarding their camp. Given this, and that the men and the lookout would be stationary while he must move, the advantage was with them.

Where, exactly, would they camp? If it were him, he would choose a place at the very bottom of the hollow. That would best hide light from the fire. And he would build the fire close to the base of a tree so that its canopy dispersed the smoke instead of allowing it to rise in a plume. He would also want his back to the steepest bit of the gully. This would prevent someone attacking from that side. At least, he would do it this way, and from what he could tell so far these men had skill.

One achingly slow step after another, taking his time to be completely noiseless, he moved deeper into the gully. Smoke was strong in the air now, and he must be close to the camp, very close, but still he saw nothing save for the dim outline of shrubby trees and a patchy sky of muted stars and scudding cloud through the foliage.

He paused. It was time to wait. Standing there, silent as the trees about him, like another trunk in the shadows, he strained all his senses for some sign of what he was getting into. But he detected nothing more than the smoke.

He had a choice now. Go ahead and try to avoid stumbling into the camp, or try for a different view on things. The trees allowed for that. He eased to the closest one, slipped his bow over his shoulder and carefully climbed it.

He did not intend to climb high. Just a few feet would give him a better view. But it was risky. He was much more likely to make noise and would be more visible. But he did it anyway. It was riskier to walk into the middle of the camp by accident and step on a sleeping man.

At last! He found what he had been seeking. A little further down the gully was a flicker of firelight. It was just the sort of place that he had expected, set up with a steep slope behind it and beneath a tree.

He studied the camp carefully. It was some fifty feet away, and there were men near the fire. He watched them closely, counting four. Two seemed to be sleeping, laying down and still, the others were seated on a fallen log and talking quietly.

There was no lookout. Or, if there were, Tainrik could not see him. Were they spies though? He could see no indication one way or the other. There were no visible axes, so they may not be foresters. But they could be hunters. Or the axes may be lying on the ground or embedded in blocks of wood elsewhere. There was no way to tell, especially without seeing the men and the camp properly.

It was obvious what had to be done, but he did not like it. Still, he forced himself to make the decision he knew he must. He lowered himself down from the tree, thankful that he made no noise, and then he edged closer to the camp.

Silently, he drew one of his knives. If things went wrong he would have a better chance to use it than anything else. The bow would be slow at close quarters.

He held the blade low before him, the steel of it darkened by a special tint during the forging process so that it did not glint in the night. Bit by bit, step by step, he drew closer. For all that he moved with great slowness, his heart raced in his chest as though he were sprinting.

Pausing, he took some long and slow breaths to calm himself. He could now hear the men talking. They were speaking loudly, or more likely he had crept closer than he thought.

"The rain will come soon," one man said. His accent was of Cardoroth.

"It'll slow the army," the second answered.

"Good."

"It'll help us though," the second man said.

"I still hate it. I'd rather be at home than stuck out here."

Tainrik listened. Both men were from Cardoroth, and their talk soon turned to the city. In particular, they spoke of an inn where the hearth-fire was always lit, the room warm and where the mead was sweet and smooth. Better there than here they thought, but they would return there when they could.

The speakers were silent for a while. One of the sleeping men began to snore, then ceased after a few moments. The two men awake carried on their conversation.

"What do you think Hvargil will do?" the first man asked.

"Kill Brand and the prince, for sure. He can do damage to the army, but he doesn't have enough men to keep it up for long. And why bother anyway? He'll want that army for himself."

"Do you think he has a chance?"

"With the regent and the prince out of the way, he does. He's in tight with many of the nobles. And he'll be the last of the true royal line then. Besides, if he kills them, he's done that black sorceress a favor. She may just leave us alone with *him* in charge. The nobles will know that, and those that don't he'll soon tell. It's quite a bargaining point."

Silence filled the gulley again, and Tainrik thought hard. The rumors were true, and these hills were where Hvargil and his outlaws hid. Given that these four men were hanging back behind the army, it seemed likely that another of their number had already left to take word to Hvargil. The old king's brother will know that Cardoroth's army was on the march.

What to do about it all was the problem. Tainrik had learned what he needed most to know, and his first priority was to give warning to Brand of a probable ambush and assassination attempt. The men in this camp were not so important now. And there were too many for him kill anyway. He must leave, and then come back with a larger group of scouts.

He took a step back, testing the ground lightly with his toes before putting his weight down. At just that moment he heard a whisper of movement behind him. He dropped to the ground, but he was too late. A thrown knife struck his left shoulder and pain flared. There was a lookout after all!

The game was up now. He had been discovered, and silence and stealth were useless. He rolled, sprang to his feet and ran.

516

It was hard to see, and he feared a thousand obstacles that he could trip over or run into, but speed counted now or he was dead. At the last moment he saw a fallen log and leaped it. He dodged left around a tree trunk and saw a shadow loom up to his right. The lookout!

He flung his dagger at the dark figure, and heard a grunt and saw the man go down. But he did not think he had killed him. It was just a wound and the man had dropped for cover as much as anything else.

Tainrik sprinted on. He heard shouts behind him, and crashing noises through the trees and underbrush. All the men were up, and they were coming after him.

13. A Game of Dice and Truth

The rain fell without relent. But the army was higher up in the hills now, and had reached the plateau. It continued on until late afternoon, for stopping was no better than proceeding.

All about them the forest grew thickly, but there were large patches of grassland too. Wild cattle, long-horned and wary, watched them from a distance. There were herds of horses too, likely escaped from Cardoroth through the long years. These wheeled away and filtered into the trees when the army came in sight.

The generals called a halt. This time, Brand was not unhappy. The army had traveled well, especially in the conditions, and where they had come to was a good place to camp. Because of the open space, the tail of the army eventually caught up and they were not spread out and vulnerable.

It did not take long to establish a camp, and it was formed in a great square. This offered good defense in all directions, and the sentries and scouts would provide warning of any attack. Water was to hand, and a clear view of the surrounding countryside.

Gil rubbed his horse down. It was common practice to dig a trench around the camp and throw up an earth wall when in hostile country. This was not being done, but he supposed there was no real reason to consider this hostile territory. Then again, he knew that was an assumption. They had not yet received any word from scouts that Ginsar's army had marched, but such a message may not reach them much before Ginsar. Or not at all if the enemy scouts had found and killed Cardoroth's.

By the time he had finished with his horse the camp was more or less established, and where once was green grass was now a sea of mud, people and tents.

He walked back with Brand and Elrika to where their own, and quite large tent was now set up.

"I'm worried, Gil," the regent said. "Tainrik is reliable, and I still have not heard from him."

"I know. But he would have to cover much more ground than the army did, and perhaps you'll see him tonight. He must sleep as well, at some point."

Brand retrieved a dry cloak and suggested Gil and Elrika do the same. Then they went out into the rain again. There was no sign of the generals. They had gone into their even larger tent, and there, likely, they would stay. But Gil had an idea that neither he nor Elrika would be under cover for a long time yet.

He was not surprised when Brand led the way back into the army again. They moved through the ranks, talking with men here and there, sharing a cup of water or a bite of food as they spoke. As always, Brand was just one of the soldiers, and though they knew who he was, they treated him as such, offering heartfelt opinions or boisterous jokes in turn.

Brand, for his part, was more at ease than ever. Gil studied him, and after a while began to adopt the same easygoing attitude. Elrika seemed to enjoy this, for she too was like Brand. But the soldiers loved teasing Gil good naturedly about his fine clothes and how wet and muddy they now were. He shrugged those comments off with a smile and a joke at their own expense. This they seemed to love above all, and he left many a tent of laughing soldiers behind him.

Yet there was something more serious going on here. Brand did this because it was in his nature to do it, but it was also a way of staying in touch with the men and assessing their morale. Even, perhaps, lifting it. This was a lesson the generals should learn, instead of staying dry and aloof in their tents.

They moved on, from tent to tent, and here and there ate of the cold rations the soldiers were given. There were no fires tonight, and it was a cheerless dinner mostly of hard-dried biscuits, but food was food and the men made their own cheer.

Gil noticed that no matter Elrika's casual attitude, she was always close by his side and alert. Brand noticed it too, and though he said nothing he seemed pleased. The story of the sword she carried had made a strong impression on her.

A man stopped Brand just as they were about to leave a tent. "Why are we here and not in Cardoroth?" he asked. It was an honest question, posed without malice, and Brand gave an honest answer.

"If the generals had their way, we *would* be in Cardoroth. And we'd be warm and snug too. But when Ginsar comes, she will bring sorcery with her. Powerful sorcery that would destroy us. We go now to meet her, to claim victory before the power she summons is too much. We go to surprise her."

"Will we win?" another soldier asked.

"I'll not lie," Brand answered. "I don't truly know. But I'll try my hardest, and I know too that every man in this camp will do the same. For what it's worth, I think that will be enough."

"It's good enough for us," the first man said. "We don't know magic and sorcery, but we trust you. You'll do your bit, and we'll do ours."

"I know it," Brand said.

They left the tent and moved on. Several times men asked the same question, and Brand gave the same honest answer. After a while, Gil realized it was not the question that counted. It was that the men felt they could ask it and that Brand gave them a truthful answer that counted.

After a few hours, they retuned back to their own section of the camp.

"Come with me for a few more moments," Brand said. "I want to speak with the generals."

They came to the generals' tent, and the guards there announced their names and guided them inside. All three of the generals were accommodated here, for it was a very large tent. There were inner partitions, rugs on the floor and a long table that ran down the center of the room. Upon it were the remains of several meals and three wrought-iron braziers, giving off warmth and light.

The generals lounged around the table, sipping wine and playing dice. Several piles of gold coins lay on the table.

"Please," Garling said. "Have a seat."

"We won't be staying long," Brand said. "It's late already."

Gil noticed that Brand remained standing, so he did not move either.

"Has there been any word of significance from the scouts?"

"Nothing of note," Garling answered.

"They have all returned? No one is missing?"

"Indeed not. All is well, though we're still waiting on reports from those scouts monitoring Ginsar's army. There's no word on her movements yet."

"I see," Brand said. "That's all I wished to know. Have a good evening gentlemen."

He left the tent, his expression neutral but the signs of anxiety were there for Gil to read. He did not think the generals knew him well enough to detect them.

They went to their own tent, smaller and less luxurious than that of the generals but still large. The Durlin opened the flap for them, and Brand said goodnight and immediately went to his own partitioned area. There were other partitioned rooms for Taingern and Shorty, but no sign of them.

Elrika looked at Gil with wide eyes. "Brand's trying to hide it, but he's very worried about Tainrik."

Gil nodded. He began to fear that something very bad had happened.

14. A Hunted Man

Tainrik continued to run. But he was no great sprinter, and he feared his pursuers would catch him. Nor would they have any trouble locating him in the dark because the sound of his flight as he crashed through the undergrowth could not be missed.

This could not go on and end well, so he made a swift decision. Even though his instinct was to try to run away, he paused abruptly and crouched down behind a large tree trunk.

The trunk was at his back and a large fern ahead. Between them both, the night-shadows were deep, and there was a fair chance he would not be seen. Stealth must serve him once more.

He sheathed the knife and nocked an arrow to his bow. Then he waited, trying to breathe as softly as he could. If all went well, they would run past and then he could slip away in the opposite direction.

The crashing noise of his pursuers came close. They were all around him in the dark. Then one of them yelled and Tainrik felt cold seep into his bones.

"He's stopped! Stand still and look!"

Tainrik felt a sense of dread threaten to overwhelm him. He forced himself to breathe smoothly though, and to remain perfectly still. The place of concealment that he had chosen was good, and he would not be spotted easily.

Silence fell. He heard nothing of the men, for evidently they dared not move just as he could not. To move was to chance revealing oneself, and that might mean sudden death.

He began to wonder how skilled these men were. The one who flung the dagger at him was good, for he had approached with silence and crept close. Unless he had been there all along, watching and waiting for his best chance to throw.

The wound to the shoulder that the man had given him began to throb. It had been a glancing strike of the blade only, but it had cut deep and he felt the blood from it trickle down his arm and begin to dry and cake. He wanted to check it to see just how bad it was, but he did not dare to move.

The temptation came upon him to run again, for natural instincts were hard to suppress. But it would be foolish. The men were closer to him now than before and would catch him swiftly, perhaps even kill him before he took more than a few steps. No, he must keep playing the game he had chosen.

Patience would serve him here. If they moved first, they would reveal themselves. Then he must throw a knife or fire an arrow. The first allowed him multiple opportunities for it was swift and he had the knives. The second more likely to kill, but he would likely only have one chance. He was ready with bow and arrow though, and that was perhaps the best. If he could be sure of killing one of the enemy, his odds against the others would improve. Somewhat.

A new thought came to him, and he did not like it. They may wait patiently for the dawn, still hours away, and let light reveal him.

He waited, his thoughts drifting and he lost track of time. He eased back slightly until he rested against the tree trunk behind him. He could not maintain a crouch forever. But it was not safe to stand, and nor could he sit because then he would be slow to move when movement was necessary.

His thoughts ceased to drift and he became suddenly alert. He was not sure what had changed, but his instincts were warning him of something. His gaze searched the shadows, and he concentrated on using his peripheral vision. In the dark, that would reveal something better than a direct line of sight.

There! A man, crawling on the ground. At least he thought so. But then there was nothing. Yet in a minute or so in the same place the movement began again and he was sure. His stalker was moving only a few feet at a time. And he was good for he made no noise.

At the current angle the man was going, he would move past him. But if Tainrik could see him, soon the man would spot him also.

Tainrik tested the fit of the arrow that he had notched to the string. Satisfied, he drew slowly, with as little movement as he could manage, and prepared to shoot. He let out his breath ever so slowly and at the end released the string.

The arrow flew. Its sudden flight hissed through the air and the crawling man half jumped up and then fell. He did not move again.

What to do now? Tainrik's mind raced. He may well have given his position away. Even as he remained where he was, the other men could be moving in on him. Yet to move was to highlight himself for attack. He remained still, moving only enough to slip another arrow from the quiver and nock it.

Tainrik's hands trembled. He had been trained for this, but the reality was different from the teaching. Every choice he made was one of life or death. And the throbbing in his shoulder made it hard to think clearly.

But he waited, knowing it was the right move, and he took some satisfaction from the fact that if he were to be killed tonight he had taken at least one of the enemy with him.

It grew darker. The cloud cover was building, and the stars were blotted out. There! It was a noise to his left and he flicked his gaze in that direction. He rose ever so slightly, drawing back on the string once more. But there was nothing to be seen.

What had he heard then? The answer was swift in coming. It was a thrown rock and he had exposed himself. In one smooth motion he dived and rolled. Even as he came to his feet again he felt an arrow slam into his left arm and then glance away into the night.

It did not stop him. Better the arm than the body it would have been if he had not disrupted his enemy's aim. With a burst of speed he sprinted again, leaping over the corpse of the slain man and crashing through the shrubbery.

Another arrow flew at him, whistling away well wide of his position. Yet one more thudded into a tree close to his head. But he was up and away and already lost to sight. They must chase him again or fire blindly into the dark.

He sped on, snaking between trunks. The ground began to rise, and this was not good. He would be more exposed above his enemies. He changed direction, veering abruptly to the left and following a downward slope.

Noise of pursuit gathered behind him. A small stream loomed ahead and at the last moment he leaped it. Straightaway he veered right, hoping to somehow evade those who hunted him. His maneuver was not successful. Arrows hissed through the dark, unseen but deadly. He had dodged in the wrong direction and brought himself back into view.

He could not turn left, for that would be predictable. Instead, he veered further right and up the slope again. More arrows hissed, but these went wider of him.

His chest heaved now for breath, and the slope did not help. But swifter than he had anticipated he found himself at the top of the gulley again. He raced away with a burst of speed, but his legs were giving out.

Ahead, the forest grew thicker. At least, so he thought because the shadows were even deeper. This offered greater chance of concealment, and he did not change direction.

The forest swiftly grew near-impenetrable, but he pushed on for another fifty or so paces, hearing his enemies enter the same area of thicker growth somewhere behind him.

It was time to rely on his skills as a tracker and woodsmen again, rather than try to run. Ahead, he saw the dim outline of a branch about head high and an idea occurred to him.

With trembling hands he tore off his cloak and looped the top portion over the trunk so that the remainder draped down near the trunk, and then he ducked and crawled a dozen feet away, coming up behind a fallen log. He waited, trying to breathe quietly.

In moments, his pursuers were close, but they slowed and then stopped too as they failed to hear him anymore. Once again, a game of patience had begun. This time there was one less of them, but they still outnumbered him.

There was no noise. Once more the forest was silent, yet the dark carried a feel of unmistakable malice. Danger and death hid in every shadow. But Tainrik gritted his teeth, vowing silently that he was as dangerous as anything in the woods tonight. Perhaps the *most* dangerous thing there.

Time passed. His hunters were wary of him now, and well they should be. But they had not given up. That, he knew. They would wait and watch, and perhaps try to move silently, searching for him as they had before.

Blood dribbled down his left arm. The arrow wound hurt less than the shoulder one, but was more of a problem. His arm felt weak and useless now. But he would not bleed to death from it.

He checked his bow. As he feared, somewhere when he rolled or ran through the trees the string had caught and been damaged. He felt loose strands and severe fraying. Dare he risk using it again? If it gave out on him when loosing an arrow he would be at great risk. He had a spare string in his pocket, but he did not think it wise to unstring the bow and string it again. That would be too much movement.

Softly, he placed the bow on the ground and drew one of his throwing knives. And waited once more.

15. More Terrible than You Know

Gil talked softly with Elrika in the tent, and the White Lady joined them. "You all seem anxious," she said.

Briefly, Gil explained to her about Tainrik. She closed her eyes momentarily, as if in deep thought.

"I wish I could help, but I cannot. Many things I can see, but not all. I seek him out, but find only blackness."

"He'll return," Gil said. "Something has happened, but he's the sort of man who overcomes any obstacle."

The White Lady opened her eyes. "But the absence of this scout isn't your only concern, is it?"

Elrika hesitated, then spoke. "It's not my place to say it, but I'm worried about Brand. He does not show it, but I sense that he feels enormous responsibility."

Gil nodded. "I feel it too. The generals wanted to stay behind the Cardurleth. Coming out to face Ginsar was his idea. If it fails, he will bear the blame."

"The answer to that is simple," the White Lady told them. "We must not fail. Though until we succeed, Brand will be under great strain. But he, like this Tainrik you know, is a man who overcomes obstacles."

"Do you really think we can win?" Elrika asked.

The White Lady turned to her, and her gentle face was determined. "We *must*. And this is in our favor. Brand is a canny man. He has endured and survived dangers that would have destroyed most people. More than that, he has luck. He is a man who makes his own luck by courage and skill and the sharpness of his wit, yet fate also smiles upon him. Nor is he alone. We will each play our part to help him. So, yes, we can win. But it will not be easy."

"The Horsemen will be the worst of it, won't they?" Gil asked.

"They are more terrible than you know," the White Lady answered. "Worse, the spell that binds them weakens. Ginsar can feel it. Should the worst happen, they will possess her. Then they will control their bridge into this world and using Ginsar, they can summon more of their kind."

"And this world," Gil said, "whence you and the Horsemen come, what is it like?"

The White Lady grew quiet, and Gil did not think she would answer. But eventually her reply came, though it was softly spoken.

"Our worlds should not be in contact. It is best not to speak of it. If all goes well, then the gateway will be closed and things shall return to how they should be."

"And what of you?"

She gazed at him, her eyes sad but lit with determination. You will see, and you will understand when the time is right."

She excused herself then, going to that portion of the tent partitioned off for her.

Elrika watched her go, then spoke quietly. "I like her, but she's hiding something. Something big."

Gil agreed, and it troubled him. But what it was they would not discover this night. He and Elrika said goodnight and moved into their own rooms within the tent.

By himself, Gil became thoughtful. But lying down on the thick rug that was his bed, he went to sleep swiftly, lulled by the constant patter of rain on the canvas roof.

He slept well, waking before dawn the next morning and feeling refreshed. There was movement within the main room of the tent, and he dressed and went outside.

Brand was there, moving slowly through some exercises. They were of a kind that Gil had not yet learned and his interest was piqued.

The regent moved slowly, as though fully relaxed, and yet Gil saw the slight tremble of his hands that indicated, despite the smooth stretching and grace of each movement, that muscular force was being used.

He saw that the White Lady and Elrika were already there, watching also. But of Shorty and Taingern there was no sign.

Brand breathed out softly and finished.

"That was beautiful," Elrika said. "Would you teach me?"

"Of course," Brand said. "But we have little time before the march begins. So I shall teach you some, and then if you are interested we will make time daily hereafter."

Elrika stood up and Gil joined her. He too wanted to learn the movements.

"Each exercise has a name," Brand said. "But don't be fooled by their slowness. There is within them a kernel of the warrior's art, and though the movements are for health, they will sharpen your combat skills too."

Brand stilled himself, standing with his feet shoulder width apart. "This first exercise is called *Scoop the Stream and Press the Stars*."

He bent down smoothly as though cupping water in his palm and then straightening to drink. But he did not stop. Instead, he pushed upward toward the sky.

"It's important," he said, "to link the motion of your body with your breathing. Breathe in as though you were

531

scooping air into your lungs and breathe out as you press upward."

They did that a few times. "Now," Brand continued, "do the same thing, but gently flex your muscles as you move. Do not be stiff though."

"How much tension should there be?" Elrika asked.

"Stop just when your arms begin to tremble," Brand said. "The movements stretch and limber the body, but at the same time they build muscle."

They practiced for a little while and then a soldier brought in some food. They sat down around the table and ate, glad to do so even if it was only the same army biscuits that they had eaten last night.

The White Lady noticed the ring on Brand's finger that he always wore, and Brand saw her looking.

"It's an ancient piece of jewelry," he said. "The spirit of Carnhaina gave it to me."

"You earned it," she said. "That much I know, but may I look at the ring closely?"

Brand removed it and handed it to her. She held it up and studied it carefully, turning it to and fro in the pale light of the lamps that lit the tent.

"It is ancient indeed," she said. "But there is power in it too."

"Magic?" Brand said. "I've never sensed it."

"Yet it is there, though buried deep and of an unusual sort. In time it may reveal itself to you." She turned it again, pausing. "There is a word inscribed inside the band. *Carngin.*"

"Ah, I had forgotten that was there. Of old, the royal family of Cardoroth had two names. One was for private use among friends and family, while the other was for public use. Carnhaina's real name was apparently Carngin."

The white Lady handed the ring back and Brand slipped it onto his finger again.

"It is a marvelous piece of craftsmanship," she said. "But the magic in it is greater still. One day you will use it for its purpose, I am sure."

Gil was surprised. "I've never sensed any magic within it either," he said.

The White Lady turned to him, her eyes intense. "Sometimes the best hidden remains in plain sight."

He thought she was trying to tell him something, but had no time to consider it. At that moment the tent-flap was pulled open and a Durlin entered.

"The generals want to see you," he said to the regent.

16. A True Warrior

Tainrik continued to wait, but it was becoming harder. The wounds in his arm and shoulder were throbbing, and the muscles all over his body had stiffened.

But then he heard a noise, and all his aches and pains were forgotten. He looked and listened for what seemed a long while, but there was nothing else. Yet someone was close, and had moved. That he had begun to do so meant it likely that he would continue.

Waiting with all the patience that Tainrik had developed through long years of training, he calmed himself as best he could and remained motionless.

Eventually, his patience was rewarded. There was a scuffling sound close by, and the hand that gripped his knife became slick with sweat.

Then he saw what he had been waiting for, hoping for. A little more than a dozen feet away a man slowly rose and drew a bow. With a twang he unleashed the arrow and it whistled though the air, striking the cloak.

Tainrik was already moving. The man was further away than he hoped, but with a swift motion he flung his throwing dagger. It arced and spun through the air.

The man was turning, realizing he had been tricked. But he was too slow. The flashing blade thudded deep into his belly.

The man grunted with pain. But he made to pull a second arrow from his quiver. Tainrik ran at him, drawing another knife. There was no time for the man to loose the arrow he had retrieved. Tainrik thrust his blade forward, but even as he did the man smashed the bow against his face.

Pain erupted in Tainrik's head, but he felt his blade drive deep in the other man's groin. His enemy screamed, then reeled away and fell to the ground. He was dead, or soon would be when he finished gushing blood.

Tainrik darted forward, grabbed his cloak and sprinted again. He had hoped to kill the man and stay hidden where he was, but luck had not favored him. The man had been too far away to risk a killing throw to his neck. Instead he had been forced to throw for the body, which had not been an instant kill.

Blood ran down his face, and the fresh injury hurt with a sharp pain. Skin was torn, but no bones broken. Yet his legs were unsteady and he felt a wave of nausea. He leaped a log and nearly fell, for dizziness swept over him too.

Stumbling, he tried to right himself but staggered to the side. It saved his life. An arrow hissed past him and he felt the wind of it.

Fear drove him on, and despite dizziness he staggered ahead. But the dizziness soon receded even if the nausea did not.

Another arrow whined nearby, slamming into a tree trunk. He veered left, fell, came to his feet with a roll and sped on.

The ground changed swiftly, and he nearly fell again but adjusted quickly. He was heading downhill once more. He slowed a little, but another arrow flashed past him and he put on a burst of speed.

It was a mistake. He lost his footing on the slope and crashed into the ground, tumbling and spinning through ferns and underbrush. He had tried to break his fall with his arms, but his left had given way beneath him and sent a jab of pain like fire through the whole limb.

He staggered up, wet and muddy, somewhere near the bottom of the gulley. It must have been the same one that he had left earlier, but he was becoming disorientated.

Moving ahead he plunged into water without seeing it. He fell again, righted himself and stumbled ahead.

Water soaked his clothing. His wounds stung and now there was mud in them. If his enemies did not kill him, blood loss or infection might. He pushed ahead anyway, hearing his hunters come down the slope somewhere behind him.

Coming to the bank at the other side of the gulley he ran uphill. An arrow sped through the air, but it was well away from him and he guessed that his opponents were becoming frustrated and loosing arrows at him too quickly to aim properly.

He reached the crest and dared to turn for a look. He cursed his luck, for he saw a man climbing up after him but he had no bow to shoot with, and even if he had not left it at his last hiding place the string may have broken.

But he chanced another knife throw even at such a distance, and sent a blade flashing through the air. The man screamed and fell back. Tainrik turned and ran on wondering if perhaps his luck was not all bad.

He went a little ahead but soon the landscape changed. It was much more open, becoming a little clearing, and he decided to stop. It was not a good place to hide, but his strength was nearly gone. Better to fight now before it all drained away, than to prolong things.

He slipped behind a tree and drew his sword. It was not a place of good concealment, but it was dark and would have to do. The men behind him outnumbered him two to one, but he had brought the odds down greatly, if still not in his favor.

Quickly he discarded his quiver. It would only hinder him now. But no sooner had he placed it on the ground than he sensed his hunters close by.

They knew he was wounded and tired now. That much they would have been able to tell by the way he moved, but they may also have seen blood where he had hidden. There was certainly enough of it left behind.

He swayed slightly, feeling blackness descending over his mind, but he fought it and stayed on his feet. He would not die by having his throat cut as he lay unconscious on the ground. If he were to live and bring word back to Brand he must force a swordfight, and then somehow win it against two men. He was not even a great swordsman, but he was skilled, and he doubted his opponents were as good.

He saw them approach, but they had not yet seen him. They stayed together now, sure that they were near to hunting him down and determined not to be picked off one by one as their companions had.

Tainrik smiled grimly in the dark. One of the men moved forward, his hand held up and pressed against his shoulder. He was the lookout who had been wounded when the chase began.

So far so good. That improved the odds a little, but both men had drawn their swords just as he had done. They *knew* he was close.

Slowly, Tainrik drew his last knife. He was right handed, but his sword was in that hand. He used his left, and though not as good with that arm he had practiced hard and gained skill with it.

The two men saw him. He reacted instantly, flinging the knife at the unwounded man. Better to face the wounded one in a swordfight.

The man dodged to the side, but not quick enough. The blade tore at his throat and a spray of blood erupted. Arterial blood.

Tainrik stepped from the shadows, sword high. The enemy he had struck stumbled away, pressing his hands to his throat, but the wounded man leapt at him, trying to ensure nothing could be flung at him.

With a crash of steel against steel Tainrik met him. Out in the open, the first pale glimmer of dawn showed him his enemy. A large man, red-haired and bearded, as skilled with a blade as he was at woodcraft.

The first touch of their blades revealed to Tainrik that they were closely matched. They were also both wounded, yet the other man far less so. But the injury was to his enemy's sword arm, and that was an advantage.

They circled, but the red-haired man seemed angry and he charged in swiftly with an overhead strike.

Tainrik almost fell for it. He began to raise his own blade to block the blow but then stepped to the side. He was just in time. For all his enemy's size he was quick. Even as he swung his sword his other hand flicked out a knife.

The blade sailed away harmlessly through the air. Tainrik, seeing an opportunity, drove forward himself. He launched a vicious flurry of blows, and his enemy retreated but blocked and deflected the attack until Tainrik began to slow. Then he retaliated with his own attack.

The big man came at him, sword flashing and eyes cold with the promise of death. Tainrik retreated now, trying to conserve his strength and using his footwork to keep out of reach and minimize the effort he put into blocking.

The attack petered out and the two men circled each other warily now. Both were short of breath. Both were in pain from their wounds. Both were uncertain of the outcome of this fight.

But the big man regained his breath more quickly. His blade sliced the air, flicking unexpectedly toward Tainrik's neck. Tainrik jumped back, but only just in time. Then a series of other blows came at him, and he suffered glancing slashes to his right shoulder and left flank.

Tainrik did his best to defend. He was weary now, more than he had ever been in his life, and he knew that was blood loss as well as tiredness. Nor had the dizziness completely left him. The sense of blackness engulfing him was never far away, and several times it threatened to send him to his knees. But he stayed upright, and he staved off the killing blows that came at him.

His red-bearded attacker circled once more, and for the first time he spoke.

"You're nearly done, dog. I think I'll cut you apart, piece by piece."

Tainrik grinned. This was good! The man was taunting him now, which meant that his continued survival had gotten under his opponent's skin and frustrated him. It also meant that he too was tired.

Now, if ever, was Tainrik's chance. This could not go on for much longer, and he wasted no effort on replying. Instead, he darted forward thrusting at the man's face.

His opponent backed away, which was what Tainrik had hoped for. He skip-stepped ahead once more and flicked his sword using little more than the power of his wrist. It was a swift move, and unexpected. Brand had shown it to him long ago, and now it worked.

His blade glanced across his enemy's neck while the man began to swing a mighty blow, thinking Tainrik fully extended. Instead he jerked and reeled away as he felt the blade.

Tainrik knew instantly that he had not delivered a killing blow, but the man had been cut and surprised. Tainrik pressed forward, changing tactics now and striking at his enemy's sword arm.

His opponent rallied, fending off the blows but he did not see the left fist that cracked against his skull as Tainrik simultaneously struck at his wrist and punched.

Pain roared through Tainrik's injured arm, but his enemy had turned to the side exposing his flank and Tainrik lunged forward, sliding his blade between the man's ribs.

The red-bearded man jerked away and collapsed, nearly pulling Tainrik's sword clear. Red foam frothed at his lips and his expression was one of surprise as he died.

Tainrik stood still, watching him. It was all he could do to keep a grip on his sword without letting it fall and remain standing upright. But he had won, defeated all his opponents. He was just as surprised as the dead man at his feet.

He tried not to, but he turned and kneeled on the grass and vomited. A long while he retched, and he felt so weak that he feared he would not be able to stand. Eventually, cold and shivering in the dawn light, he staggered upright.

His sword still drawn, he moved over the man he had brought down with the thrown knife. Checking that his enemy was dead, he cleaned his sword blade on the man's cloak and sheathed it. Then he retrieved the knife from the grass nearby, cleaned it also, and sheathed it.

Feeling somewhat better, he retraced his flight and went down in the gulley. There was water there, and he needed to clean his wounds. He did not look forward to it, for it would hurt.

The body of the man he had killed down in the gully made him feel sick again. But he retrieved another of his knives. Of everything that had happened, killing this man had been the luckiest. It had been a long throw with little real chance of success. But somehow he had accomplished it, and it was the turning point. Had three men confronted him up in the clearing it would now be him lying on the ground, dead eyes staring up, unseeing.

He knelt down by the small stream. The water flowed, but it was not brisk. There was risk in using it to clean his wounds, but they were covered in mud anyway. They *had* to be cleaned, and the water was the only way of doing it.

He peeled off his tunic and bathed as best he could, being sure to remove the mud while at the same time not opening the wounds further. They bled again, which was no bad thing for the flow of blood would help remove more dirt. Then, retrieving thread and needle from an inner pocket he stitched the cut in his arm. It was hard to do, but he gritted his teeth and endured the pain.

His shoulder was harder, but he managed at length. It was his headwound that troubled him most though. He could not see it and did not know if it needed stitches. Regardless, it was a job beyond him, and all he could do was cut a strip of cloth from the dead man's tunic and wrap it around his head. It would have to be enough, at least until he could get back to camp.

The sun was well up now, its light penetrating even into the forested gulley. Tainrik felt sick, and desperately tired. All he wanted to do was lie down and sleep, but he must go on.

He shuffled forward, moving through the thick timber carefully. His bow could not be that far away, but he did not have the energy to search for it. He would risk travel without it, because it seemed unlikely that he would encounter further enemies.

What counted now would be catching up with the army, if he could. In his current state that was going to be very hard. He was well behind it and it would travel faster than he could. To reach it, he would have to travel by the open road. That was potentially dangerous. And he would also have to walk into the night long after the army had camped.

He came to a small clearing and shivered even in the sunlight. What lay ahead was going to test him. But Brand had to know what he had learned.

Moving into the trees and seeking the road he gritted his teeth and shuffled forward. He stumbled, righted himself and moved on again. He had hoped that walking would ease his sore muscles, but instead they began to cramp.

He pressed forward. He had just endured the longest night of his life. Now, the longest day lay ahead.

17. Dismissed

All three generals entered the tent, and Gil could tell that they were determined on some purpose.

"Welcome," Brand said. "Have a seat."

They pulled up chairs around the table, and there was much awkward shifting and scraping of chair legs against the canvas floor. Just as they were sitting, Taingern and Shorty also arrived in a rush. Gil could tell from their expressions that they were angry, but they said nothing.

As the Durlindraths took seats, Gil noticed that the generals looked displeased. He realized that they may have arranged to have someone lure Taingern and Shorty out of the tent in order to isolate Brand from his supporters.

"What news?" Brand asked.

"None," Garling answered. "And that is the problem."

"How so?"

"Our scouts report no sign of the enemy, and they have ventured far ahead of us."

"*How* far ahead?" Brand inquired.

"A day or so. They have found no indication of an army before us. Not even enemy scouts."

Brand shrugged. "That doesn't really mean much. We're still close to Cardoroth, and elugs aren't renowned for military strategy. They may not even use scouts."

"Preposterous!" Druigbar said. "All armies use scouts."

Brand's attitude seemed to cool, though he remained courteous. "Preposterous? I don't think so. In

Cardoroth, you have had little dealings with elugs, and what dealings you have had has mostly been with those of the south rather than the north. And mostly you stay behind the Cardurleth. The Duthenor, on the other hand, have had more trouble. The northern elugs often come down out of the mountains and raid our lands. They have never used scouts, though I concede that does not mean they aren't now. In short, they may or may not. We don't know, and we shouldn't judge them by our standards of warfare."

"It does not matter either way," Garling said. "We don't think there are scouts because we don't think there's an elug army. It will have proceeded down the Halathrin road."

"Has there been any word yet from the scouts watching the area where Ginsar gathered the army near Auren Dennath?"

"No."

"Then we know nothing yet, either way."

"Those scouts may have been killed," Druigbar said.

"That's possible," Brand conceded. "But not likely. Nothing has changed to alter the strategy decided on in Cardoroth."

Garling slammed a hand down on the table. "Everything has changed!" he said. "The men are unhappy to leave their homes only weakly defended. They fear Ginsar will strike while we're out here. And it was just the wrong strategy to begin with."

The other generals nodded their agreement. Garling went on, but his tone softened. "It's party our fault. We are the military experts. We know what we're doing. We should not have been swayed by you, or the Durlindraths or the prince. But it's not too late to remedy that. We can fix this, while there's still time. We can turn around and go back."

"No," Brand said softly.

Garling looked like he was holding a great anger in check. "You can't just say no. That's unacceptable."

Brand seemed relaxed, but Gil knew his moods well. Just now he was a very dangerous man indeed.

"I'm the regent. I have the authority. I can say no, and I do say no. It's that simple."

"Are you an idiot, Brand!" Garling stormed. "You've never led a campaign before! You don't know what you're doing."

Brand sat back in his chair. "I appreciate your honesty. But, respectfully, you have never led a campaign either."

Garling clenched his fists. "I'm a general! I've lived and breathed war all my life. Cardoroth is like that. I've fought in many battles and I've—"

Brand interrupted him. "I'll say it again, respectfully. You have never led a campaign. Always, the old king was the strategist. He had full control of the army and you carried out his orders. Nor did you *fight* battles. You commanded men who fought battles. From a distance, those men tell me. Now, the decision has been made and we have no further information that would make us change it. The army will continue as planned."

Brand turned his gaze to look all three generals in the eye one at a time.

"Gentleman," he said. "In war, disunity is death. A divided leadership will do us more harm than the enemy could. We must be of one mind in all that we do. Can you commit to this?"

Garling shook his head. "No. If we are to be of one mind, you must change yours."

"I'm resolved on our current course of action," Brand told him.

Garling shrugged. "Then we are at an impasse. We will lead the army forward no further."

Brand leaned forward and spoke earnestly. "I ask you to reconsider, not for me but for the benefit of Cardoroth."

Gil studied the generals. They looked smug, as though they had maneuvered Brand into a position where he must give in. Gil wondered if they knew him at all.

"We three are of one mind. We will not lead the army further forward into folly."

Brand sat back in his chair. "A divided leadership is poison. I just cannot let that continue."

Garling seemed pleased with those words. "Then I'll give the order to turn around and return to Cardoroth."

"That's not what I meant," Brand told him.

"But you just said—"

"I said that we cannot continue with a divided leadership. Therefore, you are dismissed from your positions. You will play no further part in forming the strategy of the army. You are dismissed, gentlemen."

The generals seemed dumbfounded. "We were appointed by the king!" Garling said. "You can't dismiss us!"

"I've heard that phrase too often," Brand said. "I can dismiss you. I just have dismissed you. You, and many of the other nobles of Cardoroth, aren't quick learners."

Garling half stood in his chair and thrust a finger at Brand. "You'll cause a revolt," he said. "The men won't follow you forward. They'll return to Cardoroth with us!"

Brand seemed very calm. "Be careful. You're treading close to treason there."

Garling sat back down, uncertain. He seemed about to speak, but did not. Instead, Taingern did.

"You're wrong about the men," he said quietly. "There will be no revolt. They'll follow Brand's orders, and gladly. They love him, and they'll fight for him to the death. He is one of them, as you could never be, being nobles."

Gil knew that was true. He also better understood Brand's long walks through the camp. He had guessed the generals would try something like this and assessed the mood of the men to follow him instead of them.

The generals stood, and they seemed shocked and uncertain. This meeting had not turned out as they expected, and their bluff had been called. Only Garling managed to speak.

"You'll regret this, Brand. Time will prove us right."

"It may, Garling, but I don't think so. Anyway, this conversation is over. You may leave."

The generals stalked out. Brand waited until they were gone before he spoke.

"This isn't what I really wanted, at least not yet. But so be it. What it means though is that I must now rely more heavily on you all."

"Will you appoint new generals?" Gil asked.

"No. I'll now lead. You will take on a greater role, and I shall seek your opinions. That's as it should be. I'll also seek input from others in the army. I'll think on who they should be. For the moment, it's time to ride."

They left the tent, and soldiers swiftly began to dismantle it. The rain had cleared, and the army was prepared to march. Going to their horses, they found the generals mounting and ready to ride.

"If we're not wanted here," Garling said, "we'll take a guard and return to Cardoroth."

"I don't think so," Brand answered. "You'll stay where I can see you, and that will be riding close by me at all times."

547

He signaled Shorty over. "Keep an eye on them. They're to ride in our group and not leave it. Pass the word to the Durlin."

"As you wish," Shorty answered.

Brand turned to Taingern. "Bring all the colonels over to me. I'll speak to them before we set off."

Taingern left, and the generals fumed silently while the others saddled and mounted their horses.

Taingern returned soon after with the colonels, and Brand addressed them.

"Men, you will be aware that the generals and I do not agree on the strategy for this campaign. I have therefore relieved them of their command, and I now lead. You will take your orders directly from me now. Are there any questions?"

The men seemed uncertain, and one voiced his doubt. "Is this really going to help us win?"

Brand turned his gaze upon him, and smiled. "A good question, and a brave one. I am regent, but let no man here follow my orders without question. If you see something you think is wrong, say so. I will consider all your views. But once a decision is made, I expect you to follow it perfectly." He paused, looking around at the men, then glanced back at the man who had spoken. "To answer your question, yes, this will help us win. I could give you all the reasons why, but they would be mere words on the wind. Instead, I'll say this. I'm Brand. You know who I am and what I've done. Do you believe in me?"

Some of the men cheered. Others seemed in doubt. "That is enough for now. You will believe more as each day unfolds. Now, give the signal to the army and we'll march."

Garling fixed Brand with a knife-like stare. "I know, beyond doubt, that you'll regret this."

"It is possible," Brand answered calmly.

Ahead, the carnyx horn that signaled the commencement of marching was blown. The horn gave off an eerie sound, a sound out of the ancient past of the Camar people. Gil thought back to his ancestors who held the horns to be sacred. They had winded them in the tumult of battle and believed the sound scared their enemies. Well might it be so.

The army surged forward, some of the cavalry holding high the varied banners of Cardoroth, and Gil felt a surge of pride. These were his countrymen, marching to protect the nation, willing to risk their lives to do so. He would do no less. And he, like they, would follow Brand.

Onward the army marched and the morning passed. Gil had felt a strange thrill run through him at the sounding of the carnyx horn, as though it had stirred something ancient in his blood. That feeling had not left him. Rather, it intensified as the army went forward.

He rode ahead, less and less mindful of what was happening about him. The world receded and a vague dream-state took its place. He tried to shake it off, but could not. Unease rippled through his consciousness, but he seemed powerless to speak or signal Brand.

All at once the dream focused. Ginsar appeared before him, standing tall and regal as she always did. The sorceress was clad in white, and a silver crown was set upon her head. It gleamed and shone, contrasting against the midnight black of her long hair that streamed behind her in a breeze that did not touch Gil.

"Hail, Prince of Cardoroth," she greeted him.

"Hail, Queen of Sorcery," Gil answered. And though he spoke and knew that she heard him, he knew also that no one else could see her nor hear his voice.

"It is time that we talked again," she said. "And this time I shall say things that you most need to hear."

"Speak, then. I'm listening."

"Ah, that is because you must. This is no vision that you can banish as you did last time. I'm sure that frustrates you. But no matter. You will find it instructive to listen. Firstly, you should know that this magic is within your power. And so much more. But you do not delve into the gift you have. That is a mistake, for few have your talent and it should not be thwarted. I could teach things to you, such things as would make your soul sing."

Gil tried with all his willpower to break free of the spell she had cast upon him, but he did not know how.

She smiled at him. "Does that not tempt you, young prince? To learn the Mysteries? To have power such as few could even dream of? To unravel the secrets of life and death? Look me in the eye and tell me that it is not so."

Gil gazed into her eyes. He could not help it. "Who does not wish these things?" he replied.

"Yes indeed. But they are denied to you. Instead you must one day be king. That is your duty." She paused and looked thoughtful. "But it need not be so. You could be king, yes. But you could also learn the Mysteries. You could be a sorcerer king."

Gil could not stop himself from looking at her, but some part of his mind rebelled. "I learn lòhrengai – I would never learn elùgai. Sorcery such as that is of the dark, and I reject it."

Ginsar considered him, and her expression was neither worried nor angry. "You are quite correct. I would teach you dark ways. But it is just a word. Elùgai is just a different expression of the same power. And in the end, it is just as much your heritage as the throne of Cardoroth."

Gil shook his head. He did not wish to argue with her, for he sensed that in this waking dream he could win no debate. But he knew it was important to resist.

"None of that is true," he said.

"Oh, it is true. And you know it. I see it in your eyes. Carnhaina herself was of the dark. She was very nearly an elùgroth, but she failed at the last. It need not be so with you…"

"It will *never* be so with me. I swear it."

She smiled at him again, and he sensed that in some way she had changed, but he was not sure in what manner.

"So sure? Wait and see. You will learn by the end that fate cannot be defied. It is in your blood, even as it is in mine."

Gil decided that this had gone on long enough. He could not break out of this dream, he did not have the strength to oppose her will. But was that the right approach? Brand had always taught him that strength against strength was not the way. Perhaps subtlety was needed instead.

He gathered the magic within him, felt it come alive with his thought. Then he sent out tendrils, felt them work their way around him, sensed the riders nearby, the army and the hills and forest. Then he hooked onto those feelings, the sensations of reality rather than dream, and let them pull him out of this waking dream, for great though Ginsar's power was, reality was stronger still.

Ginsar receded as the real world came back into focus. But he saw her throw back her head and laugh, and the whisper of her voice slipped into his ears before she disappeared.

"We will meet again, Prince of the Blood."

18. A Man out of Nightmare

On through the day the army proceeded, following the routine of march, rest and march again relentlessly. Of the waking dream that Gil had experienced and the words of Ginsar, he said nothing. Brand had enough to worry about as it was.

Finally, the end of the day came in a sunset of ruined clouds and rising mists on the high hills. The land seemed desolate, wild, born of ancient magic. It was not tame like Cardoroth, and Gil began to love it. For once, he envied Brand that he had traveled widely across Alithoras and seen the sun rise and set over unfamiliar views like this.

Here, the plateau of the hills seemed wide and open. But they were on its edge. Tomorrow, the road would plunge down through thick forests again, where the trees would crowd close and invoke a sense of unseen eyes watching. Thus it always seemed in the forest, but with Ginsar about and her army coming, those eyes may be real rather than imagined. And the army would be spread out and vulnerable once more.

The march ceased, ended by a wavering blast from the same carnyx horn that started it all those hours ago. Gil dismounted, taking off the saddle and rubbing down his roan, now a fixed part of his daily routine, and perhaps the best part of it.

By the time he finished, the posts for the picket lines had been prepared and attendants came with feed for the horses. The tent was also erected, and to this he returned with Brand and the others. There was little rest to be had though, at least not for Brand. Almost immediately scouts began to return, bringing with them news. The regent had instructed that they now reported directly to him. There was an endless stream of them, and though the reporting was time-consuming, Gil knew that intelligence of the land around an army and the movements of the enemy were critical to success.

The general indications were that signs of people in the forest had been discovered, though no one had actually been seen and it was unknown who, or how many, they were. There was a large village many miles to the west, though it had recently been abandoned. Whoever dwelt there would know the forest well though, and it was more than possible that they had learned of the marching of the army and dispersed.

Brand asked if it were possible that significant numbers of men could be nearby. The scouts assured him it was not, though there could easily be small groups that remained undetected.

Of the elug army, no evidence had been found, and there was still no word from the long-range scouts monitoring it.

Overall, Brand seemed relieved at the news the scouts brought, and the regent treated them well offering each one of them watered wine as they reported and words of thanks for their good work. Nevertheless, he gave instructions for the camp sentries to be doubled and extra precautions taken against possible attack by small groups.

When the influx of scouts ceased, the small group in the tent drank their own wine and enjoyed a simple but beautifully hot meal of stew and vegetables on stale bread.

Conversation was sparing, and there was a distant look in Brand's eyes. Gil wondered if he were analyzing the next steps of the army, or worrying about what had happened to Tainrik. Both, he concluded.

The evening passed quickly, and they soon retired to their separate compartments in the tent. However, Gil had barely gone to sleep when he heard a commotion outside and raised voices. Swiftly he pulled on his boots and belted his sword, and then he went out into the main room of the tent.

The others came out too. A single lamp still burned, giving off light to see by, and their faces were confused and worried. Was an attack on the camp underway?

Brand drew his sword and stepped forward toward the tent flap. He never reached it. The canvas was pulled open before him, and several figures entered. There were two Durlin, and they supported between them a man who staggered, a man covered in dried blood, his features twisted in pain and his body wracked by shivers and spasms.

"Tainrik!" Brand said hoarsely.

Gil recognized him now, though he was changed greatly. Not only had he been injured, with one eye swollen shut, but he was ill also with some fever that wracked his body and shone in his one open eye. His clothes were torn and ripped, and in some places the damaged cloth was caked by dried blood. These were not injuries, but battle wounds. He was a man walked out of nightmare, and how he had survived it Gil could not guess.

The regent sheathed his sword and retrieved a chair. Gently, the Durlin eased the man down upon it.

"What happened to you, my friend?" Brand asked, kneeling down and taking his hand.

Tainrik struggled to speak, but his voice was a dry croak.

Swiftly Gil fetched a goblet of water and made to hand it to the scout, but Tainrik's hands trembled too much to hold it properly. Gil helped him, steadying the goblet as they lifted it to his mouth to drink.

He gulped it down, and then looked like he might vomit it back up again. But he rallied and his shivering reduced.

"Trouble," he croaked. "Be careful, Brand."

Elrika had retrieved a blanket, which she wrapped around the man's shoulders, and Brand looked up at one of the Durlin. "Fetch a camp surgeon, and swiftly."

Tainrik shivered again. "I have news, friend."

"Wait," Brand said. "Drink some more water first."

Gil took the goblet and moved back to the table.

"Wine," Tainrik croaked, and Brand nodded his approval as Gil looked at him.

"Make it red wine, unwatered," the regent said.

Gil knew that red wine was supposed to help the body replace lost blood. If nothing else, it should make Tainrik feel better anyway. He filled the goblet and returned.

This time the scout sipped it, but he still needed help to hold the goblet steady.

"I have bad news, Brand," he said.

"It can wait. The surgeon will be here shortly, and when he's done then we can talk."

Tainrik shook his head. "Can't wait," he said softly.

Brand pulled up another chair and sat opposite him. "What news then?"

"We were followed ... Found their camp ... Heard them talk," Tainrik said breathlessly. Every word seemed to cost him to speak it, and Gil wondered at what the man must have endured to reach his present state, but how strong his willpower was to keep moving and reach the camp. Other men would have laid down and died somewhere back in the hills.

"Hvargil is here. In hills. He knows you're coming because a message was sent ahead." Tainrik coughed, his whole body shuddering, but he went on. "His men think if you and Gil are killed, he is a chance of being king."

Brand looked thoughtful. "It's possible," he agreed. "More than possible. And you think there may be an ambush?"

Tainrik coughed again, unable to speak for a moment, but he nodded vigorously.

Brand reached out and placed a hand on his shoulder. "Then we'll be ready for it, thanks to you. You've done well, and I'll not forget it."

Gil considered how loyal Tainrik must have been to Brand. It had nearly killed him to bring this message. In fact, it might kill him yet. He knew he should not be surprised though. Brand had that effect on people. They knew he would do the same for them.

Taking the now empty goblet, Gil filled it with some more wine and returned. He helped Tainrik sip at it, but he looked at Brand.

"Hvargil is of the true line, as am I," he said. "Only the nobles like him. If you and I were both killed, I could see them turn to him."

"I think so," Brand agreed. "But Hvargil doesn't have the men to attack this army."

"No, but he could launch an ambush as you said, directed at you and me."

"Quite possibly. These large tents make us obvious targets at night." He turned to Taingern. "Warn the sentries that an attack is possible. And increase the guard."

Taingern left the tent and Brand turned back to Gil. "I would think though that an attack during day is more likely. There's a place ahead where an ambush could be set. The trail enters a gorge as it winds down the hills. If I were Hvargil, and had few men, that is where I'd snare my trap."

The White Lady bent over and whispered for a few moments in Brand's ear. A slow smile lit his face.

"That, lady, is exactly what we shall do." He beckoned Shorty over. "Alert the scouts," he ordered. "Tell them to avoid that gorge and the area surrounding it. The enemy know the terrain better than them, and they will be at risk of being killed for nothing." He paused, and then added angrily. "I suspect Hvargil is the reason we haven't heard any further word from the long-range scouts monitoring Ginsar's army. He'll come to regret that."

Gil was about to ask what plan Brand had, for certainly he and the White Lady had conceived one, but the surgeon arrived.

The healer was an older man, tall and strongly built. He looked more like a warrior than anything else, but his sharp eyes took Tainrik in at a glance. "You should be dead, son. But I've seen your type before. You'll live."

Gil looked at the scout, and was not so sure. But he hoped he survived, for he was the kind of man that Cardoroth needed, the kind of man that a king would draw to his side.

19. War!

The night was old, and mist rose like groping fingers from the river. Ginsar returned to the camp of her acolytes and wasted no time. More must yet be done before the darkness died and birthed the new day.

"Awake!" she cried, and the camp stirred to sudden life.

They came and gathered to her then, all her acolytes and the Lethrin and elug representatives. She paid the elug no heed, for his kind were of use to her only in large numbers. Not so the others.

She stood tall and regal, a figure of command. "The time has come. I have this night spoken with the dead and learned of the future. Time hastens. We will hasten with it, and rise over the land like a wave surging to victory. And when Cardoroth is destroyed, then why should all Alithoras not follow? And then, the very world! It is ours for the taking! Is this not what you have dreamed of?"

They answered her then with gleeful cries and cheers and clenched fists thrust into the air. All except the Lethrin who remained untouched by her words. She turned to him, and the others grew suddenly quiet.

She lowered her voice and spoke in little more than a whisper. "Why do you not cheer?"

The Lethrin gave an impassive shrug. "The words of the dead are always two-edged. Such is the lore among my people. The shade you spoke with would have uttered no words guaranteeing victory, and the import of what it did say would be couched in double meanings and dark riddles. Is it not so?"

Ginsar hissed, and the acolytes moved away from him, but the Lethrin stood his ground, unperturbed.

She smiled then, a sudden dazzle of genuine good humor. So few stood up to her. The Lethrin was *perfect* for her plans.

With a gesture she summoned an acolyte to stand close before her. "Olekgar, you are the youngest, and yet, the greatest among your brothers and sisters. Ever you grasp the subtleties of what I teach, and your mind nimbly moves to other possibilities building a tower of knowledge from the foundations that I provide. Therefore, you shall be rewarded."

Olekgar bowed, his fair hair spilling out from beneath the dark cowl. He straightened, and began to step back. No doubt he intuited what was coming next, but no matter.

Ginsar pointed at him and he stilled, held by invisible bonds.

"No, Mistress. Please. Not that."

She smiled sweetly at him but did not answer. Instead, she pointed at the Lethrin and cast a net of dark magic over him. The creature stiffened, not knowing what it meant but sensing danger. He tried to back away, but found himself stepping forward until he stood side by side with Olekgar.

"You shall be brothers," she said. "So different, and yet so much the same."

She pointed a finger at each, willing them to kneel before her, piling upon their shoulders a weight of irresistible sorcery.

Olekgar muttered some spell, trying to break free of the entrapment. She felt the force of it, the depth of his mind and the power that he summoned. She smothered it with her own dark power and his knees crumbled, sending him crashing to the ground, fear lighting his eyes.

The Lethrin did not move. There was a store of determination in his mind that surprised her. It would be easier to topple a mountain than him. But there were ways.

With a swift movement her hand flashed out, slapping the creature across the face. He staggered back, for she was far stronger than she looked. And in that moment of surprise she sent numbness into his legs and piled a redoubled weight of magic upon him so that he too, proud though he was, bent down before her and crashed to his knees. Rage burned in his eyes and his desire to reach out and kill her filled the air with palpable intent.

Ginsar drew her knife, a relic from ancient Cardoroth, and savored the moment the Lethrin saw it. His eyes locked onto hers and there was a rage within them terrible to behold, yet impotent. He could not move. She smiled. Oh, he was *perfect*.

The acolytes were silent and motionless, daring no movement that might draw attention to themselves. The mist on the river to her left stirred sluggishly. The higher ground to the right hulked like a mass of watching shadows in an amphitheater, bent forward and leering at a spectacle below.

The knife gleamed in her hand, and she licked her lips. The curved blade seemed a thing of shadow, but etched into the metal were runes that gleamed amid the dark. It felt good in her strong grip.

The mouth of Olekgar worked mutely, as though he still sought to voice some spell to thwart her. Fool. The Lethrin looked at her, the anger in his eyes a light as hot as the sun.

She moved to him. Slowly, like a lover's caress she ran the blade across his neck. A thin red line appeared. Then blood flowed, faster and faster. All the while he held her gaze, unflinchingly.

Next, she turned to Olekgar and did the same thing. He closed his eyes but his mouth still worked soundlessly, and to no purpose.

Blood spurted now from both sacrifices. Red, vivid, intoxicating to her as wine. She shuddered, and opened the wounds a little wider by the force of sorcery.

Crimson sprays erupted from pulsing arteries. Slowly, Olekgar collapsed to the ground. The Lethrin remained defiant, his eyes locked on hers until she reached forth with her hand and pushed him down. He resisted, but as life left him his body no longer obeyed his burning will.

She bent and drew a dark basin from behind her, and set it beneath the bleeding necks one at a time. The blood of the sacrifices mixed and swirled within it. The bodies were empty of life now, suitable vessels for what was to come. And though empty of life, the vestiges of their mind remained and would shape that which was about to enter into them. The strength of will as well as of body the Lethrin possessed would endure. So too the nimbleness of mind the acolyte enjoyed.

She ignored the bodies for the moment. What mattered now was their blood in the basin. She studied it, reveling at the sheen on its surface and the play of light within it that gleamed and glistened as the fluid congealed.

Ginsar breathed in of the night air. Power coursed through her and she laughed with the sheer joy of it. But her night's work was not yet complete.

She removed the basin from the corpses and sensed the eyes of the acolytes upon her, watching wide-eyed with anticipation. They knew what came next, for they had seen it before. Ignoring them, she turned her gaze to the thickening blood. This she stirred with her knife, shaping runes with each cut and stroke of the blade. Letters formed, and then dissolved back into the blood. But the power she drew forth slowly grew and took hold.

The air turned cool. An icy breeze stirred, sucking heat from those gathered there, and they pulled their cloaks tightly about them. The tendrils of mist creeping up from the river leaned one way and then the other as the breeze shifted direction.

Ginsar intoned words now as her blade moved through the blood. They were harsh and guttural, and as she spoke them she heard in her mind the voice of her master speak them also. Shurilgar had long ago taught her what to say, and it was as though he was in her head now, his voice one with hers.

She chanted more loudly, no longer muttering but boldly casting the words into the air. The knife handle grew hot to her touch, and the breeze turned into a gusty wind that tore the river-mist into shreds. The river itself churned and tossed in its banks, and a spout of water erupted high into the air with a cough.

And then there was more. Two voices rose in a chant of their own, and Ginsar felt the gateway between worlds tremble and the brush of something otherworldly on her mind.

"Come!" she commanded. "Come, for you are called!"

Vapor, red-tinged and wraithlike, rose from the basin of blood. The wind took it and cast it wildly into the air. And the two voices answered as one.

"We come, sorceress. We come, and your world shall be ours."

The blood in the basin caught fire, and Ginsar dropped it. The red mist formed around her, seeking entry into her body and she screamed.

The wind died. The river stilled. But the vapor churned around her, wrapping her in its dark intent. Fire dripped from her finger tips as she summoned her own power. Then she wrapped the mist within it, screamed once more as she tore it from herself, and sent it streaking into the corpses at her feet.

The acolytes scattered, fearful of falling victim to some stray tendril of magic. Even Ginsar felt panic rise within her, for she sensed the intent of the spirits she had summoned. They wanted to possess her, and nearly succeeded in doing so. Yet they had moved readily enough into the corpses when she forced them too, not bothering to continue to fight her. Why was that so?

The red mist clung to the two bodies, melding with them. After a moment, the corpses twitched and spasmed as renewed life entered them, changing them into their new forms. The Lethrin, or that which had once been the Lethrin, roared in pain and anguish. Almost, Ginsar thought, as if it still retained his defiance and hatred of her.

Ginsar stepped back. The acolytes dared come closer again to watch the transformation take place, to see the culmination of the dark magic even as they had watched its birth.

The bodies began to thrash. Skin tore where muscles swelled. Eyes popped and bones cracked, sharp edges showing before knitting together again in an altered shape. And then finally, the bodies stilled. For a moment they lay on the ground, and then slowly they rose to stand before her.

Her heart skipped a beat. Olekgar had become a Horseman. He was now Betrayal. Golden-haired he was, and beautiful. Tall and slim, his shoulders wide and his body athletic. Strength was in his every muscle, and they rippled beneath his fair skin. There was power in his blue eyes also, and they gleamed with their own inner light. Swift of movement he seemed, young and lively. But when he moved she saw knives in his back, blood constantly dripping from the wounds.

War was beside him. He was clad in armor, and possessed the full accoutrements of battle. In one mighty hand he held a great broadsword, saw-toothed and deadly. In the other was a shield of back iron, spiked in its center. A helm rested on his head, winged and cruel of visage. It too was of black iron, and a spike rose also from its top. A baldric of knives hung down his massive body from one shoulder to the opposite hip. And above his head fluttered two carrion crows that cried and cawed.

Ginsar raised her arms above her head. "We go to war!" she proclaimed to the acolytes. "We march tomorrow, and this I have learned from the dead. Brand comes to meet us." She smiled slowly. "Let him beware! We shall crush him, and all shall fall before us!"

20. You have Failed

The army moved forward for another day's march. Gil studied the country as he rode, aware that at any time an attack could be launched, and he and Brand would be its target.

It was hard to see much, though. Fog draped the hillsides, thick and eerie. Through it he caught glimpses of the lush forests that grew on the slopes. Everywhere was a potential ambush site, but he tried to trust in Brand's judgement that if one were prepared it would be in the gorge further down the trail.

He glanced over at Tainrik who now rode in the leadership group. The man was tough, of that there was no doubt. The surgeon had worked on him some time, properly cleaning and dressing his wounds, stitching the gash in his forehead that the scout had not been able to do himself and adding an infusion of herbs to the wine he sipped to reduce his fever.

And while the surgeon worked on him the scout had spoken with Brand and provided details of what had happened. Tough did not begin to describe him. It was not even a start, and Gil was sure he made light of some aspects that were the hardest and most difficult. It was the way of such men.

Brand had wanted to have him carried forward in a litter, but Tainrik had laughed. "Give me a horse," he told the regent, "and keep me awake so that I stay in the saddle. That's all I'll need."

Gil shook his head, amazed but at the same time proud. Tainrik was the sort of man that said little but achieved much. That was the best sort, and there were never enough of them but too many of the kind that spoke much and achieved little.

The scout looked better than he had last night, but still not well. When Brand had invited him to ride in the leadership group, Tainrik had joked that he had already risked his life, and survived. And now he was sure to be struck by an arrow fired from the fog and not even intended for him. Brand had just winked at him, and Tainrik had accepted the offer.

Gil considered what had been said as he rode. Loyalty was at the bottom of it all. It was the reason Tainrik had ventured out on Brand's request to look for the spies in the first place. It was why he endured so much. It was why he was here now, and not in a safer place of the army that was less likely to be the target of an ambush. The question was, how had Brand inspired such loyalty?

The regent never asked a person to do something that he would not do himself. He led like a true king, doing everything for the people and not expecting the people to do everything for him. He would have been like that as a captain also, when he had first met Tainrik. He was one of those few people who meant what they said and said what they meant. These were all simple things, but they were the hallmarks of good leadership, and Gil noted them.

Some while later they halted on a steeper stretch of road for their hourly break. Ahead, Gil saw the gorge. It ran between two high ridges that were smothered by a growth of forest and cloaked by shadow and the last vestiges of fog that had still not burned away under the long-risen sun. Just looking at it gave him goosebumps. The place reeked of danger.

Gil dismounted and saw Brand beckon him over. The regent led him a little way from everyone else.

"I have sent word back through the army that we expect an ambush here. They know that I have a plan, and that magic will be used. I have asked them, and now I ask you, to stay calm and act normal – no matter what you see."

"Of course," Gil said.

"And will you lend us of your strength? Of magic?"

"I'll help in whatever way I can."

"Then join the White Lady, and be ready to summon your power."

Brand moved away and retrieved his staff from where it was attached to his saddlebags. Then he wandered over to where Gil had joined the White Lady.

"Be seated," she said, offering Gil one of her most dazzling smiles. He had an inkling of an idea that she was going to enjoy whatever came next.

They sat upon the grass, looking out toward the gorge. "I'll shape the magic," she said, "but I'll draw on your power to do so. Summon it, and relax."

Gil allowed the lòhrengai within him to stir to life. It pulsed through his body, straining to break free as it always did, and he felt the joy of its presence but also the danger that too much use of it could bring. It was like a living thing itself, and it wanted to break free.

He sensed Brand to his right and the White Lady to his left. He felt also the summoning of their own power. The White Lady seemed different to him, her magic of a kind that he had not felt elsewhere. And it was strong, strong as iron but subtle also. But her mind was closed to him, and he gained no insight into her personality or purposes.

Brand was different. He too was strong, and though Gil sensed none of the subtlety of the White Lady, he felt the indomitable will of the regent, the unbreakable determination that had seen him survive struggle after struggle. He felt also the responsibility that weighed on him. It was an immense feeling, made up of the lives of every single person in the realm, for every decision that Brand made could save or condemn them, and he knew it.

Separate, but also as one, their combined strength began to flow together. And of their power the White Lady formed an image. It was a glint of light at first, a stirring of fog and shifting of shadows. But it grew swiftly and took shape.

A wedge of cavalry headed it, for it was a replication of the army. Brand and Gil rode behind, surrounded by the Durlin. Then came the army itself. Nor was this illusion an image only, but each part of it moved and acted as though it were real. Gil was astounded by the skill that had produced it, by the seeming reality of it as it passed down the road and toward the gorge.

But the illusion did not come without cost. Gil felt the power drawn from him and the sapping of his strength. He began to breathe slowly and paid little heed now to the illusion. He concentrated instead on drawing forth his strength and keeping steady the bond between himself and the others.

The illusory army moved forward, and fog drifted down from a slope to obscure the real one, which had not moved. Gil felt a cold sweat break out on his skin and his concentration wavered. This was hard, but however hard it was for him it was more difficult for the White Lady. But he felt the joint determination of them all. To falter now was to waste their effort and fail to spring the trap, if indeed a trap had even been set in the gorge.

Deep down into the gorge the illusion moved, but nothing happened. There was no attack, no ambuscade and sudden flight of arrows and hurling of spears. It had all been for nothing.

The false Brand and Gil had nearly disappeared from sight when a burst of activity occurred. A hail of arrows filled the dark air of the gorge like a deadly storm. One struck Brand in the back, another pierced Gil's eye. All around them the white surcoats of the Durlin blossomed red. Screams rent the air and horses bolted. Bodies littered the ground, and a wild cheering came from men hidden on the ridges above the gorge.

But even as they cheered the bodies on the ground and the bolting horses and the survivors left milling around faded into nothing. Of the army, and the victory the ambushers thought they had won, there was no sign.

The mist around the real army dispersed, and silence fell. Brand stood, and into the quiet he spoke. By an art of lòhrengai his voice, neither loud nor soft, carried for miles around.

"Hvargil!" he called. "You have failed. And your treachery will catch up with you! Flee back to your outlaw den, while you can. And there wait, for you have set in motion your own doom this day. Cardoroth will no longer suffer you. We will come for you one day soon, and all we find with you."

Brand gave a signal and several hundred foot soldiers split away from the army to climb the rough terrain either side of the gorge.

The regent seemed tired, but he smiled at Gil. "They'll clear the outlaws out, if they remain. But they'll be gone before the soldiers reach them. They had thought to set an ambush and not fight a pitched battle. This was all a surprise for them, and I don't think they'll trouble us any further."

Gil nodded. "But you've done more than that. You always have an eye to the future. What you said to them will worry Hvargil. But it will worry his men more. And you did not threaten them, only him. All they have to do to escape his doom is not be with him. I should think he will have less followers back at his camp tonight than he did this morning. And in the days to come more will desert him."

Brand reached out and placed a hand on Gil's shoulder. "You always were a quick student. What you say is true. We'll march back this way, and what I did will make it safer. And one day, you will have to go after Hvargil. You cannot allow his treachery to go unpunished, nor let him continue to incite treachery among the nobles. And the fewer men he has, the easier it will be to bring him to justice."

Gil knew that was true, but he did not like it. Hvargil was a relation, sharing the same blood and also a descendant of Carnhaina, just as was he.

Brand spoke again, but this time not to Gil. The generals were close by and they had heard his last words.

"You seem unhappy gentleman. Why is that?"

Gil gazed at them, and saw indeed that all three were scowling.

"Magic, Brand. It has no place in warfare."

The regent laughed. "You'd better get used to it. There'll be more before the battle is won, and most of it will come from the enemy."

That would likely prove correct, Gil knew. But was magic the real reason for the unhappiness of the generals? Or was it because Hvargil had been thwarted? He glanced at Brand, and sensed that despite his light tone he too was wondering the very same thing.

"It would have been better to just send troops as you did in the end anyway," Garling said.

Brand shrugged. "Perhaps. But then the outlaws would have merely tried again somewhere else. Now, they'll be disheartened. Perhaps even scared. Hvargil will sit back and await the outcome of the war with Ginsar. He will hope that Cardoroth wins, but in the process that Gil and I are killed."

He looked at Gil and winked. "We'll thwart that wish."

The rest break ended and the army commenced to march again. The gorge was secure, though it was slow going for the road was in ill-repair.

It was dark, with the ridges rising up to each side and the forested slopes blocking out the sky. The gorge was a menacing place, and Gil had the strange sensation that he had avoided death here. It was somewhere along the trail where he now rode that the ambush had been launched against the illusion. Arrows had hissed through the air and spears quivered in flight. It was a sobering feeling, and it brought home to him that he had enemies that wished him dead. That was not a good thought, but one that Brand had experience with, and Gil better understood the advice the regent had given him in respect of Hvargil.

They moved on, passing over ground littered by arrow shafts and spears. Gil shuddered at the thought of being here in the middle of the attack, at the very focus of it. Soon, however, the sense of menace passed and the gorge widened. The sky came out above and the sun shone once more. To Gil, it seemed a moment of rebirth and new opportunity. He was not dead, no matter what his enemies wanted. And he would make the most of that.

They were not quite out the other side when Brand unexpectedly called a halt. Whatever had disturbed him, Gil was not sure. But he felt a sense of unease himself, and a moment later understood why.

Sorcery. He felt it in his bones, and his own magic stirred to life in response. Just ahead, a slab of rock upon the road, perhaps toppled from the ridge above for it was cracked and fissured, began to exude smoke from its crannied surface.

The smoke, black and greasy, swirled and twisted through the air to form an image. In moments Ginsar stood there, beautiful and terrible as always.

"We meet again, Brand."

The regent sat relaxed upon his black stallion. "Only because I'm hard to kill, a fact that has taken you some while to appreciate."

The sorceress flashed him a smile. It even seemed genuine. "You *are* vey hard to kill. I know it better than most. But it's bad manners to mention my attempts on your life."

Brand bowed his head, but never took his eyes off the sorceress. "I apologize, lady. I'm only a rustic Duthenor tribesman."

"You're learning though," she said. "And I like that. Perhaps one day you would be at home in the throne room of Cardoroth."

"Ah, lady, you and I both know that isn't my fate. But, if you don't mind, time presses. What do you wish here?"

She shook her head. "So abrupt? The nobles of Cardoroth would never like that."

Brand did not answer, and Ginsar sighed. "I suppose you don't care much about the nobles. A pity, but never mind. What do I wish? Well, I want for nothing. I came here to tell you something, not to ask for anything. I know that you march to war and seek to surprise me. Did you really think to hide such a thing?"

"Ah, lady, did you really think that my purpose?"

Ginsar studied him. "You are quick on your feet," she said. "Another favorable quality, but you don't deceive me. I know exactly where you are, and where your army is. As well as your purpose."

Brand held his reins close and leaned forward in the saddle. "If you say so."

"I *do* say so! Come to me Brand, and we shall see just how good at staying alive you really are."

The sorceress turned to Gil, and he felt the power of her gaze. Evil she may be, and likely insane also, but there was a strength of will to her that he could not deny. And though she stood in the garb of a sorceress, with her dark boots tightened by silver buckles, her robes black and flowing, her cloak draped over her like a shadow, yet still she stood as proud as any queen and certain of her destiny.

"Savior or destroyer?" she said to him. "You will see soon enough which it shall be. I know the answer, as I know many things hidden from you. I know your true path, the fate and heritage that awaits you. Accept it willingly, for to struggle against it is futile. Destiny cannot be denied."

"You don't know my destiny," Gil answered. "And even if you did, I would not trust you to speak it truthfully."

Ginsar held his gaze for a moment, and then she sighed. "We shall see."

She turned then to Elrika, and Gil was surprised that she had spent little effort trying to convince him to believe her.

A moment Ginsar studied Elrika as though with curiosity, and then her eyes hardened. "Who are you to carry *that* sword? It was not forged for the likes of you."

Elrika did not seem cowed by the sorceress, and Gil was amazed at her reaction. She drew the blade with a hiss from its sheath, and held it before her.

"It may not be for the *likes* of me, but I would gladly use it anyway to spill your guts, hag."

Gil could not believe that she had said that. It was Shorty's influence on her he knew, for he heard an echo of the Durlindrath in them, yet she was the one who voiced them and his heart swelled with pride.

Ginsar's eyes blazed, but her answer was softly spoken. "You will regret that."

She cast her gaze over the others, ignoring the generals and lingering a little while on Taingern. Then her glance fell on the White Lady and remained there, transfixed.

"And who are you?"

"A secret within a secret. But you shall know soon enough. For now, think on this. To kill me is to doom yourself. To let me live, is *also* to doom yourself. You have overreached yourself, and there is no way back. The end draws nigh."

Ginsar was about to reply but the White Lady casually raised her hand and the image of the sorceress dispersed in a puff of smoke that drifted away on the breeze.

Garling was the first one to speak. "Are all you people mad? Why do you antagonize her so?"

"Better to antagonize her than fall thrall to her," Gil replied.

Garling shook his head. The other generals, Druigbar and Lothgern whispered to each other.

"One thing is clear," Lothgern said aloud a moment later. "Ginsar knows we are coming, that the army has left Cardoroth. Brand's plan has failed, and even as we speak the enemy may be hastening down the Halathrin road. If we don't turn back now, it will soon be too late."

A tense silence fell, but the White Lady broke it. "No. Ginsar's army is coming this way. I feel the Horsemen draw close. They and I are connected. And the sorceress acts in haste now, even as Brand had planned." She gazed at where the image of Ginsar had stood, her expression thoughtful. "Our coming could not be hidden from her for long, but it was long enough. She has summoned War and Betrayal earlier than she would have. She marches to a battle and not the siege she expected, and she is not one who likes to react to others. Brand has made her act in haste and change her plans. This is all to our advantage."

"More magic," muttered Garling. "All conjecture and intuition."

"We shall see," Brand answered. "But there is this too. She need not have revealed herself at all, and merely let us come. That would fit better with your view."

"Or she could be trying to deceive us," Garling said, "and make us *think* she is coming this way."

"She came," the White Lady said, "because she wanted to learn something. And she has, though by the time she understands what she has learned, it will be too late."

Gil hoped that was the case. But he understood where the generals were coming from. It seemed impossible just now to know what was true and what was false and what was going to happen. It was not a good feeling.

21. A Message

The next day the army of Cardoroth descended out of the hills and the forested ridges gave way to slopes of rolling grass. Scouts had been sent out during the night, and they began to return. By mid-morning they reported a massive army of elugs lay ahead. If Brand was relieved, he did not show it. Nor did the generals comment.

The scouts advised the size of the enemy. Their figures differed somewhat, but the averaged tally came to thirty-five thousand elugs and a thousand Lethrin. Against this, twenty-five thousand soldiers of Cardoroth would pit themselves. Small wonder, Gil thought to himself, that Brand showed no relief. Being right did not compensate for being outnumbered. And yet the elugs were not equipped as well as the men of Cardoroth, nor were they likely to be as disciplined.

Gil considered what he knew of military strategy. This was a great deal, yet it was all theoretical. He had never fought in a battle, let alone commanded one. Yet this was the golden rule: avoid engaging the enemy unless victory was certain.

The golden rule was easy to understand, in theory. Applying it was more difficult. What weight should he give to the elugs outnumbering the soldiers of Cardoroth? How should he assess the impact of the better equipment and greater discipline possessed by his countrymen? And what role would elùgai and lòhrengai play?

He could not measure those things, and he did not envy Brand who must. Nor could he weigh the greater strategy behind it all, which was to defeat Ginsar before she drew in too much through the gateway and gave the Horsemen power so great that they might usurp her. Any attempt to defeat her now must be a single and final role of the dice. To fail was to ensure no further opportunity arose. But if rivalry existed for the preeminence of a golden rule, it would come from this quarter: never stake success on the outcome of a single role of the dice.

No, Gil did not envy Brand at all.

A scout spoke to the regent even as Gil considered the situation. He had brought some new information and approached as the army rested.

"Are you sure?" Brand asked.

"Yes. Ginsar was seen, or at least a person who matches her description. Her acolytes were with her too. They are now encamped at the top of a large but gently sloping hill. It's a good defensive position."

"Very well then. Thank you for your good work. Best get something to eat and have some rest now."

The scout hesitated. "There's one last thing."

"Go on, then."

"I found the bodies of half a dozen scouts. They are not far from here, hidden away in a place where the road goes through some thick timber. They have been there some time."

Brand sighed. "Then they are the long-range scouts originally monitoring the enemy rather than any we have sent out in the last few days?"

"Yes, sir."

"Did you know any of them?"

"All of them, sir."

"I'm sorry lad. When we've done with this battle we'll retrieve the bodies and give them a fitting burial."

"Thank you, sir."

The scout left and Brand looked at Gil. "Hvargil has a lot to answer for. At least we know now why we didn't get word sooner about the enemy's movements."

Gil nodded. "You were right in what you said before. Hvargil must be dealt with, once and for all."

Soon after, Brand gave the signal for the carnyx horn to be blown, and the army marched again. It would not be long before the enemy came into sight, and it was possible that battle may be joined today.

Gil nudged his roan close to Brand's stallion as they rode. "Are we going to attack them?"

The regent pursed his lips. "We're outnumbered and they have the advantage of the land. On the other hand, the sooner we strike the better for us. We no longer have surprise, but the enemy, at least until recently, were not expecting a field battle but a siege. That is to our advantage."

Gil considered that. "This is all true, but you didn't say whether we would attack or not."

Brand gave a tight grin. "That's because I haven't decided yet. Best to see the enemy and the terrain first. It is not a decision to be rushed."

Later that afternoon, after marching many miles, both terrain and enemy were in view. The army of Cardoroth came to rest on a gentle rise opposite the enemy force. A mile of green grass separated them. It seemed peaceful now, with the sun out and a few white clouds drifting across a blue sky, but the threat of violence hung in the air and the green grass might soon be trampled red.

Brand rode a little way ahead, inviting the Durlindraths, Gil and two army officers with him. Gil studied the enemy, and his blood ran cold. This was a watershed moment in the history of Cardoroth, and what happened now, or soon, would shape the future.

He squinted against the angled rays of the afternoon sun and scanned the enemy formations. There was no cavalry, which was an advantage to Cardoroth. But after that, reason for hope was limited. In the center Ginsar and her acolytes were gathered. Sorcery would be used, of that there was no doubt. And there was only Brand, the White Lady and himself to defend against it. They were outnumbered on that front. And the numbers of the enemy as given by the scouts seemed accurate by his quick estimate. They would be better at that than him though.

On either side of Ginsar stood the Lethrin. They were few but they stood over seven feet, and though he had never seen them before, he had heard much. They were immensely strong and filled with an implacable hatred of their enemies. Folklore told that they were born from the stone of the mountains, and for all Gil knew it could be true. But irrespective of that, they were miners that hewed tunnels in the rock beneath their mountain homes with massive picks and unwearied arms. Because of their size and strength they usually formed the vanguard of elug armies. It was so here, and their mighty hands gripped massive iron maces, studded with spikes. To be struck by them was to die.

To either flank, like the unfolded wings of a great bat, were the seething masses of elugs: lank haired, ungainly, their dark skin tinged green. They were smaller than Lethrin, smaller even than men, but they were vicious and fierce fighters, never to be underestimated and especially so in large groups. They were prone to fleeing a battlefield, but they were also known to fight to the death should their leaders inspire bloodlust within them. If that could be done, Ginsar would do it.

"What do you think, Taingern? Should we attack?"

"There's no easy answer to that. But you know I'm cautious by nature. The fact that there's no plain answer of yes suggests to me that we shouldn't. Not yet, not here."

"And you, Shorty?"

Shorty grunted. "No one has ever accused me of being cautious. My heart says to attack and get it over with. A delay will not change the inevitable. The enemy will always outnumber us. But still, Taingern may be right."

Brand looked back at the army officers. "What do you say, gentlemen?"

The first shook his head. "I agree with the generals. It would be best if we had the Cardurleth between them and us. We should not fight, but return to the city."

"And you?" Brand asked of the second.

The man looked a moment longer at the enemy, and then he met Brand's gaze. "You were right about Ginsar's strategy. She sought to come upon the city by surprise and besiege us. By marching the army out, you have confounded her plans and expectations. This is an advantage to us. As for the enemy army, I think that despite their superior numbers we can defeat them. But not by attacking uphill into their current position. We should wait her out. We have a direct route open to Cardoroth and supplies. We can delay. She, on the other hand, cannot. I do not believe the elugs are organized well enough to maintain food supplies over a lengthy period."

The man's view was interesting to Gil. It was something he had not considered before.

"And you, Gil?"

"I think we should wait. It will force her to move against us, especially if the enemy is not as well organized as we are."

Brand rubbed his eyes. It was a sign of uncertainty and anxiety, and one of the few times Gil had ever seen him reveal either of those states of mind. After a moment the regent nudged his horse a few feet ahead. By himself he studied the enemy in silence a little while longer.

Gil sensed the weight of responsibility he must feel. It was enormous. But even as Gil watched, Brand lifted his head a little higher and his features became set. He had made his decision.

The regent turned his horse around and trotted back to camp. The others followed. They dismounted, and Brand issued instructions to the army officers. "We'll camp here," he said. "Send out sentries at full strength. I also want roving bands of cavalry further out, to ensure we have good warning should the enemy move."

"Yes sir!" the two men said in unison. They made to leave, but Brand stopped them.

"One thing more. We shall dig a trench and throw up an earth wall. Set the soldiers to digging immediately."

The two men saluted and Brand turned once more to study the enemy. Gil looked as well. He could see Ginsar, recognizing her by her height and the acolytes all around her, yet keeping a reverent distance. They worshiped her, but they feared her also.

"So," Gil said. "We're going to wait her out, try and see if we can force her to attack us."

"Is that the impression you get?" Brand asked.

Gil was confused. "Well, we're obviously not going to attack. Otherwise we wouldn't waste the effort of the men in digging defenses."

Brand winked at him. "Maybe. Then again, in warfare the aim is to ensure the enemy believes anything, anything at all except the truth."

The regent moved away to speak to the commander of the sentries. Gil was stunned and did not follow. Were they really going to attack this afternoon? Or would Brand rest overnight, and then try to surprise Ginsar in the morning?

What remained of the afternoon passed swiftly. The enemy did not attack. Nor did Brand. The earth rampart was built after much labor, but many hands made light work as was often said in the city. Tents were erected, and horses and pack mules tended to and fed. Night fell, camp fires sprung up and the scents of cooking filled the air.

But even as the camp began to settle down after dinner was eaten, Brand was issuing orders. Gil saw him speak to several commanders. They saluted swiftly, and when he came back to the command tent and rejoined them all Gil asked him what was happening.

"War," the regent answered.

A cold chill ran through Gil. "You mean that we're going to attack now? At night?"

"What is the one thing that an army must do if it is to win a battle?"

"It must outfight the enemy," Gil answered.

"Many would say that, but it is not so. The one thing an army must do is *outsmart* the enemy. Strategy is everything, and without it courage and skill and determination wither like unharvested grapes on the vine. Strategy is the master of war, and deception is always the goal until victory is obtained."

"Then if we're not fighting now, but the men seem to be decamping, does that mean we're returning to Cardoroth?"

"The men are moving, but you will note that it is being done quietly and under cover of dark. The roving cavalry will keep enemy scouts away so that Ginsar

583

should not discover that we have left until daylight. We will be gone by then, and be out of sight. But no, we're not returning to Cardoroth."

"Really?"

"No, but Ginsar may believe so after what we have done this afternoon. She will think that perhaps we received news from Cardoroth. Maybe a revolt of the nobles and another attempt for the throne. She will not know, but she will seek to work out why we came all this way, established a camp and then left despite all expectations. An emergency back in the city is the best explanation, and she will consider that possibility most carefully."

"Could she not discover the whereabouts of our army by magic?"

"Perhaps. But if she does…" Brand glanced at the White Lady.

"I will prevent her, should she make such an attempt," the White Lady announced.

"The enemy scouts will be key," Taingern said. "They must not be allowed to follow us or to discover that we're not returning to Cardoroth."

"Precisely," Brand agreed. "The roving cavalry have instructions to that end. And, to ensure Ginsar believes what I want her to, I have a plan."

"What plan is that?" Gil asked.

"The simplest of all," Brand said with a faint smile. "I'll leave her a message."

22. We March!

Ginsar woke to the gray light of dawn and a fading sky of stars. She loved the night, but the pinprick of a million lights ruined the perfect dark. She did not like that, and suddenly she knew that if it were it in her power she would burn the stars to ash.

She sat up. Strange. She had not always hated the stars, but that version of herself that liked them was long since dead. Yet still, she knew that she had changed more recently too, and it made her uneasy. Could she really burn the stars to ash? From whence had that thought come? And was such power even possible?

An acolyte approached. She felt elùgai stir within her. If she could not yet destroy stars, yet still she could burn this creeping sycophant…

With a wrench of will she calmed herself and let her power subside.

"Mistress," the acolyte said, bowing low.

"Speak!" she commanded.

The acolyte kept his head down, not looking into her eyes.

"They are gone, Mistress."

"Who has gone, worm?"

"The enemy, Mistress. They left during the night. Their camp is empty."

Ginsar stood and fury was in her eyes. The acolyte fell to his knees but she ignored him. Instead, she looked out over the long mile of grass that separated the two encampments. The fool was right. Brand was gone. The army of Cardoroth was gone. There was nothing there of the enemy save the dirt ramparts they had constructed, dim and shadowy in the muted light.

But Brand would not leave. No, not him. There was no give in the man, and he would fight to the last breath without stint. Yet the impossible had happened. He *had* retreated.

She turned to the acolyte. "Worm. What do the scouts say?"

The man groveled on the ground before her but answered. "They don't know what happened, Mistress. Many have failed to return and those remaining report they have found some of their comrades dead. The enemy made sure the scouts did not get near enough to see what was happening."

Ginsar gritted her teeth. They were all fools. It was the purpose of scouts to monitor the enemy by stealth. They should not have been found and killed.

She allowed herself a small smile. One day, she would have a better army than this. Bigger. Better. This was but the beginning of…

The urgency of the situation pressed itself upon her. "Fetch my horse," she instructed the acolyte. "And gather the others."

The man scrambled away and she tried to calm herself. She considered the destruction of Cardoroth, of the sacking and burning of the city. The smoke would rise high into the sky. She had never seen the funeral pyre of an entire city before. That would be something new.

After a while she grew more tranquil, and the acolytes arrived mounted on their black horses. One led her own mount forward, but it was not black like the others. It was milk-white. Long ago, as a child, she remembered her father had given her a pony colored in the same manner. She had loved that pony.

She crushed the memories of her past. They would not help her. She mounted the horse and kicked it forward into a trot. The others followed and they left the army behind.

The grass flowed beneath the hooves of the horses and some sense of privacy returned to her. She hated being crowded in by the army, so many eyes looking at her when she was not looking at them. So much noise as well. This was no substitute for the secrecy of her dark forest, yet it was better. But soon they came to Brand's camp, and she looked around warily.

It was deserted, and had a sense of utter abandonment. The earth ramp set up a perimeter, but nothing was within. Deciding to walk rather than risk injury to the horses by jumping the trench and clambering up the loose soil, she dismounted and left her horse with the acolytes to hold. She brought only three of them with her.

They crossed the rampart and strolled through the remains of the camp. All about them the ground was rutted by wagon wheels, hoof marks and the tread of thousands of boots. The grass was mostly gone, trod into the earth and killed. In the air hung the smell of animal manure and the scent of smoke from the campfires that were stoked up and allowed to burn through the night long after the enemy had gone.

The sun was well up now, and its light glinted from a sword driven into the ground. It was the one thing out of place, the one thing left when all else was taken. Why?

Ginsar saw that attached to the hilt was a leather strap and she paused. What did it mean? But there was only one way to find out.

She gestured to the nearest acolyte. "Fetch the blade."

The man moved away warily, perhaps fearful of some trap of magic set by Brand. But there was none. She would sense it if there were.

Hesitantly, the man approached. He studied the blade momentarily, then cautiously reached down, grasped it and drew its point from the earth.

He returned and handed it to her. Glancing momentarily to the blade she saw that it was of no importance. It was an ordinary sword such as some common soldier would carry. She removed the leather strap and cast the weapon from her.

Burned onto one side of the leather were several words. *We will not surrender.* She knew they came from Brand, and she read them to the others. "What does it mean?" she asked them. "Why has Brand gone?"

"It makes no sense," said one. "They came here to fight."

"It makes sense to me," another said. "They have seen our army now, and they know they cannot beat us. They have returned to hide behind their walls of stone."

"And what do you think?" Ginsar asked the third acolyte.

The man hesitated, but he answered after a moment. "I don't know, Mistress. Brand would not give up ... and yet he is gone. Is it a ruse of some kind? Perhaps. Or maybe he had news from the city of a revolt. You have certainly planted the seeds for that."

"What kind of ruse?" Ginsar asked.

"One to make you leave the superior ground that you have and fight him on more even terms."

"It could be," she said. "Yet why the message? It is so much like him to fight until the end. But why feel the need to tell us? Unless perhaps he had news of a calamity of some sort over and above our army. I think he wanted me to know that no matter what, he would not give in."

588

She stood in silence a moment, considering. The acolytes had not added anything that she had not thought of herself. They were of little use to her, and as always she must bear the responsibility of making all decisions herself. So be it, she thought.

"Well," she said eventually. "We'll not find out standing here all day. Wherever the enemy has gone, and *why ever*, it makes no difference. I'll follow them and destroy them! We march to war!" She strode toward her horse, but called out over her shoulder. "And send out more scouts!"

23. All things Die

Gil sat on a camp chair, slowly sharpening his sword. The rasp of the whetstone cut the air, and he worked with methodical strokes, honing the best edge to the blade that he could. But though his hands were busy, his mind was free to wander.

He looked out beyond the camp. They were in the last of the hills. Or the first of them. Everything was a matter of perspective. But what mattered most was that they defended the route back to the city, and that the landscape was lightly forested. This offered concealment for the army.

"Here come the cavalry captains," Brand said.

The regent was sitting beside him, enjoying what had been a momentary break from the constant stream of decisions and reports. But Gil knew he was waiting on the cavalry report with eagerness.

The three captains saluted.

"What news, gentlemen?"

One of the men stepped forward a pace and answered. "We found many elug scouts during the night. They were all killed."

"Good work. And what about since dawn?"

"A new wave of scouts came out from the army. There are many of them. Fewer now, of course. And we are keeping them at bay. They have not yet slipped close to our position and cannot suspect where we are."

Gil put down his whetstone. "Would Ginsar not deduce our position though by the fact that we are killing her scouts? Wouldn't that indicate we're hiding here?"

"It might," the captain replied. "On the other hand, it could just as easily be taken as normal practice. A retreating army doesn't want the enemy coming up too close behind it."

"Exactly," Brand said. "It could be either, but we can do no more than hope our message convinced her and that she thinks we're returning to Cardoroth."

Gil knew that was true. Brand had rolled the dice, but there was no word yet if the ploy had worked. Their own scouts had not yet returned.

"Good work, gentlemen," Brand said. "Please pass on my commendations to your men. They've had a long and sleepless night."

The captains saluted and left.

Gil watched them depart. They and their men had done a difficult job well, and he felt once more the stirring of pride. The citizens of Cardoroth were good people, but they were often let down by their leadership. He would soon, if Cardoroth survived the coming battle, be in a position to do something about that. He would continue Brand's work of promoting people on merit rather than aristocratic connections.

But that was a problem for the future. First, they must live. He sat back in his chair and glanced at the regent.

"Do you think Ginsar will come after us?"

Brand rubbed his chin. "I don't know. But I *do* know this. Either she will or she won't. Which it will be, I can't control. But, if I had to guess, I'd say she fell for the bait and is even now marching this way."

"I think so too," Gil said. "And it might be a good thing. Our soldiers are now resting and the elugs will reach here after a march. They'll be less fresh than us."

They sat for some while longer in silence. The camp was quiet around them, for the men rested. They had marched hard and fast overnight, but they had come to a good defensive position, and they had blocked the way through to Cardoroth. Ginsar could not go around them except by taking a long route around the hills.

Within the hour though fresh news came to them from the cavalry. Ginsar had indeed left her defensive position and was proceeding toward them.

Brand acted swiftly. He ordered the army to decamp from the thin forest in which they were concealed and into the open. He explained his tactics to Gil as they moved forward.

"We could remain hidden," he said, "but the enemy would be suspicious of terrain that could hide an army and that their scouts were prevented from entering. Ginsar would not march into a trap, and we would be in a stalemate for no purpose other than delay."

Gil had guessed as much, and he knew also where Brand favored the battle to take place. As they came out of the trees they reached a long slope of grass and Brand signaled a stop.

The gradient was not especially steep, but it advantaged the army of Cardoroth over the enemy. That advantage was not so great, however, as to cause Ginsar significant concern. Given her superior numbers she may well attack anyway. At least Brand would hope so.

"The intent is to engage her," Brand said. "We may force a victory here by our greater skill and discipline. I think we will. And I think, having been tricked to leave her own chosen field of battle, she will be angry. She will attack us."

Gil felt unease in the pit of his stomach and his palms were sweaty. He knew a fight was coming, one such as he had never seen before. Brand seemed unconcerned though. This was a mask however, and Gil knew it.

Brand gave instructions. Flags were used to communicate, and horns also. The army soon formed its fighting position.

The front ranks were bolstered by picked regiments of doughty fighters. These were men who had fought before and proven their courage and skill in battle. The left flank was left to the cavalry. They could play a decisive role, for the enemy had no cavalry of their own.

Behind the ranks of the infantrymen were archers. These would fire over the heads of the squatting men before them until the enemy drew close. Then the infantry would stand, lock shields and form a shield wall to halt the advance of the attacking enemy already decimated by the barrage of arrows. So much, at least, was the basic theory. What would happen in reality was yet to be seen. He was not even convinced that Ginsar would attack, though his nausea and sweaty palms told him otherwise.

Brand and the leadership group remained at the rear of the army on a higher part of the rise with a good view of the situation. The Durlin were all around them, but despite their position of relative safety, it would not last. Soldiers liked to see their commanders fight, and fought better themselves when that happened. Brand would at some point do so, and Gil made his own decision in that regard.

The enemy was now visible. They marched toward Cardoroth's army and halted less than half a mile away. Their array was as it had been previously: in the center rode Ginsar and her acolytes, while to either side of Ginsar stood the Lethrin. Then, forming the long outer wings to each side were the great masses of elugs. They milled about with little discipline, and they were short, ungainly and fidgety, but that did not mean they would not fight well.

593

Both armies were still, tension rising between them like a storm that might discharge a lightning bolt at any moment.

Ginsar was seen to make a sign, and from the ranks behind her four horsemen, cloaked and hidden, rode out. One came ahead, taller and larger than the others, and the remaining three followed. These were her heralds, though Gil had an uneasy feeling that they were more than that. No doubt Brand sensed it also, but he called Gil forth to come with him, and Taingern and Shorty also.

They rode forward to meet the heralds at the halfway point between armies. As they neared, Gil saw just how large the lead rider of the enemy was. He was massive, and not a man at all but a Lethrin. Gil had never heard of that race riding before. Nor had he seen a mount of such size either. It too was massive, and its black eyes had a dead look to them.

The two groups came to a stop some ten feet apart. The first enemy rider reached up with a gauntleted hand and pushed back his cowl.

"I am War," he said. His head was protected by a great helm of wrought iron, black as midnight and ornamented with cruel wings. On his arm was strapped a shield. It too was of black iron, spiked in its center. Armor he wore over his massive body, spiked and scaled. And a sword hung to his side, a massive blade that seemed as though it could fell trees, and that the rider possessed the strength to wield it so was apparent.

A black cape hung over War's mighty shoulders, and this seemed to catch the breeze and quiver. Yet Gil realized that it was not so. Two crows fluttered into the air from behind the rider and wheeled above his head.

Brand paid no heed to all of this. He sat relaxed in his saddle. "I'm Brand, leader of those who oppose Ginsar."

War inclined his head gravely. "Of you, I have heard. And I wonder why you lead the rabble behind you to destruction. But perhaps you do not know there is a choice. Kneel before me now and swear allegiance. You and your army may join us, and we shall conquer the world."

Brand's black stallion grew restless, but the regent patted his neck and calmed him. "And to whom would I swear allegiance? You or Ginsar?"

War laughed, the sound muffled by the great helm. "You know the answer to that, warrior."

"Indeed I do. And you should know that I will not forsake Cardoroth, nor Alithoras. I will fight, and so too will the army behind me."

War answered, and his voice betrayed neither anger nor surprise. It was merely cold. "Then you shall die, and every soldier in your army also."

Brand did not seem perturbed. "All things die."

"Not I. Nor my companions."

War made a gesture and the three riders behind him came forward. One by one they removed their hoods. The first was a young man, and his face was bright and his eyes clear. Golden-haired he was, and tall and slim. He moved with the grace of the warrior born, and his muscles rippled beneath well-tanned skin. Yet as he moved Gil saw knives in his back, blood constantly dripping from the wounds. It was Betrayal.

The next that Gil looked at was no living man. Where a head should have been there was only a skull. Tufted hair sprouted from it. Skin clung to it in patches and hung loose in others. Maggots fell to the ground from squirming orbs where the eyes had once been. Yet though no eyes were left, still the orbs, writhing pits of horror that they were, locked on Gil's own gaze. This was Death, returned to Alithoras though previously defeated by Brand.

Gil knew what he would see next, but turned to the last rider anyway. He seemed a tottery old man. His back was twisted and hunched, his eyes red and rheumy. His gnarled hands trembled with palsy, and the skin that covered them was thin, hanging like ragged cloth from little more than bone. But power was in the man's gaze, power that took the breath away. For this was the horseman Time. And he too had once been defeated.

Gil's mind reeled. How could they defeat an enemy that returned from defeat itself?

He glanced at the regent, and saw there was a tight smile on his face. "I shall repeat myself," Brand said. "All things die. No matter their strength. The good and the bad alike. Those who desire death and those who do not. Even worlds grow cold and spin into dust. Tell your mistress we do not surrender. Or rather, tell your slave."

War inclined his head. With no further word he turned away and beckoned the other horsemen to follow. A few moments Brand watched them go, and then he rode back to the army in silence. There was nothing to say.

Once there they took up their positions on the rise above the army once more. Brand called Gil and Elrika to him.

"The battle will begin now. I want the two of you to stay close to me, and to each other."

They both nodded solemnly, but neither answered. At that moment the enemy charged. Across the grass one half of their army raced, churning it into dust as tens of thousands of boots pounded the ground, and the drumming of their footfalls and clash of sword on shield sounded as thunder.

"Ginsar is a fool," Brand said over the tumult. "There was no need to charge until they came within range of our bows. It serves only to tire a soldier before battle is joined."

"And why hold part of her army back?" Gil asked.

"This is but a test before the day is done, and she does not care how many soldiers she loses. She will wait until tomorrow to come against us in full, and she does not think she can lose."

Wise or unwise, the enemy rushed toward them and the thunder of their coming was a noise Gil would never forget. Perhaps the fear of it was another reason why she ordered an early charge, and he was not so certain that Cardoroth's soldiers would stand against the enemy. There might not be a tomorrow.

As the enemy came within range a new noise sounded. The foot soldiers of Cardoroth kneeled. Behind them the archers drew their bows and sent forth a great volley of arrows that blackened the air and hissed like an angry wind.

Elugs fell. Some were killed by arrow, others merely wounded. But all died as the great army surged forward treading over those who fell and churning the earth red with their blood.

On the enemy came, and another volley of arrows thickened the air. More than a dozen times this occurred, and it took a dreadful toll upon the elugs. At the last, the bowmen withdrew and the spearmen cast a shivering mass of javelins that hit the enemy like a wall.

The enemy faltered, for the javelins were heavy and thrown with power. Yet after the wounded fell momentum reasserted itself and the charging army surged on.

Now, the foot soldiers of Cardoroth stood. The first rank stepped forward a pace and locked their shields together into a wall. They did not fight as individuals, but as a unit of men. Shields on the left, a short sword stabbing forward on the right above the wall or through small gaps to the next shield.

The two forces crashed together in a horrendous clash of weapons. Screams and battle cries tore the air. Blood sprayed. And men and elugs died.

On the elugs came, a mad rush of them climbing over their dead and attacking in a mad fury. They wished to win, to defeat the men of Cardoroth in the first rush and sweep them into oblivion. Under the fury of the assault the front line of Cardoroth gave way a little, stepping back against the onslaught. And many of them died. But as they fell others stepped in from behind plugging up the shield wall once more.

The line buckled, but did not break. Then, slowly and surely, the line straightened and formed an impenetrable barrier. The momentum of the elug charge was lost, and now they died in greater numbers.

Far away and dim, Gil heard a horn blow. It was the signal for retreat and had come from the enemy leadership. The elugs, attacking in a mad fury one moment turned and fled the next. Away they streamed, and clouds of arrows followed them. It was the price to pay for retreat, because shields held to the front did not protect against arrows in the back.

The space between the two armies was empty now, save for the dead and dying. Brand sat upon his horse, and strain was on his face. Gil thought he would signal for a charge of his own, that he would counterattack now that the enemy had retreated. But the regent let out a slow breath and smiled grimly.

"The sorceress made an error, yet it was not so great as it seemed. Nearly I went after her, but her force still outnumbers ours, and she has not yet committed the

Lethrin nor the Four Horsemen to the fight. This she hoped I would do, and then we would face our greatest enemies while at the same time giving up our advantage of ground."

"I thought you would," Shorty said.

"And I also," Taingern agreed.

Brand relaxed. "I nearly did. And perhaps we would have won too. But perhaps not."

They watched as stretcher-bearers went out and assisted wounded men. At the same time soldiers moved out onto the field retrieving arrows and javelins. But they came back soon as a stir went through the enemy.

Gil strained to see. "Something is happening, but I can't see what."

Brand also was looking hard, one hand shading his eyes from the sun. "She is sending the Lethrin now, I think. I expected her to wait until tomorrow."

In a few moments Brand was proven correct. A thousand strong the Lethrin stepped forth. They did not run yet, for they were better disciplined than the elugs, or else Ginsar had learned from her previous error.

They formed a wedge, pointing themselves at the men of Cardoroth, and it was clear what they would attempt. Using their strength and momentum, they would pierce the shield-wall of Cardoroth's soldiers and drive through the ranks. Then, the elugs would follow. Should that happen, they would win the battle.

The Lethrin wedge moved forward. Behind them several thousand elugs gathered, less disciplined perhaps, but if the Lethrin broke through the shield wall the elugs would pour through after them, widening the gap and ensuring it could not close. Then Ginsar's whole army would charge.

The marching pace of the Lethrin grew into a trot as they approached. And as they came into range of the bowmen they broke into a run. At that moment Brand ordered a flag signal given. It was an instruction to the cavalry.

Cardoroth's horsemen streamed forth from the left flank. They were positioned here for they were right handed, and they carried long and heavy spears. This was their weapon in a charge, and they streamed forth, spears ready to strike the enemy to their right.

Each of the cavalrymen also carried a curved sabre for fighting in a melee when their spears would not be useful. But their role here was to use the speed of their charge and the added power that gave them to harry the Lethrin. That, no doubt, was Brand's plan. But Ginsar had foreseen it and the elugs behind the Lethrin would have the role of protecting the backs of their massive companions while they tried to break through Cardoroth's shield wall.

The Lethrin wedge hurled toward the men of Cardoroth, and the stamp of two thousand booted feet rumbled over the earth like thunder. Arrows darkened the sky, and the hiss of their flight was as a sudden gust of wind. The storm was about to break, and Gil felt the fear of the men on the shield wall. Could they stand against such a charge as this?

The volleys of arrows had little effect on the Lethrin. Their skin was tough like the stone from the mountains in which they had been born. Yet here and there one fell, stricken in the eye or neck. More succumbed to the javelins. But not enough. They could be killed, but not easily. On they came, mostly unaffected by the hail of missiles, and they smashed into the shield wall.

Screams tore the air. Men died and the Lethrin fell upon Cardoroth's soldiers like a hammer blow. Where they hit, the line dissolved, the first rank falling as wheat beneath a scythe. So too the second rank. And also the

600

third. But the charge of the Lethrin slowed and men fought them now. They died, but the Lethrin died also.

Gil watched in horror. There was so much death, and the Lethrin were mighty beyond the ability of men to combat. Yet still the men fought, and working together they brought down their great opponents gradually. But it would not be enough.

"Watch!" called Brand, and his arm swept out to point at the cavalry. Gil had forgotten them, transfixed by the Lethrin, yet now he looked further back.

The cavalry neared the rearguard of elugs. These had turned and prepared to fight, but at the last moment scattered and fled before the charge of horses. Few were the warriors who had the heart and skill to stand before a mounted attack.

The elugs raced away, leaving open the way to the back of the Lethrin wedge. The horsemen thundered toward it, spears held high in their right hand, guiding the horses with their left hand on the reins and their legs.

With a battle-cry that tore at the sky and rose above the clash of war, the cavalry struck. These spears were not for throwing, but long and heavy, and driven by the momentum of the horses they pierced the stone-like flesh of the Lethrin and killed them by the score.

The first of the cavalry to hit them rode past, and the next in line had their turn. Yet Gil watched as the first riders began to wheel around. They would ride in a circle, keeping a constant and deadly pressure on the Lethrin.

The rear of the Lethrin wedge was forced to turn and fight the cavalry. This stalled their forward momentum. The battle raged on, and some of the Lethrin, though impaled by spears, leapt forward in their death throes and dragged riders from their mounts.

Gil looked at Brand, and he saw the regent was pale-faced, and his fingers white on his clenched fists.

Brand did not take his eyes off the battle, but he spoke. "Watch Ginsar," he said. "What matters now is that she does not act swiftly."

Gil looked out over the battle to the enemy ranks in the distance. He saw movement there, and picked out what he thought was Ginsar's tall figure among the acolytes who milled about her. Intuitively, he knew exactly what Brand meant. If she acted decisively and ordered a charge against the cavalry she could disrupt their attack on the Lethrin. But had the tactics of mounted spearmen caught her by surprise? She would likely have been expecting them to use sabers or perhaps light bows. Neither would have been greatly effective against the Lethrin.

The battle drew Gil's eyes again. The Lethrin continued to press forward despite their losses. The shield wall wavered, beginning to buckle backward. There were not enough men to keep coming forward and fill the gaps left by the slain.

Garling stalked over to Brand. "Send reinforcements, fool! Or we are lost!"

"No," Brand said, turning his cold gaze on the general. "Ginsar is waiting for that. If I peel men away from the flanks, she will attack. We would not turn her back then."

"If you don't, then we are lost anyway. Once the Lethrin are through our army will flee!"

"You are wrong, general," Gil said. "These men have courage! Look and see!"

Even as Garling debated the matter, the men of Cardoroth rallied. They did not panic. They did not flee. They changed their tactics and men came forward with javelins. These they did not throw, but rather used them as stabbing weapons, driving forward with their bodyweight behind them.

The Lethrin, assailed on all sides and suffering heavy losses, gathered in close together and attempted a retreat. But that was a fatal error, for now that the men of Cardoroth saw that they had the upper hand they redoubled their efforts. Between the ranks of infantry and the cavalry, the Lethrin were slain to the last man. He went down with a great bellow and three spears through him.

The cavalry wheeled away and returned to their position on the left flank. From the whole army erupted a mighty sound of yelling and cheers. They had survived. They had defeated a charge of Lethrin, which few armies had ever done. It was an act of defiance against death, and an act of defiance against the enemy who wanted to overrun them but had failed.

Garling said nothing. Gil looked at Brand as the sun sent westering rays of red light across the sky as it set. "Will they come at us during the night?"

The words were addressed to the regent, but it was the White Lady who spoke. "No. But tomorrow will be bad beyond your imagining."

24. The Prince!

Gil slept poorly. There was much noise from the army as they celebrated into the night, singing and cheering. And the words of the White Lady proved correct; no enemy attack was initiated through the night. Yet her other words haunted him: *tomorrow will be bad beyond your imagining.*

He rose in the predawn light, unrested and worried. He dressed, and then donned his cumbersome mail shirt and a plain helm. He had one of silver, decorated and inlaid with threads of gold, but should the worst happen it would not prevent a sword from splitting his skull any better than the plain one.

He met the others in the main room of the tent. They were somber. Each one of them knew that the battle would be won or lost today. Each one of them knew that they might die. They also understood that if they did not defeat Ginsar, tens of thousands of innocent people would be slain, and the city razed to the ground. Somberness was appropriate.

There was no speech from Brand. There was no attempt to lift their spirits or distract them from the situation. "Good luck to one and all." He said simply. And he meant it. That was enough.

They moved out of the tent, and Gil felt Elrika's hand clasp his own. "Good luck," she whispered into his ear.

Despite the movement of men all around the camp, there was a stillness in the air. The last stars faded from sight, and the leadership group took up their positions on the rise above the army of Cardoroth.

The sun rose. It had set as a fiery ball of red light the evening before. Now it slipped above the horizon, golden and bathing the east with a pale glow. The sky gradually turned blue. The grass became green and the air was fresh upon Gil's face. It could be his last day to see and feel such things, and he looked about him at the wonder of the land.

But the elug army had its own view of the world, and it was nothing like his. Over the gulf of trampled grass that separated the two armies a single drum began to beat. And then the chanting of the enemy began. The cruel words had been heard outside the walls of many besieged cities before this, and on open fields of battle too. The words carried to Gil, and he knew and understood them. He feared them also.

Ashrak ghùl skar! Skee ghùl ashrak!
Skee ghùl ashrak! Ashrak ghùl skar!

The chant flowed, seemingly without beginning or end. The drum hastened. Stamping boots thundered, swords clashed against shields, and dread thrummed through the air.

Death and destruction! Blood and death!
Blood and death! Death and destruction!

Thus chanted the elugs, and their dark words seemed to fill the world and block out sun and sky and grass. But Gil straightened even as he heard them. He was the son of kings and queens, and he would not be bowed by the dark.

His hands clenched into fists and his eyes shone. This was a day like no other, and it seemed that his whole life

605

had hurtled toward it. Afterward, he would be dead. Or he would become the king his people needed.

Beside him Brand gave a signal. A score of carnyx horns sounded. The men who bore them were tall, and the bronze horns matched them foot for foot. The soldiers held them high, the mouths of the instruments twelve feet above ground, and from their metal mouths issued an unearthly moan that sounded like an otherworldly beast.

The elug army gave a final roar, and then they rushed forward screaming. None were held back this time, and everything hung now on the outcome of this final battle.

It was no measured charge that surged across the field toward the men of Cardoroth. There were no marching ranks, no phalanxes, no shield walls. What came against them was a surge of screeching enemies, waving swords and clubs, a primaeval wave of destructive hatred.

As had happened before, the front ranks of Cardoroth's army knelt and the archers behind them unleashed swift-flighted death. Elugs fell in writhing heaps to the ground but the rest came on. Now javelins tore into them, but still the enemy rushed forward, screaming their hatred and heedless of their slain comrades.

The seething mass crashed against the shield wall. The men of Cardoroth stood their ground. Gil glanced along the line and saw that everywhere a wave of elugs hit it, sought to tear it down, and died in the attempt. Yet the mass of elugs kept clambering forward. The air seemed like a crimson mist while blood sprayed and spurted. But the shield wall held and the enemy spent themselves against it.

Nevertheless, they still came on and the men of Cardoroth grew weary. When the captains could, they signaled by whistle for the front rank of their units to fall back and the next rank to step forward. But moments of respite were few.

The elugs gave no quarter. The men of Cardoroth did not expect it. This was a fight to the death and only one army would walk from the field.

"There," Brand pointed. "The line is bucking."

Gil looked to the right side of the battle where Brand indicated, but saw nothing. But the regent was proved correct, his eye for battle keener. In moments, Gil saw it too. The shield wall began to give way. Yet even as he watched the soldiers of Cardoroth rallied and pressed forward once more.

Brand looked over at him. "Do you feel it?"

"What?"

"The malevolence. Sorcery is being used. It empowers the enemy and weakens us."

Gil realized it was true. It was something that had been on the edge of his consciousness, but subtle enough that it did not bring attention to itself. Perhaps it came from the Four Horsemen, but more likely it was Ginsar's work.

The line showed signs of buckling again in the same region as before.

"Shall we use magic of our own to oppose her?" Gil asked.

Brand shook his head. "Not of the sort you mean, but of another kind. Between Ginsar, her acolytes and the Horsemen we are outnumbered. We must preserve our magic for when we need it most. Courage is called for now, a means to give the men heart."

Brand was about to ride into battle to rally the soldiers, and Gil knew it and understood why. But he reached out and put a hand on his shoulder.

607

"No. They have seen you fight before in other battles. But they have not seen me. And I am their prince, their king to be."

Gil tightened the strap of his helm and then mounted his horse. Without another word he galloped down to the line on the right side. There he handed his reins to an archer and drew his sword.

A cold thrill ran through him. There were no Durlin now. No guards. No protection. This was a battle, and this was what it was to look death in the eye. But he was needed here, and without facing death a man cannot live.

He pushed forward, and his voice rang out above the clash of battle. "Hold the line, men of Cardoroth! We'll teach these elugs to fear us for a thousand years!"

They were not the finest words he had ever spoken, but they had the effect he wanted. Some of the men in the rear ranks turned and looked at him. And they knew who he was.

A cry went up. "The prince!" some called. Others yelled "Gilcarist," using his full name. More heads turned in his direction. More men called out, rallying to his name.

He pressed forward, and the soldiers let him through. Before he realized it, he was at the front and a man died before him, his throat torn out by a curved elug blade and bright blood spilling onto the trampled ground.

A soldier from the second rank jumped into the gap, holding back the swelling tide of enemies that sought to overrun the defense.

Gil bent down and swept up the shield of the dead soldier. He ran his left forearm through the straps and fixed it in place. Then he drew his sword. It was a longer blade than the soldiers carried, meant for swordfights rather than the simple jabbing use of a shield wall, but it would do.

Around him men called out. "The prince! The prince!" The cry was loud now, taken up by many mouths, and it surged behind him when another man died a little to his left and he leaped forward to take the dead man's place.

Gil stood in the front rank now. His shield was up, locked in close to the man at his left. Against him came a wave of elugs, all snarling faces, hideous cries and bent swords slashing. Gil felt a blade smash into his shield, felt the weight of the elug trying to bear him back. His sword jabbed out. The elug screamed. Blood gushed from his groin. One of his own kind pulled him down and leapt into the gap. He brought a club to bear, a massive thing of gnarled timber, and it heaved through the air at Gil's feet.

Gil lowered his shield. It blocked the blow, but his head was now exposed. A second elug slashed at it, but Gil ran him through. The first elug heaved high his club again, but the man to Gil's right jabbed a sword into the side of his neck. The elug screamed, and in turn went down like the one he had replaced moments before.

The battle went on. The sound of sword striking shield and the screams of agony and hate filled the air. But Gil noticed it less than the stink of death, of opened entrails and the pungent odor of urine. This was battle. This was death, and for all the horror his mind went swiftly numb. All he knew was block and jab, but some small part of his mind also knew the line was being pushed back and would soon buckle again.

"Hold!" he cried. "Hold for Cardoroth!"

All about him he sensed the desperation of the men. They were tired and weary, sick of death. But they gave just that little bit more of themselves. And the tide turned. They pressed forward a few steps. The elugs washed against them like a spent wave now, the surge of

609

their hatred sweeping along to another part of the shield wall. For the moment, this section was in less danger of being overrun than others.

Gil stepped back when he could and a man behind him slipped seamlessly into his place. All around him men cheered. They knew it was his first taste of battle. And he had survived it, becoming one of them in a way that nothing else could ever achieve. Suddenly, he understood better why these men loved Brand and trusted him, and why the regent in his turn felt the same way.

He cleaned his bloody sword on his trousers, for he had no other means of doing so, and nearly vomited. Then he made his way back through stretcher-bearers carrying dead and wounded men. He came to his horse, where the archer who still held the reins clapped him good-naturedly on the back. "If we survive this, you'll make a fine king," the man said.

It was the sort of thing that no one would ever normally say to a prince, yet it was not out of place at this moment.

"We'll survive," Gil said. He swept his arm out toward the ranks of soldiers. "With men such as these, how can we lose?"

He nudged his horse into a trot and made his way back to the leadership group. He felt their eyes upon him: grim but proud.

He dismounted, and silently Elrika handed him a rag. He took it and looked down at his sword arm. It was slick with blood. He knew his face was spattered red as well. He nearly vomited again, but instead rested his shield on the ground and methodically cleaned himself as best he could without water. He looked again at Elrika. She did not speak, but returned his gaze with somber eyes.

The regent broke the silence. "The blood of your line runs true," he said. "You did well. The shield wall would have collapsed had you not buoyed the warriors."

"Battle is fickle," Shorty said. "Minutes ago we faced defeat, but now we hold strong and the enemy throws all their might against us without success. Perhaps we should advance and attack them in our turn. We might route them just now."

Brand considered it, but then slowly shook his head. "It's too early. We have yet to see the Four Riders enter the fray."

The White Lady stirred uneasily. "It will not be long."

25. Day of the Durlin

The battle raged on. The elugs swarmed against the shield wall, but they did not break it. It weakened though, and at times Brand went down to fight. At other times Gil returned to the fray. Each time the soldiers rallied and held off the enemy.

In Gil's mind, the cold fear of defeat and death still had a grip, yet slowly the thought crept into his mind that Cardoroth could win the battle. Against an enemy who outnumbered them, they had held their own. And the elugs died in greater numbers than the men did. The tide had begun to turn with the destruction of the Lethrin, and it kept flowing now in Cardoroth's favor.

But no sooner had he begun to hope for triumph than a dread seeped into his very bones. A sense of wrongness wrapped itself about him and infused the air.

"It begins," the White Lady said. "See there, behind the battle the Four Riders are moving?"

"I see them," Brand answered. "And I will go to meet them." He turned to Shorty. "Will you come with me?"

"I wouldn't miss it."

The regent looked at Gil. "It is not wise for both of us to battle at once. You must stay here. And you Taingern as well. I leave you both in charge."

Taingern nodded. Brand and Shorty prepared to ride down to the lines, and the White Lady spoke. "Not all is as it seems, I think. But the Horsemen are moving, and I feel them prepare some sorcery. I must oppose them." She looked at Gil. "Be careful, young prince. Your hour is coming soon."

She mounted her white horse and they rode down to the back of the army. The three of them would oppose the Four Horsemen, and Gil thought he should be with them. But though the Horsemen had moved, they had not yet entered the battle.

Tainrik watched them go. "I think I'd better help," he said.

Gil was not sure that the scout was well enough to fight. But loyalty to Brand drove him, and it was not Gil's place to stop him. "Be careful," he advised.

After they had all left, a cool wind began to blow. Gil paid it no heed, but after a while it turned very cold and his unease stirred. The horses, tethered close by, stamped their hooves and flicked their ears. Then the wind died and the air grew deathly still. A white mist gathered on the ground and sent wavering tendrils upward.

"Sorcery!" Gil cried, and the skin on the back of his neck tightened. He went to draw his sword but discovered the mist was about him and had suddenly tightened like chains cast over his arms and body. He could not move. He felt the magic within him come alive, but it fluttered and died down again as though some influence of the mist dampened it like water on fire.

It was then that he saw forms within the swirling mist. They rose upward, groping figures of terror driven by dark magic. Drùghoth they were called. Sendings. He remembered their description from Brand's teachings and what they were capable of.

He could not move, chained by sorcery as he was, but he could see. The drùghoth came for him, rising up like dead men from earthen graves and lurching in his direction.

But Taingern was suddenly there, and beside him Elrika and the Durlin. To his surprise the generals also

613

sprang into action, drawing their swords and standing between him and the sendings.

Dozens of wraithlike creatures pressed forward, and the vaporous fog eddied around them. The creatures glided on tall legs and their long arms reached forward like creeping fingers of mist. Worst of all, the drùghoth had faces: gaunt, cold-eyed and cruel. A pale light lit their hollow cheeks and glimmered silver-white in their trailing hair.

Taingern leaped toward them and yelled the battle cry of the Durlin: *Death or infamy!* Elrika was only a step behind him and then the Durlin and generals charged as well.

Taingern attacked. His sword sliced and cut and stabbed. The sendings were more solid than they appeared, and Gil heard them cry as the Durlindrath's sword bit into them. So too with the other defenders. Yet though the wounds drew forth shuddering screams, yet their cries came as though from a great distance, and the creatures did not die. Instead of falling, they came on, slowed but not deterred.

Gil struggled to free himself from the sorcerous chains, but the cold of them bit through his flesh and stilled his magic each time. He watched in horror as Durlin after Durlin died, sacrificing their lives so that he had a chance to live.

One of the drùghoth slipped between the thinning ranks of guards and came for him. Gil saw his death in the creature's pale eyes as it reached for him, but suddenly Elrika was there, the ancient sword in her hand flashing.

Three times she struck it. The sending shuddered and screamed, but did not die. Then with a wicked slash of its clawed hand it struck her back, raking long nails across her left side and sending her spinning.

Once more Gil tried to summon his magic, but failed. He knew he must try something new, and instead of summoning his own power he reached forth with his mind into the surroundings. He felt the fog roiling about him, thick now, billowing like a cloud, but beyond it was something else. Beyond the sorcery he felt the warmth of the sun, and he felt that he could use that.

Elrika stumbled, but she righted herself and swept her blade at the drùghoth's legs. It lurched back, and Gil felt the sun and drew its warmth to him.

Light flared. The fog rolled back. With a trembling movement, the magic within Gil stirred once more. It became one with the light of the sun, the sunlight one with it. Then Gil summoned all his will and let fire burst from his body.

The sorcerous chains fell with a screech like tortured metal and then hissed away in a cloud of steam. Gil drew the magic to his hands, feeling the marks on his palm throb, and he lashed out at the creature struggling with Elrika. It screamed, and then fell apart and drifted into the thinning fog.

Gil scattered his magic around him, feeling it grow and expand, feeling it obliterate the sendings and burn off the last remnants of fog. When he was done, he drew in a breath and let the magic falter. Looking around, he saw the devastation that the sorcerous attack of Ginsar had wrought.

Only he, Taingern and a handful of Durlin still stood. Elrika lay sprawled on the ground close by, blood smearing her clothes. He felt a sense of dread, and was about to go to her, but instinct warned him that the attack was not yet over.

The last of the fog hissed away in a puff of steam and a wave of heat rolled over the bloodied grass. A figure shimmered, tall and ethereal. At first Gil thought it was

615

Ginsar, but as it took form he realized it was not. This was a thing of nightmare instead.

It was a summoning of fire, standing some ten feet tall and towering above the men who stood there and watched it in awe. Smoke rose from beneath its cloven hooves. Ash fell from it in a shimmer whenever it moved. Its eyes burned and shifted like pools of molten metal, white-hot and deadly. In its giant hands it gripped two swords that flickered like tongues of red flame. And the head was crowned with curved horns that sparked fire from their tips.

The summoning took a step forward. Taingern moved to block its coming, and the handful of Durlin gathered behind him.

"Stand not in my way, mortal."

The voice of the summoning throbbed like the bellows of a furnace and smoke curled from its flared nostrils.

"Leave this place," Taingern answered. "It is defended."

The creature looked down on him. "You cannot defend against such as I. Flee, or I shall send your soul to an eternity of burning pain and agony. Flee!"

"Eat dung and die," Taingern said quietly.

Gil had never heard Taingern speak like that. And he saw that the man trembled all over, but also that he did not step away.

The menace of the summoning was a palpable force. The air was alive with it, and it grew. Gil felt the pressure of it, felt a primal fear so strong that he worried it would still his heart. It beat against him in waves, and he saw the Durlin fall to their knees, overcome. So too did he fall.

But not Taingern. The Durlindrath had stood his ground against threat and sorcery both. Not only that.

His sword was in his hand and he leaped forward to attack.

The twin swords of the creature flashed through the air, cutting arcs of fire. Taingern dodged and ducked, then leaped high and rammed his own blade into the neck of the summoning.

With a howl of sparks and smoke the creature wheeled away. But it lashed out with its blades again. They whistled through the air like lashes of fire. Taingern leaped and ducked, coming at the thing with courage and skill. The blades sought him out. He dodged and weaved, smaller and more agile than his enemy.

Several more times the Durlindrath hammered home blows to the summoning, but nothing stopped it. Taingern's white surcoat was scorched and smoldering, but he himself had avoided contact with his enemy's blades.

But it could not last. Almost like a dancer Taingern moved about his opponent, spinning, withdrawing, leaping in to attack. Yet one error would see him dead.

The error came. Taingern ducked left to avoid a massive blow. He was about to step in and deliver another strike but the creature had foreseen his intent. With a heave of its giant body it kneed the Durlindrath and sent him flying to land on the ground several feet away. There he lay, his sword fallen from his grip, and though in great pain he tried to rise.

Stepping forward, the massive summoning trod on him, smoke billowing from the cloven hoof. It came on toward Gil then, and Taingern lay still behind it.

The remaining Durlin tried to rise, but they did not have the strength of will of their leader. The flaming swords of the creature cut them down. Gil watched, stricken to the core of his being and wondering if death would be a merciful release from what he had seen. Everyone had died to try to protect him.

The creature moved toward him. In his wake, he left tread marks of singed grass. With horror, Gil realized that Elrika lay before him. She might be dead, but even so he could not allow this abomination to trample her body before it killed him.

Some flicker of defiance stirred within him. It rose up, and it contended with the dark sorcery that weakened his mind and body. The creature drew closer, a massive and ponderous thing whose shadow darkened the ground.

Gil remained terrified, but he staggered up and came between the summoning and Elrika. Like a pillar of shadow and flame the thing stood before him, and it heaved high both its flickering swords.

Time slowed. Gil sensed death hover above him, but from behind the summoning there was movement. Somehow Taingern had risen. Blood soaked his surcoat, but he staggered forward and reaching upward thrust his blade into the back of the creature's neck.

The summoning howled, but not even this was a killing blow. It spun around, knocking Taingern backward with one arm. The Durlindrath went flying, but landed and rolled groggily to his feet. The creature strode toward him.

Yet in the howl of pain that the thing had vented Gil heard hope. It had not been a cry of the creature, but rather it was the combined voice of many men sounding as one. And finally Gil understood the nature of the sorcery. It was not a summoning, but a creation of dark magic, made of the thought and directed by the purpose of Ginsar's acolytes. This was how they had pinned him down and held him in chains. Together, they were too many for him. Defying the creature, the sum total of

618

their power, was too hard. But one by one would be a different thing.

His sword was of no use to him, and Gil let it drop to the ground. He held high both his palms, and from them he allowed his own magic to flare. Tendrils of power shot forth and wrapped around the creature. But it was not an attack.

Gil worked quickly. He felt the nature of the creature, sensed its powers and from what it had been made. Lastly, and most importantly, he found the thin trail of sorcery that commanded it from afar. He concentrated and dived deep into the feeling that gave him.

His body slumped to the ground and he felt it no more. But as a glimmer of spirit and magic he raced down the trail of sorcery and into the midst of the acolytes.

The acolytes sat in a circle, chanting. In the center of the circle he formed an image of himself, clad as a warrior with a sword that glittered like starlight. It was made of his memories of the constellation of Halathgar, which was fitting because it was the Sign of Carnhaina, their deadliest enemy, and he was her heir.

The chanting faltered as they saw and knew him. But it was too late. He leapt among them, sword flashing, wreaking death and destruction with a cold fury he had never felt before. They died swiftly as they tried to rise and flee, the last thing they saw being the blaze of his eyes and the glitter of his starry blade.

He sensed the fire creature back in his camp billow away into sparks and smoke as the sorcery that sustained it died. Casting his eyes about he saw the dead bodies of the acolytes, but of Ginsar there was no sign. It was foolish, for she was stronger than he, but he wished she were here so that he could challenge her, stronger or not.

One of the acolytes moved to Gil's side. The man tried to stand and flee, but Gil's anger was not spent. The glittering sword in his hand flashed. Blood sprayed and the man's head toppled from his body.

Gil looked around once more. The acolytes had chosen a place to work their magic that was distant from the battle. He saw it now from the other side, and he wondered what damage he could do appearing behind them. But he felt his strength fade also, for the magic he had worked came at a price. All magic did.

Weariness flooded through him. The sword faded away and so too the image of himself that he had made. In spirit form he fled back to his body.

Back in the camp his eyes flickered open. He scrambled up to a standing position, but swayed with dizziness and fatigue. Looking around he saw that Taingern knelt on the ground, gasping and pressing his hands on his ribs. Some of them must be broken from the weight of the creature stepping on him. All around him were the dead bodies of the Durlin. And the three generals also. They could have fled, but had not. They were better men than he had thought, but he would never be able to tell them so now.

He heard a groan behind him and turned. Elrika was struggling to her feet. She had survived! A flood of relief washed over him, but with it came a towering anger. Ginsar had wrought this destruction, and she would pay for it. He swore it would be so, no matter the cost.

26. This is the Hour

Brand, Shorty and Tainrik stood in the first rank, playing their part in the shield wall. They fought side by side, the enemy falling to them, the men around them rallying. It was at this point that the Four Horsemen directed their malevolence, and all about him Brand sensed the fear of the men. But they did not succumb, would not succumb while he was there.

A little further back he sensed the White Lady. She had invoked her own magic, and it spread through the ranks of Cardoroth's soldiers. It shielded them from the worst sorcery of the Horsemen, though she was careful to mute their power only, rather than confront them. That time was close, he felt it drawing on apace, but it was not quite here.

A wave of elugs rolled up against the wall. Their hate-filled eyes gleamed, madness glinting in them. The Horsemen drove them on, lashing them into a frenzy with their sorcery, and the elugs, even when wounded to death and their entrails spilled upon the earth, still crawled at their enemies and tried to stab their feet.

"For Cardoroth!" Brand yelled. And though the men around him were near to panic, yet still they fought by his side and did not retreat. Moreover, the longer this went on, and the more the enemy threw themselves against the shield wall with all they had, yet failed to break it, the greater grew the confidence of the men.

The line that had been buckling straightened and the fury that drove the elugs lessened. Still they were driven by sorcery, but their fear was growing for sorcery could not blind them entirely to the destruction wrought upon their own army. The frenzy of their attack subsided.

Within the midst of the enemy horns sounded, and Brand knew their purpose. It was a retreat. Ginsar had thrown everything against them and failed. Soon would come a reckoning. The army of Cardoroth now outnumbered the elugs, and the spirit of victory infused them.

The elugs streamed away. The hiss of swift-flighted arrows followed them, killing them as they fled. Brand withdrew from the shield wall, and Shorty and Tainrik joined him. Blood spattered the scout, and some of his stitched wounds bled again.

The regent shook his head. "You should still be resting, old friend."

"Time enough to rest when we've won," Tainrik answered.

The White Lady interrupted their conversation. "I'm sorry, Brand. The push by the Four Horsemen was a ruse. They are yet to unleash their full power, but while we were occupied, the enemy has struck. Somehow, Gil has survived the attack."

Brand felt a chill within his bones. Everything depended on Gil, and he had left him alone. Quickly he strode to his horse, mounted and galloped back up the slope. The others followed close behind.

He saw Gil from a distance. But all around him were bodies. The enemy had wrought havoc, and dread settled over him.

As he drew closer, that dread intensified. There were few survivors here. Smoke coiled from dead bodies, and he knew the Durlin were dead. All of them except for Taingern. And he looked badly injured. Brand could tell from a mere glance that he had broken ribs.

Brand reached them and leapt of his black stallion. He took in the scene. The stench of sorcery still hung in the air, but he felt lòhrengai also. Somehow Gil had found a way to beat opponents that were stronger than he. The prince seemed angry, an emotion that Brand had rarely seen on his face. But Brand understood why. Yet there was relief too, for Elrika had survived as well as Taingern.

The prince turned to him. Anger burned in his eyes, but there was a coolness too. In that moment he reminded Brand of Gilhain, the old king. The blood ran true in his veins.

"It is time to attack," Gil said softly.

Brand answered solemnly. "It shall be as you wish, Gilcarist. And we will make them pay."

He turned then to Elrika. "I don't know what happened here, but I see that your wounds are to the front and not on the back. You earned the sword you carry today, and he who bore it first would be proud of you. For today, you are a hero worthy to walk by his side. And in the days to come, you shall also be a Durlin. If you wish it."

The girl turned her gaze to Gil. "I wish it," she answered.

Brand put a hand on Taingern's shoulder, but he had no words for him. It was Taingern who spoke.

"They gave everything they had," the Durlindrath said.

Brand knew who he meant. He looked at the dead Durlin, men that he had known and worked with. They were his warrior brothers. "We will avenge them," he said to Taingern.

They mounted their horses then. Even Taingern. The broken ribs would hurt now, but he could still fight and would not hang back. Tomorrow, he would be barely able to move. But by tomorrow victory would be theirs, or they would all be dead.

Brand withdrew his staff from where it was tied on his saddle bags. Battle was coming now, and one of magic as well as blades. The purpose of the White Lady was drawing to fulfillment, and so too Gil's destiny.

They cantered back to the army, and Brand gave his orders. Signals were issued, and the cavalry set upon a charge. They thundered off from the left flank to sweep their spears across the enemy.

The elug army had retreated, but they had not fled the field. They were in disarray though, and the cavalry, on reaching them, killed and scattered many in the front ranks as they passed.

Brand watched as the cavalry pivoted neatly on the other flank of the army and swept across them again. This attack was not so successful. Many of the riders' spears were broken, and the men fought with their sabers. This brought them into closer combat with the enemy and some were killed. Also, the elugs had brought forth their archers. This too began to cause devastation.

Brand signaled for the cavalry to retreat and return to the flank once more. At the same time he also signaled for the army to march. It was time to attack.

As a single unit, the men of Cardoroth pressed forward. They did not run, but marched. The shield wall came first, locked in a long and impenetrable line. Behind them the other ranks.

When they came within range of the elug bows they marched at a faster pace. The shield wall did not alter, but the ranks behind lifted high their shields to form a roof. Against this a hail of arrows fell, volley after volley, yet few men were injured or killed.

The elugs possessed no javelin throwers, and soon the army of Cardoroth crashed into the enemy. The elugs hacked and slashed, fighting with fury and wild strength. The men of Cardoroth held the shield wall together and relied on discipline.

Screams tore the air. Once more men and elugs died. Brand signaled, and the cavalry galloped out again, but this time they went to harry the enemy from the rear and cause confusion. It was the price Ginsar paid for not having cavalry of her own.

The two armies were locked together now. Cardoroth did not advance, nor the elugs retreat. And death continued unabated.

Brand moved into the ranks, but he remained mounted. The others followed him, forming a wedge. "Forward!" he cried, and the men heard and saw him.

The soldiers of Cardoroth drew of their great courage and fought with all their might. Slowly, ever so slowly, the shield wall advanced. Brand came to the front of the line and he used his staff as a spear. Elugs leapt at him, but his great stallion reared and tore at them with his hooves. Upon his back Brand swung his strange weapon. An elug went down, blood running from an ear. Another fell, his head snapped back by a thrust from the end of the staff. The great stallion trampled both.

There was space about him now. The elugs feared him, moving away. Taingern and Shorty rode beside him, their swords slashing. Tainrik and Gil likewise. So too Elrika, but Brand noticed she stayed close to the prince, protecting him as best she could.

The mounted wedge penetrated deeper into the enemy ranks. The elugs began to panic and chaos reigned among them. "Forward!" cried Brand again.

"We come! We come!" came the answering roar from the men of Cardoroth, and the shield wall advanced more swiftly.

The White Lady was among the mounted wedge also. She did not fight, nor was she attacked. She rode as though unseen, and there was a mask of determination upon her face that gave Brand pause. Something was afoot, and even as he realized it she called out to him. "To the left! Strike to the left!"

Brand smashed an elug away, feeling the thrum of contact jar his arm, and angled his horse as she had advised. Then they all saw what the White Lady had sensed. War was there, and the other Horsemen also. Of Ginsar there was no sign, but Brand knew she would be close.

He raised high his staff and allowed his magic to flare. Light flickered about him. "I come for you!" he cried, and pressed forward. The elugs gave way, and War turned his own steed toward him. A challenge had been issued and accepted.

They came together. The battle raged all about them, but a space opened for the two combatants. War swung his great broadsword, saw-toothed and deadly. It moaned as it cut the air, and red fire glinted on its edges like sparks of blood.

Brand deftly guided his mount back. Yet even as the horse moved he thrust forward with the staff. White fire burst from its tip and ripped into the Horseman. His black helm glittered with light and sparks flew from the spike at its peak and flowed down the vulture-like wings of its side.

War shook his head and laughed. But massive as he was he moved swiftly, feinting with his sword and then pressing the rim of his black shield with the side of the blade. The wicked spike in its center detached and sprang forward with great force.

Brand summoned lòhrengai again, forming a barrier before him. The missile struck it and bounced away.

Quick as thought Brand let the force dissolve and nudged his mount forward. He struck with his staff, bringing it down in a whipping motion against the sword wrist of the enemy.

War cried out, moving his mount to the side. The two crows that fluttered above him screeched, flapping madly in the air.

What their purpose was, Brand did not know. But he did not trust them and guessed they may be used as a weapon. He sent a blast of fire into them and they burst aflame, sparks showering down onto War. Then they fell to the earth, two bones that were not those of birds but looked like sun-bleached ribs.

Brand readied himself to attack War, but the Horsemen kicked his mount forward and the beast charged, smashing into Brand's stallion. Brand nearly fell, but righted himself in time to see the great broadsword hammer down. But it was not directed at him. Instead it bit into his horse's neck, near severing it.

The horse screamed and toppled, blood spraying from one of the great arteries. Brand leapt from it, barely escaping being crushed as it fell and kicked in its death throes.

Brand felt a surge of sorrow. Tears sprang into his eyes. That horse had been dear to him, had been with him since his first days in Cardoroth. But there was no time to mourn; War came for him, his own steed jumping the dying horse and his great sword raised high once more. It fell over brand like the shadow of doom.

But though Brand was disadvantaged, a man on foot facing a mounted enemy, he would not allow himself to be beaten.

The great sword swung down. Brand shifted left and ducked below its deadly sweep. Then, gathering his legs beneath him, he leaped high. He did not try to strike with his staff. Rather, he thrust it in front of the rider while he landed behind him. There, he nearly fell, but he got his knees under him and found purchase atop his enemy's mount.

With a deft move, he gripped the other end of the staff with his left hand and pulled it up beneath War's black helm. War sensed what was coming, and he elbowed backward with his sword arm. The massive elbow struck Brand and winded him, but his enemy could not reach him properly to deliver a full-strength blow.

Brand pulled the staff as tight as he could, and then he allowed himself to fall back off the horse. In this, War's steed helped him for the extra rider jumping onto his back and then toppling caused him to rear.

It almost did not work, but Brand was a large man and his weight, though nowhere near that of the Horseman, was enough to pull them both down from the horse.

They fell in a ruin of tangled limbs, and Brand had to roll to avoid the weight of his enemy crashing atop him. He lost his grip of the staff with one hand, but kept it with the other. Scrambling away he stood up.

War was just as quick to his feet and the speed of his opponent's movement surprised Brand. Nothing that big should be able to move so fast.

The other three Horsemen moved forward. Brand took this as a sign that they thought War vulnerable. Seeing them, he could not help but wonder how Ginsar had brought the two defeated ones back. At what risk to the world had she done so? And what would she risk now?

He knew he would soon find out. The sorceress stepped from behind the riders, defiant and determined though her army was being swept away around her.

Defeat was imminent, yet she did not seem anxious. He admired her then, but he feared her also. Now would come the great moment of this conflict. Now she would seek to draw greater power through the gateway to aid her and stave off her downfall. Now, Gil would come into his inheritance and the purpose of the White Lady would be revealed.

And even as he watched, he saw Ginsar begin to chant and felt the power of her sorcery thrum through the air and sink into the very earth.

Gil felt the White Lady close beside him. "Now, prince, is the hour come for which you were born. This is the time of your great choice."

Her words were true. Gil felt it, but he still had no idea what he would do or what was expected of him. The White Lady had told him once that he would know when the time came. But he knew nothing.

The battle raged on, moving away from this island of a battle within a battle. He sensed Ginsar invoke her power, and he heard the harsh thrumming of her voice as dark magic filled it. The gateway between worlds was opening like a spinning vortex in the sky above the field of battle. Ginsar widened it, began to draw more force through from the other side.

Gil looked at War. He could tell the Horseman sensed the same magic at work, or at least the thing summoned into the body of a dead Lethrin did. He felt the Horseman's anticipation, even yearning for what was about to happen. Gil did not know what he was meant to do, but he understood that he could not allow Ginsar to continue.

The great battle of men and elugs receded. Brand and the Horseman were stilled as though their fight was no longer of significance. And into that momentary peace

629

Gil strode. He did not raise his sword, but instead summoned the power of lòhrengai. It burst into life inside him.

Ginsar turned to him. Her eyes were alight with her own dark magic, and there was no surprise on her face. She had known this moment was destined, and perhaps knew better than he what it meant.

"Come to me, my prince," she said.

"Never," he answered. "Turn away from your intention. Do not open the gate wider, or we shall all be lost."

She gazed at him as though considering his words. "I was born lost," she said. "As were you. Elùgrune they called you. And they did so for good reason. You were born to be one with the dark. Embrace it, and know peace. Embrace it, and the power that it brings. It is like nothing you have ever felt. Come to me!"

"No. You tried to kill me a little while ago, and now you place the world in jeopardy."

She smiled at him. "I did not try to kill you. That was my acolytes, and you gave them their reward. You are greater than they were, greater by far. Nor would I ever truly hurt you. I understand who you are." She swept her gaze over the others and lingered on Brand before fixing her eyes back on him.

Gil felt unease surge through him. "You know nothing of who I am."

"I know this," she answered. "They would make you nothing but a mere king. I, on the other hand, would teach you sorcery and give you your heart's desire. *Magic*. It is your birthright as much as kingship. I would make you a sorcerer king. Nor would I let you settle for a stinking city full of vagabonds and traitors. Not I. Instead, I would guide you to rule other cities … other lands. A king? Nay. You would be an emperor!"

Gil felt the call of his magic then. It *was* his heart's desire. Being king was a duty, and one that he had never wanted. But magic could make the world a better place. He could achieve so much more with it than he could as a king. Yet he had no wish to conquer other lands, no desire to be a king at all, much less an emperor.

"No," he said. "You don't understand me in the least."

Within him his magic stirred restlessly. He still did not know what he would do to stop her, but if needs be he would attack her and try to kill her. Even as he thought it, he knew that she was vulnerable now. Perhaps that was why she was talking to him. She would not like to risk taking her will and power off the gateway to defend herself, or the opening would begin to close again.

Ginsar tilted her head. "I do not understand you? How wrong you are. I understand you better than anyone else in the world. Shall I tell you why?"

Gil did not give an answer. But Ginsar needed none. Slowly she raised her hands. Gil saw then what he least expected – two pale marks upon her palms, twins to his own.

"I know you, Gil. I understand you as no one else ever could. We share the same heritage. We possess the same blood, and verily, the same magic from days of old before the first stone of Cardoroth was ever laid."

Gil shook his head, stunned. "It's not true."

"True? Are you so wise as to determine truth from lie? I do not think so. Not yet. But I am not lying to you. I am of the same line as you. Even as Hvargil is. Why else do you think he has my favor? We are all of the same ancient blood. And blood calls to blood. Come to me, Gil. And I will teach you the mysteries of the universe."

The world seemed to stand still. Everything that Ginsar said rang with truth, but he could not believe it.

"No," he said, a third time. "It cannot be."

"It is. And it is good. You know me as Ginsar. But once, long ago, I was Ginhaina, sister to Carnhaina from whom you descend."

She held him then with her gaze. And he stood, transfixed by her revelation. Blood *did* call to blood, and he felt the kinship with her. He also sensed the great depth of time that separated them. She was born long ago. She was the daughter of the first king of Cardoroth. Who was *he* to judge her? Who was *he* to know the truth of events from so long ago?

"Come to me!" she commanded.

Gil did not know what to do. He felt the gaze of everyone upon him, and most of all Elrika by his side. He thought of the time he spent with her in Carnhaina's secret library. He felt who he once was and who he wanted to be.

"I will say it again, Ginsar. The answer is no. I will not join you. But if you wish, you may join *me*. Close the gateway. It will destroy you. But I will stop the Horsemen, one way or another, before that happens."

The sorceress looked at him. A moment she stood still, as if in doubt. Then she shook her head.

"Fool," she said regretfully. "You could have had it all. Now, you will have nothing. You cannot defeat me. The power is in me now, a part of me. It is beyond your strength. And I protect the riders. Even if you had the power, you could not send them back. We are one now, linked by forces you do not understand."

But Gil did understand. The Horsemen were bound to her, for she was their anchor in this world. She protected them, fed them strength. But she was also

632

bound to them by the same force. It was a closed circle of magic. But...

A new realization came to him. The White Lady was drawn through the gateway too. She was balance. They were all bound together, and they could not exist apart. If she went back to her own world, the others would be pulled through with her. But for her to go back, the body she had in this world, the physical form that she had incarnated herself into, must die. It was made of this world, not her own, and could not pass back with her.

Suddenly, the White Lady was by his side and she whispered in his ear. "Do what you must, Gil. It was never a choice between savior and destroyer. You are both. To save all you love, you must destroy me. I cannot do it by myself."

Gil's mind swam with the enormity of the choice before him. The Horsemen were called into the world by sacrifice. Only sacrifice could send them back. Only the death of the White Lady...

27. I have Failed

Ginsar screamed. Her wail rose, high-pitched and keening over the battle field. When it ceased, her eyes blazed. "No!" she said. "I will not allow it." But Gil was not sure to whom she spoke. She could not have heard what the White Lady had said.

Even as he hesitated the Four Horsemen advanced on Ginsar. They moved neither swift nor slow, but with a unified purpose. And he sensed a greater vigor about them. The spell the sorceress had begun was starting to work, but already the Horsemen had too much power and were beyond her control.

One moment the Horsemen moved, and then the next their bodies collapsed. A terrible stench of corruption filled the air, but four clouds of red vapor rose from the crumpled corpses and shot like arrows at Ginsar.

The sorceress shouted defiantly. The red vapor enveloped her, pouring into her through nose and mouth and ears. She screamed once more, this time in agony. And she began to change. Her face and body twisted and contorted. At one moment she took on something of the appearance of War, but he in turn was overthrown by Death. So it went through all the Horsemen, all vying to possess her and control the others, slipping down and rising up again in turns as they struggled. But another visage appeared also: dark of hair, grim faced with wolfish eyes that burned with desire.

Gil watched in horror, and as he did so a voice whispered in his mind. It was no more than a thought, but it was not his own. And he felt the presence of the great queen herself, of Carnhaina. *It is time. Shurilgar also seeks to possess her, to return from the dead. One of them will prevail and possess all the power and knowledge of the others. Alithoras will fall in smoke and ruin if that comes to pass.*

Ginsar screamed again. "Master! Help me!" But Gil knew he was not there to help, and that the sorceress was suffering unspeakable torment.

He felt Brand's gaze upon him, sympathy in his expression. The regent understood. And Carnhaina whispered in his mind once more. *There is only one way. It must be done.*

Gil looked at the White Lady. She was so beautiful and yet so sad. She brought joy into the world, and yet he was supposed to destroy her?

She took hold of the end of his sword, raising the tip up toward her. And then she leaned in to speak to him. "You must, Gil. Or everything you love will be destroyed. Alithoras shall fall, and the world after. You must."

"I cannot."

"You must!"

He felt her hands on his where he gripped the hilt of the sword. He felt her magic also, alive and roiling within her. His own responded and leaped up to join with it.

Ginsar screamed. Fire burst from her mouth, and she strode toward him. But he turned his gaze back to the White Lady and looked into her eyes.

"I forgive you," she whispered.

He did not understand, but then he realized that she was stabbed, the length of his sword piercing her body.

635

Dread such as he had never felt settled over him. Had she pushed herself upon the blade? Had he stabbed her?

The White Lady fell to her knees. Ginsar, close by, toppled also to the ground. Her eyes blazed fire and she hissed. Then she spoke, the words she spat formed of many voices all at once. "I hate you!"

Gil was not sure if she directed them at himself or the White Lady. But the White Lady spoke also. "I love you," she whispered. "And this fair land. Protect it. Guard it. Nurture it. And … remember me."

Tears ran down Gil's face. "Always."

"Remember me, but do not mourn. Though I die in this place, yet still I live in that world whence I came." Blood dribbled from the corner of her mouth and she grimaced. "You will be a great king."

"No. I have failed. I have let you down and everyone else."

"You have done what you were born for. Yet there is more yet to come. Remember me … my true name is Halabeth."

She died then, and the light faded from her eyes. But he felt her magic still, felt it rise up and spear through the spinning gateway, dragging the spirits of Ginsar and the Horsemen with her.

There was a flash of white light and a sudden sense of peace. Then it was gone and the world was different from what it had been. The gateway was closed, and grief weighed upon Gil as heavy as a mountain.

Brand leaned on his staff, but he looked out over the battlefield. "It is done," he said. "We have won."

Gil looked around at the devastation of the battlefield. The elug army was routed, pursued by the cavalry. Ginsar's body lay close by, twisted and broken by the powers that had contended to possess it. Of Halabeth, nothing remained save her memory. And that was bitter sweet. He felt a hand on his shoulder and knew by its touch that it was Elrika's. He reached up and put his own hand over it. Then he stood and answered Brand.

"We have won. But at a terrible cost."

Epilogue

Gil sat in Carnhaina's library. The ancient crown of Cardoroth, cut by mystic symbols and decorated with myriad gems, still rested upon his head. Tradition dictated that the new king wore it until midnight on the day of his coronation. He was not going to breach that custom.

Elrika sat with him, and Tainrik also. They both wore the white surcoats of a Durlin. It was a special day for all of them.

He held the diary of the great queen in his hand, unopened.

"Read something," Elrika suggested.

"I'm not sure that I want to. It always seems to fall open at—"

"Yes. At a page that you need to read. Do it, Gil. See what she says to you."

Gil opened the book. It felt heavier in his hand than usual, and it fell open at a point near the beginning. He had read that part before, but he knew he had not ever seen this page. It was neatly written, with lots of white space around the words.

"What does it say?" Tainrik asked.

Gil read aloud, his voice subdued. "Hail, Light of the Realm, for thus is the king of Cardoroth called. Hail, and congratulations. You have triumphed, for now, over the forces of evil. This means you have also won the battle within your soul. And just as there is good and evil in the world, so too that battle plays out inside you. It plays out in all men and women, but especially so in those with magic. Be wary of the dark, but do not fear it. Come to understand it so that you may defeat it when it rises. And it will. I triumphed in the end. My sister did not. Your time of testing is not yet over."

"That's not exactly reassuring," Elrika said.

"You wanted me to read it…"

"Yes. Now keep going. What else does it say?"

Gil did not argue with her. He read on. "And remember, Brand is your friend. He does not believe the two of you shall meet again. He is mistaken. It will not be soon though, for he has many grave trials ahead of him. Spare a thought for him now and then, for while your battles are over for the moment, his are beginning anew." There was a signature, and the name given was Carngin. It was her informal name.

"What else does it say?"

There was a postscript, and he read it out. "Remember, always, that I'm proud of you and love you."

Gil closed the book, and noticed Elrika's gaze upon him.

"Was that so bad?"

"No," he answered. "It wasn't. Though now I worry for Brand."

"Ah," Tainrik said, drawing something from his pocket. "This would be a good time to tell you. He gave me a note for you before he left. I know he's already said his goodbyes, but he gave it to me anyway."

Gil was intrigued. "What does it say?" he asked. "Read it for me, please."

Tainrik cleared his throat. "Gil, we have already said our last farewells, but saying goodbye is hard. Yet this

639

much I need to say, because I did not do so earlier. We may never meet again. I travel now to the land of my birth, the lands of the Duthenor. I know some of what to expect, but I sense there is much more that I do not guess. That does not concern you though. But I want you to understand this. The White Lady was not of this world, nor could she have been happy here, even as I was never truly happy away from my homeland. Yet she lives there, as do her enemies, and the battle between them continues. What you did was ... difficult. And you have learned a truth that all of us discover, eventually. Sometimes there are no right choices. Nothing can change that. Nor will it be your last dilemma. So I say this as my final advice to you, and I hope it helps. It is the fate of kings to bear great responsibility. Trust your instincts, but heed the words of wise counselors. Most of all, keep your friends close and keep your enemies guessing ... Remember that."

Gil smiled. It was good advice, and he would not forget.

Thus ends *Light of the Realm*. It brings the Son of Sorcery trilogy to a conclusion. Yet Brand must still defeat the usurper. He returns to the land of the Duthenor, but things are not as they seem. Darker forces are at work than he knows, and his life and the future of Alithoras is in greater jeopardy than anyone guesses.

More is told in:

THE PALE SWORDSMAN

AVAILABLE NOW!

Amazon lists millions of titles, and I'm glad you discovered this one. But if you'd like to know when I release a new book, instead of leaving it to chance, sign up for my newsletter. I'll send you an email on publication.

Yes please! – Go to www.homeofhighfantasy.com and sign up.

No thanks – I'll take my chances.

Dedication

There's a growing movement in fantasy literature. Its name is noblebright, and it's the opposite of grimdark.

Noblebright celebrates the virtues of heroism. It's an old-fashioned thing, as old as the first story ever told around a smoky campfire beneath ancient stars. It's storytelling that highlights courage and loyalty and hope for the spirit of humanity. It recognizes the dark, the dark in us all, and the dark in the villains of its stories. It recognizes death, and treachery and betrayal. But it dwells on none of these things.

I dedicate this book, such as it is, to that which is noblebright. And I thank the authors before me who held the torch high so that I could see the path: J.R.R. Tolkien, C.S. Lewis, Terry Brooks, David Eddings, Susan Cooper, Roger Taylor and many others. I salute you.

And, for a time, I too will hold the torch as high as I can.

Encyclopedic Glossary

Note: the glossary of each book in this series is individualized for that book alone. Additionally, there is often historical material provided in its entries for people, artifacts and events that are not included in the main text.

Many races dwell in Alithoras. All have their own language, and though sometimes related to one another the changes sparked by migration, isolation and various influences often render these tongues unintelligible to each other.

The ascendancy of Halathrin culture, combined with their widespread efforts to secure and maintain allies against elug incursions, has made their language the primary means of communication between diverse peoples.

For instance, a soldier of Cardoroth addressing a ship's captain from Camarelon would speak Halathrin, or a simplified version of it, even though their native speeches stem from the same ancestral language.

This glossary contains a range of names and terms. Many are of Halathrin origin, and their meaning is provided. The remainder derive from native tongues and are obscure, so meanings are only given intermittently.

Often, Camar names and Halathrin elements are combined. This is especially so for the aristocracy. No other tribes of men had such long-term friendship with the immortal Halathrin, and though in this relationship they lost some of their natural culture, they gained nobility and knowledge in return.

List of abbreviations:

Azn. Azan

Cam. Camar

Comb. Combined

Cor. Corrupted form

Duth. Duthenor

Hal. Halathrin

Leth. Letharn

Prn. Pronounced

Age of Heroes: A period of Camar history that has become mythical. Many tales are told of this time. Some are true while others are not. Yet, even the false ones usually contain elements of historical fact. Many were the heroes who walked abroad during this time, and they are remembered and honored still by the Camar people. The old days are looked back on with pride, and the descendants of many heroes walk the streets of

Cardoroth unaware of their heritage and the accomplishments of their forefathers.

Alith Nien: *Hal.* "Silver river." Has its source in the mountainous lands of Auren Dennath and empties into Lake Alithorin.

Alithoras: *Hal.* "Silver land." The Halathrin name for the continent they settled after their exodus from their homeland. Refers to the extensive river and lake systems they found and their wonder at the beauty of the land.

Anast Dennath: *Hal.* "Stone mountains." Mountain range in northern Alithoras. Source of the river known as the Careth Nien that forms a natural barrier between the lands of the Camar people and the Duthenor and related tribes.

Arach Neben: *Hal.* "West gate." The defensive wall surrounding Cardoroth has four gates. Each is named after a cardinal direction, and each carries a token to represent a celestial object. Arach Neben bears a steel ornament of the Morning Star.

Arell: A famed healer in Cardoroth. Rumored to be Brand's lover.

Aurellin: *Cor. Hal.* The first element means blue. The second is native Camar. Formerly Queen of Cardoroth, wife to Gilhain and grandmother to Gilcarist.

Auren Dennath: *Comb. Duth.* and *Hal. Prn.* Our-ren dennath. "Blue mountains." Mountain range in northern Alithoras. Contiguous with Anast Dennath.

Betrayal: One of the Riders, also called Horsemen, summoned into Alithoras by Ginsar. He represents and instigates betrayal. Yet, in truth, the Riders are spirit-beings from another world. They have been given form and nature within Alithoras by Ginsar. The form provided by her is part of the blood sorcery that binds them to her will. In their own world, they do not bear these names or natures. Yet they are creatures wholly of evil, and though bound by Ginsar they seek to break that bond. Even if defeated, the bond from the summoning persists and the Riders are capable of rising again, even though they are considered dead.

Brand: A Duthenor tribesman. Appointed by the former king of Cardoroth to serve as regent for Gilcarist. By birth, he is the rightful chieftain of the Duthenor people. However, a usurper overthrew his father, killing both him and his wife. Brand, only a youth at the time, swore an oath of vengeance. That oath sleeps, but it is not forgotten, either by Brand or the usurper.

Camar: *Cam. Prn.* Kay-mar. A race of interrelated tribes that migrated in two main stages. The first brought them to the vicinity of Halathar, homeland of the immortal Halathrin; in the second, they separated and established cities along a broad stretch of eastern Alithoras.

Cardoroth: *Cor. Hal. Comb. Cam.* A Camar city, often called Red Cardoroth. Some say this alludes to the red granite commonly used in the construction of its buildings, others that it refers to a prophecy of destruction.

Cardurleth: *Hal.* "Car – red, dur – steadfast, leth – stone." The defensive wall that surrounds Cardoroth. Established soon after the city's founding and constructed of red granite. It looks displeasing to the eye, but the people of the city love it nonetheless. They believe it impregnable and hold that no enemy shall ever breach it – except by treachery.

Careth Nien: *Hal. Prn.* Kareth ni-en. "Great river." Largest river in Alithoras. Has its source in the mountains of Anast Dennath and runs southeast across the land before emptying into the sea. It was over this river (which sometimes freezes along its northern stretches) that the Camar and other tribes migrated into the eastern lands. Much later, Brand came to the city of Cardoroth by one of these ancient migratory routes.

Carnhaina: First element native *Cam.* Second *Hal.* "Heroine." An ancient queen of Cardoroth. Revered as a savior of her people, but to some degree also feared for she possessed powers of magic. Hated to this day by elùgroths because she destroyed their power unexpectedly at a time when their dark influence was rising. According to legend, kept alive mostly within the royal family of Cardoroth, she guards the city even in death and will return in its darkest hour.

Carngin: See Carnhaina.

Conhain: A watchword in use in Cardoroth. Refers to one of the great kings of the Camar peoples who founded a realm in the south of Alithoras.

Death: One of the Riders, also called Horsemen, summoned into Alithoras by Ginsar. He represents and instigates Death. Yet, in truth, the Riders are spirit-beings from another world. They have been given form and nature within Alithoras by Ginsar. The form provided by her is part of the blood sorcery that binds them to her will. In their own world, they do not bear these names or natures. Yet they are creatures wholly of evil, and though bound by Ginsar they seek to break that bond. Even if defeated, the bond from the summoning persists and the Riders are capable of rising again, even though they are considered dead.

Dernbrael: *Hal.* "Sharp-tongued." By some translations, "cunning-tongued." A lord of Cardoroth. Attempted to usurp the throne from Gilcarist. It is said that he is in league with the traitor Hvargil, though this has never been proven.

Drùghoth: *Hal.* First element – black. Second element – that which hastens, races or glides. More commonly called a sending.

Druigbar: *Cam.* A general in Cardoroth's army. In his youth, a runner of extraordinary ability. He possessed speed and endurance, and won the annual race that circuits the Cardurleth seven times out of eight starts.

Durlin: *Hal.* "The steadfast." The original Durlin were the seven sons of the first king of Cardoroth. They guarded him against all enemies, of which there were many, and three died to protect him. Their tradition continued throughout Cardoroth's history, suspended only once, and briefly, some four hundred years ago when it was discovered that three members were secretly in the service of elùgroths. These were imprisoned, but committed suicide while waiting for their trial to commence. It is rumored that the king himself provided them with the knives that they used. It is said that he felt sorry for them and gave them this way out to avoid the shame a trial would bring to their families.

Durlin creed: These are the native Camar words, long remembered and greatly honored, that were uttered by the first Durlin to die while he defended his father, who was also the king, from attack. Tum del conar – El dar tum! Death or infamy – I choose death!

Durlindrath: *Hal.* "Lord of the steadfast." The title given to the leader of the Durlin. For the first time in the history of Cardoroth, that position is held jointly by two people: Lornach and Taingern. Lornach also possesses the title of King's Champion. The latter honor is not held in quite such high esteem, yet it carries somewhat more power. As King's Champion, Lornach is authorized to act in the king's stead in matters of honor and treachery to the Crown.

Duthenor: *Duth. Prn.* Dooth-en-or. "The people." A single tribe, or sometimes a group of closely related tribes melded into a larger people at times of war or disaster, who generally live a rustic and peaceful lifestyle. They are breeders of cattle and herders of sheep. However, when need demands they are bold warriors – men and women alike. Currently ruled by a usurper who murdered Brand's parents. Brand has sworn an oath to overthrow the tyrant and avenge his parents.

Elrika: *Cam.* Daughter of the royal baker. Friend to Gilcarist, and greatly skilled in weapons fighting, especially the long sword. Brand has given instructions to Lornach that she is to be taught all arts of the warrior to the full extent of her ability. He is grooming her to be the first female Durlin in the history of the city.

Elùgrune: *Hal.* Literally "shadowed fortune," but is also translated into "ill fortune" and "born of the dark." In the first two senses it means bad luck. In the third, it connotes a person steeped in shadow and mystery and not to be trusted. In some circles, the term has an additional meaning of "mystic".

Elugs: *Hal.* "That which creeps in shadows." Often called goblins. An evil and superstitious race that dwells in the south of Alithoras, especially the Graèglin Dennath Mountains. They also inhabit portions of the northern mountains of Alithoras, and have traditionally fallen under the sway of elùgroths centered in the region of Cardoroth.

Elùgai: *Hal. Prn.* Eloo-guy. "Shadowed force." The sorcery of an elùgroth.

Elùgroth: *Hal. Prn.* Eloo-groth. "Shadowed horror." A sorcerer. They often take names in the Halathrin tongue in mockery of the lòhren practice to do so.

Esanda: No known etymology for this name. Likewise, Esanda herself is not native to Cardoroth. King Gilhain believed she was from the city of Esgallien, but he was not certain of this. Esanda refuses to answer questions concerning her origins. Regardless of the personal mystery attached to her, she was one of Gilhain's most trusted advisors and soon became so to Brand. She leads a ring of spies utterly devoted to the protection of

Cardoroth from the many dark forces that would bring it down.

Esgallien: *Hal. Prn.* Ez-gally-en. "Es – rushing water, gal(en) – green, lien – to cross: place of the crossing onto the green plains." A city founded in antiquity and named after a nearby ford of the Careth Nien. Reports indicate it has fallen to elugs.

Felhain: First element is of unknown *Cam* etymology. Second is *Hal* for "hero". Youngest son of the first king of Cardoroth.

Felargin: *Cam.* A sorcerer, and brother to Ginsar. Acolyte of Shurilgar the elùgroth. Steeped in evil and once lured Brand, Lornach and other adventurers under false pretenses into a quest. Only Brand and Shorty survived the betrayal. Felargin, however, fell victim to the trap he had prepared for the others. Brand was responsible for his death.

Forgotten Queen (the): An epithet of Queen Carnhaina. She was a person of immense power and presence, yet she made few friends in life, and her possession of magic caused her to be mistrusted. For these reasons, memory of her accomplishments faded soon after her passing and only small remnants of her rule are remembered by the populace of Cardoroth.

Garling: *Cam.* A general of Cardoroth's army. Distantly related to the royal family by marriage.

Gil: See Gilcarist.

Gilcarist: *Comb. Cam & Hal.* First element unknown, second "ice." Heir to the throne of Cardoroth and grandson of King Gilhain. According to Carnhaina, his coming was told in the stars. He is also foretold by her as The Savior and The Destroyer. The prophecies mean little to him, for he believes in Brand's view that a man makes his own fate.

Gilhain: *Comb. Cam & Hal.* First element unknown, second "hero." King of Cardoroth before proclaiming Brand regent for Gilcarist, the underage heir to the throne. Husband to Aurellin.

Ginhaina: First element native *Cam.* Second *Hal.* "Heroine." Youngest daughter of the first king of Cardoroth.

Ginsar: *Cam.* A sorceress. Sister to Felargin. Acolyte of Shurilgar the elùgroth. Steeped in evil and greatly skilled in the arts of elùgai, reaching a level of proficiency nearly as great as her master. Rumored to be insane.

Goblins: See elugs.

Graèglin Dennath: *Hal. Prn.* Greg-lin dennath. "Mountains of ash." Chain of mountains in southern Alithoras. Populated by the southern races of elugs.

Halabeth: Etymology unknown. See the White Lady.

Halathar: *Hal.* "Dwelling place of the people of Halath." The forest realm of the immortal Halathrin.

Halathgar: *Hal.* "Bright star." Actually a constellation of two stars. Also called the Lost Huntress.

Halathrin: *Hal.* "People of Halath." A race named after an honored lord who led an exodus of his people to the land of Alithoras in pursuit of justice, having sworn to defeat a great evil. They are human, though of fairer form, greater skill and higher culture than ordinary men. They possess a unity of body, mind and spirit that enables insight and endurance beyond the native races of Alithoras. Said to be immortal, but killed in great numbers during their conflicts in ancient times with the evil they sought to destroy. Those conflicts are collectively known as the Shadowed Wars.

Harath Neben: *Hal.* "North gate." This gate bears a token of two massive emeralds representing the constellation of Halathgar. The gate is also called "Hunter's Gate," for the north road out of the city leads to wild lands of plentiful game. It is said that a stele of Letharn origin was found buried beneath the soil when the foundations of the gate were excavated. No one could read the inscription, but the stele is kept to this day in the gate tower.

Hvargil: Prince of Cardoroth. Younger son of Carangil, former king of Cardoroth. Exiled by Carangil for treason after it was discovered he plotted with elùgroths to assassinate his older half-brother, Gilhain, and prevent him from ascending the throne. He gathered a band about him in exile of outlaws and discontents. Most came from Cardoroth but others were drawn from the southern Camar cities. He fought with the invading army of elugs against Cardoroth in the previous war.

Immortals: See Halathrin.

Letharn: *Hal.* "Stone raisers. Builders." A race of people that in antiquity conquered most of Alithoras. Now, only faint traces of their civilization endure.

Lethrin: *Hal.* "Stone people." Creatures of legend sometimes called trolls. Renowned for their size and strength. Tunnelers and miners.

Lòhren: *Hal. Prn.* Ler-ren. "Knowledge giver – a counselor." Other terms used by various nations include wizard, druid and sage.

Lòhrengai: *Hal. Prn.* Ler-ren-guy. "Lòhren force." Enchantment, spell or use of mystic power. A manipulation and transformation of the natural energy inherent in all things. Each use takes something from the user. Likewise, some part of the transformed energy infuses them. Lòhrens use it sparingly, elùgroths indiscriminately.

Lornach: *Cam.* A former Durlin and now joint Durlindrath. Also holds the title of King's Champion. Friend to Brand, and often called by his nickname of "Shorty."

Lothgern: A general of Cardoroth's army. Also a breeder of some of the finest horses in the realm. These he sells, at exorbitant prices, to cavalry soldiers. The soldiers complain bitterly about the price, but most do not stint on the fee. The reputation of the horses is paramount. The black stallion owned by Brand was foaled in Lothgern's stables.

Magic: Mystic power. See lòhrengai and elùgai.

Nightborn: See elùgrune.

Olekgar: *Comb. Cam & Hal.* First element unknown, second "star." A disciple of Ginsar. Born outside Cardoroth yet descended from the city's aristocracy.

Otherworld: Camar term for a mingling of half-remembered history, myth and the spirit world. Sometimes used interchangeably with the term "Age of Heroes."

Raithlin: *Hal.* "Range and report people." A scouting and saboteur organization. Derived from ancient contact with, and the teachings of, the Halathrin. Their skills are legendary throughout Alithoras.

Sandy: See Esanda.

Sellic Neben: *Hal.* "East gate." This gate bears a representation, crafted of silver and pearl, of the moon rising over the sea.

Shorty: See Lornach.

Shurilgar: *Hal.* "Midnight star." An elùgroth. One of the most puissant sorcerers of antiquity. Known to legend as the Betrayer of Nations.

Sorcerer: See Elùgroth.

Sorcery: See elùgai.

Stillness in the Storm: A mental state sought by many warriors. It is that sense of the mind being separate from the body. If achieved, it frees the warrior from emotions such as fear and pain that hinder physical performance. The body, in its turn, moves and reacts by trained instinct alone allowing the skill of the warrior to flow unhindered to the surface. Those who have perfected the correct mental state feel as though they can slow down the passage of time during a fight. It is an illusion, yet the state of feeling that way is a combat advantage.

Surcoat: An outer garment usually worn over chainmail. The Durlin surcoat is unadorned white, which is a tradition carried down from the order's inception.

Taingern: *Cam*. A former Durlin. Friend to Brand, and now joint Durlindrath. Once, in company of Brand, saved the tomb of Carnhaina from defilement and robbery by an elùgroth.

Time: One of the Riders, also called Horsemen, summoned into Alithoras by Ginsar. He represents Time – specifically as manifested by the aging process. Yet, in truth, the Riders are spirit-beings from another world. They have been given form and nature within Alithoras by Ginsar. The form provided by her is part of the blood sorcery that binds them to her will. In their own world, they do not bear these names or natures. Yet they are creatures wholly of evil, and though bound by Ginsar they seek to break that bond. Even if defeated, the bond from the summoning persists and the Riders are capable of rising again, even though they are considered dead.

Tower of Halathgar: In life, a place of study of Queen Carnhaina. In death, her resting place. Unusually, her sarcophagus rests on the tower's parapet beneath the stars.

Unlach Neben: *Hal*. "South gate." This gate bears a representation of the sun, crafted of gold, beating down upon an arid land. Said to signify the southern homeland of the elugs, whence the gold of the sun was obtained by an adventurer of old.

Ùhrengai: *Hal. Prn.* Er-ren-guy. "Original force." The primordial force that existed before substance or time.

War: One of the Riders, also called Horsemen, summoned into Alithoras by Ginsar. He represents conflict and battle. Yet, in truth, the Riders are spirit-beings from another world. They have been given form and nature within Alithoras by Ginsar. The form provided by her is part of the blood sorcery that binds them to her will. In their own world, they do not bear these names or natures. Yet they are creatures wholly of evil, and though bound by Ginsar they seek to break that bond. Even if defeated, the bond from the summoning persists and the Riders are capable of rising again, even though they are considered dead.

White Lady: A being of spirit drawn into Alithoras as an unintended consequence of Ginsar's summoning of the Riders.

Wizard: See lòhren.

Wych-wood: A general description for a range of supple and springy timbers. Some hardy varieties are prevalent on the poisonous slopes of the Graèglin Dennath Mountains, and are favored by elùgroths as instruments of sorcery.

About the author

I'm a man born in the wrong era. My heart yearns for faraway places and even further afield times. Tolkien had me at the beginning of *The Hobbit* when he said, ". . . one morning long ago in the quiet of the world . . ."

Sometimes I imagine myself in a Viking mead-hall. The long winter night presses in, but the shimmering embers of a log in the hearth hold back both cold and dark. The chieftain calls for a story, and I take a sip from my drinking horn and stand up . . .

Or maybe the desert stars shine bright and clear, obscured occasionally by wisps of smoke from burning camel dung. A dry gust of wind marches sand grains across our lonely campsite, and the wayfarers about me stir restlessly. I sip cool water and begin to speak.

I'm a storyteller. A man to paint a picture by the slow music of words. I like to bring faraway places and times to life, to make hearts yearn for something they can never have, unless for a passing moment.

66130050R00402